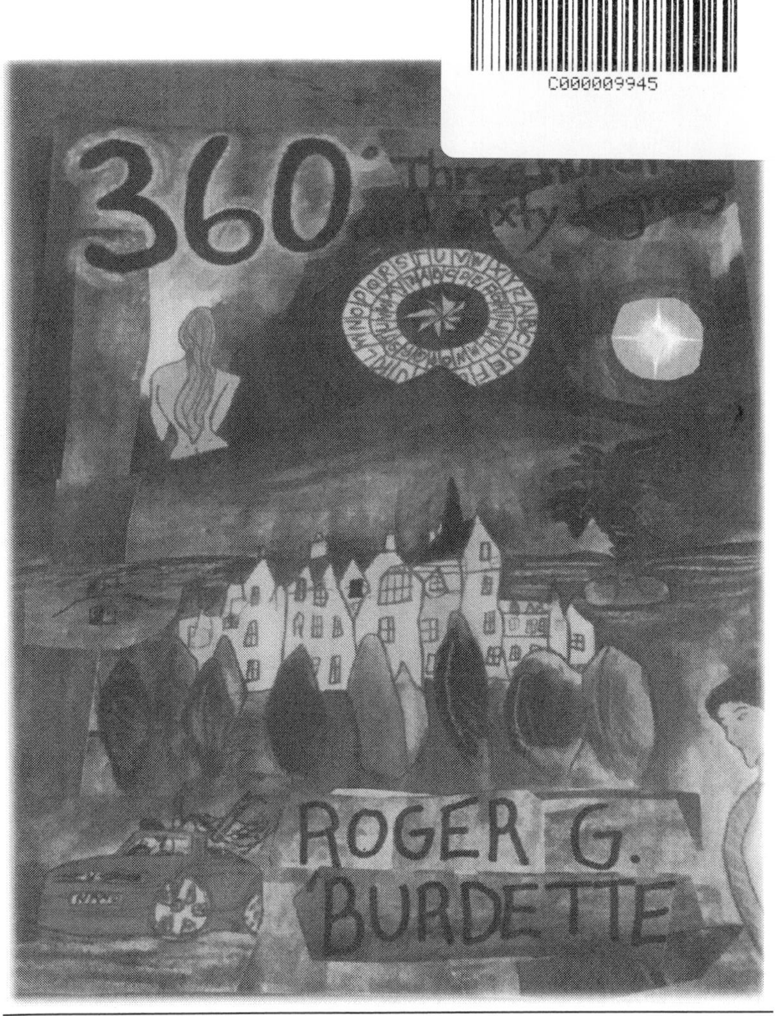

360 degrees Michaelmas

KaldeoaXplddsAtnocmOsT
brcPstnrnYtsbelreraQorb
elnhaomnrnhVayetrrjhF
bfroauWtnOtrlbefjdadal
JaaurrahVmnrliawrwriua
naannilbnedirdoeimmrti
tgrQlnedirdinstonnsueA
arcsttaimkKiAniptnucit
hmenKietneoAligirYitmr
liebodrmGrenaeibzrYeea
QrpiiwhlleatCotccueeph
ancniedaoFnJrwsakcachH
viWdGecdXawdeeeeperinr
ehgodbrunsrrTePefaoeew
jJeiknnshidijanonjGmmc
dnXoinnnSrLneoqGUnoawY
tmaSundrycnYiiunhytbtN
OdliavarQyiyutjgdnXfQj

360 degrees Michaelmas

360 degrees

Michaelmas

To my Beautiful Rose

Roger G. Burdette

IN LOCO PARENTIS

Children but not of Flaxden Brig, the greater care
Deserve, our charge to be detached, apart,
Unburdened by the kinship parents bear,
Their special love
And largesse of the heart.

The better way, for them affection flows
And does not claim requital-as is just,
Expected, and of duty owed to those,
Who bore, who gave, and loved as parents must.

Theirs the quintessential gift; my role
Vicarious and deflate, merely steward,
Yet some may count it virtue since my soul
Has lightly met travail, her pains endured

When separation comes, all human dues are spent,
Yet, parents, this I crave,
A tierce of your content.

0 degrees

1 degree

The Straight Line

'I'm looking out at the Export Ship Canal down by the Quay, on another glorious flaming June Saturday morning, forget about that bumper to bumper traffic! Be a slugger head just stay in bed! This is your favourite radio station, in your favourite City down by Export Quays, the City that is rocking, and the City that is NEVER stopping!'

The voice filtered through his head, eyes closed but he could still hear. 'Good morning! Good morning! Good morning! It's 5 am and here is the news! Prince William is in Vietnam for two days with the Duchess of Cambridge and today will be having talks with the Vietnamese Prime Minister to voice his concerns over wildlife extinction in the area. Better watch out for those snakes over there Wills! Don't forget to bring me back a Pot Bellied Pig! It's the rage down our way! Prime Minister May is in talks with European leaders over Britain's decision to leave Europe, get your best shoes and lacy frock on Tess, I hear those continentals love a well-dressed woman with a bit of leg! It'll get you on the front of Playboy maybe Vogue! ......At least! There is a sale on at ANGELIQUE'S LINGERIE, great place girls! I can vouch for that, I never get my under crackers from anywhere else! Closer to home now and we just have breaking news that Toddles the little cat has been rescued by the Fire Brigade, it took 8 hours and an army of volunteers to do but Toddles is now purring away on Mrs Barnet's knee! Nice one Toddy, worth it to get that saucer of free range milk we are now being given! Cow, goat, sheep or pig, I'm sure you don't care or even know! That will be a bill for £600 please Toddles, that will make a dent in your Vet bills! On a more serious note Export City, our Shakers are now out of the cup, beaten at AFC

Derrychasel by 5 goals to 0! Oh dear, oh dear, OH DEAR! They'll be crying on the pavements and pubs in Export this morning, the end of the world has come, how will we all cope?! How will we get over it!? The weather for today will be raining in the morning, the afternoon and evening, so just look out your window for the most accurate and up to date version to save me doing it! And now to start your day is the latest number one from the top one million, 'I do like Mondays from the SM Band which was better than their last effort! Take it away Doris!' The music started and a hand reached out and banged the button on to sleep, the radio crashed to the floor with a thump.

BEEP! BEEP! BEEP! BEEP! The loud piercing alarm rang out throughout Cliffton's apartment. The extra 10 minutes sleep had gone so fast, it always did. His arm slung out of the bed, he was in a sort of recovery position, 'UHHHHHHH!' He groaned, as the electric sounds of the milk float stopping and starting drifted into his head, stop start, stop start as the milkman from Express Dairy got out delivering his pints, the chink chink of the bottles in the milk basket clearly audible through the silence of the morning. 'What happened last night, UHHHHHH?' His head felt numb, a part of it missing. 'What had gone on?' Forcing his eyelids from his eyeballs, 'OWCH!' It slowly started to come back. Yes. He remembered Portia had come around; he had not expected to see her till the following week. 'Yes!' She had announced she didn't want to see him anymore; it was over, she was moving on, couldn't wait for him to make a decision anymore. 'Here is your ring!' But why do this to him so near to his final exam? Could she not have waited till after?

'OUT! Get out and don't come back!' He had told her in mind numbing shock, as she quickly dressed... Her lacy lingerie left draped over the bedstead. Beer cans strewn all over the floor, some DE CLARE cider, a bottle of Red Horse, a bottle of Rosé wine with a glass half empty, one on its side a stain from its mouth, lipstick on the rim, a pizza box with a slice left, the solitaire diamond engagement ring had been placed strategically on the slice of vegetable medley , he could see the spinach and ricotta through the ring itself fastening it to the stone baked base, a half eaten piece with teeth marks clearly visible, his or hers? He couldn't say but it was probably hers as the ring was just above the perfect teeth marks, as he had told her to go, chips and a half eaten quarter pounder with cheese and

on the floor, sitting with his back against the bed, he ate a slice of the left over pizza, hard and brittle with a bland taste.
‘OUCH!’As he nearly broke a tooth, closed his eyes and slowly opened one, no, still there, it’s not a dream, and there in the pizza box was the ring. solitaire diamond flanked by an empty bottle of Red Horse and a half full bottle of Rosé wine, Portia’s bra draped over the bedstead as though making a statement of conquest. Hers or His? He recognised the make, Lejaby, something he had bought her on Valentine’s Day, but it hadn’t been enough. Had it ever been enough? He didn’t even remember her leaving, his promise of marriage, he had paid £1,999, funny that the ad people think they are doing a favour by knocking a pound or a penny off, for that, it sucks the punters in though, and even then he had the feeling that it wasn’t enough, should’ve paid £2000 but that would again never be enough for her or maybe her Mum more like it, her Dad, not good enough for his little girl maybe? He was nearly there, could she not wait? He had been working so hard for a means to an end, just about to breakthrough, really achieve. He closed his eyes and shook his head, couldn’t, shouldn’t, would not let this get in his way, no, she had made her mind up she didn’t want to see him anymore, it was over. ‘Forget it Cliffton, her loss is your gain.’ He thought to himself. All was to be confirmed through e mail, her usual way of doing things, always on her computer or I phone 37, was that it now, perhaps 56? But she had decided to come round, do the decent thing, she wouldn’t answer her phone, but he had to get himself together, it was 5am, he needed an early start with just over a week to go there was much to do, he would have to take the hits when the chips were down as he had done before. His hand stretched out for his phone, the radio alarm was still bleeping and BANG!! He fell out of bed, SPLAT! A pain came on his side and he peeled away his mobile phone which he had been lying on throughout his short sleep. He had been the prey, Portia the predator. The sun filtered through the partly drawn curtains, he was never one to draw them completely, always liking to see the sky turn, to dusk and then to dawn, it was his favourite time of day just before the dawn. Getting to his feet, wearing only boxer shorts, he started moving round his place, taking a look in the mirror he saw the indentation of his phone, a complete mould with precision detail the numbers and screen could be clearly seen... ‘I’m going to change my clothes, my hair, and my face. I’m now getting somewhere and soon I will be in another place other than this. There’s

something happening somewhere and I'm not going to be dancing in the dark.' Cliffton hummed to himself as he changed in to his sports gear and headed out for his morning run. 'I'll run this off.' He concluded. 'It's over, life is a bitch, deal with it man! She's gone'. Off out round the block, waving at the other early risers, the milk man, the paper boy, bread lorry, even a leaflet distributor, waving to each as they all began their day, a lone man was on the other side of the road staggering, was he on his way home or going to his next halt? The stench of alcohol fumes could be smelt for miles, whilst the rest of the population were lying in their beds snoring their heads off. It is he who is up first and last in that is successful, they can look themselves in the mirror and know they can get better and better, he reassured himself, kept telling himself. Back home he showered, a good soaping and a 15 minute cold blast. 'That'll wake anyone up in the morning!' The water jumped off his bare skin, the droplets bouncing high, his corpuscles were now in full flow, dried himself and took his breakfast, grapefruit, wholemeal toast and a cup of tea-no milk or sugar, that will keep him alert, clear his mind. Feeling good he sat down at his desk, opened his laptop. He had an important letter to write before he started his final revision. He looked at his computer, soon he would escape this yolk around his neck, constantly backing things up, constantly paying for it all too, his contract coming to an end, not necessary he thought, but this needed to be done today, not delaying he started his parchment. It had to be short and to the point, on one page only.

Cliffton Breeze,
Apartment 385,
Strawberry Gardens,
Green Foot,
Export, NAN 6PH

Dear Sir/Madam,

I write to you with a certain sadness, regret and trepidation, as I am informing you today that I will no longer be supplying a service to you with immediate effect. It is no longer financially viable for me to do so, as your payments to me are always missing, delayed or

incomplete. I have now decided to focus on other projects and will be moving on to pastures new. It has been a privilege to have served you and wish you and your staff best wishes for what will be a successful future for you all. I realise that this must be a disappointment to you all but I have no choice in this matter.
All my work was completed and records are up to date, you should be able to find a replacement easily.

Yours Sincerely

Cliffton Breeze

After printing out he signed and placed the neatly folded letter into an envelope and put on a 2nd Class stamp, no point in a 1st as they always got there the same anyway, he strolled to the nearest post box and heard the letter drop to the empty bottom. This triggered an enormous weight being lifted from his shoulders; an uneasy part of his life had gone for good, a feeling that has to happen to someone to understand. Feeling relaxed he went home made a cup of tea, sat down at his desk, with his final exam coming up there was still work to be done and he had got himself set up. He had been lucky to have been able to work, earn some money while studying, although not easy, full time study and full time work, he was looking forward to be focussing in one direction only from now on. Cliffton had been happy to. 'There is no gain without pain!' He kept reminding himself over the last few years, unless you are born with a silver spoon up your backside being stirred all the time and that was not him, it is what you make and does, no show boating get up and make it happen! He had his own place, decent clothes and his beloved MG. Many couldn't understand how but he had worked a 'double shift' over the last 3 years. 'Impossible!' Many had said but he had done it. Next week it would all be over, all change and a brand new direction in life, it was a reinvention it was what he wanted all along, his goal achieved, the world would literally be his oyster, even though he preferred mussels and smoked ones at that!
The next day was a Tuesday, up at 5am, run and after a quick breakfast of cornflakes and mug of tea he buried his head in his books until lunch when

he took a break. Things were moving smoothly, then the phone rang, the answer phone was on so he decided to leave it, but listened. 'Hello this is Anita from Headstone Pokes!' Exclaimed a bright enthusiastic young voice, on the other end. 'I'm just ringing up to let you know I'm following up your claim for PPI!'

'Never had it in my life!' Replied 'Cliffton in a frustrated tone, voice directed at the answer phone. He had been getting many of these calls over the last few weeks and he really did need to get on. He picked it up, 'Hello? Sorry I have not made an enquiry.'

'Well have you ever had PPI or any.......?'

'Bye!!!' He had to do it he needed quiet, but a part of him felt guilty at his brusque behaviour, she's only trying to earn a crust, but there again she'll be right on to her next call already, he was history, forgotten, maybe she'll get something from that. He dropped the phone back on to its receiver and turned the ringer off. Fifteen minutes in and it's going good, concentration is total, when CLICK, CLICK, CLICK, WHIRRRRRR! 'Must be one of those PPI calls again.' He thought out aloud. 'I'll ignore it.' He decided. The answer phone clicked in.

'Hello Cliffton, are you there? This is Janet; can you ring me as soon as you can? I have to speak with you, it's urgent. Bye.' Before he could intercept, the phone clicked off. Quickly he pressed recall and Janet answered almost immediately.

'Hi Janet, I'm sorry, couldn't get to the phone in time!'

'Cliffton! I've been trying to call you for weeks!' An upset Janet exclaimed. 'Rupert has died.' A month ago their close friend Rupert had passed away but she had only just heard and his family had laid him to rest within 24 hours. Poor Rupert. It had been half expected as he had been fighting cancer but Cliffton had been under the impression that he was doing well. His disease as he called it had gone into remission, he had been told back in January, the last time they had been in contact, exchanging e mails on a weekly basis, but the information had turned out to been untrue. How cruel one can be, giving a false hope, they didn't, couldn't care, deliberate lies, how could you not see the difference, only about their pay packets so they can buy cheap booze, fill their shopping trolleys and garages with worthless junk. Look what happens when there is a threat to that, they bellyache like crazy, 'Well I went to University for 5 years!' They would always say.

'Turn off the record! You've worn it out!'
They agreed to meet up as soon as they were able. He couldn't study any more, not today anyway. His mentor and good friend was now gone, there were so many voids in life that couldn't be filled, he sat in his chair sinking into the leather upholstery and drifted in and out of his memories with Rupert for the rest of the day, remembering his long drawn out stories that were so absorbing that time seemed to last forever, nothing existing out of that space. When he needed any advice he could always rely on him to be there. His idealism was a credit to all. His area of expertise was in dangerous infectious disease of animals and he believed that the developed world's current policies for detection and management of such disease, based on culling the host animals rather than stamping out the pathogen involved, were not only outdated, inhumane and uneconomical, but also rendered the countries concerned susceptible to potentially devastating introduction of pathogens by terrorists. 'Bioterrorism!' He would warn whilst banging his fist on the desk, his tea jumping in his cup. 'Is a cheap alternative to nuclear war and, chances are that is how the civilised world will be ultimately be attacked.'
The key to tackling infectious diseases of livestock globally, he believed, was to eliminate them at source. He advised the Defence Departments of many countries on multibillion pound programmes to establish a system of public health and veterinary and public health disease surveillance in the former Soviet Union, and coordinated a linked series of laboratories across Central Asia to track diseases such as bird flu and foot and mouth disease and to keep tabs on Russia's decaying arsenal of biological weapons. The threat of animal-borne pathogens, even leaving aside terrorism, verged on the apocalyptic.
'People have no idea what's out there!' Cliffton remembered he had told a seminar back in 1995. 'It's all so blasted crazy. There's something called mad cow disease here that we are keeping a close eye on. We've got Ostriches from Namibia that could be carrying ticks with Congo-Crimean haemorrhagic fever. We've got Vietnamese potbellied pigs that seem to be a trend for the Yuppies, Alpacas and Llamas, you name it coming in just to satisfy the fads of the two bob millionaires.'
'We've Romanian immigrants trying to smuggle in crates of their pigeons or hide them under their coats. We had one millionaire a few years back who had 28 Giraffes flown to his own private airstrip, just smuggled, right

in under our noses, and right under our feet as we all continue to go about our business. God knows what he wanted them for. Trying to keep pace with all of this, even with all our technology, it's like we're running around sticking fingers in a leaky dyke unable to stop it. A quick fix, that's all that seems to be what Governments want, put a band aid on and hope for the best, it seems to be what most want as long as it doesn't affect them but it can and it will. But it is not right! It never will be!'

The tools for implementing more effective strategies, however, were already to hand, he would confidently reassure. 'We now have rapid results, on farm tests for these diseases, effective vaccination strategies, internet based command, control and communication systems, and the means to track animal products from farm to the table, even internationally…..if we choose this way forward there will be little point in deliberate attacks, because the outcomes that terrorists want to see will not be possible and inadvertent introduction now will be eliminated with scarcely a footprint. Once you start something you have to finish it, there is no going back. There is always a way!! Take this as your benchmark!'

Cliffton remembered all his seminars well, had attended everyone even though some questions asked went over the top of his head!

What a man Rupert was. What a man!

Up early the next day he decided to get up and go to the library. First taking a stop at the Gallery tea room, he could rest here surrounded by Turners and Lowry's, away from the moans and groans other cafés seemed to have at that time of day. 'HAVE YOU HEARD?'

'JUST PICKED UP MY PRESCRIPTION FROM THE CLINIC!'

'BETTER GET HOME IT'S GOING TO SNOW IN FIVE MINUTES!'

'BLASTED BUS WAS A MINUTE LATE! AGAIN! IT'S EVERY DAY! EVERY DAY!'

There would be peace there for a few hours at least and it would get him out of the house. From 10 till 3 he got some work done, not enough, he had intended to do more but better than nothing with Rupert's departing still heavily on his mind. It was a hot day, and walking down the steps of the library he decided to go and have a drink at a newly opened sports bar across the road. It would be peaceful at this time of day. Ordering a half of cider and some pork scratching he sat by the bar and pulled out his notes. Tried to read them but nothing was going in, no use so he picked up the Metro free newspaper someone had left on a table. 'OI! YOU!' A female

voice shouted loudly from the other side of the bar. Cliffton looked up, and a woman was looking at him from the other side peering between the hand pumps. 'What's your name?'
'It's Cliffton, what's yours?' He replied involuntarily.
'Hmmmmm you look familiar.' The girl continued, the movement on her mouth seemed to be a friendly smile.
'And yours? Come over and sit here, have a chat and tell me who you are, I might know you.' The barman handed her drink to her.
'That will be £2.57 please.' The girl took some loose change out of her purse, inspecting the coins, handed her money over she picked up her drink and as she turned, pirouetting on her heels said.
'YOU RAPED ME!!' And off she went up to the sun terrace. A stunned Cliffton said to the barman,
'Did you hear that?'
'I heard nothing.' He replied. Shell shocked at the events he looked at the others near the bar, expecting some sort of response as there were about five older, hard core drinkers, taking their daily food, looking deep into their pints as if they had fallen in love or drowning in their sorrows, nothing else to look forward to. Shrugging his shoulders.
'Nutcase.' He thought to himself shaking his head, he continued to read his newspaper, sports section first. What a crackpot he mused shaking his head again, then out of the corner of his eye he noticed a woman heavily tattooed with a walki talki in her hand on the stairs to the sun terrace and looking in his direction and speaking into the device. 'Hey up! I'd better wait and see what's going on.' The intention had been to leave after he finished his drink. Ten-Fifteen minutes later a Police meat wagon turned up outside. Two Old Bill crossed the road and swaggered straight up the stairs directly to the sun lounge. There was a big one and a small one, Little and Large, Laurel and Hardy, crossed his mind, good cop, bad cop maybe, they were Police, not Police community support officers, Kevlar vest, latest truncheons, thinner and longer, handcuffs hanging over their backsides, POLICE in bold letters embroidered across their chests looking more like paramilitary thugs, not your old school Bobby these two but the present day version, why don't they write UNDER COVER he thought. He decided he'd better wait and about ten minutes later they came back down with the girl who bore a wide grin across her face, as if enjoying her moment of fame, they were appearing to escort her out not even looking in

Cliffton's direction. Another ten minutes later the smaller Copper came back and walked over to an elderly chap who had not stopped staring at his beer in the whole time Cliffton had been sat there.

'Are you the gentleman who's just been accused of raping someone?'

'Eh!' The man replied scratching his head and his crotch at the same time completed with a puzzled look in his face. Cliffton thought he must've been a helicopter pilot in his day!

'No, it's me.' Cliffton volunteered, he couldn't have left or denied who she had accused as there was CCTV everywhere, if he had left he would have been on the six o'clock news. 'HAVE YOU SEEN THIS MAN?' The Copper came over and took his details down.

'Name, address, home telephone number and mobile number, Sir!' He demanded, taking out his notebook.

'Sure you don't want to know my rising sign?'

'Enough of that lad!'

'I'm the one who's been falsely accused. Who is she anyway?'

'Not saying anything much really.'

'She can't do that, come into a public place and accuse an innocent man of doing something he hasn't done!' Blurted out Cliffton.

'You can take out a civil prosecution if you want to. We get this 6-8 times a day. We'll be in touch if we need to.' All very business-like, and off he went back to the van, probably to tick all his boxes and eat his bacon butty. Cliffton had a couple of more drinks, to calm his nerves and left, but decided to stop again, the shock of what had happened had just sunk in, this had never happened to him before, now he knew full well what it was like to be falsely accuse of something. At the Five Forks he ordered a tomato juice with a dash of Lea and Perrin sauce, no more alcohol, he'd already had more than intended and continued to read his paper when he became aware there was a woman standing next to him.

'HAVE YOU GOT A PROBLEM?' She screamed, her eyes piercing into him a with a crazed expression that you see when someone is really angry, mad or even on the point of being sectioned, blood vessels expanding like crazy.

'What's your name? What do you do for a living?' He was just about to reply when the barman suddenly interrupted 'He's got loads of problems this fella!' This appeared to defuse the situation, but Cliffton decided to go. Would he ever get any peace? He was not ready to go home yet so walked

over the road to the Mouse and Fox, his head was now beginning to spin around, but he wasn't drunk. Sitting in the corner with his coffee, surely he would be okay here. He had decided to give alcohol a wide berth; again he attempted to read his paper. Looking up he noticed a man who had been sitting at the other side of the room making a bee line for him. 'Oh no! What now?' Almost in Clifton's face the man yelled.
'I'm only going to warn you once, stop eye balling me!' Cliffton put up his hand
'Stop now! I don't even know you and I haven't been looking at you!' Cliffton got up not even finishing his drink, the coffee still warm and virtually untouched, a waste of £3.50, leaving as the man continued to hurl abuse. Three times, in the space of, 90 minutes. He'd experienced the other end of Export's evolutionary scale, in a very brief time. 'Dysfunctional lot.' He thought to himself. 'They must have problems but they can't help it. Ach it's not my problem. You have to get out of here!' A cold sweat had spread over his brow, enough to have to mop with his hanky. Feeling lonely and isolated. He had to get home; this was not an ideal way to prepare for his final exam, and such an important one at that. At home concentration completely gone he tried to look at his books but no use. Couldn't even get to sleep and when he did he had only a small few hours. Stupid, why did you go out, you never go into pubs these days, should've stayed home, not long to go now, don't flag.
Getting up early still feeling the need to get out he decided to go on to the moors, he had to clear his head. Beside him on the hills the sun was shining, the larks were singing, but down there he knew there were a hundred thousand grown people, he hadn't included the children, but they were all struggling for a little sun and air, toiling, moiling, living a life of suffocation, dying as the sanitary reports constantly reported through the medias only too clearly show but we see how filthy the street is, fly tipping piles of rubbish in the back streets now spilling onto main pavements, of diseases caused by foul air and want of light – all for what? Tapping away on their computers, always inside, on their I phone 23 or is it I phone 51 now, he remembered Portia had a 37, ah yes Portia, watching the television not even realising they are only making a few people rich? The Fat Cats. All you get is that they are doing nothing wrong. Well they are conning the living daylights out of good kindly honest hardworking people. The Cons were outstripping the pros and at a fast pace, so plastic, impossible to

recycle, was he the only one who could see it and if so what did everyone think of him? He looked around...........he was the only one there.
Five different buses later he realised his house keys were missing. 'What's happening to me?!' He telephoned the bus company and was told that he could telephone back the next day and he can see if they have been handed in. 'What about today?'
'Can't do, if they are handed in they will be put into the safety deposit box and there is only one key available and it is at the HQ of the company in Goostrey the next town.' He explained he couldn't get in and will have to sleep at the bus station. Sorry they can help no further. He thought hard and suddenly realised he could have left them on the 471 and waited at the terminus. A few hours later he managed to intercept the bus driver before she went off duty. First bit of luck, otherwise it would've been the next day. Last bus put all things into a safe deposit box and with only one key it is only opened the next day, she explained to him, he thanked her but the pressure is now building, his hemispheres at bursting point. Can things get any worse for him and there is less than one week to go to before his final exam. Soon he gets home sinks into his beloved chair; it has now been sometime since he has studied. 'Am I losing it? Remember Cliffton there is no such thing as stress! That is when you can't cope. 'AND YOU ARE COPING!' He took a bath to relax his muscles, Llang Llang. 'I'M GOING TO BUST A BLOODY BLOOD VESSEL!' He screamed at the top of his voice, he needed to, must focus. Let it out. He knew!! He thought and decided to tidy his place up. 'I've been told that it's therapeutic, I'll try! Christ I'm talking to myself now!' Four hours later, kitchen, bathroom, living room and bedroom are all done, he sat down feeling better. 'Wow! What a roller coaster I'm having. I know I'll finish the stairs! Hey I like this talking to myself! I can sort things out!' Gets to the 2nd bottom step and stumbles.
'OWCH! That is sore!' As his ankle swelled. And soon a limp develops. No more study today. Another restless night and Cliffton forced himself out of bed the next day, no morning run, he now can't even drive! Takes the bus into the city library, it will be quiet there. He does this but it is difficult, his ankle is twice the size. No point in taking the car even if he could, car parking and can't stretch out, plus the vandals could be out, maybe not they'll all be in bed after collecting their benefits.. Central library brilliant but through pain he gets some meat done and hobbles

home. After all this time and no food he went to Channing's Bakery. There was one pie left, cold; no time to heat up shop was closing. £1.54 He bought this and a bottle of Red Pull, the energy drink, which everyone at this time seemed to be drinking. He could go to the 24 hour cluster, naaaaaah! All there will be there are students asleep at their computers surrounded by pizza boxes, kebab trays and empty cans of energy drinks. He fell asleep on the bus home, ignoring his surroundings. On arrival at his last stop there is his next bus is there and Cliffton started to run for it but just as he gets to the stop the door shuts and the bus pulls out. 'OI!' But the driver ignored him and the bus continued to move away. After looking at the timetable he resigned himself to a 30 minute wait. 'THIRTY MINUTES!!' This is due to the cuts made to public transport he thought; the government's austerity measures were now affecting him. Leaning against the stand he sees 5 people sitting in the waiting area, no seat for him. All five are on their mobile phones. Another girl came up and sat on the floor next to him. Pulled out her mobile phone. 'You'll get sore fingers using that!' Remarked Cliffton. The girl smiled not even looking in his direction. 'Why are you lot always on your phones?'

'Nothing else to do!' Replied the girl. Nothing else to do but log on to social networks. Sad. Big problem social networking, people mark out their territories, causing arguments, jealousies, setting family against family, friend against friend, good for many but dangerous for the few. 'I'VE GOTTA GET OUT OF HERE!' He then decided to pop into the pub for a half cider and a bag of nuts. Enough time for the bus. Across the road he orders his drink and sits down. Suddenly a woman comes up by the side of him.

'Have you got a problem?' Stunned he looks up and sees it is the same woman as the previous day, about to reply when a listening bartender says 'That's enough!' The woman with the same crazed look in her eye leaves, heading off to her next pub, Cliffton leaves just catching the bus this time.

'You'll never learn. You never learn.' He said to himself.

The next day he chose to get out again to the same library and felt better after a good night's sleep. At the library it is quiet, a few other students and people reading, directly in front of him there is a man with his back to him, a book open, pen in hand, writing. Working solidly until 2 30pm he gets a sudden cramp in his stomach twisting, knotting and his salivary glands suddenly his stomach starts to move up, fizzing overtime, about to retch.

'Quick the bog!' Rushing leaving his notes, rucksack and coat at his desk and dashed to the toilet, but where is it? 'Second floor up the stairs, left then right then right again, straight on and to your left.' Said the lady behind the counter not even looking up. Setting off right and left make no sense as the building is round! Just in time he got to the lavatory. He projectile vomited, pissed and shit all at the same time. Luckily he had got his pants down, off and there was a small sink by the bowl. Retching and straining he thinks he has emptied himself, what more can come out? It takes a lot out of him, he felt dizzy and weak. He dropped onto the toilet seat. 'Can anyone have this much bad luck?' He was sweating and looked up to the ceiling; the light is bright dazzling his eyes. He breathes heavily and rests a while when there is a knock on door.

'Are you alright lad?' After a brief moment Cliffton replied.

'I'll be fine; I'll be ok thanks for asking.'

'You don't sound good lad, must've been a bad curry, a tindaloo? Out on the pop too? I had one of those last Saturday and was never off the can!'

'I'm ok Sir; I'll be fine thanks again!' Thirty minutes later after gaining confidence to leave his sanctuary, he washed himself down the best he can and cleaned what he could, then headed back to his desk, nearly everyone is gone, nearly 7pm closing time. 'This isn't where I sat; my jacket and bag are not here.' He checked with the librarian, no not handed in she informs him, still not even raising her head. Stolen, must be no other explanation. He dropped into the Captain's chair and his head slumped into his chair Cliffton like a defeated boxer who can no longer continue to the next round. Slowly he picked himself up and rose holding his head level and put his hand into his pocket. He still has his keys in one, that is a relief and in his other £1.67. His bus day ticket, where can it be? He doesn't have enough to buy another; his wallet was in his jacket. Resigning himself to the long walk home, at least 9 miles, he left the library put his hand into his back pocket and there is his ticket. A sense of small relief comes over him, mercy. Arriving at the stop he sees the underclass coming out from the backstreets into the night, but are they any different from what is now on the streets during the day he ponders as he got on to the crowded bus but is aware of himself giving off that horrible shitty smell, a dirty nappy maybe but there are no babies on the bus. People move away from him and he feels terrible, lonely, and isolated, nobody wants him, but sees that he can stretch out and put his feet up. The 45 minute journey feels like 45 hours, his stomach undergoing resonance with the boneshaker of a bus. Feeling sick, with the next bout of diarrhoea about to involuntarily arrive and dehydrated he finds he finds his way home. After emptying himself again he grabs a glass of water and falls into his chair instantly he was asleep. Throughout the night he is back and forth to the toilet. Eventually it stops and he gets some sleep and lies in till 11am. In the afternoon a sudden asthma attack comes on, with no warning. Can't find his spray and curls into the foetal position. 'I have my final exam on Monday, what can I do? I can't study, must rest now, I can do no more.' After a long sleep he gets up on Sunday turns on his pc and reads an e mail hearing his cat in the Philippines has been missing a month. Just over a year old and when Cliffton had last seen him, Fatso was his name; he was no bigger than his hand. Fatso's first few weeks alive had been awful for a newly born, savaged twice by dogs, one nearly losing his tail and terrified by a Gecko Cliffton had helped him and given his name due to his long hind legs. A perfect mouser. He thought of him purring away on his knee, meowing when he was hungry, this helped him to relax.

Switching on the World news, Cliffton watched a devastating Typhoon unfolding in Asia, a hurricane in the US, famine in Africa, War in the Middle East, many, many, many people dead, men, women, children dead, children orphaned, families wiped out. He thinks how fortunate to be in the position he's in and sits in silence thinking about those less so or privileged. His week has been bad but not as bad as it could have been and it was not as bad as others. He'll be ok, he was here to recover.

It was now 10pm and there was a big day tomorrow. The preparation was over. What a way to do that! Had he done enough?

♪

I'M DOING FINE NOW

I'M DOING FINE NOW

WITHOUT YOU BABY

SO STOP IT BABY

JUST STOP IT

GIRL YOU REALLY DIDN'T THINK I COULD MAKE IT

NOW I'M ON MY OWN

360 degrees Michaelmas

THINGS ARE REALLY GOING ON................

He hummed as he strutted down the street putting in three twirls as he headed towards the underbelly of the single tower. Feeling good, his stomach was tender but fine, no knots or even crosses, no chance of the runs. The final day had arrived and he felt good, it was nearly over, gravy all the way from now.

♪

IN THE COOL LIGHT OF THE DAWN WHEN THE SKY WAKES
AND THE SUN SHINES ON THE BOULEVARD
IN THE TOWN WHERE I WAS BORN I AM SITTING
THINKING ABOUT WHERE YOU ARE......
♪ WELL YOU CAN TELL HOW I DO MY WALK
I'M A WOMAN'S MAN NO TIME TO TALK........

He hummed as he walked, his confidence was back, but it had never really gone, nothing was going to break his stride today, nothing, as he walked down the street. Dressed in his favourite Croix Sept jeans, belt on the last notch ensuring that the jeans hung well, tan ankle length boots, his favourite Lions dress shirt with buttons, dog tooth grey blazer, hanky in the breast pocket all cut and everything hanging well. Feeling good he headed towards the room six for the final time, heads turned, and beaming smiles.
'WOW! This is my day! I'm on fire! This is it! This is the real thing!' A group of around ten were gathered outside the block. Some were grossly focussed on bits of paper, cards with summarised notes, devouring every last drop of information from their final prepared minutes, others just staring at the floor, maybe hoping the ground would swallow them up, wide eyed through lack of sleep or maybe high on the caffeine, he heard pro plus was some peoples food but he had never tried, touched, never had to, possibly they had done enough or just resigned to the fact that there was no more to be done accepting their fate.
'CLIFFIEE! CLIFFTON!!!!' Shouted Emma and Geoff respectively in unison. They were relaxed leaning against the staircase; beaming smiles

greeted him as he walked towards them. 'I see you've made an effort today! PHOWARRRR! LOOKING GOOD! GOOD BOY!' Said Emma.
'Well this is the real me!' Replied Cliffton as he pulled out his mini PINK rugby ball and threw it in Geoff's direction. 'Catch Geoff!'
'Yeah right! Makes a change!'
'This is it. You ready?'
'Ready for what?! Is something big happening today? What's the big occasion? Yes, course I am! Have, well stopped revising a couple of days ago, nothing going in, nothing coming out so I thought I'd watch the TV. Corrie to be precise, that Vera what a woman!'
'Can't believe they've got a young character being persuaded to take the contraceptive injection. Think they are dealing with issues what a joke, causing an issue more like!'
'You! A Corrie fan Cliffton??!! Yeah, right!' Exclaimed Emma.
'Just keeping up with you, Emma! For Geoff I read the Beano!'
'Steady on Guys! We've still got one more to do!' Interrupted Geoff, handing the ball back. 'You know I'm a footie man!'
'Then it's party time! Gharry's bar! Yay hey!!'
'Can you lot be quiet I'm still revising!' Commented one of the more serious students, she was sat crossed leg on the pavement.
'You'll get piles!' A sarcastic grin was directed at Cliffton.
'Well if you are not ready now, you never will be!' Emma's comment was greeted by another deadly scowl.
'Hey look there's Dan! Wonder how many cans he collected last night?'
A small hairy man, portly with a slight limp, long unkempt hair, gapped teeth, rags for clothes a tattered and torn leather coat with a wool liming, was rummaging through the bins outside, next to the railway arches, filling an old sack with Royal Mail written on the side of it, with cans, an old bike, probably not even 3 speeds, or even any speed was propped up by the bin with a basket on the front filled to the brim with his worldly belongings. 'Hi Dan, how's it going? Made your fortune yet?'
A toothless grin beamed towards the three friends.
'Wait I'll just give him a quid to get a brew or something!'
'Here give him this too.' Geoff and Emma contributing, this would enable him to get a breakfast at least.
'Hi Dan! Here have this. Can't stop, got our final exam today!'
'Cheers lads!' Dan cheerfully spoke in a braw Scottish accent.

'I'm going to your place climbing after all this is over.'
'Well say hello tae Nessie frae me! Maybe we'll meet again?'
'I'm sure we will!'
Cliffton moved quickly back to his companions, their years of companionship almost at an end, and only about 10 minutes left now.
'Hey look! It's those two horrible new security guards moving Dan on! He's taking his sack away and kicked his bike on the floor!'
One security guard appeared to be wrestling with him and Dan shouted out. 'Get off you can't have it, it's mine!' as he struggled with the guard, seemingly keeping on to his sack of cans.
'Leave him alone! Have you lot not got anything better to do, he's only trying to earn a crust like all of us?'
'Watch what you're saying or I'll cart you off too!' Loosening his grip on Dan, he glared at them. This momentary lapse enabled Dan to wriggle free.
'HE'S GETTING AWAY! GRAB HIM THORSV...............YOU...' Screamed one of the guards to the other.
'....OK.......OU...........OUGE........' The exclamation of the second guard were drowned out as the 9 29 thundered overhead.
'RUN DAN, RUUUUUUN!'
'Pick on an old man won't you! Leave him alone, you saddo!'
'Freaks!'
Realising his lapse the guards turned back to Dan grasping at thin air but too late Dan was away, peddling away as fast as his small legs would allow him, his sack slung over his back. As he was getting away and mounting his bike he appeared to drop something. Seeing this Cliffton dashed up, sidestepping the guard and picked up what was a pouch fastened tightly with string in one movement, 'Going back to my rugby days' he thought pleased with the way he ran and picked up at the same time, dropping the pouch into his back pocket and headed back to his friends The confused guard looked from Dan to the three but decided against chasing Dan and now made a bee line for the 3 friends, his sidekick taking a back seat, but following faithfully behind.
'Come here you three. Right! I want all your names, I'm taking you to the Principal you are in trouble!'
'You can't we're going into an exam! Anyway who are you? Not seen you two before!' Shouted Emma, sticking her tongue out at them.
'Who am I? Well you should have thought about that before...........'

The door opened. It was time.
'Where are you going? Come here! Now!' Nostrils flaring out and his knuckles turning white, he was fuming!
Ignoring the guard every one filed into the exam room. They were now focusing, anyway who did that prat think he was?
'I'm going to have you!'
'But we've only just met!' Cooed Emma, infuriating the two men even more.
'You little shits!'
'Now, now Mister!!'
'After this we're leaving here!'
'They're right about here you know!' Exclaimed Geoff. 'Dull it isn't!'
'Never has been!'
'No not for us anyway!'
'What was that accent? It sounded like a German voice.'
The doors closed behind them, sealing them into their immediate destiny. 'I'll have you!' The security guard's voice faded away.
'SILENCE! All mobile phones to be left at the rear and switched off. If your phone rings the culprit will be banned from this test! And you will not pass your degree!'
Everybody sat down quietly, carefully placing their pens, pencils, rulers, calculators on to their desks. Cliffton taking off his jacket and slinging it over the chair, settled down. Emma was behind him, he could've have sworn she was focussing on his butt! Wishful thinking! The papers were already set out on the desks which were all set out regimentally, six feet between each, no chance of cheating here. The invigilator none other than Professor Brown stood authoritatively at his desk, hand in one pocket and the other tapping his chest.
The clock above the blackboard tick tocked towards 9am and on the final tock Brown commanded out. 'You can now turn over your papers and start!'
There was a flurry of papers opening, as though coming out of the blocks, rustling, gasps then sighs were heard across the room as some resigned themselves, others heads in their hands to what they had and had not prepared themselves for. Cliffton read through the questions carefully, focussing, deciding on which 3 out of the 5 questions he needed to do, or even was able to do in the 2 hours permitted. He would have to get his

skates on. Not much of a choice but he could do it, he knew more than enough for 2, 3 and 5, he closed his eyes, 'Thank you Lord!' It was going to be ok. Having barely come to his decisions he could hear Timmy Tien writing, scrawling across his paper without any interruption. What could he be writing? He couldn't see anyway so settled into his task. He could hear glug glug behind him. It was Emma having her drink, the end of her desk were her pens and a teddy bear, her mascot which had been with her throughout the finals. He tried to focus, forcing information out from his hemispheres. Not easy with the industrious Timmy, the sighs, the shifting of chairs, coughs, sniffles somebody nervous perhaps? Then somebody let out a loud fart and it stank! Phewww! A nervous disposition, perhaps. There were no giggles this was no laughing matter, careers and futures now hung in the balance, this was the hardened exam room of the undergraduate, all pros, well nearly all, and they must be after all the exams they had taken here. Fifteen minutes later he could see the person to the left pushing his chair back and leaving the room. Brown glared at him as he made his way out. How could he have done it all so quickly he must be good and know his stuff? Timmy continued without looking up pen not losing contact with his paper, totally focussed. Another gulp behind him as Emma refreshed herself with the smacking of lips. He returned to his paper and continued on his first question, when BANG! A heavy thud hit him on his right rump. Quickly he turned and looked at Emma but she was focussed on her paper. Braun glared at him so he quickly continued with his exam feeling a numbness spreading on his side.

Another hour passed tick tock, it seemed to go quickly. There were only about 10 left in the room now. Cliffton was on his final question now and was feeling content as the hands approached 10 45am, as if by military precision.

'You have 15 minutes left; no one may enter or leave the room now!'

5 minutes before time he finished and went over his paper, checking over and over, it looked neat and tidy and he was happy with what had been done, no more could be done. Timmy was still furiously writing and had already asked for extra pages. 'Is he writing a book?!! How can he write so much?' Cliffton thought to himself when BAM! Cliffton felt another sledgehammer thud on his rump. He quickly glanced behind, Emma had finished too, arms folded comfortably under her ample bosoms, 36, he had decided, which he now focused his eyes on. Realising a set of eyes was

burning into him he turned back to the front to see the stare of Professor Brown drilling deep into his head.
TOCK! TICK!
'Put your pens down NOW!' Barked Professor Brown with God like authority. 'NOW! NOT TOMORROW!' Directing his wrath from Cliffton to Timmy from Hong Kong seated directly in front of him who had been writing without pause during the last 2 hours. What could he be writing about Cliffton was thinking as he tried to focus on his own efforts. 'Was there that much to write about the Genome?' He asked himself. Geoff, Emma and Cliffton glanced over at each other with confident smiles. The Genome, their final exam was over and a champagne sense of joy filled everyone in the room, the popping of corks everywhere. Better than bungee jumping, better than sex well better than……everything for that one brief moment only, the tension release was incredible, like a sigh on milk white flesh. Everyone piled out of the room, they were free! There was no sign of Dan or the security guards.
'I firmly believe before many centuries more, Science will be the power of man, the engines he will have invented will be beyond his strength to control and someday Science will have the existence of mankind in its power and the human race commit suicide by blowing up the world wrote Henry Adams April 11th 1862 when he witnessed the first battle of Ironclads during the American Civil War an event that rendered all other Navies in the world obsolete overnight. Did I get that right Geoff?' Cliffton broke the silence.
'Exactly!' Said Geoff as they headed out of the block.
'Yes there is something in that you know. It's not an accident all this, carefully planned all through greed, through mechanics playing on emotions. All controlled by vacuum tubes, diodes, transistors, and unfortunately such a beautiful tool of electronics has become the mechanics of disaster. Scientists have and do warn us but no one listens, building into these monstrous wars, we must find ways to go on living.'
'Come on let's go! It's all over! We have some serious celebrating to do!' Interrupted Emma.
'Hey Emm why did you thump me back there?' Cliffton exclaimed incredulously.
'I didn't do anything but I saw what you were looking at you dirty sod! Gharry's Bar here we come!'

360 degrees Michaelmas

‘But I wanted to check on Dan!’ Said Geoff.
‘He’ll be fine! He’s a survivor and will outfox the security guards! Besides if they catch us …………!’
‘Have you ever seen them before?’
‘Nope but come on, as long as they keep out of our hair!’
They all headed for Gharry’s bar in the Union to drink themselves to oblivion one final time and into their new land of confusion.
‘Sorry to hear about you and Portia, Cliffton.’ Said Geoff, as they headed towards the bar. ‘Somebody not too far away, little ears pricked up when she heard that!’ Nodding in Emma’s direction.
‘Boy Geoff! News travels fast!’ The bar was full, the release incredible, their time over, impromptu tunes like ‘I have survived’, rang out, the atmosphere was electric, laughter filled the air and the drinks flowed. Emma, Geoff and Cliffton grouped themselves with other faculties who had been befriended by them during the years. ♫I have survived!♫’ Sounded out from a group of engineering students in the corner in tune to, ‘I will survive!’ on the jukebox next to the two life like figures of the Blues Brothers. They talked about what they were going to do until their results came out. Emma was going to drive around Europe with a couple of girlfriends for 4 weeks, Paris, Rome, Madrid, Berlin, Prague, Amsterdam, the lot! ‘Keep out of the Hostels Emma you don’t want to be taken!’
‘No men! Girls just want have fun! I’m saving myself for the right one!’ She would say but this time she looked at Cliffton. ‘Yeah right Emma!’ Geoff was going back to his Mum in London. Finances would not permit any extravagance and he would look for a job till results day. Cliffton was luckier than most, he knew and was grateful for it. He had planned a 2 week break to the Scottish Highlands, climbing and visiting relatives and old friends. After a few hours the parties began to break up.
‘We won’t be coming home tonight! Our generation will put it right! We’re not just making promises that we can’t keep!’ Screeched the remnants in the corner.
‘We’re away Emma, I’m going to see Geoff off at the station and catch my train home, you coming for a coffee?’
‘Awww!

♫

WON'T YOU STAAAAAYAAAAY
JUST A LITTLE BIT LONGER!??????

Pleeeeaseee!! I'm staying Cliffton; see you both on results day!'
'You're one on your Emma take care! Just do everything we would do! Keep off the wacky backy!'
'Never touched it in my life! I'll send a postcard!'
'You'd better!'
'And Cliffy.... don't worry about Portia, her loss is MY GAI....... whoops! I nearly did it there! I'll see you right next month!' And with that she was off turning briefly to give a seductive smile.
'Told you so my man!!!'
'You mean she's interested in me? Never!'
'Yes my man! Told me herself many times!' Geoff and Cliffton made their way out of the bar. When suddenly a tearful Emma cried out. 'Cliffton! Geoff! This is really it!' She ran up to them with tears in her eyes and they all hugged. Cliffton could feel Emma's voluptuous breasts against his chest, a couple of pencil erasers pressing into him, what a feeling, but that pleasure was over far too quickly. 'Thought you'd like that! You can have that on account!' Emma teased, wiping the tears in her eyes as she scampered back into the bar. It was finally hitting them. As Cliffton turned WHAM! He was knocked to the side. 'Wow Cliffton! You OK? What was that about! You've only had soft drinks!'
'What was that? I thought someone had kicked me up the backside!'
A glance around and he could see nothing. 'It must've been coming out into the fresh air! Strong stuff that!'
'Forget about Portia Cliffton, she certainly got her pound of flesh!'
'Portia? Who is she?' He lied. Although he knew, he couldn't help but think of The Merchant of Venice.
'Got your ball Cliffton?'
'Sure have!' As he pulled the miniature rugby ball out of the side netting on his rucksack. 'Never leave home without it!' His pet possession had it all the way through University. 'Come on let's go, I've a lot of energy to get rid of!' The two friends started an impromptu scrimmage in the street and headed as a wrestling match up the street into a crowded shopping centre, sweating and getting gLowering looks from the shoppers maxing

out their credit cards. The boys scrimmaged through dodging the shoppers miraculously, some think it was funny others did not. Then Geoff broke away saw two young women ahead. 'He sees the posts and WHAM! Straight! Up 'n' Under!' He kicked the ball between the two women who shrieked, it headed straight between them! 'He scores!' Then it all fell silent as a loud booming voice shouted out, 'HOWZAT!' Stood directly in front of them was a very tall Policeman! 'Now, now, boys having some fun here?! Rugby players? Well there are plenty of rugby pitches around here, I suggest you go there!'
'No sir we've just finished our final exams!' Said Cliffton realising this was his second run in with the Law.
'Ok, ok, here's your ball. No more rugby in here ok? Good luck with the exams!'
'Thank you!' Cliffton took the ball and put it back in his rucksack. 'Close shave there Geoff! But all part of the game!'
'Yes if it had been a younger Copper he'd have hauled us off to the clink to impress his Superintendent! We'd have been arrested, for something or other. Not many of the old school Bobby left these days!' They trot off to the cafe, they see students and school kids all over the place, eating their snacks, sausage, chips and gravy, panini's and pasties, dribbling everything on to the floor, chucking their litter where they pleased.
'Do this lot never do any other studying?'
Geoff smiled and they walked towards the station with each other for a final time stopping at Nero's for a last latte.
'Did you see that girl coming out of the shop?'
'Where?' A young woman about 23 had come out of Tosco's and pulled her mobile phone out of her pocket like a gunslinger at the ok Corral.
'HIYAA!!' She said at the top her voice in a broad Northern accent. 'Yeah Hun I miss you too!' As though she'd not seen whoever she was talking to for months. 'I love you loads and loads! Yes I know! Oh yes I know!'
'Eeeeeee bah gum luv! Well why don't you go and see him.....or her! We don't want to know!' Shouted Geoff.
'UP YURS!' The young woman countered, sticking her middle finger in their direction. 'Not you Hun! Just some pricks who need to get a life! Yes I know!' She continued now sticking two fingers in their direction as she continued down the street.
'Not very ladylike that!'

'You know if you do that walking across the road in New York, it's a serious fine? Life is just a video game to most now.'
'How about the fine in Singapore, if you are caught eating chewing gum you get fined $300, Singaporean, there!'
'Wow! Look at this on the pavement!'
'Yep you could do a page on social behaviour studying that! Get a PhD!'
'You mean I could be a Doctor of Bubble gum!'
'If you can get the funding!'
Sitting down in the cafe, from behind another phone rang, sounded like Zen spirit Cliffton thought. For what seemed like an eternity of ringing and a rustling and folding of newspapers a man answered his mobile phone, 'The bill is HOW much!' He stood quickly up, phone in one hand and newspaper folded under the other, then suddenly a thud on the floor with the magazine opening in the centre displaying June playmate of the month!
'You know Geoff these phones are a detriment to all, even indirectly!'
'Yes I know Cliffton yesterday I saw a young mum pushing a pram, two kids in the pram, baby on her back, with another clutching her Mum's coat whilst she with two hands is frantically texting, playing a game or something.'
'Yes the internet is an evil thing, you put something online and people go back and back and stew over it.'
'Hmmmmm! Yes, did you see that article in the Metro? Where Sarky Crookenturder the founder of Mybook said he is going to eradicate disease in the world with his millions!'
'Unbelievable!'
'Well he should start by eradicating his site; it's a putrid disease and gives all his money to charity!'
'It is a tool, like the interne, that is way out of control. The mobile is now the most important single item in modern living, it is an instrument of freedom, opportunity and convenience, a symbol of essential day to day living but it has now become a dangerous obsessive shackle to many, many people and they don't even know it. The best bit is that it is never mentioned how much drain these two so called technological advances are doing to the energy system.'
'Nobody seems to give a toss anymore. It's a free for all. Technology is killing us!' Just a way of controlling the masses. What did the Romans say? Control the mob and you control Rome?'

'Yes if we were more sensible, like placing restrictions on the use of mobile phones. Our visual awareness would not be impaired by these things. In this modern world the ability of all to have good awareness is paramount but it is deteriorating rapidly through the nature of mobile phones, i pads and when you look at your phone you are losing awareness because you are focussed on the screen all the time, there are no eye movements happening-everything is completely static, you don't know what is going on front or back and left or right. It is a shame because we all know this yet do nothing about it.'

'Can't fault you there Geoff. Most people wear blinkers these days only tunnel vision of what is going around them. I remember when there was none of this. Remember the petrol strike? Well I was in Tosco nearly 3 weeks into the strike and the shelves were getting bare and I could see a circle of people so I went to investigate. In the circle were two women fighting over a loaf of bread, when suddenly the loaf split right down the middle, the slices of bread just shot everywhere as the women landed on their backsides ending their tug of war. Then it went silent, you could hear a pin drop. It must be because of the stark reality of what was going on around us at that time. And, all because of that idiot running the country.'

'I don't know about you but it drives me crazy!'

'Me too.'

'All we need is one serious eventuality and there will be anarchy everywhere. Darwin's Theory of Evolution will be fully realised and come into full play. Only the fittest will survive, I saw one kid crying because her battery had run out on her phone! Just couldn't cope or communicate. And she was 18!'

' A sad world, It's a shame really social media divides us and brings us together, but unfortunately it is also used for marking out territory, developing online rivalry, an instrument of mass destruction that can bring anything down.'

'Yes a click of a switch is life changing. Unfortunately we are stuck with it now! Make the best of a bad job or is it good job?''

'I asked directions for a place in the City not long ago and was told to Google it! Crazy!'

'I'm going to miss our daily confabs, weekly coffees Cliffton, discussing current affairs, and putting the world to rights.'

'Our rights!'

'Exactly!'
'Any idea what they are?'
Two elderly ladies sat down with their drinks and buns, next to them. One squeezing her big bottom into her chair. A conversation was struck up almost immediately between them.
'We'll have to be quick Audrey; our bus is in 10 minutes.'
'Yes I know!'
'Did you see your Doctor?'
'Yes, what a complete waste of time. Waited for 30 minutes only in for two minutes.'
'What did he do?'
'Well, he referred me to the Nurse who referred me to the, Rheumatologist, who referred me to the Dermatologist, who sent me to the Gynaecologist.'
'Gynaecologist? At your age? Whatever for? Are you pregnant?!'
'Women's things Audrey love, women's things, but she said I was in the wrong place and sent me to the Proctologist.'
'Proctologist? What's that?'
'Bum Doctor Love. I've been getting these horrible.............'
'Hey I'm going to get my future told next week. With one of those clairvoyants.'
'Really? What are you having read?'
'Well I can have my cards read, my palm read, my face read and something read by an anthologist.'
'What's that?'
'Don't know. Anyone here know?' The lady asked around the cafe, to which someone chipped in,
'It's having your arse read! Pretty accurate reading actually reading from your arse apparently. Personally I think it's a load of S H ONE T!'
The lady changed direction back to her original discussion with her friend and continued to give a graphic description of her examination at the top of her voice.
'I've gotta get out of here!!!!!!' Cliffton cried out in multiple exclamations, dropping his forehead with a bang onto the table.
'Be careful what you say Cliffton it might come true!'
'Only if I'm really lucky!! I haven't told you about my last couple of week yet!'

Nero's was abuzz with laughter, even porno man was laughing, yet the two ladies were oblivious to their show, cocooned from the outside world, good companions, inseparable friends, it was good to see.
Cliffton looked into his coffee mug it was empty. 'Pity it wasn't tea maybe they could've read my future!'
'Don't you need leaves for that?!!Go with this lady and you'll get your arse read!'
Geoff finished the dregs from his drink. 'You don't want that really!? Come on it's time to go. We have a good future ahead! We've never had such an opportunity!'
'Yes we have worked hard for it.'
As Cliffton stood up he put his hand into his back pocket. 'Oh Geoff, Dan dropped this when one of the security guards grabbed him outside the exam room.'
'What is it?' Cliffton opened up the pouch.
'No idea? Not seen anything like this before, have you?'
'Could it be the guards? Maybe that is what they were after.'
'Well if it is he's not getting it back!'
'Maybe this is what they wanted from him?'
'You know I've never seen them before. Strange. And their accents.'
'Yes, EMM thought he looked pretty slimy, really creepy. And she is a good judge.'
'What is it?' Cliffton undid the string on the patch and dropped a round coin like object into his hand, approximately 4 centimetres in diameter, with another coin 2 centimetres diameter on top of that, a bright white star was in the centre of the middle piece. Letters surrounded the periphery of both discs, the centre disc which could be bevelled like the diving watch on Cliffton's left wrist.
'What do you think this is for? Not seen anything like this before.'
'Dunno. I'll keep onto it; give it back to Dan on results day. He's bound to be knocking about!' From behind he could hear a foreign accent,
'***Apare apa nu madada ate paramesure ne tuhanu karana Vica madada karega.***' He turned around and could see a group of Pakistani women chatting in their own tongue.
'That's if that security guard hasn't nailed him! Do you think one of the guards dropped it?'

'Naaah!! Dan is too sly for him! Anyway I am sure I saw Dan drop it! Maybe an heirloom or something valuable perhaps?'
'Yes maybe!'
'Seventh of July then?'
'Yup! The seventh of July. Did you know the results are being listed differently this year?'
'How so?'
'Well bring your id card as you can only identify your grade through your number.'
'I am not a number! I am a FREE MAN!'
'Yes me too, apparently this is to avoid the shame of not seeing who got what!'
'Last year there were complaints and tears as others could see who didn't do as well as they thought? Tears everywhere!'
'Well as long as get what I want I don't mind who sees my result!'
'Well if I do really crap I'll tell everyone I got a First!'
'Do you remember that guy whose parents turned up for his graduation and he had been booted out after a few months?'
The miniature ball dropped out of Cliffton's bag, picking it up slowly and looks longingly at it. 'How you managed to get all those girls involved in a scrimmage these past few years I'll never know!' Quipped Geoff.
'I'll miss this, miss it all. It's goodbye to this then.' As he balanced the ball in his right hand.
'Why do you think we have a culture problem Geoff? It's because, we have evolved socially from the days of the hunter gatherer. It has become an us and them where the us's want there to be more, if not all us than them and vice versa. It is easy for each to mobilise one or the other and that in turn creates the problem because it is not the individual who is thinking for themselves.'
'Yes but at the moment we are them and soon after results day we will become us's, going into our new careers, we will soon forget about the them's.'
'I don't want to do that! Must never forget how we got here.'
'And why do we do what we do?'
'What?'
'To make a difference.'

'Well if everybody actually carried out their intention of being a better place it would certainly be a better place.'
'Can't fault you there!'
'Let's go in here for one!'
The TV is on behind the bar in the Orange House and a group of men and woman are watching an ice hockey match.
'GO ON GET IT IN! YES! HE'S SCORED! HAVE IT! YA BAS!' The group cheered wildly at their team scoring when suddenly a fight breaks out between the players.
'GO ON! KILL HIM! SMASH HIS TEETH OUT! TEAR HIS FUCKING HEAD OFF! KICK THE FUCKIN' SHIT OUT OF HIM!' Continued the group, men and women, when suddenly blood was seen on the ice.
With a huge roar. 'YESSSSSSSSS! GET HIM FINISH THE FUCKER OFF!!!!' Shouted one of the women at the top of her voice.
The crowd on the TV could be heard baying for more, as did the group at the bar. The woman screamed!
'COME ON TEAR HIS BALLS OFF!'
'Stop that! Right NOW! Or I will have to ask you to leave!' Intervened the girl behind the counter, in a quiet firm voice.
'What of it?!I'm not doing any harm!'
'You are swearing and disturbing the other customers! It is painful to the ear.'
'So what!?' Replied the woman confrontationally and aggressively, eyeballing the girl.
'Ok, ENOUGH, that's it, OUT!'
'What? What did I do?'
'I said… LEAVE!' And with that she turned off the TV. An argument broke out and the woman became more aggressive but eventually her friends managed to calm her down and they leave but not without a parting shot, a last word. Geoff and Cliffton watched in amazement. Struggling to comprehend how a respectable looking woman could behave in this way.
'Who wants to drink in this shit hole anyway with all you yokels?' The venom with pure spit was directed at the girl who seemed to take the whole episode in her stride, obviously seasoned in these matters.
Geoff and Cliffton looked at each other blankly and shook their heads.
'You wouldn't think respectable looking people would behave like that.'

Cliffton looked in the direction of the girl and smiled, nodding approval of her resilience. She returned this with a smile and said to Cliffton.

Suddenly the familiar voice of Emma was heard. 'Now listen here Mr Speakers! Let's enjoy the time we have till results day! Are you two coming? Come on be a sport! Please Clifftonrrrrr! I NEEEED YOU!'

The two boys politely declined, Cliffton had to get back to prepare for his

'*Helfen sie sict selbst und Gott wird Ihnen helfen*!'

trip, Geoff was on his way to London, and he didn't want to miss the last train. His Mum was excited too, she hadn't seen him for a while, since before New Year and he didn't want to disappoint her. Good woman, came over from Antigua and did all the jobs nobody wanted, never off work, the last Bus Conductress in town.

♫

THE BOYS ARE BACK IN TOWN
THIS CHICK SHE GOT UP
AND SHE JUST SLAPPED CLIFFY'S FACE!
MAN WE JUST FELL ABOUT THE PLACE,
IF THAT CHICK DON'T WANT TO KNOW
FORGET HER!

'Thanks for that piece Emm!'

'I'll make it up to you Cliffton, I PROMIIIISE! We'll have a big party to celebrate our success! Even Timmy will come along!' With that she said her farewells and skipped joyfully on to her next pub!

'Told you! You're in there!' Behind the two there was another girl on her phone....... 'YAK YAK YAK YAK YAK!!!!'

'Does she not realise she is more pathetic than she looks?! Social media shite!'

'Shall we ask her?'

'Nah! Let her getting on with having no life!'

'Now where were we? Yes! Just like a burglar alarm salesman.' Cliffton continued.

'How so?'

‘Well the alarm salesman comes around to your house gives you all the crappy spiel and then says £5,500 pleas sign on the dotted line! You disagree and he drops it a little, you still disagree so he drops it more, again you say no so he asks if he can phone his boss on your phone he agrees. So he goes into your hall he is heard talking. He comes back in I have just spoken to my boss and he says that a customer over ordered on a Canary Wharf luxury flats and they have exactly the system I have personally designed for you and can sell them at ....£2500, now you can’t do better than that can you. ‘Sorry no, No!’ He argues some more, ‘Well I have no commission on this.’ ‘No still don’t want it!’ ‘Please leave.’ ‘Can I use your toilet?’ ‘Well if you must!’ He comes back and tries again. So you ask him to see something else. He has it in his car and as goes to get it but as he is in his car you put his bags at the door and close it. He screams through your letter box ‘Well don’t blame me if your house gets burgled!’

‘Come on Geoff I’ll treat you to a burger.’

‘Thanks Cliffton buddy, my student loan has maxed out, as is my bank account, overdraft n’all!’

‘They really stitched us up with that one Geoff, free loan my arse! Don’t worry we’ll soon be on the road to recovery!’ They go to McLain’s and order a Big Mac for Cliffton and a Fillet o Fish for Geoff with two Cokes.

‘That’ll be £3.59 please!’ Cliffton puzzled at this says.

‘Are you sure?’ Yes I am, you think I’m trying to rip you off!’ Replied the cashier in almost aggressive tone.

‘No, no!!! It should be £7.59!’ She tried again, no, £3.59 once more. She called the manager, the manager came in,

‘What’s the problem?’ They explain, no problem, you are undercharging,

‘No I’m not. It’s £4.59!!’ Cliffton rolled his eyes.

‘It’s simple, it all adds up to £7.59.’ The manager says,

‘Tell you what I’ll let you off the £3!’ As if he is doing them a favour! ‘How do you add up?’ He showed them. It is pictures on the till! No wonder things are getting like they are! These days’ people want others to do the thinking for them; soon they are going to want you to push the buttons for them on the damn things. Cliffton paid £3.59 and they eat their meal. He takes his change from the lady at the till, said thank you. ‘***Pomz sobie sam, to i Bog ci pomoze***!’ Cliffton glanced up, ‘What did you say?’

‘I said thank you!’

'Sorry I thought you said something else.'
After they walked to the station chatting and reminiscing about their time over the previous three years, suddenly it would be all over. As they arrived at the station the Northern Belle pulled in. A group of French girls skip excitedly past them, one looks directly at them. '***Aide toi et Dieu l'aidera***!' Smiles and carries on her conversation excitedly with her friends.
'What did that girl say to us Geoff?'
'What girl? I didn't hear anything. Now that's a beautiful sight!' The steam train pulled in filling the air with white smoke and on coming to a halt the band started up, splendidly turned out in their uniforms, the red carpets rolled out of the doors on to the platform as the staff, Chef with his tall hat, waiters and waitresses even the driver, stoker and guard stood by this marvellous monster of a bygone era to welcome her passengers.
'Well Geoff this it.'
'Yes old buddy it is.'
'One last thing.......all these deaths in the world cannot be for nothing, we get numerous chances, somehow we must embrace wisdom, instead of greed and ignorance past present and future technologies we have will free the mind of mankind.'
'Yes see you in about a month. We'll deal with it then!!'
'The seventh of July buddy, can't forget that one!'
They shook hands and headed for their respective platforms. Cliffton turning around just as Geoff did.

'OI! CLIFFTON! WE'LL PUT IT RIGHT!'

Shouted Geoff raising his hand in the air and he filtered into the crowd heading for platform 11. All around were oblivious to his shout tunnelled onto their devices, most with ear phones, some with the new headphones that filter out all noise, not knowing anything outside their village bubble, a danger to all let alone themselves. He should've asked him to go climbing with him, he'll sort something out after results day, go to Anglesey for a weekend, dinner at the Lobster Pot, and maybe Emma would come to? That sounds good, yes he would suggest that. How fickle he could be! Emma hmmmmmm......!

Cliffton caught the train back to his apartment, while watching the passing scenery he sees the passenger opposite him reading the paper.

EIGHT RUSSIAN WARSHIPS ESCORTED THROUGH THE CHANNEL.....
FLEET SET TO REFUEL IN SPAIN

RAF SCRAMBLES 8 TYPHOONS

He turned over his page to reveal......

CLINTON AND TRUMP TRADE INSULTS IN LIVE DEBATE,

Z LIST CELEB GETS HOUSE BURGLED
AND IS TERRIFIED!
EXCLUSIVE

Cliffton thinks to himself.....It's a crazy world, madness is prevailing, promises are made but what more can be done and the media is to blame just inciting everyone. All they want is copy. They are not helping anyone they have provided a dangerous platform. George Orwell in 1854, no truer words are ever written. The passenger drops his paper and glared at him.
'***Hjelp deg Selv og Gud Vil hjelpe deg***!'
'Excuse me Sir, I didn't quite catch that?' The man glared back.
'I said what the fuck are you looking at!' And raised his paper continuing with his reading. He dozed off and is woken by the guard.
'Let me see your ticket.......you should've got off two stops ago!' He lets him off the excess fare, realising the mistake, leaving him to walk the 3 miles back and decides to take a short cut, through the local council estate, it'll shorten his trip, dangerous but it was light. He sees the backstreets littered with rubbish, overflowing bins that the bin men have refused to empty, wrong stuff in the bin, beer cans, wine bottles strewn across the street, readymade meal cartons, M&S, ASDA, MORRISON'S, ALDI, energy drinks, Lucozade, Red Bull, he remembers the day when Lucozade was only to be taken when ill and could only be got from the chemist, glass bottle with a refund on it. Settees, TVs, a parrot's cage all dumped in the street. Suddenly SPLAT! A small package Lands in front of him, he stops

and looks down and is about to pick it up thinking someone has dropped it and rears back because of the stench, on closer inspection he discovers it is a dirty nappy. He glanced around and at his left there was a woman cigarette in her mouth, glass of wine in hand looking at him.

'*Msaada mwenyewe na Mungu atakusaidia*!'

'Excuse me?'

'What are you looking at, you stupid cunt?!' She shouted at him. Cliffton rose up to his feet and stepped over the nappy and headed to his apartment block shaking his head as more torrents of abuse were directed at him. Taking in his surroundings he sees that these people are no hopers, on benefits, been that way for so long now they are unemployable. No industry anymore, the country doesn't make anything, no jobs, no real money no chance to get respectability anymore, no chance to live life, earn a living get respectability for themselves or even to go about it or build, used to handouts. A few doors down the street he slows down as he approaches a commotion in the street. He can see at the end house a man with a breeze block and he is smashing against the door. 'LET ME IN YOU FUCKING BITCH!!!!' He was so lucky he thought to himself as he walked to the other side of the road, getting deeper and deeper in thought as he turns the key in his lock. Suddenly there is a downpour and he sees a lady pushing her pram struggling through the deluge and over the uneven pavements and kerbs. 'Here let me help.' As he took hold of the pram he wondered who would see him. 'Do you think this will affect my street cred?' He joked with the lady a Grandma helping out here Daughter who was at work.

'Affect it? This will make it!' He was witnessing the good and the bad of society in all its glory; it had always been there but was coming to the fore, distinct in the now widening gulfs.

Cliffton watched the maddening crowd heading down the street, god knows where. 'I remember when, I remember when I nearly lost my mind! You're driving me crazy, you're driving me crazy! Yeah!' It sure was a crazy scene.

'You'd be a great critic Cliffton! Tell you what I'd be a critic of the critics! You are quite a literary man. 'Only quite? I'm a literary genius!!' He commends himself. After the last few weeks he deserves this pat on the back!

Cliffton was luckier than most, a mature student with a good job with income, his exams over and now a new future!
His pride and joy an MG TF 135 in metallic Tango Red, the colour of his favourite team. He was now moving into pastures new and as soon as his results were out his life would be changing forever, he had prevailed but he looked at the pizza box with the ring on it, still there from the previous week. 'Lucky escape that! I'll see if I can flog it when I get back.' Three days later with the celebrations and hangovers from finishing his final exams over he headed for the Highlands of Scotland. A treat to himself which he had planned to the finest detail months before during the dark nights of winter, he had hoped she would come but that was now all over, she, not Portia now, that is all she had become, the idea being to rest, recuperate dream and plan the rest of their lives together. Now it was only himself, alone, single, unattached, in his head at least! The journey north was like a flight, surreal to say the least, Preston, Lancaster, Carlisle, City, Stirling and Perth, Butterham and the village. He could see the change in topography as he drove through the mountain landscape; he intended to do a few of those over the next few days, very relaxed he was on a high! The Lake Hotel was an ideal base for what he had planned for the next two weeks. Hill climbing, swimming, sailing, looking up old friends even fancying a go at water colours, maybe even oil paintings! Just complete relaxation after the previous 3 years, and the last couple of weeks. He had the world at his feet. He arrived about 4pm, the sleek sports car gliding into the car park of the Flaxden Lake Hotel with that distinctive MG sound. There was a few staff outside clearing up tables from the afternoon lunches, their heads looking up as he came to a halt. Cliffton checked in and headed straight to the little beach at the end of the lake. He was alone walking on the soft sand at the head of the lake, a favourite spot for him over the years, with the warm sound of the waves moving behind him as he gazed as far as the eye could see, he could feel his aims were now finally within reach and the sun was smiling and shining just to remind him, Export seemed a million miles away. He gazed down the Lake stretched and reached for the sky. 'Reach for the stars!' He remembered Grandma Hoyle used to say. 'Let the party begin!!' Cliffton screamed at the top of his voice, then quickly did a 360 degree turn to see if anyone was looking, but there was no one, a sigh of relief when, BANG! A thump on his rump knocked him off balance; 'What the?!' There was no one there, no one

around the beach deserted, the sun still smiling. 'I must be tired,' Cliffton thought to himself. He had been stopped for the last year, had recovered from a horrible week, finished his exams and completed a long journey, fatigue he concluded and decided a well-deserved libation was now in order, unpacking his bags could wait till later. Heading straight for the hotel bar, he ordered a pint from the barmaid a lady called Henrietta late twenties in appearance, single she told him, from Durban South Africa, just finished university like himself, a good looker with a trim curvy figure, hair tied up and crazy about sport. The main talk was of the 1995 rugby world cup and her hero was Francois Pienaar, his type of girl, he told her he was a Lions man and couldn't wait for the tour to New Zealand. 'It's the only thing that gets me really excited, passionate, you know, gets me going!'

'Really?' Commented Henrietta with a smile. 'Are you sure?!' They had hit it off much to the annoyance of her fellow staff, in particular a tall grease ball with long hair and a pony tail and some residents, a group of men staying at the hotel he was probably expecting an easy lay. He thought, 'I'm in here-definitely, it was so obvious!' The promise of his escape was coming true! Not a care in the world. The grease ball disappeared so he told her a joke. 'Why can't you trust men with a ponytail?' She smiled back at him, seemed to be thinking.

'Hmmmm? No I don't know.....you tell me!'

'Coz there's an arsehole underneath it!!!' She split her sides giggling away when the Devil himself returned.

'What's so funny?'

'Oh nothing.' Said Henrietta biting her bottom lip.

'You're to go into the restaurant bar now!' A sarcastic smile followed and was directed at Cliffton.

'Oh right.' And she disappeared out of view.

'Yes? You want something......can I help you? Another drink?' The grease ball said looking at Cliffton's three quarter full glass.

Cliffton thought this over and sensing an atmosphere decided against another.

'No thank you.........I'll be back later!' The glare from the grease ball burrowed like a channel tunnel drill mining its way into Cliffton's forehead. He finished his pint and took his leave.

Cliffton headed for a swim in the hotel pool, forget about the gym no weights today, he's on holiday. He loved this pool, had been here many times, usually after exams, and after a few laps he looked out the big open plan windows whilst still in the water, his arms resting on the poolside and could see the Sleeping Giant in the distance. He never knew much about this except that it was a few Lower hills positioned in such a way that it looked like a giant lying down. He was really winding down, that feeling that people yearn for, the pressure of exams had gone, results a million days away, when there is just yourself and no one else about like the girl in Cadbury's flake advert, you know, the girl in thin summer dress in a pontoon with her curly hair flowing in the breeze as she glided her boat passed the 'Only the crumbliest flakiest chocolate tasted like chocolate never tasted before!' Par! He now was switched off with no pressure away from it all and as he eyed the peaceful looking giant in the distance, he felt that he had now reached Utopia having traversed the Indian village and previously the Savage. After his swim, followed by a sauna he returned to the bar, the Henrietta had gone, shift probably over or maybe consigned to the restaurant for the evening. 'BLAST!' He thought to himself, another girl another day! Well he had another couple of weeks something was bound to happen. The grease ball stood behind the bar grinning smugly at him, polishing a crystal whiskey glass. Surely not?! He ate his favourite meal of haggis, tatties and neaps washed down with a pint of Jaffrey's, a ritual on his visits north. Should he have another? Nah! Why spoil the next day?! Then as he was leaving a bang on his rump! 'Again! What is this?' He turned abruptly to the grease ball,

'***Aiutare se stessi e Dio Vi aiutera***!' He appeared to say.

'What was that?'

'To you? I said nothing!' Looking down on Cliffton as though he was some sort of peasant.

It was 9pm early but it had been a long day and only adrenalin was keeping him going so he took off to his bed, a little room above the porch of the hotel where he always slept when staying here. From the window he could see his intended tramp for the next day beautifully mirror imaged, like left and right gloves, in the lake as it was still light being a warm balmy, early June evening. He showered, drew the curtains switched off the light got into bed, turned on the TV and watched the news, TRUMP WINS ELECTION! CHEMICAL ATTACK IN IRAQ......He quickly switched the TV off and with the room pitch black drifted into a most contented perfect sleep.

The knock, slight tapping on his door came just after midnight. 'Cliffton?' The voice, a whisper, was Afrikaner in origin. It was Henrietta the barmaid! RESULT! He could not believe his luck. Bolting upright in bed he was about to get out of bed to answer the door but there was no need she was already within. How was that? He didn't hear the door open. Surely enough it was her. 'Am I dreaming?' He said.

'I think you are.' She softly replied. Dressed differently from the afternoon, out of her hotel uniform, in a thin white summer dress, her lacy white lingerie, a teddy perhaps, seductively visible underneath, she came over, her wavy dark hair cascading around her statuesque shoulders and down her back and sat next to him on the bed, the aroma of her beauty, consumed him, giving a rush like a rolling ball of thunder, he could feel his body, sinking, sinking under. 'I don't usually do this!' She said. I bet you don't! He thought to himself.

'Neither do I!' Said by someone who considered himself to be an honourable man! Well believe it or not they just talked and talked for what seemed like forever eventually deciding to meet up the next evening when she wasn't working and go for a drive. Henrietta told him that she had seen nothing of the area since she arrived, she must've seen him arrive and it was the car, chicks love the car right? Well it couldn't be him! Cliffton didn't care as his holiday was turning into every man's dream. The promise of marriage had been returned, the exam room was a million miles away! The night was not over. There was a silence, not awkward but a longing. Gazing into each other's eyes they moved closer to each other and she softly whispered into his ear. 'It's time to make you mine!'

She brushed her lips against his scar on his cheekbone. 'Mmmmmmm!' She purred. 'Give me one sec!' And with that she glided into the bathroom, knowing the way, no need to ask; well she worked there after all! Cliffton sat back in his chair listening to the music drifting in through the open window from the bar below, a Ceilidh was in full swing. The night was warm, balmy, and exotic to the extent of an event that he was sure to come when subconsciously his stomach started doing flip flops coinciding with a movement reflected on the TV screen as Henrietta came back into the room closing the bathroom door behind her. She was dressed in a big white bathrobe, her hair was done up with a clip and she had that flushed look of someone who had just got out of the bath or shower. Moving over to the bed, undoing the tie on her robe as she turned around with her back to and slid the robe of her shoulders, slowly revealing her magnificent body on turning her dark pink nipples were already at attention, firm, straight and as the robe fully dropped to the floor a neatly trimmed, downy, dark coloured triangle could be seen between her legs.

Pulling back the top cover, she gracefully manoeuvred herself up and onto the bed and lay down on her stomach, next to Cliffton. Then as if to tease she reached back and pulled the sheet over her body. Although she was modestly covered the sheet left little to the imagination, the sheet moulding itself to every curve and valley of her body. Cliffton swallowed in awe. Henrietta gave a contented sigh as she settled herself on the centre of the double bed, turning her face to her left, resting her arms above her head she smiled at the struck Cliffton. 'All this, to yourself?'

'Did you enjoy your shower?' Cliffton blurted out, struggling for something to say. Gulping as he did so.

'Mmmmmmm! It was heavenly! I could get used to this! Loosen me up! Or are you just all talk.' She commanded, giggling with her tease, holding out her hand, beckoning him to her.

Cliffton smiled as he towered over her. Taking the cream from the bedside table and rubbed the smooth substance into the palms of his hands, 'I certainly will!' He said, wondering if the growing bulge in his boxer shorts was starting to show. 'Is there anything special you'd like me to work on, any areas that have been bothering you?'

'Damn!! Don't be so matter of fact! Look what's in your face!' Cliffton said to himself.

Henrietta looked deep into his eyes, her pupils were dilating 'Nope, I've never done this before, nor wanted to, I have never had a massage before, I'm in your hands, and you are in charge! You have the power!'

'Okay, that's good,' Cliffton said 'Just relax and leave it all to the expert!' With that he sat himself beside her on the bed and folded down to expose her lovely back, keeping her booty modestly covered, he began rubbing her with firm strokes, using both of his powerful hands up and down the full length of her back.

Soon the strokes expanded to cover her entire Upper body, including her neck, shoulders and arms. This went on for quite a while in tune with the music coming through the window but in complete silence between the two. A couple of times Cliffton's fingers strayed to the sides of her breasts, where their firmness bulged slightly out as she lay on them, but she made no protest or move to stop him. Cliffton figured everything was cool and relaxed further.

After a while he moved down her body so that he could begin to work on her legs. He kneaded and stroked every inch of them, from her calves past her delicate inner knees, up the backs of her thighs. His hands almost circled her entire leg as he worked the cream deeply into her skin of that athletic body.

As his hands moved upward they began to brush against the bottom of the sheet, moving it up little by little with each contact, until his fingers were just grazing the hint of rounded peach flesh visible beneath the covering. His strong movements now caused her hips to move up and down beneath his touch. As he worked the tops of her inner thighs, his hands moved together in between her legs, only centimetres away from heaven. Henrietta was obviously in enjoyment with this sensation. She was sighing deeply and even panting a little. Her head had moved to the other side and Cliffton could see her hips were moving on their own.

Cliffton now leaned over and without a word and with their eyes locked on each other in a longing stare; he folded the sheet over in the middle of her back exposing one entire side of her body. Preparing himself with fresh cream he started to work directly on her uncovered cheek, moving his hands over its entire surface. There was hardly room for his two hands as his slide fingers started to probe down between her cheeks and even further.

Suddenly Henrietta gave a sharp gasp, 'Ummmmmm......are you sure this is what we should be doing?' Cliffton thought to himself

'Well it was going great Guys and suddenly she froze!'

'I'm just getting to the deep tissue areas.' Cliffton murmured softly 'If you are uncomfortable with this I can stop.'

There was a pause 'No!' Henrietta said, then, 'I'm just a little embarrassed, shy if you like. Nobody has touched me like that before, I mean in that way, you know, there!'

'Don't worry,' Cliffton reassured her 'I have never touched this way before.'

Henrietta said nothing to that, but after a moment she seemed to relax even more, placing her head down closed her eyes and smiled contentedly, the corners of her mouth curling. There were no more protests. Cliffton obligingly moved across to the second beautiful peach, repeating the process. He was soon moving his fingers deeper between her legs with each stroke. This time there was no doubt about it-Henrietta's hips began a slow grind up and down as one of his hands moved up to stroke her back, the other stayed busy on her bottom, gliding around and then dipping down, more and more deeply each time. Henrietta's breathing was getting heavier and heavier with each passing movement. When he stopped caressing her booty and most of his hand disappeared between her legs, there was no resistance as she began to moan and gasp again. She was getting closer and closer to fulfilment but then Henrietta straightened up, pulling up, his hand was soaked in her juices.

'Why……why have you stopped?!' Henrietta breathed almost whimpering.

'We've still got plenty of time,' he told her. 'Besides I still have to work on your front!'

'You are wicked!' Henrietta countered with a deep sigh of contentment.

Now in complete control Cliffton pulled the sheet over her body and told her to turn over. When she had done so, he moved to the end of the bed and started massaging her neck and shoulders. With her arms raised above her head he had complete access to her Upper body. He gently worked around her ears and soft throat, then held up each arm and worked the length of it to her hands. Henrietta had calmed down a bit by this time and her breathing was almost normal and slowly Cliffton peeled down the sheet down to her waist, revealing her lovely breasts in all their glory. He started at her collarbone, stroking in a slow circular motion that progressed gradually down her chest. It wasn't long before his hands reached her breasts, but he danced around them, never touching them directly or going near her erect nipples. Her breath became heavy again and she made soft noises in the back of her throat as his fingers moved around her quivering breasts, without granting the now direct contact she was now aching for. When he did allow his fingertips to graze ever so slightly over her mounds, she moaned and arched her back as she strained to meet his touch.

Finally taking pity on Henrietta he moved to the other side of the bed and placed both hands on her stomach and moved them up over her breasts, his flat palms, dragging across her nipples. Henrietta made a meowing sound. He then took both of the hard little nubbins between his fingers and began to roll them back and forth. It was as though he had given her an electric shock. Henrietta's head jerked up, her eyes tightly closed and her mouth wide open as she let out an animal cry. The look on her face was one of pure pleasure. 'Yes, Oh yes, like that! That's the way!' She cried out her hips began to rise and fall again as she raised her knees and planted her feet on the bed. Overcome with passion she shouted 'What are you doing to me? Don't stop! Don't stop!'

As Cliffton enthusiastically continued to stroke and tease her nipples, Henrietta brought one hand down to slide it between her parted legs under the sheet away from Cliffton's eyes. The movement of the sheets could be seen as her fingers began to do their own work on her pussy. Her other hand reached out blindly for , encountering his shirt, sliding instinctively down, undoing the button on the fly of his boxer shorts in one swift movement. At that point Cliffton took a step back swivelling his hips away from her. 'Please! Please!' Moaned Henrietta. 'Unh unh!' He teased her with a grin. Henrietta smiled back with smile like a cat about to get her cream, wetting her lips.

'No touching me yet!'

'Cliffton you're such a tease!'

The sheet had almost fallen clear of her body now as he released her nipples and moved his hands down her stomach, whisking the sheet away onto the floor revealing Henrietta's stark naked body writhing under the hands of Cliffton. 'Ohhhhhhh.....Your hands I want them! I must have them! I want to keep them!'

Cliffton withdrew to the end of the bed giving him an unobstructed view between Henrietta's widespread legs. He continued to rub her stomach, making circular motions with his palms as he continued to move downwards, until his fingers brushed over her manicured bush. Now she was humping her hips up to meet his movements as he moved ever Lower, sliding his hands down to her inner thighs, he massaged the outside of her pussy lips with his thumbs. Each movement pulled the succulent lips apart giving him a glimpse of her inner pinkness. Henrietta was now moaning continuously, at this point, but when Cliffton slid a finger between her moist labia her moans turned to gasps. 'Aaahhhh!' she cried out. 'Oh God! Oh please! Please!' She bucked up and down as his finger went deeper and then was joined by another. Soon he was pistoning his digits in and out of her open lady purse with increasing speed. When he began to stroke his thumb across her engorged delight as well, Henrietta started to shake and shudder she was on the verge of orgasm. She shook her head wildly from side to side her hair spilling out everywhere cascading down as the butterfly clip came undone and fell to the floor.

'Yessssss! Ohhhhhh yes! Right there! Ahhhhhh.... yesssssss!' She hissed as he continued like a man possessed. Her hands flew to her breasts and she began to tweak and pull at her nipples. Her mouth was wide open as she struggled to pull air into her burning lungs. What he did then surprised himself as he put his hands on her thighs spread her legs leaned down and swiped his tongue over her clitoris. He kept his tongue there lapping and swirling his tongue over her burning lady purse and suddenly Henrietta's moans and groans merged into a shrill scream of ecstasy as her body arched almost completely off the bed, going rigid for a few long seconds before exploding convulsively in climax.

Cliffton straightened up and Henrietta sat up unbuttoning his shirt, his face was covered in her juices. His firm body rippled as he slid down his boxers inch by inch. He was very hard now and his very proud manhood came into Henrietta's view for the first time. She lay panting, out of breath, spread eagled as though she'd been shot. Her hips were still making small involuntary movements, her nostrils flared with each ragged breath.

Cliffton grabbed her hips and pulled her booty to the edge of the bed, raised her knees and pushed her thighs apart. Henrietta reached down grasping his engorged member and started to rub his tip up and down her soaking slit lubricating him for entry. 'He'll slide straight in!' Henrietta purred. Suddenly through the fog of her lustful arousal she raised her head and her eyes fluttered open.

'Relax Henrietta,' He said soothingly. 'I won't do anything you don't want to do. If you want to stop we'll stop. Is that what you want Henrietta?' As he said this she was still rubbing his tip up and down **between her** glistening lips, while his hands continued to caress her outstretched body.

'Nobody has talked to me the way you do Cliffton.' She said as she gave out another moan. The desire was too much for both. Her hips began to move once more in response to the stimulus at her entrance and after a brief moment she closed her eyes again and laid her head back. Her legs now of their own accord, spread themselves apart even further in apparent invitation.

Cliffton accepted and putting his hands on her hips slid slowly and deeply inside her. Henrietta gasped out loudly as though a wind was being forced out of her, as his proud member slid into her. 'Oh my God this is absolutely amazing! Unbelievable!' She wailed.
'I'll be gentle and go slowly!!'
'Gentle, slow, hard, fast Just don't stop!' The line had now been crossed and neither wanted to turn back. Henrietta's eyes were scrunched tight and her knuckles had gone white as she grasped his shoulders and entwined her toned thighs around him. As he moved into her she started to pull back achieving a rhythm, exalting sounds from her open mouth that were of pure pleasure.
They continued to fuck slowly as Cliffton's mouth took one of her rigid nipples into his mouth, giving out a sharp yelp Henrietta brought a hand to his head holding to her quivering breast. He worked on the other nipple then straightened up, hooked his arms under her legs pushing her knees back almost to her shoulders with her thighs still wide apart. This not only raised her pelvis for deeper penetration it also gave a view of what was happening to her. She whimpered as he brought his hips back and she could see her juices glistening on his engorged phalanx. pushed in again and Henrietta gave a soft grunt as he began to rock back and forth with each forward motion pushing him further inside. They, together had established a rhythm, a bond now, the strokes became longer and smoother. She was now beginning to breathe more heavily too as his body gleamed with sweat. 'Ahhh.....Ahhhh....Ahhhhh!' Henrietta began to chant in a hoarse breathy voice in time with his even strokes. Her hands now clutched at his biceps as she bucked her hips more strongly now to meet his powerful thrusts. He was fully inside her. His balls began to make a soft slapping sound against her booty as their bodies came together.
'You have all of me now Henrietta!' Cliffton panted. 'How does it feel?'
Her words sounded strangled as she forced them out of her panting mouth, 'Unnnnnnh...... Oh God......It feels so.... Soooooo good! I .... never felt .... soooooo gooooood!' Through her words one could hear the wet squishing sound her tight pussy was making as he ground into her. Cliffton now moved up a gear as he grabbed her ankles and pulled them up, slipping her legs on to his broad shoulders. Her booty was now completely off the bed and nestled onto his rippling thighs. He then had a direct shot and was in complete control over her and began to pound into

her like a jackhammer. The solid firm bed held firm and Henrietta's breasts shook back and forth as she neared another orgasm. Henrietta then let out a keening cry that could've been heard throughout the hotel, but they didn't care. Cliffton continued to grind and rotate through her cries, thrusting with all his strength, the sound of their bodies slapping together got louder with every stroke.

Cliffton began to grasp and grunt he was coming close. 'Damn this is good!' He shouted as Henrietta shuddered, yelped and clawed beneath him, bucking in the throes of her own orgasm. Cliffton pulled himself from her as she gave out a yelp. They collapsed into each other's arms embracing, quivering; as Henrietta reached down to hold his still hard member. They kissed, their tongues battled intensely, sucking and swirling as they thanked each other for what had just happened. She leaned down and kissed his tip.

Only in his dreams has this event happened but now he could see this is going to be. 'Yeahhhhhh, I've reached Utopia!' He thought to himself as he lay back arms behind his head.

'I've waited for this moment all day, the moment when we would share ourselves, this moment can't be thought about it has to be felt.' She purred as she entwined herself around him, blending them together. He had no control, mesmerised, hypnotised by the vision unfolding in front of him, seeming so wrong but feeling so right.

They had got closer to each other, closer than they'd ever been, seeing things they'd never seen before.

'I've dreamed your fingers touch me a thousand times, dreamed the warm skin of your body burning next to mine. I can see our light.'

He then kissed her sugar lips, caressed her hips. Now they were together,

'Now it's time, time to make you mine, mine all mine.' She breathed into his ear. The sweet anticipation of her hands he knew would touch him soon. Two fascinating shadows now moved in time. 'I know what it's going to be, me and you, you and me for a moment I thought it would never be.'

He had never thought or felt such a feeling. It was beautiful! Back and forth, back and forth......in and out......in and out......a little to the right.....a little to the left......she could feel the sweat on her forehead......between her breasts......beads of all sizes trickling down the small of her back......she was getting near the end, on the verge of passing

out. He was in ecstasy with a huge smile on his face as she moved forwards then backwards……forwards then backwards……again ……again and again, her head was rearing now…..her back arched……her faced flushed……she moaned softly at first, then began to groan louder and louder…..finally…..totally exhausted she let out a piercing scream, as the music suddenly ceased. They had been at it for what seemed like hours.
'I only knew it in my dreams even though you are here with me.'
Was he in heaven? Was this really happening? Oh what a night! Cliffton turned in the bed and Henrietta kissed the back of his neck bringing her arms around his engine. Nibbling him down his back towards his hips.
'Cliffy how did this happen? You have a mark just above your right cheek!'
'I don't know but it's tender to the touch'
'Get it looked at, it looks sore! Please!'
'You know I've never done this before Cliffton. Never ever had a boyfriend, never been kissed or touched. My folks were strict, Church goers, but I'm glad it's you!'
'Really? Me too Henrietta! Never before!' He lied, immediately feeling remorseful, but it hadn't been as good as this......EVER!
'Thank you.' She purred and they kissed each other gently blending again into oblivion. 'Hey look out the window the stars!' Cliffton tilted his head and looked towards the window. 'See that big one shining brightly? It's as though we are being given a sign. A direction.' Cliffton looked at the star it was something he had seen before or just something he'd never noticed, but as he looked there was something about this one. Henrietta snuggled into his chest and her body became limp as she fell into a deep sleep. Brushing his lips on her forehead he drew in a deep breath taking in the intoxicating aroma exuding from Henrietta's body. They were in Utopia!

He awoke the next day about 6 30 am like a light switch being switched on, sitting bolt upright in the bed, there was Henrietta dressing. 'Good morning!' Said Cliffton as she silkily slipped on her undergarments, snugly fitting her perfect lines. 'Now that is a sight to wake up to! Why are you rushing?'
'I'm going to Cronkley, will see you later!' And with that she came over and kissed him on the lips for a few seconds and was gone. Was this all that two consenting adults were only capable of together? Surely not?

There must be more. Taking a long shower, which, he was reluctant to do so, as he would remove the smell of Henrietta from him. He dressed into his outdoor clothes and walked down to the lake side and took in the atmosphere. A wonderful day had greeted him, there was a reflection of BolyBrack in the lake, a majestic mirror image, a splendid form and he was excited knowing that this time next week he would still be here on holiday. Short breaks although a change, and refreshing are no substitute for knowing that a week later you would still be away from the cauldron of the metropolis. At 8 am he made his way to the Gitana Grill for breakfast hoping that he would be first there. He was lucky and got served quickly. Full Scottish breakfast just right for what was needed for the exertions he had had last night and what he intended for the day. He gobbled his food down being so excited. Checking out the menu for tomorrow 'Hmm! Porridge I think!' His enthusiasm was that of a schoolboy, not a bad thing, he had been told not to lose your enthusiasm as a schoolboy, when a man does that he has a problem, or lost it. He looked around hoping for a glimpse of Henrietta before she went for her trip but couldn't see her. The grease ball told him gleefully, that she had got the early bus to Cronkley and would not be back till late with his greasy smile. 'She's out of your league mate!' He said to. If only he knew! Cliffton smiled pleasantly.
Skipping down to the MG feeling good with a packed lunch and drinks in his rucksack he set off for Sugwas Pool with the hood down but just as he drove through the village he saw Henrietta sitting on the bench in the village square. 'Hey stranger missed your bus?' Henrietta jumped into the car and pecked him on the cheek. 'I thought you were going to Cronkley!'
'Changed my mind! Had to get away from the grease ball! Throw him off my scent! He's been after me since I arrived! Now what cds have you got?'
'Jump in!' It was a glorious day, clear blue sky and a warm feeling with a tiny breeze.
'Hope there is no midges!'
'Well I had marmite for breakfast on toast. That'll keep them away.'
'Yuck! I wondered what that taste was!'
'Well you either love it or hate it and it keeps the midges away!'
'Well I'm not kissing you again today!' Teased Henrietta, as she gently bit his earlobe.
The journey to the car park at the foot of BolyBrack passed many nostalgia points, pointing them out to her as they drove along. Taking the goat track

route, a small c road they passed familiar places, the Old Boys cottage, the Blacksmiths Forge and the farm at the Braes where the farmer bred sheepdogs. As the MG pulled slowly into the car park. 'GREAT!' He exclaimed with a satisfaction. 'Nobody here yet!' Hopefully they would be the first to the top. They had them themselves! Suddenly, THWAP! Cliffton reeled to the side feeling a punch to his right buttock and nearly losing his balance. Regaining his composure he looked around to see what had happened there was nothing only Henrietta, who looked at him blankly, nothing to see, nobody about, the day was warm, sunny with no wind, nothing. Puzzled and remembering yesterday on the beach, the station, Gharry's bar and the exam room he shrugged his shoulders smiled at Henrietta and they set off. Walking up the hill, usually would take 3-4 hours but he decided to dawdle wanting to take it all in, keeping looking around and taking the views at different stages in. After negotiating the last rocky lunar like stage the top was reached the view was staggering!

'Oh look at that! What a view I feel on top of the world! You see that light over there?' Forget about Jack on the bow of the Titanic they were on top of the world! Taking in the panoramic view of the area, Shunner, Little Whernside even Cross Fell in the distance and the remnants of the Great Caledonian forest that once covered the whole of Britain, but he could not see the light. The full glory of Flaxden Lake, Lake Humber encapsulating Queens Victoria's View in reverse. and Henrietta sat down at the Trig point putting a rock on it as had become his tradition whenever out on a tramp, sharing the pack lunch had brought, they had only been there a few minutes when a large man, massive protruding beard and with a rucksack on his back came in to view. Henrietta put her hand over her mouth to stifle her laughter. Taken aback they greeted the unexpected climber. 'Good morning!'

'Mornin Mannnnnn! Mornin Lassie!' Said the man in Southern American drawl, obviously picking up the lassie bit on his travels. He was wearing a kilt and kilt shirt' the whole thing, a replica of Rob Roy.

'How you doing?'

'Thought we'd be the only ones up here at this time!'

'Me too! Hey Man! Would you share a beer up here with me to celebrate getting to the summit?'

'Bit early for that don't you think?'

'Awwwwww come on!'

'Go on Cliffton, be a sport, you're on holiday! And I'm off tonight!' Encouraged Henrietta.
'Ok!' Cliffton agreed as two bottles of beer were pulled out of his rucksack.
'Here son will you video me drinking this beer on the top? Just so I can put it on MY Tube.'
'Yes sure, of course!'
The man showed Cliffton how to use the video recorder on his phone. 'I came up here to get away from all this!'
'Well I'm afraid it's with us! Nothing we can do! Here let's noooooo it!'
Positioning the recorder towards the man he took his pose with a stunning backdrop behind him and putting on the most perfect Scottish accent, he flicked off the bottle top with his teeth, 'Let it roll, ACTION!!!!' As he took a long swig from the bottle.
'Mmmmmmmm! Ahhhhhhhhh! Lovely! Just lovely! There's nothing better after climbing a wee small hill like this pile of shite than to have a drink of Shagbracky Beer!'
Then taking another long drink 'Ahhhhhh! Just like a sheep pissing straight doon yer throat! Wait!!! What's that I hear?! 'BAAAAAA! BAAAAAA!' Heck, it's Dolly! Go away Dolly I've told ye it's over. You'll find someone else! 'BAAAAAA!'
With that he turned back to the couple and with the camera still rolling, 'Drink Shagbracky beer and you too can be a randy BAAAAAASTARD!'
'Annnnnd....... CUT!'
'I've gotta get out of here!' Thought Cliffton. Then suddenly remembering what Geoff had said. 'Don't wish for what you want Cliffton! Or you might just get it!'
The three sat down, chatted about this and that with the American repeatedly telling dirty jokes from his phone, with which Henrietta seemed to become uncomfortable with. As they were leaving shouted bye and shook his hand, the man pulled him close in a brotherhood handshake and said, '**Ajudar a Simesmo e Deus ira aduuda-lo!**'
Cliffton pulled away from the powerful grip, turned and headed down with Henrietta. 'Didn't you hear that?'
'No, let's get to the car! I can hardly walk after all the exercise we've been having! My inner thighs are aching!'

They smiled at each other, embraced and headed back down the path but they were persuaded to stay longer.
They had to get away from this, it had becoming boring, as more bottles of beer were produced from his rucksack and the jokes became more vile and repeated, the man just laughing loudly at his own jokes. They left him singing to himself. Stopping about half way and after eating a biscuit and drinking some water and tea from the thermos, lunch was finished with other climbers now appearing Cliffton and Henrietta bade their farewells and headed down with their new friend thankfully heading in a different direction. Just in time as he meandered down passing groups of people with their brand new Berghaus and Karrimor equipment, spotlessly clean, looking them up and down to see what brand name they were wearing. Ah the great outdoors! At about 2 30pm he could see his car gleaming in the bright sunshine he felt a quiet pride. At the car park they took their boots off and ate the remainder of the lunch box and pondered what to do with the rest of the day as basking in the glory of conquering Henrietta's first peak and his in a long time. Using his monocle he looked up towards the summit to see the American still on his decent or was he descending. He looked to be taking four steps down to ten steps back!! 'I know, We'll go and see the Topping's at Redcliffe, the old Chaplain from my Alma Mater.' So they set off arriving 20 minutes later. Welcomed with open arms Mrs Topping prepared afternoon tea but not before Ladd had given a guided tour of the village where Pontius Pilate was born and the oldest Yew tree in the United Kingdom or even world was. At the Yew tree a Millennium timeline had been well laid out and Ladd explained the project and how the young man who had completed the project had been killed on his way back to Perth after the party put on by the villagers at the hotel to commemorate the completion of the work. The afternoon was over far too quickly and they set off smiling and waving to the Topping's as they left. Cliffton felt at ease and very happy, that he was with Henrietta, as he drove along the winding road, passing the thatched cottages and fields with their cattle and sheep grazing in the summer sun. Maybe this was the beginning of something? He thought glancing at what appeared to be a very contented Henrietta, as she linked his arm and slowly caressed his bicep.
'Never felt like this before.' Henrietta whispered, as though she didn't want him to hear. What an amazing break he was getting, only 2 days into it, he could not remember when he had been this happy, not for a long,

long time. Henrietta was enjoying herself and they seemed comfortable with each other. Dire Straits were playing and Henrietta had her head on his shoulder, her wavy hair blowing in the wind. Could this all be for real? At around 4 45pm a light drizzle had developed but visibility and road conditions were good as he drove at a leisurely pace through the splendour around them retracing their route back to the hotel that had been followed in the morning. What would the next few hours bring? A hearty supper and a couple of pints? No skip the pints, you'll spoil the evening.

'Are you working tonight?'

'No I am off! How could you forget that?' She purred, her dreamy eyes gazing at him longingly.

'Fancy a date?'

'Hmmmmmm! But I'm washing my hair.'

'Let's clean up and drive over to Cronkley and see a play, and something to eat.'

'Hmmmmmm! How about something first, then the play and something after?!!!' Maybe he could persuade her to come back to Export with him? He hoped so. A holiday romance at this age?!! It's more than that; he was so sure of it. That only happens in your teens. 'Hey Cliffton slow down!!' Driving past Outerhadden he remembered an expi he'd been on with Dude Carrington and Mike Harter where a guy called Freak had collapsed in the snow with exposure and Mental Pete had arrived before the Hill Service, wearing his Sunday suit and smoking his cigar! One of the coolest things he'd ever seen. He sank into the comfort of the MG's seat and started to think about what was waiting ahead for him. Dire Straits, 'Solid Rock' boomed out of the stereo as the car sped along the Goat track, coming up to the bridge at the old forge the car slowed down when suddenly BANG! Cliffton felt a thump on his Upper right bum and the car swung its back end around. A gasp from Henrietta, he could hear the wind being knocked out of her, Cliffton shouted, 'It's ok! Think we've got a puncture!' Luckily the skid had happened clearing the bridge and next to the entrance to the forge. Getting out, and with a slightly shaken Henrietta, looked around the car, underneath and his immediate surroundings. Nothing. Mystified at another unexplained incident he had a drink of water, settled himself down for a few minutes and started again. 'I was almost in a bit of lather then!' Exclaimed Henrietta.

'In lather twice in 24 hours! My! My!' Henrietta thumped Cliffton playfully on the shoulder. 'OUCH!' He faked. Solid Rock boomed out again as he drove past Lassintullich House where there came a straight stretch of road approach where the temptation to open up especially with a sports car could be irresistible but he didn't he was too relaxed and as at the end was a blind corner it would be dangerous, whilst Mark Knopfler had now moved on to Sultan's of Swing.

♫

WE ARE THE SULTANS....

THE SULTANS....

THE SULTANS OF SWING!!!

Accompanied by Henrietta as a backing singer along with the stereo the Beatles came on,

♪

CLIFFIE WAS A MAN WHO HAD EVENTUALLY FOUND A LOVER....

Sang Henrietta to the beat..........

♪

BUT HE HAD TO FIND THE LONG RED GRASS

COME BACK...

.COME BACK

TO WHERE WE BOTH BELONG.....

GET BACK CLIFFEEEE......

LET'S GET BACK TO ROOM TWENTY NINE!!!!

LET'S GO CLIFFTON!!!

What a lovely voice, in perfect tune, her arms waving in the air to the rhythm, he thought, as they slowed down to 16 mph dropping down to 3rd gear, Henrietta took the CD out of the player. 'Let's have some Straits!' Then just as he got just at the corner it was there, a big Tonka like eight wheeler dumper truck taking up the whole road. He got a glimpse of two men in the cab, smiling. There was nowhere for them to go, there was no panic; there was no time for any of that, BANG! The front wheel of the lorry smashed into the drivers crushing it instantly, a piece of the came through the hood catching Cliffton's crown although he could not feel it, things were happening too quickly, the trees, walls and surroundings were flashing by, he glanced at Henrietta, she was holding her seat but her head was dropped forward and she turned to him, her eyes looked into his. '***Ayundate que Dios te ayudara***!' She said clearly, blood was now coming from coming from the corner of her mouth and nose as flames began to lick all around. NOOOOOO! How can this be happening? All sinners will burn in everlasting Hell, had he sinned? Why had he brought her? This was his entire fault, was there something he had missed? Then came something like a large implosion followed by a slicing sound as two black objects approached them, there was what seemed like a tearing sound coming from the roof, simultaneously Cliffton felt a lurch forward then backwards, a heavy thud, this is the end, it's over he thought when,

POW!!!!!..

an inaudible cork popping sound in his head, he was unable to move or coordinate in any way, the car no longer responding to his touch, suspended, locked in his body like a vice, looking ahead, he tried to turn but couldn't see Henrietta anymore but was aware what was unfolding, unable to act, unable to scream or call for help, no sound just silence, trapped, yet there was no fear, no pain, he could think nor see anything except what was in front of him now, no memories, everything gone, he could now see the stage in front of him, he alone, was on it, was this all it was for, was this all he was now capable of? What had he done?

♫

MAKING MOVIES ON LOCATION..........................

Could be heard in slow sound from the stereo as his eyes slowly filled up with darkness, flooding, closing the final curtain. Nothing but..

360 degrees Michaelmas

ARRIVEÉ

45

degrees

Salvette

Stirring.........his eyes still closed, he could feel he was moving in some way, floating, suspended, being driven, a Magic Carpet? He felt nauseous, a dull headache as he felt movement in his body, toes, legs, arms, fingers, neck. Opening one eye then the other without moving he could see he was in the back of a car. Voices from the two people in the front could be heard a woman and a man's.

'You know Hazel, Walt asked me the other day. 'Dad why do I have to go to school?''

'And you said, Hoss?'

'So you can be moulded into a state approved homogenous drone that cannot think outside of the prescribed consensus. You will learn to repeat information instead of how to think for yourself so that you don't become a threat to the status quo. When you graduate you will get a job, pay your taxes in order to perpetuate the corporate system of indentured servitude for your political overlords.'

'What did he say?'

'Well Dear he just looked at me! Thought a bit and said 'Dad I don't want to be a parrot!!!!!!'

'I want our children to develop, I want him to do what he wants to do instead of someone crushing his ideas before they even start and it is a **serious form** of neglect to keep children out of the education they should have and deserve.............'

At his side he could see a newspaper half folded.

SWAZILAND GAINS INDEPEDENCE
FROM GREAT BRITAIN

ROW OVER DECIMILAZTION COSTS RAGE ON

Was blazoned in bold across the headline and underneath in smaller but still bold letters:

NORTH KOREA SEIZES USS PUEBLO

FRANCE PERFORMS NUCLEAR TEST on page 2.

EGALITÉ! LIBERTÉ! SEXUALITÉ!
4 MONTHS ON EXCLUSIVE
WILL IT HAVE EFFECT ON THE UK?

JOHNSON NOT TO SEEK RE-ELECTION

None the wiser looking up he could see the back of two heads. There were no headrests on the seats. On his left he saw trees and stone walls flashing by and on his right he could see water and hills at some distance. On further inspection he could see that he was wearing a pure blue blazer with a green tie and buff shirt. Slowly his eyes scrolled down to what he could only describe as a coloured pattern which looked like a dress. 'A dress! What am I wearing a dress for?' He blurted out as he sat bolt upright in shock horror.

'It's your kilt silly! You've been sleeping for hours! I think you were dreaming!'

The voice was a gentle Scottish female voice.

'But where am I? What am I doing here?'

'You are on your way to Flaxden Brig lad! We're nearly there! You've been asleep since we left Stirling.'
Said the man who was driving the car.
'Where?!There's nothing here!'
Sitting back in his seat he looked at his surroundings. He saw his 'Kilt' and what looked like a leather bag belted around his waist. A pair of green socks, matching the tie and jacket and black laced brogue shoes.
After some thought he recognized his Mum and Dad's voices and started to take stock.
'We'll soon be there!' Said his Dad.
The new diamond white Wolsey sped steadily along the south side of Flaxden Lake, he could see it was new. It had now become very quiet in the car, not a word from anyone, deafening. Mum was in the passenger seat with her hanky, her little boy was about to be displaced from the nest, maybe a Cuckoo or the Spartan Mother letting her first male born off to the Agogi Dad enjoying zipping along the narrow road, away from his veterinary practice and all the pressures that that involved. He couldn't understand where he really was. He looked over into the back the car and a large silver box was filling the area with N. W. FLANNIGAN stencilled on it in large black capitals.
'What's this with my name written on it?'
'It's your uniform and clothes. Don't you remember me helping you to pack?' Said his Mum as he sat back to take stock this was all new to him but in a way familiar. He now recognized his Mum and Dad and was being to remember the area, leaving home.
'Morag, Phillip, Fairlie, Chirsty, Iain where are they?' He exclaimed
'All home being looked after by Mrs MulQueen.'
'How long will I be here for?'
'Thirteen weeks but you'll be home for a break after seven.'
Bemused he started to accumulate all this, it WAS new to him. Was he in a bad dream? Had he been asleep for long? His previous 11years now all came flooding back, he must've been having a bad dream.
He had never been away from home on his own before but to him it was all a big adventure beginning. He most definitely didn't understand that he was soon to be saying goodbye to what he had known or was now. As the car drove up a sweeping front drive he could see rugby posts all the way to the road but no football posts or nets, a usual comfort. His Mum said it

looked like a Fairy Castle. A sign with FLAXDEN BRIG in large green letters with a picture of a cat with the words SINE PRAESIDIO underneath stood erected at the entrance to the drive. He had no understanding; he had not seen the language before. The actual building was big and white, surrounded by woods producing quite a sight. It looked good with a plethora of colour with blue flowers dotted around and greenery, large trees towering over the scattered buildings, flowering rhododendrons flanked the driveway. 'How I'd like to climb to the top of those turrets.' He thought to himself. A window on the top tower was blocked out and he wondered why and what could be behind it. Another large window on the second floor seemed to be watching and waiting. Figures were coming in and out, coming and going, other boys in the same clothes as he were with older people some with a man and woman some with male or female only Mum had not been here before, Dad having come up earlier in the year with for an interview with him he remembered. To him it was somewhere in the middle of nowhere, he was now at the end of the earth. Far away from his beloved football team, Export City from the fourth division of the football league, whom he was sure were going to finish top after being nearly booted out of the division last season and that after having won the Cup!! His big sister Morag, a constant companion for his life so far, Phillip his younger brother who he remembered being met on the way home with a bowl of rice pudding over his head one day and the 'little ones' Fairlie, Chirsty and the newly born Iain, they were being taken away from him, why? To the end of the earth where was he?

As they drove up the long sweeping driveway the large Fairy like building now came fully into view, with tiered banking, trees were space equidistantly along each bank and a large lawn in front of it.

'What are those trees? Christmas trees?'

'No they are Yew trees!' Remarked his Mum.

The car pulled up outside the main building where the Headmaster Peter Barron was holding his reception for new boys... It was a short welcome and his Dad drove around to what was going to be his new home for the next two years, Brecon House. Dad helped him with his trunk into the house, Mum followed behind, hanky in hand. Inside was a buzz of activity and excitement, chattering voices everywhere; they looked on the notice board and found he was to be put in Conway dormitory with another 9 boys. Mr Flannigan helping him with his trunk, heavy and cumbersome, backs bent they came into the dorm along a narrow corridor and had been assigned the bed in the corner, ready made with blankets and sheets, one pillow. Suddenly, it was now time to say goodbyes. They walked out of the house and he looked at Dad's new car which he would not be seeing for a while he thought. They then walked the three of them to the end of the back drive. Dad had already given his pocket money to the housemaster £3.00 for the term, a tidy sum of money! But where could he spend it? He couldn't see any shops! Mrs Flannigan then said, a big tear rolling down her cheek. 'Give him a little bit of money Hos!' So his Dad put his hand into his pocket and a jingle of coin could be heard as he pulled out a half crown, three florins, two shillings, a couple of sixpences and a few coppers and them to him. This meant a lot.

'Now remember Son it doesn't grow on trees! The tanners are for luck!'

It was time to go. He gave Mum a big kiss and hug and gave Dad a firm handshake, like men do. They walked to the car and although he didn't cry he wanted to, an upwelling was within him, his stomach churning with butterflies, he knew this was it. As they drove away he watched the car down the drive until it disappeared out of view. He must have cut a lonely figure, sad but no tears as he looked and looked for something that wasn't there, gone. Right up in the sky, a flight of birds were flying in perfect formation heading south or north, east or west who could say? Definitely not him. He then walked back into Brecon house alone, not knowing anyone or anything that lay ahead of him. A small petite lady introduced herself as Maggie Borthwick as he approached the door.

'Hi laddie! How are you? New here?'

'Yes I am, my parents have just gone.'

'Och that's a wee shame, but never mind, never mind, it'll be alright, I'm new here tae! Whaur are ye frae?' Her pleasant smile reassured him that it would be.

'I'm from Lancashire.' He replied after a short delay, taking time to comprehend the new accent and he entered the house.

Nobody spoke to him as he walked towards the dorm some fleeting glances, some up and down looks, sizing him up, a big fat boy deliberately knocked him with his shoulder, nobody was giving way took it. It could be seen there was a hierarchy here, and he was at the bottom of the pile. Once in the dorm there were another seven boys all very quiet having gone through the same earlier experience, one vacant bed remained by the door, nobody saying anything. It was quiet, a new environment, sizing up each other. He took off his kilt and kilt jacket and hung them up in a big communal wardrobe. This was new, undressing in front of seven complete strangers. At this point a boy came up to him with a strange accent and asked if he would be his friend, he introduced himself as Larry MacCloon. He readily accepted he was the first person that had spoken to him besides the lady at the door. It wasn't long before they were all talking, chattering away like chipmunks, leaving nobody out. A couple of LOWER boys then showed them around Brecon, all matter of fact. The common room where there was a table tennis table and two pianos, the locker room called Clyde where they each had their own locker with key and the changing room where they were to hang their towels, rugby kit/gym kit, and adjoining shower and bath room and finally the boot room.

'Oh yes and get your daily routine from the house notice board.'

'What's that?' One of the boys asked pointing to a solitary black and white gym shoe on the top rack.

'Oh that! Yes! Well you will find out soon enough!'

Without a definite answer they trudged to the board and looked at the daily routine. It read:

DAILY ROUTINE

6 30 Rising Bell

7 55 Breakfast

8 35 Chapel

8 50-9 30 Class 1

9 35-10 15 Class 2

10 20-11 00 Class 3

11 00-11 30 Break

11 30-12 30 Class 4

12 35-12 55 Class 5

1 05-Lunch, followed by a rest period during which gramophone records will be played.

2 20 Games/afternoon activities followed by a shower

4 00 Afternoon tea

4 30-5 10 Class 6 (mon, wed and fri)

5 15-5 55 Class 7(mon, wed and fri)

6 00-6-40 activities

6 50-Supper

7 30-8 10 1st preparation period

8 30-9 2nd preparation period

9 30 Bed time

9 45 pm

LIGHTS OUT!!!

'How are we going to fit all that in?' Moaned Larry in an Australian drawl... 'I want to go surfing!'
'Gramophone records? Where are you from Larry?'
'Well I live in Australia, was born here, my folks are Scottish. Emigrated when I was 6 months old. You didn't tell me your name.'
'It's Walter, Walter Flannigan.'
It was now time to unpack their trunks. They all had cubby holes to put their daily clothes in, shirt, jerseys, shorts, underpants, socks, their kilts, sporrans and kilt jackets were put on hangers and hung in the dorms communal wardrobe. Sports gear, rugby shirts, shorts, socks and towels were hung on our allocated pegs in the changing room with a cubby hole beneath the bench to put one of two pairs of Dunlop Green Flash pumps

into (standard issue). Their shoes-leather one pair brogue and the other pair plain, both pairs black identified with their initials studded into the sole for identification, rugby boots and wellingtons were put into each owns cubby hole in the boot room at the entrance of the house.
It was in this room that one could not help but notice the solitary training shoe with a white stripe down the side of it, taking a pride and prominent place on the top shelf for all to see.
'Why is that there?' The boy showing them around wouldn't say. Asked an older boy, to see if he could get an answer, who ignored him.
'You'll know soon enough!!' Piped up a voice with a hint of humour in his tone. Glancing around he saw a few puzzled looks but it was soon forgotten as they were herded away.
Back in Conway they continued to unpack, feeling strange that their parents were no longer there, unfolded one of his towels to uncover a small radio with a note attached to it, 'So you can hear the results on Saturday! Dad!' He felt happy at this, very surprised as his Dad was always too busy with his work, he turned the knob to hear only a crackle, crackle. So along with the wash bag he put the radio into a little cabinet next to his bed.
The boys had never been away before from the bosom and comfort of their homes, but this was the done thing nowadays so off he had gone and straight into survival mode. Walter had been away with the Cub Scouts on a trip to Edinburgh, Auld Reekie, and the city where his Mum and Dad had met whilst at college. On the way up the group had stayed at a place in Carlisle where one of the boys there had told him about the place he was going to, 'That place up there!' A boy had told him, it would be cold and unpleasant, miles from anywhere, the headmaster was terrifying, there is square bashing every morning, boys who are stupid or lazy get caned on bare buttocks. It is like a prison run by sadistic sociopaths as the head enjoys beating the boys. Indeed there doesn't seem to be a crime that doesn't merit a caning on the bum. You will be beaten if you do badly at work, if you are cheeky, if you walk on the grass, if you walk with your hands in your pockets, if you slam doors, if you barge ahead of masters, if you swore, if your lockers were in a mess, if you didn't have your towels, if you were caught fighting, if you damaged the gardens, if you hide your food, the list was endless. There are two kinds of beating. There is a beating at the end of the day in the dorms or common room, when the head comes around slippers people, and the 'swish' a cane administered in his

study. A very Draconian society. It will be constant, relentless. 'The boys here are hardly traumatised' He thought, maybe he's exaggerating, making it all up, got the wrong place. He sounded eccentric but with a good heart, maybe. It is an austere building with constructed around towers and clad in white stone, the grounds are vast and include a large wooded area known as Myrtle Wood and a gigantic lake. But people didn't seem to know where this place was. The beds are rickety with springs sticking through the sagging mattress and if you hear a pair of heels clickety clacking on the wooden floor you behaved, it was the Matron. He had heard the Headmaster had a terrifying look about him but nevertheless may have a good sense of humour, sometimes and one night as he came around to say goodnight, the boys had set traps above the door so that when he entered a cascade of books and shoes rained down on him smacking off his wig to reveal a shiny pate. He would then chase around the room and give a mild slippering to whoever he caught, or believed to be the culprit. At supper in the dining room whilst gathering to eat, the head boy would read out a list of the day's miscreants who were instructed to 'come down' for some reason. The list is never short so expect your name to be on it! The condemned will stand in a queue in the corridor outside the headmasters study and the head boy would appear. To the right of the heads desk is a chair, known as the 'The Headmaster's Chair', with a long cane watching, waiting, this is Swish. The head boy then picks up the cane and carries it along the line of boys and hands it ceremoniously to the head dressed wearing full graduation outfit. For menial misdemeanours it would be a slipper, but few and far between. You will then be instructed to take down your trousers and bend over the chair and place your hands on to the arms of the chair. To many it made no difference to their attitude. Your parents may offer you money to work harder. Pass your exams or you will be there forever! Never leave!

The staff are out of a Carry On film. The Nurse is beautiful and every boys dream. There are many characters and one who seems to style himself on Hitler, same haircut and moustache and drives a Mercedes Benz car, he is called Uncle Adolf. He divides his class into two groups, imbeciles and morons and when he isn't teaching German he relates to the principles of the jam butty mines. A humorous hoax.

Each day will begin with every pupil in the house about 40 going for a morning run followed by a cold shower. At break time there will be gang warfare erupting at every opportunity. The older boys will kidnap a few younger boys like you, called squirts and take them to the wilderness where they had dug out a den and made a roof of corrugated iron. Here a kangaroo court would be held impromptu and punishment dished out for whatever. You will be guilty, so there is no use putting up a defence! There is a compulsory dip in the unheated swimming pool which has this strange Braun tea like colour in the water.

On the plus side there are many hours of freedom where you can roam the grounds, climb trees, and feel 'free'!

You will enjoy returning back after an away match as the food is better, their buildings terrible and a horrible smell of dirty laundry. There are no girls. You will learn to shrug off all the slipperings and cold showers and begin the adventure.

Walter had been aghast at this description of his imminent future, surely his parents couldn't do that to him? What had he done to be sent away to this? Yes he had failed his 11 plus and not got into to the local grammar school with his sister, but he had worked hard, moving from 38 at end of his first year at Fairfield to 9 that last year, and this was his reward? You can check out but you will never leave! At the time he had been horrified but had been told so much it had all been promptly forgotten! After all he was in an adventure at the time with the Cubs.

Well here he was, was this the place? It seemed all very Savage.

There were three other dorms, Shannon, Thames and Mersey with about forty boys housed in Brecon in all. Once back in Conway they were all told to get ready for bed. After washing and brushing his teeth **he got into bed** and then a big man with a gigantic beard appeared in the doorway, this was Big Jim Powers. The lights were switched off and door shut without a goodnight or what have you. Unable to sleep he could hear one of the other boys whimpering. He didn't know who it was but couldn't have blamed anyone in the position they were all suffering, they were all in an enforced sea change. As he started to doze back to his life in Export and Crane Hall, it was all coming back thinking about the Shakers result on Saturday how would he get the result, the most important thing on his mind that second? Suddenly there were voices in the corridor outside. Mum and Dad must've come back for him he thought, he hoped, they had dropped him off at the wrong place, made a mistake. The door opened and the last occupant for

the vacant bed came in. With his Mum and Dad stood at the door he heard his Mum say in what appeared to be an African accent,
'Are you not going to give your Mommy a hug, my honey?' The young boy willingly obliged, stretching up on his tip toes. The door closed and he made his way to his bed directly opposite, silhouetted against the full moon and pair of big ears prominent he bumped into trunks that were still at the foot of the beds. With the full moon which he could see through a gap in the curtain. Out of his pyjama pocket could feel a rolled up photograph took the neatly folded piece of paper and opened it up. Looking at the six faces, Louise, Dee Dee, Babs, Ruth, Flick and Andi. He could swear they were looking at him, he believed they were, he knew they were. A small piece of paper accompanied it; it read 'Thought you would like this! I know you liked them! Love R x' this was Rachel's picture of Pans People dancing girls who he watched every Thursday night. Dad, Mum, his brothers and sisters were not here but his Angels were, assuring him that all would be ok. Footsteps and a large shadow through the gap in the door alerted him to quickly fold the prized possession to a place of safety. The room became a hushed quietness as they waited for the next day and what it would bring. Walter lay in his bed reflecting on what happened since he woke in his Dad's Wolsey. He'd been dreaming before he woke, a jumble of places, buildings, people had been flashing through his head, familiar to him in some way yet he could not understand why. A couple of beds away more crying could be heard. It was a full moon and light was shining through a gap in the curtain onto his bed, looking out he could see what looked to be a big star high up and directly ahead of him and slowly but surely he drifted into a restless haunted sleep. The next day would come soon enough.

'WAKEY WAKEY BRECON! EVERYBODY UP!'

It was 6 30am. This was not a gentle awakening, it was ruthless! A bugle charge had preceded the voice of who they were soon to be so rudely introduced. As they were all stirring Conway's door burst open and this small man charged in and tipped unceremoniously the nearest boy out of his bed! Systematically he went from bed to bed tipping them all up, all nine! Walter was already out of his but he tipped his anyway. Introducing Mr Fowler, Brecon's housemaster otherwise known as Jimmy Crow! He

dashed out to cause destruction on the other dorms. They all looked blankly at each other. Up righting his bed and making it with two sheets and a couple of blankets and the one pillow. He undressed suddenly realising he had never been naked in front of anyone before. An awkwardness followed with everyone, turning their backs away from each other, they were all in the same boat, they all realised they were not alone.
'What do you think you are doing?' Screamed Jimmy Crow. 'Get your shorts and gym shoes on now!' Astonished looks flashed around the room.
'And assemble at the front of the house! NOW MOVE IT! YOU DOZY LOT!'
He looked at his watch, it was 6.30am! 6.30AM! Realising they had no choice in the matter all obediently changed into their identical Dunlop Green Flash pumps and piled out into the front of Brecon.
'This is crazy!' Walter said to Larry, 'I don't even know where we are!'
'Me neither!'
'What are we doing?'
'A morning run, you stupid little English shit!'
The remark had come from the fat boy who had shoved him the night before.
A loud blast of a whistle indicated to start running so they decided to follow the older boys who had distanced themselves from the new arrivals.
'Where are we going?'
'Just follow us!' Said another of the Lowers as they all hurtled towards the main building. 'Quick you've got to be quick!'
'All the hot water will have gone!'
And as they set off around the main building boys appeared from behind the trees on the banks and grabbed the first new boy they could and literally throw him down the banking. Larry got through, so did but the African who arrived the night before slipped and was struggling to get out of the grasp of two boys. 'Quick Larry Let's help!' and they turned back and pulled him away from the two boys and sprinted off.
'We've seen you! We'll get you! You've had it now!' Screamed two older boys they had not seen before, but every face was new. Glancing behind he looked up at the side of the building he could see other boys throwing stuff out of the windows, some windows had towels and shirts hanging out too.
Racing back to house they went to the comfort of the dorm, sanctuary!
'Where do you think you are going? Shower room! Now! Not tomorrow!

Take your kit off and get in!' They all plunged in and were made to stand under a freezing cold shower for two minutes.
The hot water already gone. Numbed with yet another shock. Drying off they changed and readied themselves for what lay ahead. They all appeared to be straightening themselves out but it was fast approaching breakfast time and had to be in the dining room by 8am. They didn't even know where the dining room was! The late arrival asked if Walter would help him but he was only interested in not being late himself and selfishly refused. He should've helped he knew that would've been the right thing to do and he was given his just deserts he was late and got his first circuit! That pleasure awaited him the next day.
'Name! You again!'
'Flannigan. This is my first time.' They had been here for fourteen hours only, why were they there? 'Why am I here?' It was to become a catchphrase. It all felt unusually familiar.
Sitting down at the table Brecon had its own section of the dining room. Out of view of the seniors. Suddenly. BONG! The gong sounded, with the rumbling of standing boys resonating throughout.
'The Grace for what we are about to receive may the Lord make us truly thankful!'
A clatter of benches accompanied the sitting down of everybody as breakfast was eaten
Chapel followed breakfast well congregational practice actually where the school practiced singing hymns for the regular Services and Sunday evening Service. This session was taken by Peter Barron, the head otherwise known as Mental Pete. There were about twelve of them in the first form and they were shepherded around their new surroundings that day. The first experience of the new world came in the form of an orientation lecture, given by the founder of Flaxden Brig, this was Dochan Do. Speaking with a booming voice dressed with a black cape he immediately thought of Batman and Robin. They had watched him walk to their class room in silence. Many boys were milling around waiting to go in the classrooms all dressed in pure blue jerseys, some wearing long dark grey trousers, whilst the boys in Brecon were wearing shorts. 'Still wearing shorts!' others were wearing kilts in smart contrast. Why was that he thought? As he strode down the quadrangle to their classroom there was a hush. 'Good morning **sir!'** Acknowledged by a firm nod. It seemed as

though an Angel of the lord was passing through. He entered the room and they all stood up automatically as though programmed to do so. He Lowered his free hand and all automatically sat down. The bell went it was 9am.

He began slowly. ‘Man is born a tame and civilized animal, nevertheless he requires proper instruction and a fortunate nature, and then of all animals he has the opportunity to become the most divine and civilized, but if he be insufficiently or ill-educated he will become the most savage of earthly creatures.

‘The soul of the child in his play should be guided to the love of that sort of excellence in which when he grows up to manhood he will have to be perfected.

‘He who has received this true education of the inner being will most shrewdly perceive ominions or faults in artificial or natural things, and with true taste, while he proves and rejoices over and receives into his soul the good and becomes noble and good, he will justly blame and have the bad, now in the days of his youth, even before he is able to know the reason why: and when reason comes he will recognise and salute the friend with whom his education has made him long familiar.

‘He whose happiness rests with himself if possible wholly and if not as or as possible-who is not hanging in suspense on other men or changing with the vicumtitudes of their fortitude/fortune has his life ordered for the best. He is the temperate, valiant and wise for he relies on himself, as you all know said PLATO.’

‘What is he talking about? Who is Plato? A Disney character?’ Walter whispered to Larry as the rest of the form stared at the large man dominating in front of the classroom.

‘No idea! I think Pluto is a dog in Disney! I’ve never heard any of those words before! Big aren’t they.’

‘SILENCE!!’ A long cane flashed into view and slammed on to the desk in front of Larry, leaving a cloud of chalk dust belching clouds into the immediate area.

‘It has already been said that one of the aims at Flaxden Brig are to invest a boy, each of you, gradually with responsibility and authority leading to the goal of achievement. First, however he must show that his personal standards and self-discipline justify that promotion, by listening and learning, you will then be able to lead with confidence. Flaxden Brig is the realisation of an ideal, our Services have evolved, there will always be plenty to do but it will be a lot of fun. Its philosophy and integrity working together for the common good. We are all a part of this but if you want to get out, leave, go, there's the door.' Nobody budged.

'There are five houses here at Flaxden Brig, Sperrin, Cuillin, Magillycuddy and these, as is the new house under construction called Pennine, are all out of bounds, as is Flaxden Moor, to you NOVUS who are residing in Brecon.

'For your first year you are all NOVUS and therefore each of you will all be a NOVUS and be required to submit to school and house discipline and prove your reliability and efficiency to all. When you reach the second year you will be a LOWER Boy where you will be required to keep a LOWER Log. From being a LOWER Boy, you will proceed into the 3rd year and become seniors. This elevates you to the title of UPPER boy and then you will have to keep an UPPER log and moreover be expected to show, besides efficiency, a readiness to help others. On the recommendation of his housemaster, he may then be promoted to house senior as a BREVET or FACTOR. As such he will be on probation for more important pre factorial duties. His powers of punishment will be limited but the opportunity to serve others will be great. Up to this point in his school career a boy will mix freely and share both studies and dormitories with NOVUS, LOWER and UPPER boys. The period of probation satisfactorily completed, a boy will be made a house prefect and enjoy the privilege of a separate common room. From these house prefects will be chosen a small group of school prefects amongst these will be the head of school and the head of houses. This important group will have regular meetings with the headmaster and help promote the welfare of the school.'

THE LOWER AND UPPER LOGS

'If a boy is subject to a very severe external discipline he may grow into a very efficient person whilst at school. But, once having left, there is the very real danger, that he will relax all the standards imposed on him. If on the other hand, having first to obey others, he is gradually permitted to take some of the responsibility for himself upon his own shoulders, his inner being will grow fortified by habit and by the desire to justify the trust placed in him. He will then be able to enter the world confident in his ability to care for himself and others, maintaining freely chosen standards.'

'Why is he telling us all this?'

'Yes if we are Novus, not Lowers or Uppers!'
'Yes Sir I think we are in the wrong room!'
'I am, telling you this Boy because you will be told this only once!' And again the cane smacked onto the desk, re fumigating the room with even more chalk dust.
'Hence the UPPER and LOWER logs and these logs will take the form of a diary which the owner must fill in at the end of each day. Both will contain a short, simple list of questions which must be truthfully marked with a tick or cross. These questions will be entirely practical. They will deal with matters of health, work, punctuality and co-operation. The UPPER log being more comprehensive and searching than the LOWER log.'
'Very great care will be taken to avoid unnatural introspection curbing the spirit and zest of the boy or placing a heavy burden on his young shoulders.'
Health, work, punctuality, cooperation, activities.
'Freedom and trust are privileges and like all must be deserved. The society that we live in today is jumped up, geared to success and we are all judged on how much we earn, what car we drive, where we live, it's just stuff and doesn't mean anything.
'If therefore a boy fails persistently to merit the trust placed in him by the log, the privilege may be removed until he has learnt to appreciate its purpose and show himself ready to conform to its exacting demands.
'Every clever boy is a potential candidate to go further. But if he is of idle nature he seldom reaches it, and his example of idleness is infectious and detrimental to less intelligent boys.
'Academic achievement cannot be forced. No teacher can compel a boy to work however much he may coerce him. Real achievement is gained by boys who themselves wish to work. If they live in an atmosphere where academic work is respected, they themselves will want to work and in this way will realise their potential. When all do their best, the intelligent are spurred towards academic distinction.
'Therefore FLAXDEN BRIG will welcome all who do their best.
The boys of the school have such a wide range of out of school activities that the more practical minded boy can hardly feel unhappy or unfulfilled providing he is trying his hardest.
As you are all NOVUS you will undertake the following academic subjects;

English, Mathematics with Arithmetic, French, Latin, Geography, General Science, History, Art, Music, Scripture, Physical Education and Woodwork. Once a month you will also have a first aid lesson and all will learn to swim, in the Flaxden Pool whilst the swimming pool is under construction, but most important of all you will have an hour each month with me on what is right and wrong and I want you all as a group to tell me how you would sort things out from right and wrong, your duties as men.

'And you will be examined in all these disciplines at the end of the winter and summer terms. 'Intellectual life is sterile unless it is enjoyed therefore two periods a week within the timetable are devoted to art and minimal appreciation so that boys who have not already an interest in them will have an opportunity to appreciate them. Music, Art and Literature are encouraged amongst the boys, as much are practical outdoor activities.

'Sir where do we get our timetables?' Piped up Larry.

'There is paper here and you have pencil and a ruler.' Replied Dochan Do, his voice booming with authority as he continued with his sermon.

'Again as NOVUS you will participate in activities. Sailing-all boys will be taught to handle small boats. Although the lake is considered to be exceptionally safe, safety measures will be stringent and at all times a master with the lake patrol will be in attendance with a fast rescue boat – the Flaxden Brig Cutter. The Lake Patrol is also responsible for development and maintenance. And soon you will be acquiring certain skills with The Brig Services. The dinghies/canoes will be built in the school workshop and boys will be able to share in the work of construction. By so doing, they will learn to appreciate more readily the products of their own hands and at the same time practice a valuable craft which will help them enjoy the time of their later years.

'At weekends there will be frequent expeditions into the hills/hills when boys will be taught the skills of camp craft and compass navigation and develop qualities of resource and discipline. An experienced master will supervise each expedition and the Mountain Service will be on standby.

'In winter you will have, skiing, ice skating and sledging to look forward to.

'Individual skills-boys will learn to swim. They will also be required to undertake one cross country run per week. There will be team games Rugby, Cricket, hockey, soccer, and athletics in the summer, fencing, shooting, horse riding, tennis and badminton.

'As Brecon House are not old enough for the main Brig Services, Fire Service, Ambulance Service, Lake patrol and Hill Service you will spend Tuesday afternoon working on the estate to take a personal interest and pride in these lovely surroundings. There will always be many jobs to do, and by making their contribution boys will come to know the dignity of manual labour. We are in the process of building our school, the chapel is done, but the quadrangle has to be completed, the swimming pool and gymnasium are also almost complete but there is still much to do.

'It is assured that when your parents sent you all to Flaxden Brig that you may all take part in all foregoing or in similar activities which are normal and essential features of the school curriculum and therefore no specific permission will be asked of them. As Plato once said,

'Mens sano in corpore sano'

'Remains as true for us today as it as it was for Juvenal. The Brig will aim to both, strengthen the delicate and give stamina to the robust. Boys will be measured and weighed at the beginning of each term and the diet will be based on expert advice. Physical training and athletics will form a regular part of the curriculum.

'The Brig has its own Sanatorium and medical equipment supervised by a trained nurse. The local village Doctor will visit periodically. 'This is all to encourage you in a thought and independence for the adventure that now laid before you.

'This is a new school first and foremost, for any enterprise a certain minimum amount of £ s & d has to be found. At first there has not been much to show and sceptical abound! Tables, chairs, beds, vehicles, classroom, kitchen and surgery equipment, all these items have had to be delivered in the right quantity and diversity for a given date.

'Machinery has had to be established for communication, correspondence, accounts and rudimentary business and office administration. Before Flaxden Brig could begin jungles had to be cleared, rooms decorated and painted. Every boy has taken a hand, providing growth and putting out roots. Don't think what the Brig can do for you think how and what you can do for your Brig as what Flaxden can give to the individual depends on how many its members contribute to the whole! Success of which depends on the contribution of many minds and getting up on to the feet and making it happen!'

Dochan Do then suddenly stood up and pointed out the window, 'Go now and grasp this opportunity every day henceforth , choose the man you want to be and begin to make your lives extraordinary, your activity and enthusiasm will make you all successful, get on this vehicle hold tight and don't fall off! Time is the scarcest commodity of all, don't waste a second, and use it wisely. On the table in front of me are full transcripts of this lecture so you have a record of how we work here. Collect and guard with your life and refer when you need to. This is the Flaxden Brig Bible! **SINE PRAESIDIO!** Is the Brig's motto! Use your brains and work hard, there is no substitute! And remember to prepare yourself for the ultimate test!'

'The ultimate test Sir?'

'Yes! The ultimate test! The UPPERS v The LOWERS! And for tonight I leave you with something to do for our next meeting. I want you all as a group to come to a ten point understanding on out to sort things out!

And with that he left the room, cloak getting caught in the door but then sweeping majestically behind him.

Nonplussed they all looked blankly at each other. The bell went and they could see other boys pouring out of their classrooms.

'The ultimate test? We are Novus so it won't affect us!'

'Thank Heavens that's over! I didn't have a clue what he was speaking about!'

'Where do we go now? Anyone know?'

'What was that all about?'

'No idea!'

One of the boys pulled out a timetable 'Its Latin in classroom 8.'

'Classroom eight? Where's that?'

'Well this is three must be that one.' So they all piled into what they thought were the correct room only to find a group of older boys at the desks. Wrong way! So they all trooped across the other way eventually arriving in classroom 8.

'Ahhh! You've decided to arrive. Welcome to Latin!' A man speaking with a very posh voice sat behind his desk. It was Pansy Ward.

The next period was History and waiting for them was Big Jim Powers, the Deputy Housemaster of Brecon and rugby coach, History teacher, PE teacher, Art teacher.

At 11am the bell went.

'You now have a 30 minute break and then you have PE with me in the gymnasium, 11 30 am sharp!'
With that Big Jim was off jogging as he left, brown leather satchel over his back.
'What do we do now?' All sticking together like a flock of sheep, they left the room. Outside, on what they would discover at the top of Magillycuddy Hill was the tuck shop, the 'Tucky', the building was a big shed, wooden in structure with four serving hatches. A small queue was beginning to form. 'Hey, let's queue! I've got half a Crown Let's get something before we get changed.'
'Ok.' Rummaging in his pockets Walter could feel the 3 florins and other change his Dad had given him, the ten shilling note he would save for a rainy day.
The queue got bigger and older boys started pushing in front.
'Hey we were here first!'
'Was somebody squeaking?' Said an older boy.
'You're pushing in that's rude!'
'And you are not a NOVUS you are a Brecon Hoosie! And you do what we say!'
Quietly they accepted their position and waited patiently. 'It's 11 15am we have to be at the gym at 11 30am and we've still to change!'
'One minuter Larry, nearly there!'
Five minutes later the queue gone they arrived at the hatch. 'I'll have a bag of cheese and onion crisps, marathon and a can of Banta please!'
BANG! The hatch slid down like a French guillotine, nearly taking Larry's fingers with it.
'WE'RE CLOSED!'
'But it's only 11 20 am!'
'No it is not its 11 30am. We are closed, Now... BUGGER OFF!'
'11 30?' Walter and Larry looked at each other. And ran like the blazes to Brecon House. The changing room was empty everybody else had gone! Quickly they changed into their gym gear and headed for ….well they had no idea!
'Where are ye going lads?' Asked an old man with a spade slung over his shoulder. This was Greasy Joe, Joe Delgrano, one of the grounds men. He gave them directions and eventually they found the gym. Big Jim growled

at them as they entered the gym. No words were needed they were late. The look was enough.
'Outside and run round the building and don't stop until I tell you to halt! Oh yes and take a medicine ball each and carry it above your heads!'
With no choice but to obey they did as they were told. About thirty minutes later the others came out of the gym. 'Now run back to your house, shower and get off to your next period. Completely ignoring Larry and Walter, Big Jim ran behind the others. They stopped. 'I think we'd better go too Larry!'
They changed and headed off to the dining room for their lunch. The whole school was there. The Head and Deputy Head were sat with the Head Boy Gordon and the House Captain on duty, Stoker. The food was ok but they were hungry after dinner the two friends walked over to the Top o'th' Banks and looked out around them. They could see for miles, the lake, the forests and the distant hills. It was difficult to believe if there was anywhere else or even another world apart from their new home.
'Picturesque!' Commented Larry in his Australian drawl.
'Yes it is, come on; I think we have bed rest now!'
'What rest? We go back to bed now?!!' Joked Larry. On their beds they could hear music being piped into the dorm.
'What's that tune?'
'Blue Danube Waltz!'
'What's that?'
'It's about a dance on a river..... I think! Flows through about 10 countries!'
The voice came from a small boy, the smallest Novus called Iain Stevenson.
'I'm going to join one of the Services.....the Fire Service looks good! What do you think?' Announced Larry.
Dochan Do said we were not old enough.'
'I'm game, if you don't ask you don't get, how about you?'
'Nothing to lose. Yes I'll come too.'
So the boys headed off down to the fire station and knocked on the door. A large boy with tight red curly hair opened the door. He was wearing school uniform and was wearing his kilt.
'Yes! What do you want?'
'We've come to join the Fire Service!'

'Join the fire Service? What you little runts? You are only Hoosies!'
'Hoosies? We were told that we could join the Services learn new skills and develop ourselves!'
'Well you can't! We have our full complement of crews! No vacancies until next year.'
So the boys left and headed for the Hill Service. A tall boy in breeches was gathering up at long piece of rope. 'Ye wan ta join the HS? Sorry ladies there's no room for you here!'
Heads still high the boys headed off to the Ambulance Service and got the same response.
'I'm going to try for the Emergency Service!'
'Come we can but try!' At the shed for the Emergency Service the doors were wide open and there was nobody around. No vehicle when suddenly a loud roar was heard.
'QUICK MOOOVE!' From around the corner came what looked like to the boys an armoured car!
'Just look at that, let's join this one!' A head popped out of the turret.
'Vot do you vant here? Zis place is out of ze bounds to you!'
Puzzled at the strange accent Billy replied.
'Ve vant to join the Emergency Zervice!'
'You cannot, it is verboten, now go!'
'Think you insulted him there Billy! What was that accent? I think it was German.'
'Well they don't want us in the Services what about the societies? I quite like the Biology Society, how about you guys?'
'Yes that's a good idea! I'll try the Geography society!'
'And you Billy?'
'Think I'll go for the Drama society, what with knowing how to speak a foreign language and all that!'
'Ach get away with you! Ok let's split and we'll meet at the Top o'th' Banks later. Let's go to it quick style! Also we do not tell ANYONE WHAT WE ARE DOING!' So the three boys again headed off but soon all were back at their meeting place.
'No!'
'No!'
'Oversubscribed!'

'Not fair, why do they offer all these things for us to do and no intention of letting us do any!' At this point they could hear a long creak and a door opened nearby. It was the Head. He strolled in the direction of the boys.
'Hello, it's Flannigan, MacCloon and Odhiambo isn't it?'
'Yes sir!' They all replied in unison, amazed he knew all their names...
'Beautiful spot here, I see you like it, I have seen you come here after your meals. How are you all getting along?' He said as his grey blue eyes looked at them in a gentle manner.
'Well sir......' Walter dug Larry thinking he was going to talk about the beatings.
'We're doing great sir but we've tried to join the Services and the societies that we've been told about but they won't let us!' The boys in turn explained their experiences to the Head who listened and nodded thoughtfully!
'Well boys I'm afraid you are too young for all that just now, you are the Novus and have only just arrived here. Be patient but don't worry your opportunity will come and you will be kept busy until then!' And with that he about turned and headed back to his study.

The school outfitters Cherryble & Hitchon from the City arrived in the afternoon but had everything he needed. Some boys especially from overseas still needed to complete their wardrobe. After this they got ready for games and here came their first taste of rugby. What was this? An oval ball where were the round ones? Big Jim was the coach for Brecon; he was also the coach of THE team, the 1st xv. After supper they had their first prep which was done in the classroom block. Here they did work set from the day's classes but for this one only the maths teacher had set them work, times tables, all of them. Then it was back to Brecon to wash, bed and lights out. Twenty four hours had gone since mum and dad had gone but the day wasn't over yet. After lights out as they lay in their beds discussing what Dochan Do had asked them to do.
'So come on. Has anybody any idea what Dochan Do meant?' Said Larry
'Duties of being kind to each other. 'Duties of not harming others. 'Duties of truth telling.' 'Duties of keeping promises.' 'These are good values, anything else we can put to him?' 'Duties of gratitude and reparation. 'Duties of being fair.' 'Duties of self-improvement.' Suddenly there was a loud crash.

'BRECON HOUSE! EVERYONE UP, AND IN THE COMMON ROOM, NOW!' This was a new voice to all of the Novus and came from Ian Soutar known as MZEEE. 'They must've heard us talking after lights out.' So unaware of why they had been dragged out of their beds they were soon to meet George. Once in the common room the whole house was accused of leaving the changing room in a mess and that clothes had been untidily left on the floor. Consequently all the clothes left on the floor had been put in the pound box. As all clothes were name tagged offenders had been identified and were to be called into the boot room to see George. There was a deathly hush in the room as names were read out. Then Walter's name was read out. 'Flannigan! 1 sock and 1 towel.' He was then directed to the boot room to see George. No eleven year old boy could ever be prepared for what was about to happen. MZEEE was there with George, a very worn out Puma trainer, the one that they had all enquired about during their orientation. 'Bend over Flannigan!' WHACK! WHACK! He just took it, accepting it all but not really knowing why. 'Get to bed now boy!' He was stunned! There was no defence. How did his clothes get on the floor? He had hung them up himself. Did he really deserve this? It would be, much later before he discovered the truth. He went back to Conway where he was the last to get back, two Lowers Troup and Kerr watched smugly at the end of the corridor. The late arrival from the night before had been beaten like Walter, twice. They looked at each other and realised that they all were in this together. The newcomer was Billy Odhiambo, who would become a very close friend. 'Wowweeeeee!' Billy said in a quite tone. 'That was some whacking! By the way Guys thanks for this morning!' The biggest smile you had ever seen lit up the room. The torture was over they hoped or so it was thought.

'I'm sorry for not helping you this morning.' Apologised Walter. 'It will not happen again!'

'It's ok, no worries, strange way to get acquainted, my name is Billy.'

'I'm Walter. And this sorry piece is Larry MacCloon!'

As he drifted into his sleep the same bright star could be seen from the night before. Suddenly awoke bolt upright in bed, sweating, breathing heavily, but he wasn't in bed he was on the floor. 'You ok? You were talking in your sleep, mumbling away; don't know how the others stayed asleep!' Said Larry.

Focusing in the pitch black replied.

'I thought I was having some sort of nightmare just seeing all these letters swirling around as if in a whirlpool, thought I was falling off the end of the world.'

'What letters? I had it myself, but I didn't fall out of bed!'

'Can't remember they were all in a mix.'

'Just a dream go back to sleep!'

As he was attempting to do so there was suddenly a large crash. Everybody woke up to see Darnley out of his bed thrashing arms and legs everywhere.

'What is he doing? Is he having a nightmare too?'

'No it is a fit I've seen it before, quickly switch the lights on! Clear the room, move the beds, give him space!'

'He's calming down now, put him into that recovery position we were taught in first aid!'

Soon he started to come around. 'Are you ok?' The others crowded around him.

'I...I....I'm ok....'

'Need to go to the San? We'll go with you.'

'Thanks but I'll go in the morning after breakfast.'

'But........that looked serious.'

'No I'm ok just need to rest. Thank you.' With that they all went back to their beds.

The next morning Billy and Walter were woken at 6 30am and told to go on their circuit and as they passed the boatsheds to run into the lake pick up a rock and bring it back. 'Make sure Darnley doesn't do the run Larry.' The circuit was the outer periphery of the school which was near enough a mile. That morning they were not late for breakfast. Only two days previously he had been woken up at the Station Hotel, sitting down with his parents for breakfast. It was all coming back; he yearned for them now, more than ever.

Later that day they were to report to the Sanatorium for weights and measures. The second form boys were also to go and when they asked if they had had to go they were told you will love it and see the Nurse she is gorgeous! True enough they headed for the San with the others and just before they arrived they passed the elderly man whom they were told was Greasy Joe, the man who had directed them to PE, the general dogs' body around the grounds. 'Hi lads, it's a braw day ye ken, are ye aff tae the San to see the beautiful Rose? How did ye like the haggis an tatties?'

The four boys acknowledged him. 'Who's ya fitba team lads?'
'My team is Export City!'
'Och aye, it is, is it? I used tae play for Montrose ye ken!' With that he turned and carried on with his sweeping the fallen leaves and started to sing.

♪

THERE'S A STAR WHO'S BEAMING RAY IS SHED ON EVERY CLIME

IT SHINES BY NIGHT, IT SHINES BY DAY AND NE'ER GROWS DIM WITH TIME

IT ROSE UP AT THE BACK OF THE FAIRY HILL BOLYBRACK AND DOWN INTO YONDER GHYLL

IT SHONE ON FLAXDEN'S CLEAR BROOK

A HUNDRED YEARS ARE GONE NO MORE YET BRIGHTER GLOWS IT'S BEAM

LET KING AND COUNTRIES RISE AND FALL

THIS WORLD HAS NOT TURNED

BUT BRIGHTLY BEAMS DOWN THEM ALL THE STAR O FLAX............

Joe's voice slowly petered out as they joined the queue to get measured and weighed, the Novus at the back of the queue. Whilst they were waiting Billy noticed something odd, whilst looking at the list. 'Have you seen this? We all have the middle initials JP, what does yours stand for?'
'Your turn Flannigan!' Just as he was about to say the Mum tone of the Nurse commanded his attention and not only that! She was gorgeous! A woman in her mid-thirties stood at the door, shapely, athletic with a full bodied figure enveloped in a blue uniform, her dark Brown hair tied up in a ponytail. Her face seemed unspoilt, natural with no makeup, her green eyes shone like emeralds. On her dress was a badge NURSE ROSE / SRN, SMN. What a sight! All the boys were now at attention at the vision in front of them.

'Right Flannigan, 5 ft 7 inches, now on the scales, 10 stone 9 pounds, now off you go. Odhiambo, you next!' The voice was a soft American accent, a New Yorker maybe?

Billy then Larry took their turns in silence and then joined and headed for the dining room and supper.

Brecon house had its own section in the dining room and they had the meals, 'food' served to them by waiting orderlies from the senior school, 3rd years, now Uppers. These orderlies along with kitchen staff known as the Ghylly Men were responsible for serving their mush, it was a well-oiled machine and the boys of Brecon House also known as the Brecon Hoosies befriended the Ghylly's who seemed to pity them so far away from home and gave extra bits and pieces from the kitchen.

That night during prep McIver a fellow Novus challenged Ross Monroe to a fight. All were in disbelief, could never understand the thinking here. Monroe accepted, he had no choice, couldn't back down to a Novus boy especially one who was just starting out. After prep they all trudged down to a clearing by the Blue Huts at the lake side where they formed a circle on a beach area and Monroe and McIver met in the middle, just how the Hares settle their disputes except this encounter lasted only for a few seconds with McIver consigning himself to become the weed of the house and indeed wrecking his immediate potential with that one reckless challenge. 'Make it quick Mony!' A whisper came from the silent ring, 'Keep it quiet!' There was a deafening silence with only the water from the lake washing up on the shore, and nod from Mony then a loud CLAP! It lasted all of five seconds with McIver on the floor with a bloodied nose. The audience stood quietly with the star covered sky, full moon and water from the lake lapping against the shore, giving an atmospheric setting to the proceedings.

As they headed back they could see figures moving around, some vehicles near a scattering of buildings, the Blue Huts near to the lake side but they briskly walked back with the others, it was dusk now and there was a chill in the air.

'What about McIver? He's still on the floor.'

'What about him?'

'Leave him! He made the challenge!' A Lower boy replied. The Novus were silent but the Lowers acted as though it was just like any other day. Justice had taken its course, a summary. The clear night directed them back and again this big star could be seen over the large expanse of water high in the sky, hovering, watching, guiding.

All was quiet that night. They didn't know why but it was welcomed! The next day followed a similar pattern. Get up 7am, run, breakfast, chapel, classes, dinner, bed rest, classes, games, supper, bed lights out.

The next shock was to be Friday afternoon the last two periods, woodwork, taken by Mr Davie, aka Jaw! This man was the most fearsome person the boys had ever met! The workshops were full with tools, benches and materials and the second room had a group of boys cutting metal with a large machine. Upstairs, a small stair way lead up to a loft like room, which was the technical drawing area. Once the class was over the feeling of elation could not be described yet once the weekend was over they would be worrying about next Friday's lesson and counting down the days. On the comfort of their beds, they talked about home and about the girls back home.

'Well I have girlfriend!' Walter blurted out, though he didn't really. He'd liked a girl called Prudence Blaney who he had seen riding her horse, trotting up and down the fields admiring her tight jodhpurs, smacking her whip against her knee length boots when she was angry.

Larry talked about his girl called Shelia who had come to him after four other boyfriends Ste, Dave, Nig and Baz!

'Hey Larry we can make a song out of that. To the tune of Robin Hood, Robin Hood riding through the Hill!'

'We could use these as are nicknames! You can be Baz, Larry!'

'Nahhh mate!'

'You are an Aussies right? From Australia? Well isn't Cobber another way of friend or mate?'

'Yes it is, but don't forget that I was born in Scotland! I'm Scottish!'

'Well we'll call you Cobber! Yes Cobber MacCloon! Sounds good that doesn't it?!!' With a sigh Larry resigned himself to that fate!

'But only you two mind!'

'What about you Billy? Have you got a girl back home?'

'Home......' He replied, look out into the distance.

'.......yes it's out there somewhere. There must be girls here somewhere.' Coming out of his trance Billy said.

'Well I heard there are girls on the other side of the lake.'

'Who told you that!?'

'That building you can see directly across from the boat sheds?'
'Yes?'
'Well, Mum was driving and we got lost coming here and drove past it the other day!'
'So that's why you were late!'
'Yup, Mum and dad wanted to drive around the lake before catching their flight home. Take in the scenery.'
'Great all we need is to get a boat from the boatsheds we saw this morning and sail across the lake!'
'Oh yeah! Do you not think they will miss one of their boats?! Or mind?'
'Negative waves Cobber! Negative waves!'
'So what do you propose?'
'I propose......... we do nothing!' Said Larry.
'Come on Cobber! Where's that Aussie sense of adventure?!'
'We'll build our own! A raft!'
'Yeah!'
'Yeah! I'm a genius!'
'Let's doooooo it!'
'Heaven help me I'm in the hands of madmen! I can't even swim!'
Tuesday morning began with the bugle charge, followed by the scramble to get out of bed before Jimmy Crow got to them. The morning run was completed, evading the Uppers behind the Yew trees on the banks; they were learning to escape their clutches. Billy was at the front and the first into the shower, he was athletic compared to the others, the cold waking them all up. The blood was circulating at a fast pace. The three boys met up in Clyde the locker room where Walter had just finished sweeping up, his housework chore.
'This afternoon at 4pm after games we'll take a boat and row over to the other side of the lake!' Larry announced with a positive definite edge.
'Where from?' Billy enquired.
'The boat sheds of course; there are loads of them there!'
'And you don't think they'll mind us taking one?'
'We've been through this already.'
'Well it will be quicker!'
'We'll take it after games, go over, have a look see and come back in time for tea! Nobody will ever know!'
'Genius! That will save us making a raft!'

The excitement built as the morning progressed. Latin, Maths, Science, French and PE took them to dinner time. After lunch they had bed rest and the gramophone music could be heard drifting into the dorm.
'What is that music?' Said Mad Mac McNut. Nobody replied it was the only time they knew they would get some peace and rest.
On the rugby field pitch 2 they were the only ones on the playing fields at this time as it was Service day and they could see the fire engines V1, V2 and V3 charging around the grounds, bell ringing, boys could be seen in uniform with distinctive yellow helmets on their heads, hoses spraying out water and ladders against the school building the ambulance speeding along the lake side road with blue light flashing and siren wailing. A Land Rover packed with what looked like ropes and rucksacks and a group of boys was driving down the front drive, the excitement was everywhere, there was much going on. Then suddenly Big Jim appeared.
'Right everyone on the line. On my whistle sprint to the far posts! Last one there does it again! PHAAAARP!!'Like a bolt out of a gun everybody soon shot off but soon there was a clear separation with Mony getting there first and McIver last. 'You will do it again at the end in front of everyone you slimy little shit McIver!'
Big Jim ran over to a pile of rugby balls and picked up them all up and kicked one towards the group of boys many in recovery position, others on their backs, prostrate. 'On your feet! You poor excuse for men! On your feet! I am now going to teach you to play rugby! You have a game coming up soon against Mumblemond and you are not going to embarrass me! They are a different breed from the Brig and you need to be ready.''
The next 90 minutes seemed to go on for ages, a minute seeming like an hour. Learning to pass the ball backwards, which seemed odd to the Novus boys and tackling was rough. Kerr and Troup using the opportunity to put the boot in on the newcomers at each and every opportunity, while Big Jim was not looking. 'Come on you bunch of Fairies, my Granny can pass better than that! There are no magic wands here!' Games ended with McIver doing his sprint with Big Jim who won at a canter. McIver crumpled up in a heap and the other boys mostly Lowers started to jeer. 'Shut it! You set of scabby reptiles' Big Jim barked. 'Come on son, there's no shame get up!' McIver just lay there whimpering in the foetal position.
'I said get up!'
'The Weed just isn't up to it!'

'Powers! Deal with that boy!' A large booming voice bellowed from the banks. It was Mental Pete, the Head. He must've been watching on the banks. Big Jim's head snapped a round and stomped towards a group of dive boys, Monroe, Bothwell, Frostwick, Troup and Kerr.
'Who said that?' There was silence although they knew who said it. 'Right if the guilty boy does not own up the whole house will be beaten here and now!' Again silence.
'It was me sir.' Monroe had owned up but they knew it wasn't him.
'Right Monroe you're coming with me! The rest of you games are over go and get changed! See you tomorrow!' With a broad cheesy, sadistic grin Big Jim and Monroe headed off and all now wondered what fate lay in store for him.
Larry and Billy lingered behind, soon, when they got the chance and headed for the boatsheds to look for their transport across the lake. People were heading back to the buildings as their activities had ended for the day.
'Who really made that comment? It definitely wasn't Monroe; he is a good fair one'
'I'm sure it was Kerr, the coward and Monroe took the flak, stood up for us all.' The others agreed.
'It's like that scrap the other night he had no choice but to fight McIver. And now he's sort of standing up for him.'
'Standing up for us all!'
'Let's get that boat!' They got to the boatsheds. No one was around.
'How about that one? It looks big enough for all of us.' The boat was a fibre glass dinghy with one oar and they pulled it to the water line.
'Quick down! There's a lorry coming!' Shouted Billy. Chugging along the road appeared a Thames Trader with a flat back and dustbins in it.
'Looks like the dustbin men!' Said Larry.
'No it's the pig man. He collects all the shit we don't eat and takes it for his pigs!'
'Let's go!'
The dinghy slid into the water. 'Beats making our own!' The water was very calm like a plate of glass and when they were 50 yards out. 'We've only got one paddle! What are we going to do?' Glancing over to the other side they could see little figures on the shore and behind them, there was no one about. It was now or never!
'Blow it! Let's carry on!'

'I don't think we should!'
'Are you a boy or a girl?!'
'Well we are doing this to see the girls! Hey look it's that McIver bloke by the boatsheds and four or is it three others. Do you think they can see us?'
'Nahhh let's carry on. Quick style!'
'Look he's talking to someone. Who is it?'
'Forget him, let's get going.'
By now the boat had reached about two hundred yards out, paddling furiously, taking turns until one tired as though they were possessed. A big hill towered over the buildings of their home
'Can you hear that?
'Yes it's a motor.'
A big white cutter came into view, waves splashing over its bow as it sliced through the water towards the dinghy a forlorn hope in the middle of the lake... They stopped and gawped at the boat. There were three boys aboard clad in lifejackets with the formidable stature of Puss Whiteford, his hair flowing in the breeze, not a strand out of place, at the stern. It was the Lake Patrol, with an Ambulance crew member.
'What are you three doing?'
'Well ermmm!'
'Don't say anything or everybody will want to cross the lake!' Whispered Billy in a barely audible tone.
'Get in! We'll tow the dinghy.'
The three boys were helped in and the dinghy was tied to the back of the Cutter by the Lake Patrol crew and the group set off to the shore.
'You're in trouble lads!' Puss said as he combed his hair.
'As the cutter pulled up alongside its berth at the jetty a familiar figure from Friday came into view, upright, a mile high, focussed on one thing only……the three boys!
Frightening on a good day but this was going to be worse, much worse, they could feel but knew they were in it together.
'Think I need a clean pair of shorts!' Cobber said quietly.
'Huuuuuu! What have you been doing? Where have you been? Get back to your house and change! It's the Headmasters chair for all of you!' Growled Jaw, like a Lion.
Back at Brecon they showered and changed. There was nobody there except Monroe, looking tired, slumped on a changing room bench.

'Where have you three been?' He asked.
'We took one of the dinghies and had a sail onto the lake, fancied to see the other side but the lake patrol brought us back!'
'So that's why the sirens went off! Didn't you hear? Jimmy Crow was furious you weren't at roll. We thought there was a real emergency!' Monroe started laughing out loud, smiling and contented.
'And you? Did Big Jim beat you? How many? We know it wasn't you who said that.'
'No, far worse, he took me on a run, the ACE.'
'A run?' They all looked at each other puzzled.
'No the ACE is a six mile run through the woods and up the tracks. You will have to do it sooner or later, whether you like it or not. I've done it.....loads of times I've lost count; sometimes use it to count myself to sleep!'
'Wow! We know who it was though.'
'Yes, so do I. Where are you going now?'
'The Headmasters Chair.'
'Oh. You'd better go.'
The look on Monroe's face had changed to one of pity.
Jimmy Crow came in.
'Flannigan! Odhiambo! MacCloon! Headmaster's office now!'
Jimmy Crow escorted them down to a corridor in the main building where there were two doors. 'That's the door, he's expecting you.' With that he left them to the mercy of what lay within.
Larry went up and knocked on the door. KNOCK KNOCK! No answer.
'I can hear paper rustling he must be in there, knock harder Cobber!'
BANG! BANG! BANG!
'WHAT THE FLAMING 'ELL!'
The door swung open. It was the Headmaster and it was not his office but his toilet! Jimmy Crow had set them up! All were aghast! All 3 of them shrunk back against the wall in shock at what was unfolding. Trembling in fear. 'Who was knocking on that door? What are YOU three doing here?'
'Mr Davie sent us Sir.'
'Ah Hah! So you are the ones! Who stole Flaxden Brig property? Go into my office!'
The boys trooped in one after the other. Then Mental Pete lined them up and across the other side of the room a big fireplace could be seen with

roaring flames. By this they could see a large Captains chair, with what looked like a long stick with a curved handle on it. This must be the Headmasters Chair. The adrenalin began to flow within each of them, flight or fight, but they could do neither. Riveted to the spot they listened.
'At Flaxden Brig, I have gone to great lengths to ensure we live in harmony, where we can trust and respect each other and their property and this is how you have repaid my leniency! What do you have to say? Well you give me no alternative, a removal of a boat from the boatsheds is a serious offence. I am disappointed as not once have I ever had to use my cane. I have been proud of that. Flannigan! The Chair!' Directing him to the chair he scooped up the long cane in one flowing movement. 'Bend over boy! You first Flannigan!'
Could their bottoms take this? He slowly bent down clenching his bum cheeks for whatever good that would do and closing his eyes, would he have an arse left after this? Heart pounding like the clappers, when.........
KNOCK!KNOCK!KNOCK!.......KNOCK!KNOCK!
The Heads arm was raised ready to strike, up a couple of inches, then another and another, KNOCK! KNOCK! Growling he said 'Who is that!'
KNOCK! KNOCK! KNOCK! KNOCK! KNOCK!
Realising the beatings would be heard through the door. 'One minute please, be right with you.' His voice changing to a pleasant relaxed welcoming tone as if by magic.
'You boys out now! We will discuss your punishment after evensong later!'
Quickly the three scarpered through the office back door. Shutting the door they listened, ears against the door hear him fumbling about then answering the front door.
'Ah Mr and Mrs Digweed! How good of you to come. And you must be Charles! Do come in, do come in! Welcome to Flaxden Brig!'
With this they went straight to the dining room for supper. 'Hey look there's the pig lorry!'
Hmmmmm! Walter thought to himself. All eyes were on the three at supper, chattering away. Then the Head walked in with his guests who had saved them, and the young Charles trotting dutifully behind, a late arrival into Brecon as he had come from far away. There was a vacant spot on their table and as the Head approached the table everybody stood up.
'Charles is joining us today! I am entrusting you three to look after him!'

'Yes Sir! 'They blurted out as Charles sat down with them.
'And don't forget I want to see you three later!'
With that he turned and walked away with the Digweeds. They also noticed he was walking with a very straight leg! At the top of his pants you could see the curved handle of Flash. What a scream! What an escape! Trying not to laugh,
'Thanks Charles you saved us back there!' He stared at them blankly, non plussed through his thick rimmed spectacles.

90 degrees

'Welcome to Flaxden Brig!' Welcome to Flaxden Brig! They had only been there a few days themselves!
'This is that that sorry excuse is Billy! I'm Larry, but you can call me Cobber!'
'I have another plan!!' Billy interrupted the introductions.
'Awwww! Nawww! Give it a rest!' They all cried.
Larry looked at the clock, they had now been here a week. Took a drink from his tea mug and a mouthful of toast.
'Okay, okay, we'll build our own!'
As they piled out of the dining room, McIver who was in front of them suddenly ducked towards the banks. 'Where do you think he's going?'
'Leave him, he needs time and if we're not careful we'll be in more bother.' Turning behind they walked up to the Top o'th' Banks by the front lawn to admire the scenery, the surrounding hills in particular the one looming behind this community, the forest, the lake. It was all too brief.
'It really is a beautiful place!'
'C'mon, no sentiment here!'
'Let's go!' Said Billy.
Looking up at the main building Billy said. 'Larry what do you think is behind that blocked out window?!'
'Dunno Billy. What do you think?'
'No idea Cobber, wonder about that when I arrived.'
But before he could answer……

'Odhiambo! Flannigan! MacCloon! In here now! Digweed! Go to your dorm!'

They froze, not expecting to see him till after evensong but quickly obeyed his command. 'This is it! I knew he wouldn't forget! Charlie you follow the others back to the house, you'll be ok, we'll catch up later, no honeymoon period here!'

Once inside his office he lined them up again. They glanced nervously over to the chair, Flash was nowhere to be seen.

'Now where is my cane?' They started to tremble. Suddenly he realised it was still down his pants, to his embarrassment, looking up and down in despair at his predicament.

'Well 1,000 lines "I must not use a boat without using a life vest!" On my desk by Thursday! Oh yes and "It is against the rules to take a boat out on the lake without permission!" That is 2,000 lines each! Now out!'

They needed no encouragement!

'Did I not like that?'

They scarpered! They had got away with it lightly!

'Well Mental Pete, has kept his record intact!! I wonder why he is called that.'

Back in the dorm, Charlie was being made welcome by the rest of Conway; they discussed the day's events, chatted with the others, checking if Darnley had been to the San, he had. 'That was some scare you gave us! At least we know how to help you now so don't worry.' And settled down. Billy was reading a comic and Charlie was drawing on a notepad. 'What you reading Billy?'

'A Commando, The Chef who went to war!'

'You fancy yourself as a cook then?!!' A pillow hurtled in Larry's direction.

'Quiet the Germans are attacking!'

'Wotcher! What you doing Charlie writing home already?'

'No I'm just doodling!'

'Doodling?'

'Yes I want to be an inventor!!!!'

'What's your doodle?'

'Well....... it's a toilet seat that Lowers so you are squatting when you do the business.'

'Business?'

'Yes, I picked this up from an idea on the continent. The French just seem to have a hole in the floor no seat the better the squat the more you get rid off! Want to look?' So Charlie handed it to Larry, who could see that it consisted of what looked like a rubber ring and two car jacks.

'Think it will catch on?'

'It will make me millions!'

'So shall we build a raft? Charlie's the inventor he can design one!' Interrupted Billy.

'You never give up?'

'All because you think there are girls on the other side of the lake!'

'Shhhhhhh! Walls have ears! We don't want everyone to know!'

'Damn right! Hey maybe the girls are building their own boat to come and see us?!'

'In your dreams! Who'd want to see you?!!!Let's discuss tomorrow, we have prep tonight. Remember that pig lorry? Well that must go round to the girls school let's try that! Let's follow all options.'

'Ok, I've seen it every day!'

'Do you never think of anything else Billy?!' A pillow smacked into his head as the piped music played around Conway.

'Damn right!!!'

That night they returned to the dorm, the other boys were in silence all were looking at McIver, packing his bags.

'What's going on McIver?'

'I'm leaving, escaping, not staying here, I hate it. I want my Mum!'

'We all want our Mum!'

'Where to? We are in the middle of nowhere! Don't think you are the only one who has thought about this there is no point!'

'I'm going up that track at the back of Brecon it must lead somewhere!' After lights out he waited about fifteen minutes picked up his suitcase and left! All were awake and after a few minutes Larry said,

'I think we'd better follow him.'

'Follow him where to? Its pitch black!'

'Come on let's go, we can't let him go.'

'He'll soon come back. If we get caught we'll get beaten!'

'Well we will just have to be careful then won't we?' The four climbed out of the widow after putting clothes in their beds to make it like they were sleeping. Hey a couple of you do some snoring just in case someone comes it! They headed off, blindingly heading towards the track at the back of the McInnis.

'Hey that looks steep!'

'Come on, I can see him at the top!' They headed off up the track in the dark with no torches, only the one in front a dark shadowy outline being visible.

'Must remember to eat my carrots at dinner time!'

'Don't you think we'd be better with a torch?!! Whose idea was this; we should've let him go! I want my bed!!!' Soon they came to a crossroads.

'Which way do you think he went? This looks flat both ways.'

'My thinking.' Said Larry. 'Is that he went right ahead, getting as far away as possible.' So they continued uphill through the windy track.

'Are we nearly there?'

'Stop moaning Billy just another five corners to go! We must be nearly there soon; can anybody hear or see MacIver?'

'No!'

'No!'

'Keep on going then.'

Soon they came to a clearing in the woods and the track turned into a wider track, nearly a road.

'This is different; McIver must have the right idea where do you think it's going straight on? McIver would still keep going.' And sure enough, he was tiring and they could hear footsteps in the distance, definitely him, as they could see him lugging his bag.

'Look! There! A figure ahead! That must be him, keep moving, and keep moving!' After a few minutes they came to a wall. 'Here let's rest, if we are tiring he must be too, he can't go much further, let's have a minute.'

The four boys dropped to the floor, getting tired now, they should've stayed in bed. Charlie stood up and looked over the wall,

'Look fellas, it's another lake!'

The other three stood up and looked across the lake into the dark night.

'Pretty spooky isn't it!'

'You scared Billy?'

'Me scared? Never!'

'Come let's get going.' Another crossroads.

'Right on!' Said Charlie. 'I can hear his footsteps, getting louder.' They tramped wearily up and incline and soon they notice they are out of the

forest and into a barren wilderness, soon the track starts to descend and the boys stop. Surely he can't have gone down there, it's going nowhere!
'So you think that's Wales down there Cobber? Could be Scotland or Ireland!' It was getting cold now. All they could see was hills, larger lakes and forests, no lights. Suddenly they heard the noise of panic screams and running steps heading their way. It was McIver sprinting. He saw the other boys 'QUICK! RUN!' There is a big man chasing me!' The four boys are frozen to the spot. McIver ran off ahead, his suitcase was gone and sure enough there was a large man lumbering towards them, followed by another smaller figure silhouetted in the night sky. The boys were rooted to the spot, frozen.
'RUN!!!' Shouted Larry and the boys set off in the same direction as McIver. They reached the thinner track but could still hear the heavy footsteps of their chaser behind them. They reached the crossroads and Charlie slipped and tumbled into the ditch at the side of the road, the others stopped hesitated, they couldn't leave their friend, the poor guy has only been here a day! So they all dived in to the ditch by the side of Charlie.
'You ok?
'Yes, Shhhhhh! I can hear them coming.' The two figures came to the cross roads and the boys got a clear view. A massive man with an oval face, the smaller muscular one now by his side, sweeping the area looking, looking. They all held their breaths and watched as the men looked from one route to the other, first to the left then to the right and then straight on. They came towards the direct route where the boys were hid. Larry's hand was outstretched and the giant's large foot came down close to it. Charlie closed his eyes, expecting the worst. Then the men turned and headed back the way they came. They could hear the heavy steps fading in the distance and when they could hear no more they headed back down the track and clambered back through the window of Brecon House.
'They was looking for something you know, I'm sure of it'
'McIver you fool, why did you do that?' He didn't reply, he was under the bed sheets trembling, scared stiff, and whimpering. They'll all got into their beds. 'Did anyone come around?' Then the door bursts open, it was Jimmy Crow. 'Right who's talking after lights out?' The four owned up, but McIver did not. They headed for the common room and each got one, courtesy of George! 'Now get back to bed and sleep that is what you are supposed to do after lights out! Get it while you can!'

The next day started and continued as usual, it was all becoming routine very quickly. The gramophone stopped with a continual rotating scratching sound and they could hear the rest of the house stirring. It was time for supper. 'Let's go and see if we can find that old man, the one they call Hairy Dan after supper we've got an hour before prep.'
'Ok but let's get back early!'
There was no sign of Dan or his cat Wolfie but they came across an old shed that they had been told was used by Norwegian Commandos during WW2. Inside they found some rope, old drums about twelve in all, plastic and sheets of metal and an old tarpaulin. 'We could build a raft with some of this!' Larry suggested.
'Well Charlie you are elected to design the craft!'
They decided to use it later as they were going to try the pig lorry, sure that would get them there. They had to head back for prep and took the shorter route down by the lake side.
'Shhhhhh! There's McIver!' He was climbing over a fence by the Blue Huts. They stayed quiet and still but could see where he'd walked to, the Blue Huts of Her Majesty's Armed Vessel, HMAV Caledonia. They could see three Land Rovers parked up.
'Let's explore!'
'Haven't you had enough excitement for one day Walter?!' Groaned Larry and Billy but it was clear the adventurous spirit had become embedded into them.
There were two buildings and a smaller hut. The larger one looked like a hall with accommodation. You could see bunks, mats, hammocks and a dining area below. The other building looked like accommodation too with the smaller den completely closed up with no windows. What could that be? The hum of engines could be heard in the background and revving up of vehicles. Suddenly the tops of the Landover's could be seen at the roadside.
'Quickly hide!' And they jumped over some hedges but their exit was blocked. What had McIver been doing? They had no choice but to wait. The men piled out of their vehicles unloading rucksacks. They must've been in the hills they surmised. These men were instantly recognised from men watching at the rugby match. To them the grizzled features of the men were fearsome. They entered the larger building, they thought now was an opportunity to escape unseen.

Suddenly there was a commotion. Shouting, pushing shoving. 'No I haven't you stupid fooker!' a broad Geordie accent boomed out. 'Well where are they man?' This voice appeared to be a Brummie or Welsh it was hard to distinguish. 'Well, where are they? I left them here!'
'Wait a minute it'll be those little shits from the school! They haven't paid any of you have they?'
'Nope!'
'That's a 100 quid we paid for that lot!'
With that they went inside.
This was their chance they were going to be late if they didn't go now.
'Right we go on three! You count!'
One! Two!' and Billy and shot off leaving Larry still counting!
'.....THREE! Wait for me! Come on Charlie!'
Running as though the Devil was chasing them, they managed to reach the road when they heard 'OI! It's those little shits! Let's get em!'
Hearts beating like a Stag they pounded through the trees and suddenly reached the sanctuary of the Myrtle Wood but could still hear shouting behind them. A mass panic set in. What were they to do were should they go? In the distance a blue plume of smoke was visible. 'Head for that!' It was the old man's shack. Hairy Dan saw them running. 'Help us!' They screamed as they ran towards the shack. Dan was sitting outside, a thick leather coat with a dirty fur lining was flung over a wooden tree stump, and Wolfie curled up on his lap asleep.
'Inside! Hide at the back!' He said calmly!
Minutes later they could hear voices.
'Old man have you seen a boy run this way?'
'No Sir, not seen anybody for weeks.'
Wolfie arched his back, starting meowing and spitting at the men.
'Shut that scrawny thing up!'
'Pooh! What a reek, I'm not surprised you seen no one smelling like that get a wash you filthy old git!' And with that they left heading deeper into the Myrtle Wood. Five minutes later the man peered into his hut and said they could come out now.
Cautiously peering out, hearts still beating like the clappers, 'What have you been up to?'
'Nothing!' They protested in unison and proceeded to outline the events at the Blue Huts.

'Mmmmmm! Interesting!'
'We'd better go now! Thank you sir!'
Dan directed them to the Brook and bridge where they would be safe, taking up their seats in prep with only five minutes to spare...
'Where's McIver? There he is! We want to talk to you!' He looked at them. 'Yes we do!'
'Get lost!'
'You've no choice we saw where you went.'
'Ok! Ok!' He said quietly knowing that they were on to him.
'Hey Billy, we've still 2,000 lines to do for Thursday!'
'Don't remind me!'
After prep they cornered McIver. 'Well what were you doing up to at the Blue Huts? We've just been chased by the Blue. We could see something had happened and they are mad as hell!'
McIver looked with saucer wide eyed at them. 'It's not my fault. I asked them to buy me booze and fags but when I went down to pick up and leave my money there was nothing there. Gone!'
'Well it seems the booze and fags have gone and they've not been paid. And they are blaming you!'
'Why are you buying that stuff anyway? It's unhealthy!'
'I didn't pick up somebody was there before me.'
'How much?'
'£100 worth.'
'A hundred quid? Where did you get that from?'
'Not mine, it was Kerr, Troup and Pearson who made me do the deal. I got friendly with the ratings after the fight with Monroe, when everyone left me.'
'You prick; those three had no intention of giving you a penny! Where would they get that money from anyway?'
'Where did they get the money from? Isn't all money supposed to be with the Housemaster?'
'You got involved with this and those bullies and we've only been here just over a week. Let's hope they forget. What were you thinking?'
'I don't know. I thought if I had something to trade I would make some friends? They were very friendly with me. I sunk all my pocket money into it.'

'Make friends? Who with? This could turn into a real mess! Do you know who could've done this?'

'Ever since that fight with Monroe.........'

'That was stupid too! Idiot! Monroe is a good person you saw what happened at games.'

'Yes I saw that.'

'He stood up for us all.'

'We'll just have to hope they leave it. They are not happy, chased us up to......' Billy elbowed Walter in the ribs.

'Ouch!' Realizing his near slip 'The road! You fool! They'll think it is us now!' A sly grin coming across McIver's face.

'Let's go for a walk, you're coming too McIver!' So they put on their duffle coats and headed for the Top o'th' Banks. From here they could see the smoke from the Blue Huts chimney, but now they were feeling safe in the confines of their sanctuary, 'At least they can't touch us here!' Said McIver.

'It's you they will come for! Not us, you made the deal.'

'What's that over there by the football pitch?' Six figures could be seen crawling along on their bellies in a perfect line, metal glinting in the evening sun.

'By heck! It's the Blue! They are going to attack us! Quick raise the alarm!'

'Don't be daft; they are pissed, literally legless, as hell!'

Billy set off and raised the alarm and ringing the big bell by the South door. Larry and Charlie set off to the athletic store and McIver, just set off, high tailing it.

The WW2 siren, Moaning Minnie wailed and the bell clanged as boys poured out of their Houses forming lines others racing to the Fire, Ambulance and Hill Service stations, the serene peace had been shattered.

'I hope we're right!' Walter called to Larry as they slugged their arms to the Top o'th' Banks.

Larry ran to join them when he saw McIver cowering behind a tree.

'What the heck are you doing there!?'

'Waiting for help!' Screeched McIver, trembling with fear.

'It's here!' Growled Billy leaving McIver in his safety hole. Billy, Walter Larry and Charlie armed themselves with shot puts, discus, hammers and

javelins and started aimlessly throwing them down the banks, in every direction, the shot puts were difficult but the others flew through the air.
'This should give everyone a start! Slow them down a bit! Their surprise has gone.'
'Look there's more!' Another group had started a double quick behind the ones crawling on their bellies. A javelin whistled through the air, thrown by Billy, heading towards the second phase.
'Owwww!!!!! Arghhhhhh!' A piercing scream, then another could be heard at the foot of the banks.
'BULLS EYE! Quick get those hammers!'
'Careful Billy you'll hurt someone!'
There was another shriek then another then another. They could see them all now, about twelve in all. Throwing the last of the discus, their ammo was now gone, spent. 'Look out we've been rumbled!' A shout in Cockney rang out. 'Keep going! Let's get em!' A slurred voice in Irish replied.
'Quick get into the Yew trees.' Larry could see Walter running along the mid bank and diving into a tree. Larry couldn't see Billy or Charlie but he had no sooner got into the confines of the tree when one sailor came within inches of him, heads level and he held his breath until his face went purple, it felt like life or death and he could hear some shots. 'Christ! This is getting serious! Are those real bullets's?' He muttered under his own breath. He crept out of the tree and ran along the Lower banks; other boys could be seen racing along the top. He could see pitch 2 covered in javelins, discus and shot puts and a group of three staggering back to the Huts, supporting one of the figures. Where were his friends? Walter got on to the main lawn and it was pandemonium more boys were coming out of the buildings with the V1,V2,V3, Ambulance, Quad Tractor and Hill Service Land Rover converging on the South Door simultaneously. 'Brecon is locked down!' Shouted a small man who continued to bark out orders. The Service crews were racing to their posts, boys in stages of undress, barefoot, putting on their uniforms as they went their way.
The remaining sailors, six of them were advancing on the main building armed with rifles, bayonets attached glinting in the darkening night determined and he stayed put. It was terrifying but they were staggering obviously drunk
The Head appeared at his door, 'What is going on?' The sudden appearance of so many people startled the attackers, Big Jim, Beefy Bill in

his fireman's uniform and Puss Whiteford in his Ambulance jacket could be seen racing across the main lawn and flooring 3 sailors knocking their rifles away instantly. Suddenly Tug Wilson appeared and blew on his whistle sharply and barked out some commands. The remaining sailors froze instantly dropping their guns to the floor. Who was this man? He had not seen him before. It was all over.

The word soon spread around for all boys to get back into their houses as quickly as possible. As they walked past the South Door they turned around to see the two Land Rovers from the Blue Huts screeching to a halt outside the main building. Then Minnie suddenly stopped and you could hear the silence, nobody was talking, a deathly quiet enveloped all around. It had been an awesome night.

Once back in Conway they were locked down. Lights were out. A hush followed; there was nothing to say, hearts pounding. Everyone was wide awake, it couldn't be otherwise but eventually they drifted into a restless haunted sleep. 'Think they'll come back' Whispered a voice.

Next morning there was no bugle, no run. They all trooped into the dining room and stood for grace.

The Head walked in to the centre, Dochan Do behind him and even stranger all staff were there. BONG! The Head walked into full view and everyone stood up.

'Last night we were attacked by a rogue unit of the forces of HMAV. Not happy with being on a losing side last year to our glorious 1st xv, they resorted to armed conflict to give out their own form of justice but we prevailed, you all prevailed, you all served the Brig well! Classes for today are cancelled' I am declaring this day The Brig holiday in celebration of our victory. I have just spoken to Chef and tonight there will be as much grog and nosh as everyone can eat!'

'Three cheers for the Head!' Shouted the Head Boy Piggy Gordon.

'HIPP HIPP! HURRAH! HIPP HIPP! HURRAH! HIPP! HIPP! HURRAH!'

There was a strange feeling as the entire Brig sat down when suddenly

'SIXTY EIGHT!'

'OH NO!!! NOT THE CUSTARD!!'

360 degrees Michaelmas

Rumbling followed by mass shouting and roaring filled the area. 'It's a counter attack!' Shouted someone in Brecon. Tentatively the Novus peered into the dining room and there seemed to be a pitched battle going on, between Sperrin, Magillycuddy and Cuillin. Peas, potatoes, beans, fruit, cakes, buns and custard were flying everywhere! As they watched the free for all a small cloaked figure brushed by Larry and stood in the centre of it all, food flew around him when all at once it stopped. It was Dochan Do! He stood for a while then turned around and walked out. Gordon who had been taking a full part looked towards the audience from Brecon pointed and said, 'YOU! YOU! YOU! YOU! Clear this mess up!' Obediently Larry, Charlie, Walter and Billy did so sweeping the all the debris into the spot where Dochan Do had stood minutes earlier.

'Look at that!' Pointed Billy it looks like one of those hills around us!'

'Come on let's get this done, the pigs will certainly get a good meal tonight! Hmmmm? The pigs?'

However all were subdued, unusually quiet, not venturing far from the sanctuary of the main buildings. Charlie observed a hole in the dining room ceiling, could that have been a real bullet? Through the windows and into the wood panel. It was eerie.

The four boys, Charlie was now tagging along, took a walk along pitch 2. Shot puts, hammers, discus and javelin were strewn all over the place. They could see in the light of day what they had done. One javelin had blood on it!

'Heck we could've killed someone!'

'Let's clear all this up!' So they did, putting all the equipment back into the store.

On the way back they passed by Big Jim's cottage. 'You hear that?' Said Larry.

They listened intently 'Ahhhhhh! Ahhhhhh! No! Please! NO! Stop! No don't! Ahhhhhh!' Quickly Larry went up to the window, peering through a crack he ran back to the others and said, and 'Big Jim's wife is on top of him! She's trying to kill him! Go and look!' Billy crept up and came back.

'Big Jim's on top of her! He's biting her!'

So Walter and Charlie crept up and peered through the crack and so it was, Mrs Powers was on top of Big Jim her hands around his throat and bouncing up and down! sprinted to the two guys, with Charlie close

behind. All four of them went up to the wall taking turns at peering through the window.
'She's on top of him!' Said Billy.
Larry bobbed his head up, 'No he's on top of her!' Spluttered.
Now Charlie looked through 'She's on him now!'
'What are we going to do? I know Let's smash the window! Ok I'll do it; we have to save Big Jim! Let's get Mental Pete!' Larry picked a rock the size of a cricket ball. CRASH! TINKLE! TINKLE! As the stone hit the window.
'Quick RUN!' As they ran they could hear the front door of the cottage swung open. They all glanced around and could see Big Jim with a towel wrapped around him and his wife the same, their eyes moving from left to right, sweeping across the area in front of them. Suddenly Big Jim's towel dropped to the floor, revealing all. Giggling the boys continued their flight then suddenly went flying. His knee sliding along the floor as he regained his balance and scarpered into Brecon. They went straight to the common room. Looking out of the window they could see a Blue Land Rover was parked outside the Heads study. The Head came out with a man in a peaked cap and uniform. The Officer turned to the Head, nodded his head curtly, shook his hand and drove down the front drive. The Barron walked around to the South Door saw them watching. They didn't move, lit up a cigar and stood proudly upright a plume of smoke rising into the air.
'He thinks we're something to do with it!'
'Hey he's mouthing something! It's……'
'So you can lip read now? Mr Genius!'
'He's saying……That's my boys!'
'Well they are right about this place you know……dull it ain't!'
That night they saw McIver for the first time since the night before. He was bruised with a broken nose and a split lip.
'No guessing for how that happened McIver. Look what you nearly caused. So they found you?'
'Cut myself shaving!'
'You've not reached puberty yet! Tell us what happened. We want to know!'
'I told you yesterday. Yes I was wrong to do what I did but I didn't take the booze and fags, I was going to pay.'
'Any Ideas who then?'

'Yes! But I can't say they'll kill me!'
'Who? Who are you afraid of? Tell us now or we will sneak!' Though they all knew that wouldn't happen.
'Ok, ok, it's not Troup or Kerr; it's the 3 boys, Uppers, Blare, Braun and Ztirgeon. There is another one called Horbyn but he just says nothing. Just looks at everyone in turn.'
They boys looked at each other. 'Not heard of them before.'
'We'll ask Mony!'
'You'd better go to the San.'
'No! If I do they will know and come after me!'
'Forget it McIver we've tried to help.'
So they left him alone and went for their walk to the Top o'th' Banks.
'Wow! What a few days! I'm beginning to love this place! You know, it's....... exciting!' Said Charlie.
'Unbelievable! We've got to do something. What's McIver hiding?'
In Conway that night after lights out the door opened, 'Flannigan, Odhiambo and MacCloon to Georgetown now! They waited along with Monkey MacKay and Mony Monroe. They were surprised to see these two but it was for the same reason, but for prefects to be beaten. That night Walter had three, Billy four, Larry two Monkey and Mony one each and they were very angry. Could there be a power struggle here they were thinking. Or a warning? George came out and WHACK! WHACK! WHACK! But they couldn't feel much, their bums were black and blue already.
They hadn't long been back when the Conway door opened and three boys came in, not from Brecon and took out McIver from his bed. One had a milk bottle in his hand and they could hear what sounded to be like water being poured on to the sheets. With a sadistic laugh a voice could be heard
'You don't need to piss yourself anymore McIver we've done it for you. Slasher distillery! And you lot, not a word or else!' McIver was made to get into his wet bed. It was a long night and it was a relief when the bugle sounded. Jimmy Crow true to form tipped as many beds as he could and reaching McIver's bed caught his hand on the wet sheets.
'McIver you've wet your bed! See me in the boot room in 5 minutes boy!' All knew that George would be waiting there and his shoulders slumped as a boxer does when he has been defeated. The whole house could hear the beatings six of them, and then another four but that appeared to be

someone else. All were powerless but they had to do something. McIver came back into the dorm and sat slumped on the end of his bed put his head into his hands and cried. They all looked around at each other, in silence, all of them could've cried.
'What are we going to do about this? Let's talk to Monkey and Mony, they are both fair people, I think they are approachable.'
'That's a good idea but are we going to get to see the girls today? The pig van will be here at five!'
'Billy can you not give it a rest!?'
'No!'
'Ok let's do that after games?'
'Sure!'
Games for some reason seemed to be enjoyable they were learning rugby skills quickly under Big Jim, and they were on similar terms to the Lowers. Two figures watched from the as the young boys were taught their new religion.
'The male body was designed for two things men! Playing rugby and shagging women!' Barked out Big Jim.
'Really Headmaster is this we should be saying to boys at this age?'
'What's wrong Nurse Rose? These boys are the life blood of Flaxden Brig, is there no room for encouragement in your order?'
'Encouragement, yes, but influencing young boys early on, no!'
'Well The Brig is a competitive place, I am preparing these boys for the outside world, to survive and thrive!'
'Come on! The Brig is no place for Fairies, can't use your magic wands here!' Big Jim barked out his favourite phrase, directed at the newly arrived Novus.
'Now listen to that, humiliating the weaker boys!'
'James Powers is a first class man and is doing a good job Miss Rose! He is teaching these boys a new discipline! To work together as individuals and to blend together as a team.'
A Upper boy ran past the two with a large log across his shoulders.
'Stewart what are doing?'
'6 circuits sir!'
'Who set them? How many have you done?'
'Mr Powers sir! This is my third!'
'What did you do, blow up the gym? Do one more and

then go in. If he asks tell him I said so.'
'Thank you sir!'
'Keep running, you don't get off that lightly!' With that the two figures disappeared, up the banks towards the South Door, the Head full in thought at what the Nurse was saying. He remember the hard days he had survived at school and knew that something must be done but when, just when?
Big Jim was driving them hard but fairly and nearly all were rising to the challenge even McIver, there was a purpose here. They noticed that Monkey and Mony, by far the two best rugby players had started to play very hard and had been targeting Kerr, Troup and Pearson turning into personal battles. It was a good job Big Jim was policing this as it could've got violent, seriously violent. However Big Jim was loving the physical commitment, the motivation and the enthusiasm that had developed. The end of games arrived.
'Right! Everybody line up on the 25 except Odhiambo, Digweed, Flannigan and MacCloon who will line up on the touch line. The last four will stay behind!' But the feel good factor prevailed.
The whistle shrilled and surely enough the four friends all finished last. Mad Mac McNut way ahead of everyone else. They knew why and became very nervous. 'Change into your pumps and follow me!'
'No girls tonight lads!'
'Give it a rest Billy!'
'Come on Cobber!'
Big Jim set off and they followed, 'Keep up or you'll do it again tomorrow!'
For what seemed like miles they stuck together and within sight of Big Jim. This must be the Ace track Mony had been on, thought as he gasped dragging his battered body uphill. Suddenly they were going downhill and began to enjoy the run but Big Jim was miles ahead by now and couldn't be caught. About twenty minutes later they came to a road which they were unfamiliar with.
'Left or right? There isn't that the pig lorry? Yes let's get in the back it must've been to the school already!' Quickly with a newfound energy they didn't know they had they sneaked into the back just in time as the engine started up. The lorry sped off in a direction they didn't know. 'Keep down! Look we've just passed big Jim running! Shit we're heading for the Brig!'

Sure enough the lorry turned up the back drive and pulled up at the back of the kitchens where they clambered out and dashed into Brecon. In the distance they could see Big Jim running up the end of the back drive.
'Phew! This is unbelievable! We are unbelievable! We should write a book!' They took their kit off and plunged into the showers! And were showering themselves when Troup, Kerr and Pearson came in and opened the windows. They could smell smoke but said nothing. Ignored their sarcastic comments and left the room.
'Hey what's that mark on your arse?' Exclaimed Billy.
'Looks like a love bite!' Said Larry.
'It must be the bruising from the beatings. I've had so many! Maybe a knock in games?'
'No you have a mark, round mark on your left bum cheek! Just on the top of the rump. Looks like you've sat on something, an indentation.'
'Pervert!' Said Larry.
'No look!'
The two looked and sure enough a round mark could be seen clearly.
'Is it a birthmark?'
'No I don't have one! What is it?'
At that the door flung open and a few more boys came into shower.
That night Walter was in Clyde looking at his photo of Pans People when Kerr and Troup came in he could hear Pearson telling them to make it quick.
'You have something we want!'
'What's that piece of paper you're always looking at Flannigan?'
'Mind your own business Kerr!'
'Give it to us NOW!'
'No chance you fat slob!'
'What did you say? You're going to pay for that, as are your little buddies!'
'Oh yes? You are cowards on your own. Only think you are big when you've got these twits with you!'
'Think you are hard Flannigan?'
'Think I am? I know I am!' He couldn't believe he said that but he had begun to fight back, take them on!
'Give it to me!' Kerr launched himself at Walter knocking him to the ground but he still had the paper in his hand thrusting it into his pocket. A

blood curdling feeling filled his throat as Troup's boot connected with his ribs.
'Quick there's someone coming!' Shouted Pearson. WHACK! One more kick to the thigh and they took their cowardly exit. It was Mrs Borthwick the house cleaner who he had met on his first day. She came in and saw on the floor. 'Och Sonny, are ye ok? This is wrong you must report this to Mr Fowler.'
'It's nothing. Just a boy's fight. I'm only scratched.'
The small lady looked at him.
'It happened to me lad; girls can be just as bad as boys, if not worse.'
So dragging himself up he decided to go to the Housemaster.
KNOCK! KNOCK!
'Come in!'
'Ah, Flannigan! What can I do for you?'
'Err.....'
'Yes Flannigan?'
'Mr Fowler, Sir, I'm being bullied!' He blurted out. He couldn't think of anything to say.
There was a sigh then silence. 'Where from, within or outside the house?'
'Within the house, sir!'
'Well you must first approach the prefects Flannigan. Have you done that?'
'No sir.'
'I have appointed 4 very good prefects Monroe, Mackay Pearson and Kerr, approach them and let them sort this out! I was in the same boat as you, you know but we were a different calibre of boy in those days. Next year you will become a Lower. Anything else, Flannigan?!'
'No Sir. Thank you, sir!' And left the office nonplussed, staggered at the housemasters response. When he went back to Conway Larry, Charlie and Billy were waiting for him.
'You ok? We heard you took a kicking.'
'Where were you? You're supposed to be my buddies.' Walter could see by the look on their faces they were upset at his remark.
'Look sorry fellas I didn't mean that. I'm the guilty one, I went to Jimmy Crow, and I shouldn't have sneaked. He didn't listen, not interested and I thought it would do some good but this might have made it worse, much worse. They are after you three as well. Me going to Jimmy Crow was a

mistake, he'll tell them, Pearson and Kerr are prefects and they'll make us pay.'
'Why did they go for you?'
'I think they were after a photo that my sister gave me of Pans People. I wasn't going to let them have it; they just said I have something they want.'
'Pans People! Corrr! Let's have a look see!' Said Larry.
So took his friends to Clyde and showed them the picture and could see their eyes light up.
'You know we need to build that raft!' Said Billy. Two pillows were thrown at him. 'We're going to have to figure something out.'
'I don't know why I'm here! Shall we escape?' Walter said to Larry, as they walked into the main building and started looking at the notice board, 'First thing I knew I was in Mum and Dad's car on the way here!'
'Me too, I woke up on a plane sitting next to an air hostess who was holding my hand, Landed at the airport, was called to information where they said I had to collect my luggage from arrivals. There was this big trunk with my name on it Larry JP MacCloon. I was wearing what I thought was a dress, and then I got put in a taxi and was brought here. Escape you say?'
'What about you Billy?'
'Strange I too arrived like that, woke up on a boat in a cabin, went outside to be told to stay inside, my Mum and Dad, and then took me here!'
'Charlie?'
'Well I woke up in the sleeper carriage on the train. Disembarked at the smallest station I've ever seen and cane here with my parents the other day!'
'What's the routine for a Saturday afternoon?'
'I went into the library after lessons yesterday and looked up the North Star.'
'Yes it does seem to be about every time we hear that music, Blue Danube Waltz by Strauss. Isn't that what Darnley said the music was?'
'Well, The North Star is always overhead at the North Pole.
The Earth's spin axis points close to the North Star so as we sit on the earth's surface the other stars in the sky seem to rotate around it while it is close to stationary.'
'So what does it mean Charlie?'

'I'm working on it! Something strange, the star appears to be moving!' Suddenly a clatter of boots could be heard, the grinding of studs on the road outside; 'UGGIE! UGGIE! UGGIE! OY! OY! OY!' loudly filled the room. They all rushed to the windows. It was the Firsts! A mass of men wearing pure blue shirts, a golden embroidery on the centre breast proudly stuck out, white shorts, blue socks and polished black boots, crisp and splendidly turned out, trotting, chests proudly out, knees up, heads directly ahead, they were calling the school. At a steady deliberate pace with Big Jim snapping at their heels they headed towards the expanse of the lawn in front of the main door, focussed and driven. Slowly, a straggle at first, boys and staff appeared from nowhere and followed the group across the lawn, down the banks and on to the hallowed turf of pitch one. The site was awesome, a natural stadia, what a place to play sport. Walter had never played or even watched a rugby match before here and along with Billy, Larry, Charlie and the rest of the Lowers and Novus, they followed. Each side of the pitch was swarmed with eager boys as the 'Flax Machine' was put through their warm up by Big Jim. 'COME ON FLAXDENNNN!' Bellowed a portly man with thinning comb over hair this was Mr Zaluski the French master or Allor as he was affectionately known. 'ONE TWO! ONE TWO! HUP! HUP! ONE TWO! HUP! HUP!' Barked out Big Jim, snapping at their heels, as he prepared these warriors for the battle to come. Press ups, sit ups, stretches, short sprints, ball handling, would they have enough energy left to play they thought to themselves. The theatre was a buzz of electricity! Then a quietness enveloped the arena as another set of large men jogged on to the pitch transfixed on the men in green amassed at the top of the pitch, eyeing up their opposite number with Wolf like snarls and spitting venom as Benzedrine puff adders cornering their prey, here came the opposition, Kriel, old foes apparently but a new name for the dictionary of the Novus. The tension was tight. Horns and tubas blasted away adding to the ingredients of a well stirred cauldron. Then suddenly silence and a low humming noise began followed 'brig.....brig....brig....brig....' Quietly at first building up to a' brig....brIG....bRIG....BRIGGGGGG!' A blast of a shrill whistle indicated that the referee was ready and two players jogged to the centre for the toss of the coin. The captains shook hands; a cheer went up as the tall athletic man in green, colours on his left breast returned to the team which was now forming into a circle. Brian Whiteford was the captain, known as

'Puss' Whiteford and as he entered the circle a loud cheer went up as he faced his players, looking at them, talking to them as
suddenly the rest of the team went into perfect tune 'UGGIE! UGGIE! UGGIE! OY! OY! OY!' They then turned and lined up for kick off. 'Go Cats! Go Beefy! Go Puss! Jonathon C!' Screamed the crowd.
'Hey isn't that? Yes the ones who rescued us on the lake!'
'And the ones who tackled the Blue Ratings!'
The new boys were not prepared for what was to happen next! Silence fell and a slow drum beat could be heard and the crowd broke into a loud humming noise, then a voice started to wail and one by one all joined in,

♪

WI NA DE YA HO
WI NA DE YA
WI NA DE YA
HO HO HO HO
HEY YA HO

At the blast of the refs whistle Fraser Cattel, 'Cats' kicked the ball high into the air WHAM! towards the other side, as the ball came down Puss Whiteford launched himself at the catcher SMACK! BONG! With a bone crunching, spine chilling hit, the opposing player was flattened losing his grip of the ball. The oval ball bounced and was scooped up by Beefy Bill in full momentum. YAHOO! BEEFY BILL! BEEFY BILL! The crowd was ecstatic as he ran at the opposition, muscle on muscle, bone on bone, SMASH! CRUNCH! Then with no less than 5 Kriel players trying with all their strength to bring him down BONK! CLONK! WHAM! BIFF! BOING! Beefy seemed to stumble but as he did he managed to put the ball behind him They learnt that much from the first rugby session! straight into the spade like hands of Davie FiveTrees who shouted to his team mates 'LET'S GO!' Another cheer went up as he sprinted, side stepping his way to touch the ball down in the corner. Jonathon C came up as a deadly hush came over the crowd. Placing the ball with precision as the Kriel side regrouped behind the posts. A slow chant started,

'Jonathon......Jonathon.....Jonathon....Jonathon...Jonathon... JONATHON C!!!' He then coolly slotted the ball between the posts ZOOMPH! The firsts were ahead 6-0. Bloodied but not unbowed the Kriel side came back with avenging aggression but the firsts held out PAARP! WOW! As the sides trooped off they headed for afternoon tea. Jam butties, tea and the much sought after chocolate digestives.

'Guys, I've just heard Big Jim talking about the team, he said they must have drunk C19H28O2, testosterone to play like that!'

'What's C18H2802?'

'Must be some sort of drink?!'

'What was that chant at the start?' Larry asked an Upper.

'Well Hoosie it's the Flaxden Drum, Davie FiveTrees started it last year, scares the bee jeepers out of the opposition! He's from the Cherokees!'

'Wow a real Cherokee here at Flaxden!'

'I remember Mum used have a delivery of pop from the Corona man.'

'Makes a change from the Milk man!'

'Who?'

'The Corona man, six big bottles of pop, lemonade, sarsaparilla, dandelion & burdock, orange, cola, ginger beer but we never got any testosterone!'

'Let's ask at the tuck shop, they may sell it!'

'Later, perhaps!'

'Did you hear those names being called out at the line outs? And the ball was thrown to a certain place? Well I worked out our system.' Said, Charlie. 'Oh yeah Herr Professor! What are they?'

'Well in the first half it was front, middle and back.'

'So?'

'They take a letter from each word make up another word and throw the ball to that spot, thus fooling the other team!'

'Why?'

'Well they say the code so the other team doesn't know where the ball is going!'

'Oh yeah!'

'Yeah, and then in the second half they changed it.'

'To what?'

'Tom, Dick and Harry!'

Hmmmmmm..... Harry thought, that rings a bell, familiar.

Tom at the front and Harry at the back.'

'Wait don't tell me! Ermmmm! Dick in the middle!???'
'Dick in the middle? Has a ring to it! Dick in the middle! Bit like Toad in the hole!'
The boys laughed out loud, dragging strange looks from others standing by. Then noticed that Troup, Kerr and Pearson were in deep discussion with four other boys.
'Who are they?' Larry asked an Upper boy.
'Who? Them over there? They are Horbyn, Blare, Braun and Ztirgeon, they are Sherrinites.' Larry, Billy and Charlie looked at each other.
'You recognise them, those 4? Well Blare, Braun and Ztirgeon were the ones who came into the dorm with the milk bottle the other night.' They all nodded in agreement.
'The other one I don't know, Horbyn?'
'Probably their side kick, but what are they doing speaking with Kerr and his cronies?'
'Forget that let's go down to the lake we've no time to go see Dan, plus we'll keep out of the others hair for a while.'
Can you hear that song the 1st XV are singing? What was that...... it went like this.....

♫

MUCH HAS BEEN SAID OF THE STRUMPETS OF YORK
SEEN BY THE RABBLE AND SEEN BY THE SCORE
BUT WE SING OF A BAGGAGE THAT WE ALL ADORE
THE HEADMASTERS DAUGHTER!
AND WHEN HER NAME IS MENTIONED
THE PARTS OF EVERY FIRST TEAMER JUST STAND UP AT ATEENTION!
THERE'S NOTHING MORE DELIGHTFUL
AS MUCH AS THE PART THAT LIES BETWEEN HER LEFT TOE AND HER RIGHT TOE!
SO YOU CAN HAVE ALL YOU LIKE IF YOU SWEAR NOT TO WASTE THE HEADMASTERS DAUGHTER!

'You are a real songbird Billy! I wonder if Mental Pete knows. Well he must have heard that but they did win so he is probably turning a blind eye. Does he have a daughter?'
'Not seen one so who knows!'
'Well I bet they don't sing it when they lose!'
The afternoon had shown the boys that these men of sport where not phoneys, nor were they pompous gits but honourable.
The boys headed down towards the lakeside. 'Can you see anything over there Billy?'
'Billy pulled out a monocle from his pocket.'
'Hey! Where did you swipe that from?!'
'Found it! Nope, no movement, besides its getting dark now let's try again tomorrow! Hey wait a moment; I can see something over there moving quickly along the lakeside. Heck it's a MONSTER!!!'
'What? Let me look!' Exclaimed, grabbing the monocle out of Billy's hand.
'Sure I can see it! I can see orange eyes and lots of smoke!'
'Give that to me!' Larry said taking it out of Walter's grasp.
Sure enough a Monster like figure was moving along the lake side at speed, then suddenly ....gone!
'It's not there anymore. It's vanished!!'
'Let's get out of here!!'
'But it's near the girl's school, they may need help!'
'A rule of survival! RUN!'
The boys ran at pace back into the safety of the grounds. On approaching the Service sheds they could see the stooped figure of Joe Delgrano, cap on his head, a rake in his hand prodding, stabbing at something in the ground.
'Got ya!!!' Joe shouted pleased with himself. Out of breath they ran up to the ageing grounds man. 'Mr Delgrano, we've just seen a monster, glaring orange eyes and bellowing black smoke!'
'Och lads! You've seen the Beastie then?' A large vole had been speared onto the rake, its tiny legs wriggling spatially around its body, grappling with thin air.
'The Beastie?'
'Yes the Beastie! She lives in these parts!' Joe commented in a calm way as though it was something of a daily occurrence, and nothing new to him.

'Yes she's always around here somewhere but mind how you go, keep awa frae her! She bites! She'll ha ye fer her breakfast!'
Glancing at each other the boys ran towards the South Door where a queue was forming. 'What's going on here?'
'Nobody told us there was a Monster here!'
'It's afternoon tea, jam butties and tea!'
The boys queued up and eventually were served there tea. There were only two sandwiches left so they shared. 'Ever heard of the jam butty estates?'
'Nope, heard of the Jam Butty mines, in Knotty Ash with the Diddy Men!'
'Only a jam butty estate!'
'What's a jam butty estate?'
'It's a posh estate where people have big house, big mortgage, two cars and jam butties on the table!'
'Meaning?'
'Come on Billy!'
'Two bob millionaires!'
'What's a bob?!
'The King's shilling you nit!'
'Anyway jam butties and water are the best energy you can get!'
'How do you make that out Mr Encyclopaedia Britannica?' Said Cobber to Charlie.
Well the water is the rehydration, the jam the instant sugar and the bread protein and carbohydrates or something or other that slowly break down into sugar or something like that.' Added Charlie.
'You are a real mind boggler Charlie! A great way to prepare for games!'
BRINGGGGGG! The bell sounded to indicate it was time to attend afternoon classes. 'At least it's not bed rest! I couldn't listen to Blue Danube Waltz? What's your taste in music fellas?'
'Middle of the Road, T Rex!'
'Chirpy chirpy cheep cheep! Cobber!'
They headed to the Top o'th' Banks and discussed what they would be doing after classes. Looking up at the blocked off window suggested that they could have a look if they could get to that floor. All agreed they would look later when they knew that everyone was at supper. So that was the plan, English and maths progressed with no incident and the boys headed for the main building. What a stroke of luck! 'Would you believe it there is no one about!' Quickly but on tiptoes the boys headed to the stairway,

figuring out that this must lead about to the area where the mystery room was. Surely enough they found a door. 'Sure this is it?'

'Must be!' Larry turned the door handle. It opened with a push from all four.

'Shhhhhh! They'll hear us!'

Entering quickly and closing the door they found themselves in a large room with a ray of light shining through a 3 ft long crack at the far end of the room. It was virtually pitch black but the crack offered a guiding light.

'I don't think this is the right place, the window is completely blocked out from the outside. We're lost again, come on let's go!'

'Let's stay and have a look see!' Walter encouraged, 'We are here now, let's grasp this opportunity!'

carefully treaded lightly over to the light, it was a window alright, rays of sunshine layering through the thin gap, Shuttered up and he managed to open it more with a loud creaking sound. 'Shhhhhh! Somebody will hear us!' Light poured in revealing a large room. The walls were covered from floor to ceiling with shelves, crammed full neatly with books. In the centre was a big table covered with a cloth. Sticks were in a cabinet by the side of the wall.

'It's a snooker table! Let's play!' Said Larry.

'I know the rules!' Said Charlie.

Voices could be heard from outside the room, in the distance at first but getting closer and closer. 'Quick hide!'

'Where?'

'Anywhere! Under the table!'

No sooner had all three got under the table when three people entered the room, their feet could be seen walking around the table, muffled voices in deep serious discussion, only their shoes visible, one pair black the other Braun and a smaller set of feet wearing white gym shoes like their own. Both men with trousers, one black with striped piping and turn ups, the other cigar Braun in colour, the younger feet pale skinny legs with white socks. The one in the turn ups started pacing up and down. Holding their breaths.

'We will have to do something; these people are getting too close.'

'What do you suggest?'

'We have to do everything slowly and surely.' The other man said. 'And as for you! Can you not do something about these damn........ ?!!! They are running rings around your lot, and they don't even know it!'
'But.......'
'No buts deal with it!'' None of the voices were recognisable to the boys, whose hearts were beating so fast and just as they thought their lungs would burst from holding their breaths for so long. 'Right we'll do that then!' And the two men left and a loud CLICK could be heard. Quickly the boys scrambled out from underneath the table and crept towards the door; turning the knob slowly.
'Shit!!
'Language Billy!'
'The doors locked! What are we going to do?'
'Calm down everyone, we'll figure it out!' The boys sat down in silence, a pin could be heard to drop if indeed a pin was to drop.
'Anyone got anything to eat?' Said Charlie
'Eat? Now?'
'First order of survival fellas, food! Another survival tip, don't tell us where you got that from!'
'Well I got something from the Tucky earlier, was saving it for a midnight feast! Two mini rolls and a can of Banta!'

♫

TWO MINI ROLLS

AND A CAN OF BANTA!!!!

The boys shared the feast,
'We can stay here all night. Hey look there are another two doors here. Let's try that one.'
'Funny as they didn't say anything about the open shutters.' Nervously they headed over, creak stop, creak stop over the wooden boards.
'Shhhhhh!'
'You shhhhhh! It's your big feet Billy!'
At the door Larry pulled the handle down, it opened! Revealing a small staircase, leading upwards.
'It's going up! We need to go down!'

'We've no choice it's going to be supper soon!' Taking the lead they headed up the narrow stairway, 'Stairway to heaven perhaps!' Giggled Billy as he took up the rear closing the door behind him, CLICK! 'What was that?'
'Shit! The door has locked!'
'Shhhhhh, someone is coming back in the room!' Surely a pair of footsteps could be heard in the room.
'No there is nobody there. I'm sure I could hear voices.'
'And why is that window not closed?' It was one of the voices from before. The door slammed shut and a key could be heard turning in the lock.
'Flipping heck! We're really stuck now.'
'Maybe we'll die here! In years to come they'll find our skeletons here!'
'Come on let's go up, we've nowhere else to go!'
At the top of the stairs the boys came to a tiny room with a three small windows and a small trap door.
'Hey look at this view! I can see for miles!' Sure enough they could see far and wide, the round tower giving a panoramic view as far as the eye could see. The lake, the forests surrounded by high hills, enclosing their habitat like a gigantic colossus enveloping them into a wilderness of adventure.
'Wow!'They exclaimed in unison, taking in the expanse of it all. For a brief moment they were in a utopia that was shattered with the realisation that they were in a sticky situation with time running out, they had 30 minutes till supper and they would be certainly missed if they already hadn't been.
'Quick the trap door! It's worth a try, we can't go back down.' Opening the door the boys squeezed through the doors which lead them into the rafters.
'We're in the bloody roof now!' Crawling along their bellies they got to a skylight which was easily opened. The first piece of luck of the day. Climbing through they sure enough found themselves on the roof. 'We no choice now!'
Once through they found themselves high up on the top of the building. 'Look see those planks let's crawl over and we can leapfrog down!' Doing this they came to a thin ledge that would link them to another building.
'I'm not going over there, let's go back!
'Too late my man!'
'Hurry!'

'Hey look I can see in to the senior bed studies it's those three, Blare Braun and Ztirgeon! What are they doing? We must be over Sherrin House.'
'Forget them!'
Eventually they managed to Lower themselves down to an outer building where they had to jump the last stage. Landing heavily on top of each other they lay in a crumpled heap, landing first on his rump. The pain was excruciating and he felt a nauseating sickness which seemed to vanish when Billy landed on him. 'Nice cushion!' THWAP! Larry Landed on Billy. 'You ok Cobber?'
'Yep, but I think my heels are where my bollocks are supposed to be!' Then finally Charlie.
Suddenly they were aware of a figure standing over them; it was the toothless grin of Joe.
'Now what are you lads up tae now?'
'Errr nothing!' Grinning, Joe turned and slinging his spade over his shoulder he headed for his shed.
'Come on let's go eat. I'm hungry!'
As they were last in the boys had to share a table with Kerr, Troup and Pearson. Sitting at the end of the table the food trays were passed to the head of the table where the bullies sat. The tray had been full when delivered by the waiting orderly but by the time they reached the bottom of the table there were only scraps. The boys split was left between them and ate in silence not rising to the taunts of the others. BONG!! The gong sounded to indicate that supper was over. Kerr, Troup and Pearson got up, barged their way past the boys knocking Larry and his mug of tea over him' as he was trying to drink it. Billy glared at Kerr and stood up, squaring up.
'Don't give me the stare!' Larry tugged at Billy who sat down. 'It's ok, it'll be ok. Not worth it. I can clean it up.' After finishing off and wiping down the table they headed to the Top o'th' Banks. Looking up they could see the tower where had been an hour earlier. 'We were all the way up there?'
'Yep looks like we were. I'm getting sick of these bullies.'
'What are we going to do?'
'Hey what was that all about in that room? Pretty secretive. Those two men.'
'Better keep that to ourselves!'
'For now at least!'

The boys headed off to Brecon to collect their books for prep. All thirty nine boys were sent into classrooms one and two. Initially the hour long session remained quiet until Davies a LOWER started singing 'School's out!' by Alice Cooper. Strutting up and down the desks, using a broom as a microphone. At each chorus he would stop and the desk he was out he would punch the boy sat there. All happened to be new boys, nobody escaped. The hardest punches seemed to hit on the three friends but the hardest and flurry of punches were rained down on McIver. He just took it. Cheered on by Troup, Kerr and Pearson they all took it. Suddenly an Upper boy burst through the door,
'Who is making all this noise?'
It was none other than Puss Whiteford and he was very angry, his face bursting with red and purple he had a long technical drawing ruler and as he pointed it at everyone in the room, the ruler wobbled too with anger.
'Well who is it?!!'
'It is them, the Novus!' Shouted out Troup. 'They are the noisy ones!'
'I can't study because of you lot, Shut up no more noise! Understood?'
All nodded vigorously at this leniency it could've been so much worse. Prep finished and all headed back to their dorms. At the time the boys were taking a shower when Billy commented, 'You need to get that looked at. It looks very sore!'
'What does it look like now?'
The friends took a closer look. 'Is it sore?'
'No only now and again.'
'It looks like a star in the middle of a circle.'
'You are kidding?'
'No really it does! As though someone has scratched it on you.'
'Yes, that it is in the middle and there are little squares after that and more squares after that.'
'Now you are bluffing!'
'You'd better get it looked at. Ever been to the San?'
'No, but I will go tomorrow after breakfast, is that clinic time?'
'Better check and I'll get to see that Nurse we saw the other day watching us at games.'
The shower room door swung open and in came Pearson and Troup,
'Hey what are you looking at?'

They had spun their towels into a whip like tail and where whipping everyone in sight.
'OWCH!!!' Shrieked Walter, right on his testicles. Reeling in pain he fell to the floor his head just missing the metal shower controls.
'Whoops! Nearly hurt yourself there Flannigan!'
'Quick! Big Jim's coming! Let's get out of here!'
Holding his private parts Walter struggled into the changing room and slumped down on the bench. The others dried themselves looking on in pity.
'That must've hurt!'
'It did!'
Big Jim entered into the changing room. 'Unusually quiet in here tonight! Come on boys bed!'
After lights out they waited for the summons to the common room, but it wasn't coming tonight. They had been last to leave the changing room, so all their kit had remained hanging. They now realised that they had a choice to be beaten by George or rat tailed in the shower. At least now they had the choice. It had been an exhausting day.
Next day Walter went to the San to get checked out. About five or six boys were before him, coming out with small boxes of Strepsils, different colours depending on the ailment. His turn came.
'Now what is wrong young man?' A soft voice came from the lovely uniformed woman before him, Nurse Rose.
'I fell the other day and hurt my…my…..my….'
'Well, what is it clinic has nearly ended and I don't have all day!' Her eyes were brown as was her hair tied up in a bun, a shapely figure with her perfect curves, clearly visible, any male would be putty in her hands.
'It is my bum Miss! I fell and there is a bad mark on it!' He blurted out!
'Well lie down on the bench and let me see.' Walter duly obliged, doing as he had been told. 'On your front, not your back, silly boy!' The voice was firm, authoritative yet kindly but not nasty and this reassured Walter that he was ok, and she was going to help him. Rolling over he pulled his pants down. 'I see no mark, where does it hurt? There or there or there?' Nurse Rose prodded his backside, gently. Walter put his hand on the spot where his friends had seen the mark just above his right rump. 'Nothing there Flannigan, this area looks tender and I can see you have been beaten. What have you been doing?'

'Nothing Miss.'
'Well do you think it may be better that you were beaten for something you did than didn't do?'
'Yes Miss!' He said as he gazed at her, he was falling in love, mesmerized at how her touch had been.
'I will give you some cream to rub in for the soreness but I cannot see anything wrong! Here you are, now be off with you!'
Walter now headed off to Chapel, making it just in time. On their way to class explained to his friends what the Nurse had diagnosed.
'Corrr! You lucky sod!'
'But there is a mark there I saw it last night, we all saw it! Let's have another look.' Sure enough they could see the mark.
The next day went smoothly for once, thinks seemed to be evening out the initial shock and awe over now, Geography, Scripture, Latin, break again the shutters coming down as they reached the hatch at the Tucky, double PE, dinner, piped music, games-they were now getting good at this rugby thing, afternoon tea, double woodwork, society, dinner, prep, shower. The boys looked at Walter's rump. 'You do have a distinctive mark. A birthmark? It must be.'
'I have never had a mark there before, ever, and Nurse Rose says there is nothing.'
'There is Walter, tell you what I'll draw it!' Charlie went to get a pencil and a piece of paper. 'We'll have to be quick! If anybody see's us doing this they'll think we are weird!'
'Quick! Now!' And Charlie quickly sketched what they had all seen on s rump. The results startled all. There was a circle, within this circle another circle and within the inner circle there was a star. Surrounding each circle were letters in order of the alphabet. The inner L had been lined up with an M.
'Is that what you see too Billy?'
'Yes, well not exactly.'
'What do you mean?'
'Well I see the star, the circles and the letters but the B is lined up with O.'
'Charlie?'
'That's what I see but the C is lined up with D.'
A silence enveloped the group. 'Bring that big mirror over here so I can see what it really is.' Said Walter. And placing the mirror behind him he

peered over his shoulder to see the mark on his body. He could see the star, the inner and outer circles. 'Move it closer please.' Turning his head abruptly his pallor changed to a pale grey. 'You ok?' A silence followed. 'I....... could see.........the star, the circles, the letters.........'
'And?'
'The W lined up with the F. What do you see Cobber?'
'A lined up with the M.'
'Spooky this, it looks like a Ouija board.'
'You mean to contact the afterlife? I always wanted to speak to my Great Great Granny!'
'Yes something like that, parents caught us doing it one night on a sleep over, went barmy.'
The door swung open. 'What are you four doing? Give me that!' Kerr snatched the paper out of Larry's hand, turning it over and back. 'What is this? There's nothing here! It's a blank piece of paper!' Sure enough there were no markings to be seen. 'You lot are hiding something from us and we want to know!'
Nobody replied, an uneasy standoff followed, a show down was soon to happen between these groups.
Suddenly,
'Light's out!' MZEEE's voice could be heard from the boot room, he was just about to check for pound. Troup and Pearson turned about but Kerr stared at, then pumped his fist up at him and left. The boys scrambled into their beds and waited in deathly silence for MZEEE to make the call. It didn't come the focus had been too much on them for the bullies to fill the pond box. Yet another option had arose to keep them at bay but more had to be done. 'We need to talk.' Whispered Billy. A hushed silence enveloped the dorm.
The day had been eventful and exciting. Export seemed a different planet. But what were they doing here? Walter briefly closed his eyes but could see nothing, 'Nope still here!'
'That was great fun!'
'Yes brilliant! I'm going to catch the football results. Dad got me a radio, let's go and find a spot where we'll get reception!'
Billy and Charlie declined but Larry was interested wanting to know how his team had fared that afternoon.
'No good in Conway Cobber, let's try the common room!'

No luck there, then the changing room still good.
'Hurry we'll miss the results at 5pm!' Exclaimed Larry. After trying a number of places they returned to Clyde the locker room.
'We'll have to wait till next week and try again, there must be somewhere! Here let's have one last go!'
Surely enough on turning the knob the unmistakeable voice of James Rupert Gordon could be heard.
'Newport County 3 Chelsea1- Arsenal 0 Leeds United 1......'
Amongst the crackles Gordon eventually started reading the 4th Division results. 'Port Vale 1 Export C....crackle......crackle........crackle......'
'Yes! Yes!' Blurted out.
'Torquay United 2 Bradford City 1.....'
'Missed it! Awwwwww!'
'Hang on it's the Scottish results now.'
'Celtic 1 Hibernian 4.'
'Yes!' Exalted Larry. 'We did it!'
'Shhhhhh! Keep quiet Cobber, Kerr is a Celtic fan, haven't you seen all those pictures on his locker. If he asks, better tell him Celtic won!'
At supper that night they all chattered away about the match and the film they were going to see. The meal consisted of a mug of tea, minestrone soup, macaroni cheese, piece of toast and a pear. Towards the end the gong went. BONG!!!!!!!!!! 'Remain seated everyone!' A portly man with Bryl Cream hair swaggered into the dining room. This was Boot Jarvis the science/physics master carrying a long stick.
'There's not going to be a beating in front of everyone is there?' Whispered a voice from behind, there was an audible tremble in his voice and the whole of the Novus froze. Surely not? There was a deathly hush in the room.
Boot Jarvis slowly began to speak. 'Last night in Sperrin House a 4th form boy was caught talking after lights out! As is our custom the penalty for this action is a damn good thrashing! This punishment was duly carried out last night by my good self but this thrashing will go down in the history books as the culprit was none other than a Prince of the Realm!'
'Prince of the Realm? What's that?' Whispered Billy.
'Shhhhhh! Royalty!'
'I didn't know we had Royalty here! I thought I was the only Royalty!' Said Walter.

A giggle vibrated across Brecon soon displaced by an icy glare from the Head of The Brig Piggy Gordon.
Uninterrupted in his flow Boot Jarvis continued. 'And as is customary I will now auction the applicator that was used to carry out the punishment! I give you none other than SWISH!' Holding up a long stick Boot Jarvis swished the cane in one whooshing movement.
'Now who will give me £1? 1.1,1,2,2,2,3,3,6,6,8,8,12,12,14.......................'
14 pounds!?'
'WOW!'
'40, 40, 44, 44, 48, 48, 50.........51? Do I have 51? No? Wait I have 51 pounds and 4d, 5d,6d going, going, going GONE!!!!!!!'
And with a whoosh, swish and a loud smack the cane landed firmly on the table.
'Sold to the boy at the back! Come to my office and collect this piece of history. Cabinet supplied courtesy of Mr Davie!'
Then a woman with long Braun hair came into the dining room and a hush came over all 273 boys.
'Who's this?'
'Dunno!'
'I have to report that we have a mouse in the kitchen, a rather large mouse that has been taking whole packets of Digestive chocolate biscuits. If this mouse owns up nothing now and no more will be said. If the mouse is caught he will be gated for 4 weeks, banned from the tuck-shop and if he does not own up soon afternoon tea will be suspended for 2 weeks from tomorrow.' And with a whoosh, swish of her hair and click of heels she was gone.
With that everyone began to leave the dining room, the cacophony of chatter rose to a high level as the houses streamed out of the west door. Larry, Billy, and walked to the Top o'th' Banks, Charlie joined them. It was 6 30pm and a warm balmy night, the colours, red, green and gold blending into the autumn panorama a beautiful sight.
'What was all that about?'
'The auction or the biscuits?!'
'Wow what a body!'
'Is that all you think about Billy?!'
'Are there no girls where you live?'

'I'm a breast man!'
'Awwwwww! Missing the bosom of Mummy!'
'Certainly am!! You see the size of them!'
'Word has it that the Prince is that guy called Albert, you know the one who has the two men near him all the time. Remember the helicopter that Landed on pitch three the evening we arrived? The Wessex Blue chopper? Well that was him' not only is he a Prince of the realm he is the heir to the throne! Did you not see him coming out of Cherryble & Hitchon outfitters with his servants carrying all that stuff?'
'Wow! A real life Prince! Here?'
'Yeah! And who says politics is boring!'
Laughing out loud the four friends suddenly stopped as they heard the unmistakable creaking of the Headmaster's door.
'Quick let's get going. We need to get to the film. Dirty Harry isn't? What's that all about?'
Back in Brecon they donned their duffle coats and headed for the gym. A scuffle broke out between McIver and an Upper boy called Horbyn, the side kick. They could do nothing but watch.
'McIver has a brother an Upper, doesn't he? Why doesn't he help?'
'Can't be seen to do that Cobber!'
'Is he ever going to learn?'
'Hey Cobber get us all a boomerang for Christmas!'
'Why?'
'We could use it!'
Saturday evenings they had the film in the gym. Here the whole school trooped over to the Gym on the other side of the Flaxden Brook to watch the film. The projectionist was the Head of Biology Dr Wallace otherwise known as Spy! A botanical genius too, his Biology Societies were always fully subscribed. They were all queuing outside the gym, at the head one benefit of being a Brecon Hoosie when from some direction they could hear a low rumbling whining noise; 'Out of the way! Out of the way!' Shouted an Upper boy, when round the corner came an unusual red vehicle, grinding to a halt there was a loud cheer as 5 or 6 firemen jumped out and stood in line. This was the 'Fireys' the V2, one of the school fire engines. Immediately after followed another vehicle this was the 'Ambo' the school Ambulance Service with another complement of crew lining up on parade. The Hoosies stood in awe and puzzlement. What was going on?

Was there a fire? Was somebody hurt? Names were blurted out, a roll call, 'Here!' 'Here!' 'Here!' Then a whistle whence the paraded crews filed into the gym, each taking a post at a fire exit. By now there were many boys milling about engulfing the younger boys. None of them spoke; there was a lot to take in. Then another unfamiliar sound, the marching of dominating feet, not quite in step but in unison none the less, as the sound of blakeys clattered the tar macadam path.

'MAKE WAY! MAKE WAY! 1st XV! 1st XV! MAKE WAY!' There they were, a group of rugged men, bruised faces, tall, short, fat, thin, wide, narrow, led by that storied athlete Brian 'Puss' Whiteford into the gym. Heads held high, Puss caressing his long black locks as they seemed oblivious to their adoring crowd, cheering wildly. They then moved to go up the steps when, 'Stop Boy!' It was Nick Fecitt 'Beefy Bill' his gigantic frame taking up the whole doorway, his kilt swinging like a well calibrated pendulum as he followed his band of brothers to their seats. Music struck up from the inside, it was Dance with the Devil, Cozy Powell, this was the signal that proceedings were about to begin. At last they were allowed in, the room was already humming with anticipation and excitement. The 1st xv had taken their reserved seats in the front row, a fireman was positioned at each emergency exit and the ambulance crew sat at the rear. Walter wondered how he was going to see the screen over these big men but that worry was allayed when the Hoosies were all ushered to the front where they were to sit cross legged and quiet in front of those awesome warriors. 10 minutes later nearly 300 had entered the building, the lights went down, the film started, it was Dirty Harry not Soldier Blue their first experience of an X rated film. What would Mum think? The whole audience hushed as SPY walked down the aisle and took his place on the stage.

'Before the film begins I want to inform you all at the enormous help the Tuck shop or as you all know the 'Tucky' has enabled the show to go ahead. Profits have been used for the purchase of equipment of interest and benefit to the school as a whole. In the first place the tuck shop purchased and erected its own den and paid back its initial grant of £75 from the school. It then made contribution to the dramatics department by fitting up the stage I now stand on, in this gymnasium complete with curtain runners and curtain rail. Its first major expenditure was to the contribution of £150 to the surface of the hard tennis court, this was nearly 2/3 of the cost in total. This was followed later by Bells and Howell sound projector and a pair of huge quality auditorium speakers for the gymnasium. So thank you to you all for keeping the Tucky in profit and thank you to the Tucky for tonight's show SOLDIER BLUE!' The audience roared with approval. 'However...however it has been noticed that the Tuck Shop sales are down on last year so come on! Remember your shilling is as good as mine!' He couldn't tell her about this film but maybe about the enterprise of the tuck shop or many of the things he was now experiencing, he couldn't it was not the thing to do and why should he? The film was a couple of hours long and as SPY turned on Theme One to signify the end of the film, Brecon House were told to leave. As they left the bright lights from the building illuminated the near vicinity including the forestry track road running parallel to the gym. could see in the distance what looked like a bundle of rags riding a bicycle away from them in the distance, an eerie but calm feeling came over him the as the shapes soon merged with the darkness and away from his mind, it was Dan The 1st xv hitched rides on the V2 and the Ambo back to their houses, in full voice as they went. They weaved their way back through the darkness for the comfort of their beds. On their beds they talked about home and about the plan to see the girls, as music piped into the room. Lights were put out by MZEEE with no pleasantries. Click and a slamming of the door. The moonlight still came through the window and he unrolled his photo of his Angels said his prayers and drifted into a deep sleep.

Sunday came they were told that they would get a lie in till 8 30 am. No run, no housework, no cold shower. Think again. Yet another rude awakening with a world war pillow fight that started early and lasted for ever. The pillows having a little bit more than cushions. Rocks, books and rugby boots were the main filling. After a 9 am breakfast they reported to the prep rooms where they would have letter writing. s first letter home to his family. What should or could he say? Pen in hand he opened his letter writing case, took out a sheet. He had never done this before not even a postcard. He wanted to write to have a contact, what could he say? So much had already happened, should he tell everything. Holding his pen in his right hand he started to write home.

Brecon House,

Flaxden Brig

Dear Mum and Dad,

It is now 6 days since I last saw you. I didn't cry when you drove down the back drive though I wanted to, it is difficult to describe how I felt inside. I watched the car disappear, watching till I was sure that you were no longer there. On walking back into Brecon house a little lady called Mrs Borthwick said hello to me and said in a broad Scottish accent 'You'll be fine lads!' I went straight back to Conway where Dad helped me with my trunk. I am pleased with my bed in the corner; I can see everything that is going on! I then went down to the dining room for supper where we all sat together. I have made friends with a boy from Brisbane Australia called Larry, a boy from Africa called Billy, oh and Charlie from London who arrived a few days later but really everybody is very friendly in the dorm. We have had classes all week, even Saturday morning! Played games, rugby and cross country. There was also a big game of rugby which was great! Yet I still have to learn the game myself. We are all NOVUS except the second form who are very tough. We have our own fire Service, ambulance and hill Service .There is also another vehicle called the Quad which is a gun tractor and is use for emergencies. It looks like an armoured car!

We are learning to swim in the Myrtle Pools until the main pool is built; it is one of the rules here at The Brig everybody must be able to swim a 50 yds. I am glad I did my mile at Export Baths as it has enabled to help others.

The actual building is very big and white. We have decided that one day we will find out what is behind that sealed window. I have had no time to ponder the situation of the place, there is so much to do here you know. The buildings are by no means new. The food is sometimes rather

nice, some of which we even eat! Although my science master took some home for his dogs which they refused! The hot soup is usually as cold as ice; the pudding sometimes tastes like meat. But if you take it to brass tacks, then one will surely find although this school has many lacks it is not that far behind.
The five pillars are, Service to the community, a global awareness and understanding, a concern for the environment, education for citizenship, and challenge through adventure. There is also food, clothes, home, health, education and entertainment. Food then sex in the mind of man and woman, but I am not sure of the full understanding of that.

I miss home, my brothers and sisters, our fighting, on who was to feed the animals. There is no TV here as there is no reception. Thank you for the radio Dad, but again reception is difficult. I tried to listen to the football results but when it came to Export City score the radio started crackling so I still don't know how they did but my new friend Larry did catch his teams-Celtics score. When you write to could you let me know the score and their position in the league. I wish I could phone home and listen to all your voices but we are not allowed to until we are in the 3rd form. There is a phone box at the end of the drive but I had better not as it may get me into trouble!

Life here is nonstop, even in our free time there is plenty to do, exploring our surroundings is exciting, the adventure. After the match on Saturday we went to the gymnasium to watch a film. We sat at the front and the film was Dirty Harry! It was exciting! About this Policeman who is chasing after a bad man who has murdered people. I was very happy when Harry killed him. This morning we had our first lie in till 8 30. But before that there was a pillow fight between Conway and the rest of the house though we lost, a good show was put up! I think often of being at home and what everyone is doing. My favourite time of day is bed rest, just after the lunch where we lie on our beds relaxing to music that is being played throughout the house from a gramophone. You can feel the tension ease but after the time we are all taut again with the minutes seeming like seconds but still it is most welcome!

This next Friday in woodwork we are going to start building our own boat. It is a double lesson and the master/teacher is a fearsome man, nobody misbehaves but it was a relief to end the class and yet I am looking forward to next week's lesson. The school has 3 fire engines, an ambulance Service and a hill Service. It was amazing and I could not believe my eyes when they all turned up at the gym last night for the film smartly dressed in their uniforms. However we have been told it will be a few years before we have the opportunity to join.

I have not managed to spend the 6 shillings and loose change Dad gave me yet. There is a little shop here called the Tucky but every time I come to be served it closes! We have a free afternoon today and we are not allowed to stay in the house so Larry, Billy and Charlie, and I are going off exploring! The food is ok but sometimes I feel hungry but that soon is removed from my mind with the constant activity.

I'd better go now as we will be going for Sunday dinner soon. Let everyone know I miss them. I will write another letter next Sunday.

You're loving Son

Walter

Walter looked through his parchment, checking for spelling mistakes, satisfied with what he had written. He had left out many events of that week. Why? There were far more plusses that negatives and he was ok. He couldn't say anything; he just had to deal with it. 'Better fold this up before the others see the loving son bit!' He thought to himself, not giving his friends or anyone else for that matter the opportunity to rib him. Folding the sheet in two he placed it into a white Basildon Bond envelope and put on a first class 2d stamp. Laing another Novus asked if he could borrow a stamp which gladly obliged. Mum had given him thirteen stamps, probably because there were thirteen weeks in the term. He didn't write about all what had happened since arriving seeing what was unfolding in front of his eyes. He had told her of the Services,-the fire engine and the ambulance and that there were new challenges for him.

All the letters were collected by Jimmy Crow who informed them he would post them.

'What did you write?' Asked Larry, as he handed his Airmail envelope in.

'Nothing much just about the routine, the match, the film.'

'Anything about getting whacked or about Kerr?'

'No.'

'Me neither.'

'Wouldn't do us any good!'

Looking at each other they understood that they couldn't. Who would believe them anyway?

'Come on let's get to Sunday dinner and see what the pigs have just refused!' Laughed Billy.

After Sunday dinner they had a free afternoon and were not allowed in the house until after tea. Charlie, Larry, and Billy decided to explore their new surroundings further than they had done before, so they put on their duffle coats and headed towards the gym so they could see where they had been the previous night. On the way they headed to the path, sandwiched between the Headmasters house, Mental Pete and the Bursar, Commander Wilson known as Tug Wilson, house, he was the man who had stopped the Blue ratings in their tracks. On the way they passed the Curling Hut, with overgrown pond and the Shooting Range skirting the Nature Reserve to the metallic bridge built by the boys in Jaw's shack a few years before. Here the gym loomed into view; it didn't seem as big in the light. Here they saw the track running parallel, 'Let's see where this goes!' said Billy with a sense of adventure.

'That's where we saw Hairy Dan on his bike, heading into Myrtle Wood. That must be where we were the other day.' Heading down the track the trees towered above them, a strong smell of pine and peat were evident and the fresh air was invigorating. As they walked they chatted about their families, Billy was born in Wales and now lived in Africa, and Larry was a Scot with an Australian accent and Charlie was from London but had been living in America. Amazing! Four 11 year old boys exploring a new world when a week ago they were still being nurtured! All with a connection to the United Kingdom.

135 degrees

'Stop!' Said Billy. 'Did you hear that?'
'What?' Said Larry.
'That Belling.'
'Belling, bellowing then it is what a Stag does when rutting or looking for his mate.'
'Look! Over there!' Walter said with a hushed voice. It was a majestic Stag with antlers that were so well formed. 'It's a Moose!' said Larry.
'That's a desert Charlie!' The laughter was so loud the Stag, startled shot off deeper into the wood. 'Let's follow it!' So they ran into the wood. Suddenly there were 4 boys about 30 yards in front. 'Hey you lot come here we want you Flannigan! It was the four Upper boys, Blare, Braun, and Ztirgeon with Horbyn tagging along. The boys spiralled around and ran. Their path was blocked and there was nowhere to go so they headed up by the Flaxden Brook where the path slowly petered out. 'Quick keep going they are still behind!' The pursuers were closing and their heads could be seen bobbing up and down in the distance accompanied by shouting. 'Quick let's cross the river!' So the boys crossed where they thought were a safe place but soon they were in difficulty. 'Here Let's link our arms!' And slowly but surely and soaked through they clambered across the boulders and on to the other bank. A stroke of luck came as they noticed a cave like hollow under a tall pine tree. 'Over there!' Quickly they crammed themselves into the eroded cave and stayed quiet. Soon the other boys who

now were recognisable as the boys from the other night were level. They stopped looking around.
'Where are they?'
'I think this is going to cave in!' Whispered Charlie.
'Can't see them, ach come on we'll get them later! Let's go back as long as they don't find ....' And the voices faded. But the fourth boy stopped and stared in the direction of the large pine tree. Surely they couldn't be seen? How does or could he know?
'Come on Horbyn! We have work to do!' The voice sounded like Blare's. After a brief moment he turned and followed the others back down the Brook. About 15 minutes later confident that they had long gone the boys ventured relieved to get out from their hideaway.
'Do you think they saw us? They were the ones from the night before, with that bottle of piss in McIver's bed. I recognise Blare, Braun and Ztirgeon, but who was the fourth I haven't seen him.'
'I think he is called Horbyn.'
'Yes I heard that name just then. What do you think they meant 'We have work to do?'
'Maybe they haven't done their prep!'
Battered, wet and dirty, their clothes heavy with wet they headed away from the banking clambering over mounds of heather and moss, wading through swamp like terrain when,
'Look at that!' Said Larry. It was a small den with smoke coming from a chimney. Outside the door an old antiquated bicycle was propped up. 'Let's go look. I think it is Hairy Dan's place! You remember from the other day. I think we've come from a different direction!'
'No we shouldn't, he didn't seem that inviting before.'
'Awwww come on!' So slowly they tiptoed towards the building hiding behind the trees as they ventured closer and closer. As they approached the door the adrenalin was rushing around. Larry peered into a dark room and could see nothing so he turned to his now trustworthy firm friends.
'There's nothing here.'
'Cobber behind you!' Cried Charlie and Billy in terrified unison. Swivelling round as though on a sixpence he found himself rooted to the spot in front of the most terrifying sight he had ever seen. Wearing a threadbare ancient overcoat, worn out hobnailed boots, unshaven and long unkempt hair was the bundle of rags he had seen the night before. He was

pushing a very old bicycle with a basket on the front towards them with what appeared to be a large fish tail sticking out and other bits and pieces. They all screamed and they all ran as fast as they could away but to where? They were lost! They then turned around and headed back to the den. 'Excuse me sir?! Can you tell us the way to the road please, we're from Flaxden Brig.?'

'Flaxden Brig? Aren't you the ones from the day before? Lost again?' He grunted.

'Yes sir.' He then waddled to the back of his shack, raised his hand pointing

'That way.'

'Thank you sir!'

'What's your name?'

'Dan.' He replied' confirming what they already knew.

'Quick we need to go!' Said Larry.

'Wait boys, stay, and have a tea, the kettle will be hot.' The boys agreed and in old tin cups Dan poured the tea into them, no milk no sugar, a bouquet of its own. A black cat was purring around Dan's legs. 'Ah Wolfie, I'll get your supper in a minute we have guests!' The five sat down, natural chairs placed outside Dan's shack, in the form of large boulders.

After a brief chat the tea, no milk or sugar was drunk and the boys realised that they were going to be late. They said their goodbyes and hurtled away in the given direction. Dan watched the four boys leave. 'I wonder? Could they be...Yes........... ?' He thought to himself rubbing his bristled chin. Out of breath they arrived at the track. 'Left or right?' It was getting late. 'Left!' Said Larry with an assertive ring. Trudging down the track they arrived at a stone bridge and recognised where they had come the other night after prep so at least they knew where they were. Heading back they chatted freely of the excitement in the wood.

'Let's go back another time!' Said Charlie.

'Not on your Nelly!'

At a fast pace they headed back to the house puzzled at the silence that they found, it was deafening. 'Christ! Fellas we're late! We will get another beating! look everyone is in the common room. We're for it!'

At a quick pace they ran into the boot room, George, the Puma shoe was still in his place, glowering at them. could swear he was showing a set of snarling teeth. They took their shoes off, put slippers on, hung up the soaking duffle coats and headed for Georgetown. As they headed for the door they could hear a voice repeating, talking quickly and Billy being the biggest slowly opened the door. There in the common room was the table tennis table with sweets, drinks, crisps and fruit on it.

Behind the table was Mad Mac McNut.

'Here we have a Mars bar, unwrapped straight from the Tucky, an unwanted item as the current owner has now decided to go on a sugar free diet, guide price is 3d,

Start at 1d, do I have 1? Yes I do the fat man at the back! Do I have 2d?'

Another hand shot up and McNut launched into rapid fire 3d, 3d, 3d, 3d, 3d, 3d, 4d, 4d, 4d, 4d? Hands were being put up all over the place, left right and centre. 'I have now reached 6 shillings! 6 &1, 6 &2?' The bidding was slowing down. '6 shilling & 2d to the fat man at the back, any more, take a half penny if it helps, yes I have 6 &2 ½, 6 & 2 ½, I now have 6 & 3, 6 & 3, are we sure we're done at 6 & 3? Quite sure we're done? Going! Going!' No more hands were raised; A tremendous roar went up, 'GONE!'

'Sold to the fat man at the back. We will soon reach the required target for the week!'

'You sod, Fewster, you did that deliberately, raising the price, you know I can't do without my fix, should be illegal!' Said 'Blob' Paterson.

'A 3d mars bar sold for 6 shillings and 3d!' Exclaimed Larry.

Coolly Mad Mac pointed to another item.

'Here I have lot 6, a much prized 1 litre bottle of cola TC. I'll start at sixpence.7,7,8,8,9,9,10,10,11,11,1 shilling....................15 shillings and 4d! Going! Going! GONE!' Screamed everyone in the common room. 'SOLD!'

Suddenly, 'Quick Big Jim's running along the chapel lawn!' Exclaimed the lookout.

With that warning the remaining items were hurriedly thrown into a box and whisked out through the far door. The table was put back to its place and the net put up. Two boys were then playing table tennis and the rest of the boys were cheering on every hit, as Big Jim burst into the room.

'What's all this noise?' The room fell silent as big Jim walked around the room eyeballing everyone. 'Monroe, explain!'

'Sir, we're just playing table tennis!' The ping pong ball could be heard doing its last bounce on the floor.
Big Jim growled and replied.
'Brecon in perfect harmony? Get yourselves to supper, now!'
Back in the boot room they put their shoes on and went to have supper saying nothing of what they had been up to that afternoon, returning to don their best, kilts, kilt jackets and shiny brogues for Sunday chapel Service. The dorm was inspected by the prefect on duty who was Monkey MacKay. With a smirk he quickly went around, stood at the doorway, saluted and said, 'At ease men!'
The Head gave the first lesson with the Chaplain giving the sermon; the story was fascinating about a man building himself a round square to escape from the Devil after selling his soul to him. The school then belted out the school hymn, Father Hear the Prayer We Offer and they all piled out of Chapel heading back to the house. 'Let's go to the banks fellas so we can view the scenery! Maybe see another attack!'
'Nawwww I think they've learned their lesson!'
'Let's go anyway we've still got 30 minutes before we have to be back!'
So they all trudged down to the Top o'th' Banks looking smart in their kilts and jackets with an awesome audience surrounding them, complementing them. Those autumn colours surrounding the view were spectacular. On their way down they could see various masters watching them, Mental Pete, MZEEE, Spy, Molly and Grap but they stayed in view, making no attempt to seem as though they were up to no good. Gazing out to the lake side they could see the sunset mirroring on the glass like surface of Flaxden Lake. 'Look over there, 3 figures at the lake side football pitch, no I can see another. That's the group who chased us. Isn't that in between the boat sheds and the Blue Huts?'
Sure enough there were four figures and they could see they were dressed in similar attire to Blue. The cutter could be seen at anchor just off the jetty, her white paintwork reflecting in the water.
'Do you think they are looking for our raft or are they the ones who stole from the Blue?'
'No they won't find the raft because Billy we haven't made it yet! I don't think anybody knows what we are up to!'
'Whoever they are they are up to no good, shall we follow them?'
'No time, we have to be back in 10 minutes anyway.'

'Pity! We may have found them out!'
'Let's ask Mony about them he has already been here a year and he is approachable.'
'Okay but let's go! I for one am looking forward to my bed!'
The four friends trooped back to the sanctuary of Brecon, showered and went to bed. the last to leave the changing room with Mony. It was good to see he and Monkey were looking out for them.
'Hey Mony. Who are those 4 boys from the Upper? Blare, Braun, Ztirgeon and Horbyn?'
'Hmmmmm! Well they are Upper and it's best to keep out of their way.'
'How so? I don't understand.'
'Well they appear to be a gang on their own, Braun and Blare terrorised the Hoosies, especially the Novus all last year with menaces. Blare seems to be the ringleader and he just tells the others what to do, Braun has a pocket money racket going on and this year for some reason his rates have gone up. Ztirgeon is also out for what he can get seems to be a lackey and Horbyn I don't know, he has just arrived as you have and follows the others around like a lap dog. Like to call themselves the BB Gang because at first it was only Braun and Blare, got many in their pockets, but for some reason or other they have changed their attitude this year, seems to be more covert, more cloak and dagger. But best just keep away. Oh, but we must get to our dorms.'
Walter got into his bed and pulled out his crumpled photograph and looked at his girls, happy that Kerr, Pearson and Troup still didn't know what he was hiding. He would have to be careful, and now they had the Upper boys to watch too. What did they want, what is it?
A creak wakened Larry, as the dorm door opened and 3 figures came in the room and dragged a sleeping occupant out of his bed. A loud thud was heard as the unsuspecting boy hit the floor, waking the boy up.
'Get up bed wetter!'
'Yeah! Get up Slasher!'
'What are you doing?' Whimpered McIver.
A bag was put over his head and in his pyjamas was taken out of the room.
'Where are you taking me?'
'You'll soon see! Somewhere no one will hear you scream!' The dorm door closed behind as they left the room.

'Walter, wake up, wake up! They've taken McIver out!' Larry whispered. There was silence in the room, though they knew everyone was now wide awake.

'We forgot to put the wedge in the door!'

'It was removed by Jimmy Crow. Gave Darnley hell! Said it was a fire risk.'

'Where've they taken him? We've got to go. We can't stand by otherwise we are just as much to blame as they are and we could be next!'

'It's 2 am! Ach come Let's go!' Billy was snoring his head off.

'How he can sleep through all this I'll never know!'

'Come on Cobber!' The two boys crept out of the dorm, down the corridor where they could hear whimpering coming from behind a wall, what appeared to be a sealed door next to the boot rack. A small crack could be seen and peering through could be seen Blare, Braun and Ztirgeon.

'Where am I?' Whimpered McIver.

'In the old music room, where nobody can hear your pathetic whimpering! Sneak!'

'I've said nothing!' His appeals became muffled as a gag was put around his mouth.

There was a fireplace at the far end of the room which had been lit and one of the boys, who looked like Blare, could be seen heating a tin of black boot polish over a candle. Brush in hand he approached McIver who by now was stripped waist down and legs held apart by the two others.

'What are you doing?!'

'Shut up!' Braun whispered in his ear.

'No! Please don't, leave me alone please!'

'Shut your mouth!' Ztirgeon said in a dominating way.

'Hold him still!'

'Cobber! They are going to black ball him!' Walter said.

'We must do something then, and now! Quick smash the alarm!!'

And with his elbow Walter broke the alarm and sure enough Minnie began to wail.

'Let's hope we foiled them! Quick back to the dorm, RUN!'

But as soon as they turned the house had been stirred by the alarm and boys were pouring out of the dorms, a slow rumble at first volleying into a stampede, and outside the house. The two boys followed the others, mixing with the rest as they all lined up in their dorms.

'What's going on fellas?' Asked Billy.
'Decided to wake up have you? You were snoring the house down so somebody set the alarm off! God knows who!'
Jimmy Crow came out of his house and began the roll call. Eventually coming to Conway.
'Digweed CW?' 'Sir!'
'Holt HR?' 'Sir!'
'Darnley SW?' 'Sir!'
'MacCloon LE?' 'Yes Sir!''
'Odhiambo WS?'
'Sah!'
'Sir to you Odhiambo! See me at 6 25am lad!'
'Laing CAJ' 'Sir!'
'Flannigan NW?' 'Sir!'
'McIver RDA?' There was no answer and we all looked around.
'McIver?!!!''Sir.......'
A faint voice whimpered but they could see he was alright but trembling.
'You too McIver! You have no pyjama bottoms on! See me at 6 35am along with Odhiambo!'
'Melton GF?' 'Sir!'
'McNut BW?' 'Sir!'
'Stevenson IK?'
'Sssssssssssssir!'
'Speak up Stevenson!'
'Bowles JD?' 'Sir!'
'Thom EL?' 'Sir!'
'Bartholomew TC?' 'Sir!'
'Gibson BW..................'
They could see the blue lights of the Services flashing around the main building; they could see Magillycuddy and Cuillin lined up on the Chapel lawn and Sperrin on the front lawn. The V2 pulled up alongside the house and a couple of the Fire Service went into Brecon immediately discovering the smashed alarm in the boot room. One was Harry Stoker the boy in charge of the Fire Service the other the Leading Fireman Beefy Bill, the 1st xv hero.
'Here we have it Sir!' Beefy Bill explained to Mental Pete, who had followed them into the building.

'This is where the alarm was triggered.'
The Head walked slowly to the front of where the boys were lined up. All eyes were focused on him.
'It is late. Go back to bed. I will deal with this in the morning!' He said and turned on his heels and headed for his flat, his dog Jet following at his heels. With that they all headed to their beds. Kerr and Pearson made a bee line for McIver, jostling him as far as they could before they had to go to their dorm Shannon.

'It is my entire fault!' Exclaimed Walter.
'I thought, if I went to Jimmy Crow it could be sorted but it couldn't be, it was never on, he would not listen.'
'But, it's not Troup, Kerr or Paterson who did this.'
'Yes I know but there is a link between those three and the ones who took McIver. I heard Blare said he had sneaked.'
'Don't worry. Thank you!' The voice came from an unexpected source, McIver.
'No, hear me please! I'm sorry. I thought I was being helpful, I made a mistake but we can't let this go on. We will have opportunities from these difficulties and they will come! They will come! And we will take them!'
Murmurings of unbelieving agreement came from around the room but with exhaustion setting in, limp bodies they were soon asleep. Walter could see a boy moving towards the door; it was Darnley putting the wedge into the door.
'There's no need for that. They aren't coming back now.' Said McIver, his voice firm, different with a defiance to it that had not been heard before. What does he know? thought to himself.
It was 3am. 3 am!
At 6 15am the bugle sounded, earlier than usual. With lightning speed Jimmy Crow succeeded in tipping everyone's bed.
'EVERYBODY on the lawn wearing your shorts and pumps only NOW!'
With a scramble everybody was out on the lawn within minutes.
'Right! McIver and Odhiambo over there now! Now who smashed the fire alarm?'
There was silence.

'Right all of you apart from Odhiambo and McIver run down to the lake and into the lake and bring back a blue stone and it better be wet. If nobody owns up you will do it again and again until I tell you to stop!'

With a sharp blast of the whistle they set off and on the way back decided he would own up.

'It was me sir!' Walter owned up to Jimmy Crow.

'And why boy?'

He was silent.

'Do you realise you got the whole school up at 2 30 am and for what?'

Walter said nothing, he couldn't, there was no use, he would not be believed.

'Right!' Jimmy Crow grabbed him by the ear and grabbing hold of George from the top shelf marched him into the common room. 'Bend over boy! Look in the mirror!'

He did so in front of a large mirror that had been placed in front of him. WHACK! WHACK! WHACK! WHACK! WHACK! WHACK! Six of the best.

It hurt. The blood rushed to his head, boiling up, nauseous, his knees went weak but he held his stance.

'Stand up!'

He rose slowly up straightening himself up, showing that he was undefeated.

'You'll learn from this! You'll learn Flannigan. You'll learn from this as a man does! I will take the cost of the replacement glass from your pocket money, 10 shillings for the glass and half a crown to house funds as a victim surcharge. Now look to this day, go and get yourself ready!'

In the changing room he showered to ease his pain. Mony and Monkey came in after their run. 'I see you stopped the blackballing. Could've been worse.' Said Monkey in appreciation.

'Worse?'

'Yes. He could have had the angry bees.' Said Mony.

'What is that?' There was silence, and then Mony replied.

'Best not say.'

'Can we not stop all this somehow?' Pleaded Walter to the two Lowers.

'Nothing we can. Part and parcel of life here.'

There must be something, there has to be a way.' The two shook their heads as if in defeat. At breakfast the mood was sombre and quiet as they

were served their food. There was to be no afternoon tea today, the mouse had not owned up. The four chums took their customary stroll to Top o'th' Banks. It was a cloudy day with a chill in the air. 'Think I'll get my scarf and duffle coat on today.'
'Speaking of that, we have Pansy Ward for Latin straight after Chapel. That will make your vocabulary richer Billy!'
'What, you mean we'll be able to talk proper?!'
'Yeah, that too! But what are we going to do about these blokes?'
'Blokes? You mean the bullies? Well if we stick together we'll be ok, as long as we do that they can't do anything. Just don't get separated.'
'No I mean the Uppers, Braun, Blare and Ztirgeon. They have an agenda!'
'Yes but first we need to get Pearson, Troup and Kerr off our backs and on our side. We need to unify the house.'
'Hey how about if we challenge the Lowers to something? Say British Bulldog?'
'Billy you'd be the last man standing!'
'No, it would be a free for all, we need it umpired and we need to work as a team! You said we stick together right? What about rugby, a game of rugby. Ask Mony, he's approachable; we'll force a truce and play the second form. It's worth a try, get it, worth a try, get it a try?'
'No Billy!'
'But we can't even play the game! None of us know the rules! We are still learning.'
'Yes we will have to learn more! They will love the opportunity to batter us officially, in front of everybody.'
'Maybe they will, maybe they will.'
'It's a good idea but we don't know the rules and have hardly played at all but it could work and give us street some cred!'
'Walter, you had a run in with Beefy Bill, twice now, maybe he'd help us?'
'Help us? Only heaven can help us you mean?!'
'Right that's it then. Walter you ask Beefy Bill to train us and I'll put the challenge to Mony, remember from McIver's scrap he's not going to back down with this, he is fair. From games I haven't noticed that neither Troup nor Pearson being that good at rugby, but Kerr is good, on a par with Mony and Monkey. We're bound to win!'
'How do you figure that one out Cobber?'

'Because if we don't we're screwed! We'll put it to the others tonight before lights out.'
'YOU BOYS! MOVE! MOVE!' The voice came from nowhere but they didn't look around to find out.
'Hey, Cobber, what do you think is behind that blanked out window? We still haven't got there. Maybe those two men when we were under the table.........'
'Forget that now Charlie we're going to be late for Chapel!' And with that the four scampered away.
As they went out of sight the door creaked open and the man walked over to the Top o'th' Banks, a puff of cigar smoke rose into the air. 'Hmm... what are they doing here? Why are they so interested in this spot? What are they waiting for, are they watching for something Hmmmm...' Turning on his heels cape flapping in the breeze he headed off for Chapel, hymn book and lesson for the day tucked under his arm.
This day proved busy though uneventful, the bullies kept their distance and the Novus were left alone. The house seemed subdued, quiet but with a tight tension that could snap at any time, anything could happen in the next five minutes. They were at ease during their lessons, Latin with Pansy Ward was good as he talked about Roman History, and Maths a double dose seemed to go on forever. At break they queued up at the Tucky to be pushed to the back again, nothing new there, Larry ordered a marathon bar plus a bag of beef crisps and handed a half crown through the hatch 'NO CHANGE!' Both now missing out with still having the six shillings in his pocket. Maybe he should save it, after all he only had 42 shillings and sixpence left in his bank account. After break there was English and PE. Lunch was haggis, tatties and neeps, a strange meal as many had not had this delight before, Larry had, but not Walter or Billy, Charlie thought he had but couldn't remember. After bed rest they had double music. 'Shall we ask about the old music room? Maybe we could get it converted or something.'
'Later. Let's get going first we'll put ourselves into a position of strength.'
Rugby with Big Jim followed but he decided to give a fitness session so there was no contact. To their surprise there was no punishment, Big Jim being in a good mood, confirmed when he sprinted away back to his cottage, his wife waiting at the door. 'Must have something to do!' Billy quipped. 'I heard Mrs Jim say she promised him something or another and

that her temperature was just right. 'The day was turning out quite well. They had their supper and as they headed back towards their house they caught a glimpse of Big Jim running around his house naked, banging on his door. 'Let me in. Let me in!'

The boys smirked but stayed quiet. They didn't fancy another ACE the next day. Prep followed tea and then after their shower and wash they made sure the clothes were hung up and then in the fifteen minutes before they discussed a plan with the whole whole of Conway.

'We all have to be in it. We need everybody to take part we must do something.'

'Well I don't want to! I only like athletics!' Said Mad Mac McNut.

'Come on Mac you are the fastest in Brecon here you can go on the wing we will pass the ball to you so you can score!'

'Yes Mac and if you can take out a few of their players on the way that'll be great!'

'Yes I hear Pearson will be on the wing!'

'How do you think this will help us? There are only 13 of us and 26 of them.' Said Darnley another who they knew wasn't keen on rugby.

'I know, but we have to show them we are all together, united. We can do it, put up more than a good show! Listen we are being battered around enough as it is Let's get battered around under our own terms!'

'Let's have a vote! Those in favour of taking them on raise your right hand!'

A deafening silence filled the room. Walter put his hand up, then Larry, Billy, Charlie then nobody…….. After a strained pause McIver raised his hand, and surely and slowly the rest followed.

'Great! After lights out we will have a midnight feast! Drink and eat to our success!'

'Yeah? Really?

♫

TWO MINI ROLLS

AND A CAN OF BANTA!

All the boys, launched into song glanced eagerly around at each other, excited at the prospect when suddenly the click clack of shoes in the corridor could be heard approaching.
'Lights out!' It was MZEEE on duty. The door closed firmly and the boys waited nervously to see who was going to be called for pound. Surely enough the door flung open thirty minutes later. 'Flannigan! Common room now!'
Walter got up and left the room taking his place at the common room door only to find only himself there.
'Flannigan! You have 1 sock on the floor tonight! Take the position! WHACK!'
'Thank you sir!' He held out his hand to MZEEE to the Masters surprise. It was another step in the fight back!
Walter headed back to the dorm, opened the door where everyone was wide awake.
'What happened?'
'Only 1! Couldn't believe it! Nobody else there! Strange! Sssh! Come on let's get this feast going! Well Larry what have you got?'
'Two mini rolls and a can of Banta! What else!' Everybody started laughing but realised to stop quickly, MZEEE was still around. They could be heard but the mood was good as they passed the can around, nobody being greedy with their swig. Larry cut the two mini rolls into thirteen as equal as possible sections as possible but everybody was happy as all fell into a welcome sleep. It had been a good day but still it was difficult to sleep, they were the prey and the predators could come at any time.
Suddenly the alarm went off disrupting the dreams they were having.
'Not again! I was having a dream about crossing the lake to see the girls!'
'Mine was Prudence!' Walter pleaded as he rose from his slumber, the rest of the house scrambling out of their beds and out of the house. Jimmy Crow was there before them with an anxious look on his face, everyone could tell by the way he spoke there was something seriously wrong. They could see boys sprinting towards the fire station donning their yellow leggings and uniforms as they ran. Jimmy Crow anxiously continue with the roll call as they heard the engines of the V1, V2 and V3 splutter into life, their blue lights could be seen in the distance when instead of heading for their usual muster point at the South Door they headed towards Brecon and hurtled down the back drive, followed closely by the Ambulance, Hill

Service and Quad. In the distance they could see flames sprouting high into the air towards the lake side. Jimmy Crow finished his roll call,
'Good everyone here!' The relief in his face was immense. 'Okay boys all back into the house and get back to sleep, the house is in lockdown, there will be no morning run tomorrow, you can all lie in till 7 30 am!' They all were quiet, not a word was uttered as they looked blankly at each other wondering what was going on. They knew from the sound of his voice there was something seriously wrong. Soon they were all back in their beds and you could cut the silence with a knife. Sleep was impossible, when slowly Conway door opened. And a figure appeared at the door. It was Monkey MacKay,
'The boat sheds are on fire! We've just been looking through the Matron's linen room window. One of you at a time can come and look.' Thinking it maybe a trap nobody volunteered but Walter and Larry knew Monkey was a good sort and friend of Mony's. So Walter volunteered and surely enough he could see golden flames, in the direction of the boatsheds licking high at least 100ft into the pitch black night sky with blue flashing lights surrounding the flame it could have been an alien rocket as in Quatermass taking off. thanked Monkey and returned to the dorm. He told everyone what he had seen and been told, all were shocked. 'Was the Cutter inside?' Somebody asked quietly and nervously.
'I think she was.' Said Darnley, 'I was walking along the lakeside road and saw the Lake Patrol winching her up the rails towards the shed.'
'Yes, I'd heard they were going to clean her up and give her a new coat of protective paint. Ready for winter patrols.'
Let's hope she wasn't inside. Let's creep out and have a look!'
'No we'll get into trouble.'
'Well I'm game.' All four crept out of the window, carefully working their way to the golf course at the back of the chapel and headed for the lake side. Just before the road they hid behind a large oak tree. There was much activity, the Ambo was there, HS landi was there, all three fire engines were there, the V1, V2 and V3 were around the site in an arc all spraying water with their hoses at full pressure, a Coventry climax pump was floating in the lake and six other firemen two each pump were directing their hoses at the burning boat shed. Other crews had made a chain and were moving buckets full of water from the lake. As the building burned

the outer walls began to collapse and the frame work of the cutter could be seen inside a burning mass,
'Hey! I see a body!' Shouted one of the crew standing on the Quad. The four friends froze to the spot looking at each other, shock was setting in.
'Was McIver in the dorm?'
'He was at roll call Jimmy crow confirmed it all.'
Suddenly the Quad moved up with its leader Aeronout Fabius. Boot Jarvis approached the Quad and instructed the crew to pull down the nearest outer wall. A chain was hurled over by Beefy Bill and the Quad reversed slowly pulling down the outer shell, using its winch. The burning hulk could now be clearly seen. 'Can they see a body?' There was no mention but they suddenly noticed the Head looking towards the inferno, a solitary figure deep in thought. 'Come on let's go!' The boys headed back and managed to get inside without being seen. McIver was there asleep. And with that the boys drifted into a restless haunted sleep.
They all got up at 7 30 am and headed for breakfast for 8, nobody was going to be late and as the school trooped into the dining room not even a pin dropping could be heard. As the boys stood at their tables in silence, BONG! The gong sounded. Everyone seemed to be there except a few empty spaces; probably the Fire Service, all the masters, domestic staff, kitchen helpers and ground staff all were there.
The head walked in, fully erect ramrod style as always, you could see from his ashen face there was something very seriously wrong indeed. He stood there in silence for a few moments.
'During the early hours of this morning you were all awoken due to a fire down at the boatsheds... Unfortunately our glorious cutter, the Ariahdne was inside...... there is now nothing left of her but ashes and twisted metal. Our own Fire Service backed up by our Ambulance, Hill Services and the Emergency Service extinguished the fire to a sufficient level of safety before the full time Services could reach us. This I am immensely proud of what we are and stand for at Flaxden Brig however there will now be an investigation being carried out by the Divisional Fire Department, and the County Constabulary as to the cause. Our own Services will now be excused classes if they so wish for all today and the lake side are now out of bounds until further notice. The whole school will meet in classroom 11 and 12 on Wednesday afternoon when the findings will be known.'

With that he turned and left the dining room. Everyone sat down and breakfast was eaten in silence. It had indeed been a very serious night.
After breakfast the three headed for the Top o'th' Banks and just stood there saying nothing, shuffling about, hands in pockets, the V2 and V3 passed by dropping off their crews who were covered with blackened faces , exhausted from their exploits. There was nothing to say, nobody knew what to say. As if by automation they turned and headed for the chapel. The Head took the Service and the Brig hymn was belted out, the loudest that had been ever heard. Nobody was smiling there was nothing to smile about yet for the rest of the day the school went about its business, the fire engines could be seen being cleaned and polished, the hoses spread out on the Chapel lawn, some hanging up in the trees, it was Service day anyway. A steady stream of people was seen coming and going at the Headmasters office. A Police car turned up mid-afternoon, a Fire Land Rover and an official looking car with two suited men emerging arrived late afternoon.
Wednesday arrived and the appointment for the school arrived everybody crammed into the large open class rooms which were acting as temporary dormitories whilst Magillycuddy and Cuillin new houses were finished. Once in there was silence nobody spoke. They were kept waiting for a good thirty minutes when eventually the Headmaster arrived with the Second Head, a Policeman and what looked like a Fire Officer, both in uniform, they took off their caps and efficiently placed them under their arms. The Heads next statement was to shock all in the room.
'The boatsheds were burnt down by a naked flame, started by an accelerant; there were two hotspots, identified by the Divisional Fire Brigade. Our magnificent Cutter the Ariahdne which patrolled Flaxden Lake not only for your safety but that of the general public was lost in the flames. It appears that someone or somebody or some bodies had started this fire deliberately not by accident and it has been decided to be taken as arson which is a criminal offence. The Fire Department has concluded this and a report have been passed on to the local Constabulary and an investigation has now begun to find the culprits. If this fire has been started intentionally or accidently by anybody at this establishment/community they will be expelled/dismissed immediately and handed over to the Police for prosecution. I am charged with your safety whilst here and any fire started in any building is a risk to the safety of others and will result in instant expulsion/dismissal. These people also decided to put Mr Halfa, the

skeleton from Dr Wallace's laboratory into the boatsheds, this made our Glorious Fire Service initially think and fear that there was a body in the fire, it was a sick trick to play, there are a few bad apples in our community and I want them, I want them out, I want them on a platter. I have therefore also decided without any hesitation that if the perpetrators have not been caught I will close down Flaxden Brig at the conclusion of Michaelmas.' Gasps could be heard about the room and with that the four men left the room. All could be seen looking at each other in shock and amazement.

The boys filed out in silence, not a word was uttered. 'Who do you think did it Cobber?'

'I know it's those four boys who we saw down at the lakeside. Upper boys but we can say nothing we have already been in trouble once for taking a boat, they'll think it was us.'

'I'm sure it's the ones who chased us the other day. The ones who came in to get McIver.'

'The problem with this sort of evil is that you have difficulty rooting it out, you only see the results and it is too late. Look, twice now, the Blue attack and now the boat sheds.'

'Yes and we have been near there both times.'

'Once ok, twice it can be a coincidence a third time then we have a problem!'

'Tread carefully now fellas. They will be looking for fall guys. We'll have to sort this out.'

'How?'

'Well what have we got that's good? We'll figure it out.'

'How about we go see them? You know negotiate, talk.'

'What do we need to do to change? What do we need to be /to do differently? What do you think we can do better? What didn't work as well as it should have before?'

'What are you going on about?'

'AND therefore!'

'Yes!?'

'What in terms of principle do we need to have in place to make sure that it improves?'

'WE'LL TAKE THEM ON!'

'I love it when you talk like that!'

'Let's go and see Dan at Myrtle Wood!'

'Was talking to Mad Mac. I like him, bit crazy but I like him.'
'Yes, did you know he was a Novus last year but his grades weren't good enough so they kept him back?'
'Kept him back? I wondered how he is so relaxed with the Lowers.'
He got B's, C's and D's at the yearend an average of a C.'
'A grade C? You can be President of the United States of America with less than that!'
'Eat your heart out democracy!'
Monday arrived and they were now settled into their new life, but with Flaxden Brig threatened with closure unease had developed that could be seen on nearly all faces... A welcome surprise for many of them came at break. Walter received his first letter from home written by his Mum. She told him that she nearly made Dad turn around and bring him home but he had persuaded her that was not the way. 'I want him to learn to think for himself!' His Dad had declared and that on the way back they had gone to Edinburgh, to visit their Alma Maters, after Flaxden Brig and at long last Dad had let Mum drive his car! She had only just passed her test. His brothers and sisters were all well and missing him. They had all read his letter. was missing them too. He couldn't wait for letter writing the following Sunday. He had so much to write! But he could see the disappointment in those who had heard no word.
At games that afternoon Big Jim put them through their paces,
'You need to be fit!' He barked as they all jogged in a group around pitch 2. Once it was over they crawled back to the relative sanctuary of Conway. The older boys seemed to like them more probably because they were holding their own in games.
'Hey!?' Said Larry. 'Want to go to Myrtle Wood with Billy, Charlie and me?'
'We can't!'
'Awwwww come on! Let's take some food to Hairy Dan, he made us a cup of tea remember, no milk and sugar mind but I liked it, and we can catch a fish for his cat, Wolfie was it?! We can tell him what's been going on. He might even know something.' After tea they hid some of the leftovers into a paper bag, risking a thrashing for their efforts, 3 pasties, beans and potatoes and headed over the metal bridge but couldn't find the den. Then just as they were about to head back Billy exclaimed. 'There!' Sure enough the shack was there. Strange it wasn't there before but thought nothing

more of it. Slowly with anticipation they approached the door and called out…

'DAN!'

They could hear a shuffling sound as Dan came to the door, Wolfie at his side tail in the air meowing. Leaning against the door he asked what they wanted so they said they had brought him some food to thank him for helping them the previous day. He took the food from them with a grubby hand soiled with years of neglect they thought. He went back into his hut, they followed but he stopped them at the door but not before they saw inside. Nothing more than bundles of cans, rags and papers, a Royal Mail sack lay crumpled on the floor, possibly his collection since they had last seen him. No bed no cupboards. He came back out and sat down asking about each of them in turn which they gladly told him. He explained that he lived here in the Myrtle Wood and each day would ride out up the tracks leading off from the wood to sort out his problems, talking to himself sorting a few things out for himself. These tracks were the McInnis, the Grap track and Krebs Quickie. He then revealed where he had been that day.

That day Dan had gone up Krabs Quickie to settle a dispute between Teppop KpachbiN and Rpom Traba, two Ogres of Flaxden Brig Moor. They were wicked and formidable taking delight in terrorising the people of Flaxden Brig. Many brave men had tried to attack them and braver mean had pleaded with them to spare the people, but the same fate overtook them all; their mangled bodies were found on the hillsides. The people of Flaxden Brig were desperate; they hardly had a night's sleep in their beds for the giants rampaged nearly all and every night, roaring and tearing things up. A young man of the district. A young man of the district, known for his patience and good sense rather than for his strength, decided to do what he could to rid the area of the two ogres. He made his way into the mists of the Pass of Tullygarvan, and being careful not to be seen, he observed the from a safe distance.

It was soon obvious that they were a quarrelsome pair for ever arguing about their strength, flexing their muscles and showing off to one another. Their arguments got fiercer and fiercer and they strode off to terrorise the gill and vent their anger on the people of Flaxden Brig.

When they returned, Dan chose a tactful moment to speak to the pair; he was trying to reason with them. He spoke with common sense and quietly, saying, 'I come in peace. It is silly to quarrel about your strength because you are both fine, strong men. Why don't you let me settle for you who are the stronger? Let see who can toss a log the furthest.' The Ogres were so vain, they jumped at this chance of showing off, and they readily agreed.

Dan started them off with small stones the size of a man's head. The Ogres laughed as they each picked up a log as easily as a boy picks up a stick. Soon these logs were hurtling far over the hills. They were soon tearing up bigger and longer logs, and one after another these were soaring away over the moor, and the people of Flaxden heard these whistling through the air like thunderbolts and crashing to the earth, causing the whole Land to shake, and they huddled in their houses terrified.

The Ogres, in their efforts to out-do one another, hurled hundreds of these logs. They thundered to the ground littering the countryside for miles around. The foolish Ogres continued this contest for a day and a night until they were completely exhausted.

'You are about equal', said Dan to the two panting Ogres who could hardly stand. 'There aren't many logs left now…but here are two about the same size. Take one of these each, and whoever throws his stone furthest is the winner'.

Their big craggy, ugly faces sagging with exhaustion, the two Ogres stood by their logs, each determined to outdo the other. The logs were higher than a house, as thick as a tree stump, enormous and heavy. The first Ogre, with a roar the like of which had not been heard previously, sent his projectile soaring up into the air, over Lake Ballylady to Land with a crash as of thunder at Fall of Shin.

It was a tremendous throw and the Ogre, although he had used all his strength, was proud of it. He watched his companion pick up his log. With loud grunts and much puffing he heaved it up to his shoulders, and settling it in his hand, he let fly with all his might. Higher and higher it went, whistling and shrieking as it tore through the air. It continued rising as it exceeded the throw of the first giant, beyond Lake Greevybeg, over the Glasswater river and finally hitting the top of Chickory Hill, it bounced down to earth to land beside the Brook, at Tullymachnous, at what is now called Caber town at the head of the lake.

'You've won!' said Dan to the second Ogre. But he collapsed exhausted after his effort and he lay groaning on the ground. The other one, full of hatred and jealousy at being beaten, struggled over and with his remaining

strength-it was to be his last action in the world-crashed the last remaining log the heaviest of all down on the prostrate Ogre, bludgeoning him and crushing out what little life he had left, but collapsing himself, he fell down on his antagonist. Both lay there together. Both dead.
With saucer like eyes they were transfixed on Dan. 'Right lads time for ye tae gae.' And without a goodbye he shuffled back into his little cottage. 'I'm sure I've seen Dan before.' Said one of the boys as they all looked at each other nodding in thoughtful agreement. They had had no time to ponder or tell him what had happened to them over the last few days. It was beginning to get dark so they raced back, over the bridge and just as we got to the curling Billy ran straight into Mr Cunningham aka GRAPPY. 'And where have you boys been, what have you been up to?' he said. They had already heard of this fearsome man.
'N, n, n nowhere sir!' They all replied together.
'Ok! For this time. Get to the dining room for your supper!' And off they scarpered like mice running away from the cat.
They had only been gone a few minutes when they noticed a figure about 30 yards in front of them, heading their way. 'Hey look he's coming for us!'
'Hey you lot come here!' It was Horbyn on his own.
The boys turned and started running back up the Brook. 'We're heading away from the school.' There was no choice.
'He's gaining on us keep going!'
About a half mile away they could see he was still behind them getting closer,
'Who is it? It's Horbyn!'
'What does he want from us? Keep moving, Mony told us to keep clear, keep moving! We'll have to cross the Brook to get to one of the Upper tracks.' Eventually they came to a point where they felt they can cross safely and just as they are crossing Horbyn appeared, feet behind them. The boys are shocked at his speed. 'Well I'll get one of you.' and Charlie get across leaving Billy and Larry in their wake. Horbyn reaches out and grabs Larry's hood.
'Gotcha!' As he does this Larry slips out of his duffle coat and he clambers across to his friends on the other side. Horbyn lost his balance and fell into the fast flowing torrent. The boys saw this, he is struggling, feet and arms are all over the place. No sound can be heard but his mouth is open the

rushing of the water drowning out his shouts for help or shouts of anger. 'Quick he's in trouble, he needs our help!' Without ado the boys run down the banking linking their arms and at a Lower point.
'Take off your duffle coat and use it as rope, he'll catch it!'
'Ok Cobber!' They do this as he comes down the rapids; they can see he is bleeding from his temple,
'Look! He's hurt himself. Here he comes throw the line! does that and Horbyn grabs it, clutching for anything he can. 'Quick pull him in!' With all their strength they pull him into the banking. They all collapse in a big heap, soaked to the skin and out of breath. In silence they all rise to their feet Horbyn up last. He stares them out, looking cold and wet, breathing heavily the boys offer their coats. He refuses. 'Get off me you little shits, this is your fault and you'll pay! Can't you see you can't stop anything? We'll get what we want.' The four friends group together saying nothing and Horbyn exhausted and out of breath turns and heads slumbering back down the Brook, muttering 'I'll get you all for this!' The boys rest and then go back up to retrieve Larry's coat.
'Ungrateful sod! We'll we have to watch him. What did he mean we can't stop it?' Shaking their heads they headed back for their supper.
They got to their seats just before grace so there would be no early morning circuit for any of them this time. As they ate their food they didn't talk about Dan. They didn't know why, maybe a fear of getting into trouble or just that they didn't want to share walls have ears, keep stum, don't tell anyone what you are doing. As they went back to Brecon they discussed Dan and decided that they would take him some blankets. This was easier said than done for all they had was one blanket each, one pillow two sheets and an under blanket. Without these they would freeze! It was an issue that would needed to be solved if they were to help Dan. As they entered Brecon George glowered down from his pedestal and they trooped to Conway and to get themselves ready for prep. This turned out to be a non-event and as they weren't set any homework or 'prep' for the next day they were told to go to the sanatorium for their influenza jab. Here Billy and Charlie met the shapely woman Nurse Rose with breasts the size of small hills. During this first week they had not seen many women but had heard of this beauty as had his bum looked at and this was their first close up view of one and what an eyeful or eyefuls, they could smell the perfume, what a pleasant aroma! Silently they waited their turn, like drooling

puppies waiting for their milk. Billy prodded in his back and whispered, 'There is a room there stacked high with blankets.'
'Ok you distract her and we'll whip a couple of blankets!' He said.
'How am I going to do that?'
'Use your initiative, improvise, you think you are good with the ladies!'
'Right shirt off Odhiambo!' At this Billy turned around with his eyes horizontal with her chest, his nose almost touching her cleavage! And as he turned his nose landed in her cleavage popping open her top button! Everybody started giggling.
'It was an accident! It was an accident!' Exclaimed Billy.
'Report to your housemaster! I said your shirt not mine!' It was enough time for Larry and Walter to each grab a blanket each and they scarpered off back to Brecon. Billy was quiet unsure of what was going to happen. Sure enough George with Jimmy Crow was working that night. Billy ending up with three from George.
'Come on Billy! It wasn't worth it! Just think!'
'Well when you put it that way Cobber, I have a nose for it!'
Larry got away with one from the pound box. Beatings were now becoming a matter of course, but strangely enough petering out. At lights out they talked about when they would go to see Dan. It was decided that after games the next day. During that night they were awoken at 2am by a very loud siren. It was moaning Minnie the fire alarm. 'Not again!' A voice came from the corner of the dorm. They could hear the boys in the dorms above them scrambling out of their beds so they did the same putting on their dressing gowns and slippers and piled out of Brecon onto the Chapel lawn where a roll call was taken. They could see the senior boys from the other houses outside and other boys running down towards buildings out of view. Two red fire engines appeared, the V1 and V3, the ambulance and a large Land Rover which had not seen before. This was the hill Service. As they all blearily watch the activities the crews filed into a line and a hush descended on the scene as Mental Pete strode in front of the assembled Services coolly smoking his trademark cigar. Looking at his watch he announced, '10 minutes you could all be cinders by now! Back to your beds!' There was no fire, a false alarm this time no one hurt and no one in need of rescue it was a practice. They all got back to their beds falling asleep instantly.

360 degrees Michaelmas

'WAKEY WAKEY BRECON! EVERYBODY UP!' Surely it wasn't time to get up yet. They had only just fallen asleep, but this was real, the door burst open, Jimmy Crow headed straight for Billy's bed and WHAM! His bed was turned in one fowl swoop. Only picking on another two boys Jimmy Crow headed to another dorm. They approached Larry's upturned bed and could hear an animal like moaning then 'BOO!' he was ok.

'You shit Cobber!'

'Where's Stevie?' The wardrobe was slightly ajar.

'In here!' After completing their run they all showered dressed and went for breakfast. Classes were ok and they eagerly awaited the end of games to go and see Dan but not before they had been introduced to the 1st xv at rugby practice who were to take them that afternoon. Big Jim their usual coach and as they descended down the Banks onto the pitch they awaited his arrival. Instead, Beefy Bill, Fraser Cattell and non-other than Puss Whiteford swaggered on to the pitch,

'Right!' Said Beefy Bill, 'Who knows how to really play rugby?'

'Me sir!' volunteered Billy.

'Yes!? Then prepare for some pain!'

'You hit the other player when the refs not looking!' This brought howls of laughter soon to be silenced by Puss Whiteford's roar.

'Come here Hoosie!' Subsequently kicking Billy up the behind and sending him running around the pitch! 'Since you seem to know more than we do I want you to run round the pitch and take me out, show us what you've got.'

'Go Billy! Go get him!' Came a comment from Mony, they were being accepted. So Billy set off,

'Right around the pitch!' Commanded Puss. The three 1st xv heroes then turned to the rest of the group.

'In this game you need to be fit!' Said Beefy Bill,

'You also need to have your eyes, looking ahead!' Added Cats, as Billy came from behind Puss, into a tackle as Puss sidestepped him, resulting in Billy going flying!

'And ears! They're real important too!'

They were then instructed that to start learning, they had to practice passing the ball level or backwards but not forwards. They did this for about 80 minutes before they were lined up at the end of the goal line, calling Billy to the line they made them all lie on their bellies and on

Cattell's whistle they were to get up and sprint the full length of the pitch to the other try line. Just the same as Big Jim. Games were finished. This was their chance and as everybody was dispersing they approached Beefy Bill. 'Excuse me!' Bill turned sharply round,
'Yes!' He growled glaring at each in turn. 'What do you want?'
'Ermmm! Well……'
'Yes! I haven't got all day!'
'The thing is...... the thing is…..' Larry started, 'The thing is Bill we want you to be our coach!' Blurted out Walter.
'I gave you no leave to call me familiar!'
'I'm sorry Mr Beefy!'
'What!!!!!' Beefy Bill shouted moving towards the 3 boys. Cats and Puss stood smiling behind.
'Sorry, we want you to be our coach so we can beat the Lowers in a match!!!!'
'You've got to be joking! Your tallest is the size of their smallest!'
'We must win! We have to! You can help us!'
'Cats! Puss! Come over here! These 3 want me to train them to beat the Lowers in a match!'
Cats and Puss came over. 'Beefy they have bottle and some have talent, let's give it a go!'
'You think?!'
'Yeah, why not!' Added Puss 'Could be interesting, I've actually heard the Lowers have Jonathon C and FiveTrees coaching of them!'
'Hmmmmmm...... ok!' Quickly Beefy Bill rounded on them, 'First session 5 am tomorrow! Be on pitch 4! By the lake side!'
'5 am!' Exclaimed the four boys.
'If you want to win be there! You have 3 coaches now! Be there! There will be a 30 minute session no more no less!' With that the four of them sprinted away got showered and changed and headed for Myrtle Wood. They found the shack quickly and shouted Dan but there was no reply. As it was darkening they decided to throw the blankets inside and head back for their supper.
The next day they got up at 4 45am and headed for pitch four where the three stalwarts from the Firsts, were already there to put them through their paces. 'Look at this Puss; all thirteen of them are here!' Said Beefy Bill.
'Right grab those hockey sticks!'

'Hockey sticks?' A look of puzzlement spread around.

'Team work! Team work! This will teach you how to play in a fast and ferocious sport. Get to it!' They did as they were told.

'When is this match Flannigan?'

'In a couple of weeks?'

'Not a chance!'

'We have to try!'

They were spared rugby that afternoon and were taken for a walk up the Flaxden Brook by the Art Master, Big Jim. This was all exciting as they shadowed the route they had taken when being chased the other day, diverting along a well worn track, up the Brook deeper and deeper into the wood past Sperrin's grave where there were two grave stones rumour had it that one was Heith Vernon Sperrin and the other his faithful dog, Spike. The final destination was the Flaxden Pool a serene looking pool which was supposed to be very deep, and where they had had their swimming lessons. This was a new adventure to everyone but Billy, Larry, Charlie and Walter were keen to see Dan again, they had much to tell him. Twice that week they went to the shack but no Dan and no Wolfie, The place was cold but the food had gone and the blankets were on a bed in the corner. They knew he was still around as there was always the smell of the peat fire and the blankets. On Sunday they again went to see Dan. This time the bike was there and he greeted them thanking for what they had done for him.

'Where have you been?' They all said in unison.

'Ah Boys! I've had a busy week! Do you want to know?'

'Yes please' They eagerly replied, 'but Dan we have much to tell you!'

'Ok after I tell you what I've been doing!' And Dan launched into his tale.

There were two friends who had hump backs and they lived at opposite sides of BolyBrack, this is the hill you see looming behind us here, it is the Fairy hill. One lived on the east side of the hill Sugwas Pool and the other lived on the west near Templar. Each Sunday one would visit the other and then on the following Sunday the visit would be returned.

One fine summer evening the man from Foss of Braes set off to visit his friend. Because the weather was so good he decided to make the longer journey by Capel Uchaf rather than along Deuglawdd and so it was near to midnight as he approached Dolydd and to Clachnacuddin . All was still and peaceful. He had just crossed the Brook when he heard voices and the patter of tiny feet. He proceeded carefully and there, over the knoll, he saw the Fairies singing and dancing to their Queen Titania's song. It was so a splendid sight and Blut Rotes was delighted. So carried away was he by their song that he felt like taking part. It went as follows...

'Saturday and Sunday.'

They sang this repeatedly.

It was in Gaelic and he was so pleased that he could sing their song that he joined in a melodious voice –

'Saturday and Sunday.'

And then he added-

'Monday and Tuesday'

The Fairies were delighted. They sang the song 'Saturday and Sunday, Monday and Tuesday.' Over and over again and they clapped their hands and they danced around him. Eventually three came forward, and approaching the man, they said,

'What do we wish for him who gives us such a nice addition to our song?'

'We wish that his hump will drop off and he will be as straight as a rush,' said the first Fairy.

'And that he has plenty until his grave.' Said the third.

The man went on his way light of heart, and light of step for he found himself straightening up and walking as upright as a soldier. His friend did not recognise him when he reached the house. So he told the story of how he had lost his hump. He told him of the song and how he had been able to add to it. Soon as the Fairies heard them they ceased their merrymaking and dragged him down to the ground and jumped on him and pinched him. Three angry Fairies came forward and the first one said,

'I'll do the same', said his friend hurrying away. He strode down the gill and when he reached Clachnacuddin he listened. He heard the Fairies singing and he saw them dancing just as his friend had described. They were singing with great glee.

Saturday and Sunday, Monday and Tuesday.'

Thereupon Gras Donner began adding his own lines in a loud tuneless voice

'Wednesday and Thursday.'

As Soon as the Fairies heard them they ceased their merrymaking and dragged him down to the ground and jumped on him and pinched him. Three angry Fairies came forward and the first one said,

'What shall we do to someone who spoils our Queen's lovely song?'
'Double his humps.' Was the answer.
'Let him be the ugliest man on earth.' Said the second.
'May he grow bigger and bigger unto the grave,' said the third.
The unfortunate man made his way back, disconsolate. He could hardly walk because he was getting bigger all the time. When he got home his friend could not recognise him for he had two humps, he was very ugly and he was much bigger.
Soon he was so big that he could not get into the house. He had to sleep outside and it required and it required 17 blankets to cover him. He had to stay out summer and winter until he died. By this time, says the story teller, he was so large that 24 coffins were required to hold his huge, ugly remains.
And at that Dan said 'Off you go boys! Remember there is a message to us all. Away with you! But think on it.'
Again they had not been able to relate to Dan what had been going on. Maybe he does want to know.
As they walked past the common room they saw that the room was full with boys. Had they missed a meeting? Where they in trouble? They hadn't been told of this! Quickly they raced into Brecon, George glaring at them from his position above the door, was sure he had an eye and gnashing teeth! A sense of doom came over them as they looked blankly at each other. As they approached they could hear a voice clipped in tone, then Bang! Bang! Then another and another! Bang! What was this? Another beating but it couldn't be they had just seen George. They opened the door finding themselves at the rear of the packed group; the whole house was again in attendance. In front were a couple of tables filled with food, fruit sweets, cakes, cans and bottles of coke, lemonade, crisps. It was another impromptu auction.
'Got any cash cobber?'
'Just that Half a Crown they said they wouldn't change for me.' In the centre was the auctioneer, Mad Mac with his large wooden mallet in his hand. 'What will you bid for this Mars Bar? Starting 2d! 2d, 2d, 2d, 2d, 2d, I have 2d! any advances on 2d? Do I have 4d? At the back 4d, 4d, 4d. Yes I have 4d! Do I have 6d? 6d, 6d, 6d, at the back! Do I have 8d? 8d, 8d, 8d, any advances on 8d? No? Going, Going, GONE!! To gentleman at the back.' It was an auction. New fruit parcels had arrived that morning and

many of the boys had decided to sell their contents through an impromptu auction. They were amazed! The Mars bar had gone for three times its value. The boy would get 7d and Mad Mac would get 1d auctioneers commission. Yes and the profits would go to ....The next item was a pear going for 1d, sold anyway. The seller wasn't bothered; after all he had got it for free in the first place! Bananas, apples, oranges, mangoes, jack fruit, coconut, biscuits and all types of sweets were on auction that day. They learned that whole fruit parcels could go for £'ssss! Then the entrepreneurs would take their money to the tuck shop 'the Tucky' and buy as many sweets, crisps, peanuts and TC pop. Sell some of them at the next auction and drink and eat the rest. A 10d TC bottle of cola going for 76d that day, 2d bag of crisps-Golden Wonder cheese and onion going for 15d, a marathon bar going for the same, wine gums going for a lot less.

'Gosh look at that the prices have gone up!'

'Didn't you hear? The Tucky hours have been cut down until the biscuit thief is caught!' Said Blob Paterson. 'Don't think I'll be able to afford this for much longer!' As he handed over a large bag of coin.

'Blob, do you not have anything smaller? Instead of 91 d. No half-crowns or shillings?' As Mad Mac counted out each and every penny.

Tidy profits were made all round that day, they needed to be... Look outs were at the windows and suddenly they shouted

'Jimmy Crow coming out of the South Door, heading this way!' Quickly all the contents of the tables disappeared and the table tennis table put back just in time as Jimmy Crow looked around suspiciously as the boys played table tennis cheering whoever they wished on knowing but not able to prove something had been going on. They then went for their supper collecting some pasties for Dan, Billy putting these under his baggy school jersey, Larry took some boiled potatoes and placed them in his sporran added to this took three slices of bread.

Quickly after tea they raced over to the Myrtle Wood but Dan was not at his shack so again they placed the food at the entrance and made their way back to prep.

The next day they returned with some more goodies but Dan again was not there but the food was going and it could be seen a fire had been made. They decided to go earlier after games but as they were walking by the curling hut Billy said in a quiet tone 'We're being followed!' Quickly they

hastened their steps and moved silently into the nature reserve and watched to see who was there. It was another boy an Upper, it was Horbyn.
'It's Horbyn, he's been sent by the others to watch us, what a skivvy!' But he was one of the boys who had chased them the other day, cunning and sly in his ways. Was he really following them? They decided to go back just in case. Dan was a secret and they did not want to share. As they walked back the Tucky was open and they took their turn to be served. Billy got served his usual ♫ 2 mini rolls and a can of Banta! But the Shutters slammed in Walter's and Larry's face. 'CLOSED!' Shouted the server on the other side.
'Looks like we have another feast Billy!' Just as they turned Horbyn walked past them, glaring as he did so, covered in mud and bracken and leaves all over his back, they had obviously outwitted him but he watched them all the way back into Brecon. At tea that night they talked about the day's events and their homes which seemed so far away, their brothers and sisters, their parents, animals Billy and Larry listened tentatively about life at Crane Hall.
'Hey tell you what! You can come with me at mid break? Billy you can't get home for such a short time and you Cobber, said your parents will be away on business? And Charlie?'
'Yes that would be great!' Walter hadn't heard any football results since his Mum's letter at the beginning of the week. He would have to find out this Saturday. He knew the Shakers were playing Crewe Alexandra at home oh how he wished he could be there. The more they talked, the more they thought, the more they missed so it was decided it was better not to.
The next day they headed towards the wood but this time took care that they were not being followed. The four boys they saw earlier suddenly came in to view but they were too far ahead for concern. At the shack they were relieved to see Dan sat at the entrance. 'Hello boys!' He said. 'Where have you been?' said Billy.
'Ah lads, I've been to see the two giants.'
'Like the same two as before?' Larry said.
'Nay lad! These two are called Russo Terrore and Tuono Erba.'
Dan launched into another tale as the boys took their places.
'When the world was young and Flaxden Moor was covered with trees there lived two giants Rosso Terrore and Tuono Erba. While one was

rapacious the other was destructive and they were jealous of one another. They both wanted the waters of Flaxden Moor.
'Giants are usually quarrelsome and small minded and these were no exception; they bickered and argued all day long about who should have the waters. Eventually they came to blows and their screams and curses could be heard from far and wide. They tore up the trees and snapped off the trunks to use as clubs and missiles.................................'
Dan continued, the boys listening intently
'For one hundred days and one hundred nights the battle raged. Although both were wounded and sorely bruised they fought on stubbornly until the Moor was a wilderness, not a tree was left standing. Finally, exhausted, and neither having gained anything, they agreed on a truce. They decided to divide the waters. Rosso Terrore was to take the rivers to the Atlantic by way of the High Cup, the Schill and the Wrath, while Tuono Erba was to take the easterly flow by Lake Geneva, the River Hickory, Flaxden Lake, the Roach and the Irwell to the North Sea.'
'Isn't Lake Geneva in Switzerland? Giant's in Switzerland?'
'So many names! Never heard of some of them.'
'Let's get a map!' announced Larry. 'Then we can see all these places Dan goes to.' Eagerly they headed for the Barron library which at this time was virtually empty, a couple of boys and one master they'd seen before but didn't know. And one boy with his back to them. Finding an ordnance survey map of Gill Garry and Flaxden Lake Brig they spread it out, eyes darting from coordinate to coordinate. It was confusing there were so many topographical places then Charlie noticed BolyBrack Hill or the Fairy Hill saying 'That's where the Fairies are!' Then Billy put his finger on the McInnis track.
'Here! Look! These places all exist! Well....some of them!'
'Let's go and see these places!' Said Larry. 'Why don't we just follow Dan? He seems to know where they all are.' Said Billy, opting for the easiest passage possible.
'Tell you what. Let's ask Dan if we can go?' So they agreed on this. The next day they visited Dan and he told them of his latest trip.
They took their places around Dan sitting down on the four boulders outside his shack with their tea cans. And he began............
'West of Lake Shinn on the Deepwater Moor stands the Hill Bwlch Mawr. In the olden days this area was much used by Flaxden people for their

grazing of cattle and sheep. Here, when the summer evenings light was fading the herdsmen would often see the good Witch, Demdyke MacNutter, collecting her hinds together ready for milking. At the same time she sang a wild air that the mothers of Lanfinhagel and Flaxden would use to lull their children to sleep.

I WILL PROTECT MY BONNIE RED DEER AND SHEEP
I'LL TAKE THEM TO THE HIDDEN GHYLLS WITH PASTURES STEEP
WHERE THE SWEET GRASS GROWS TENDER AND GREEN
AND I WILL LOOK AFTER MY DARLINGS
FROM ON THE HIGH HILL TOPS
AND NOT LET THE HUNTSMAN NEAR THEM
BUT WHEN THE HUNTER MEN ROUND MY DUN DEER PROWL
I WILL NOT LET THEM NIGH
THROUGH THE RENDER CLOUD I WILL CAST ONE LAST SCOWL
AND THE'LL FAINT ON THE HEATH AND DIE

'When the two evil hunters saw the Witch and heard this song they kept away from Belch Mawr. But there was living in the area at this time a famous huntsman called the Red Terror and his accomplice Thunder Grass who were renowned for their skills with the bow. They were able to stalk a feeding hind so close that by giving a peculiar whistle Red Terror could make the animal look up so that they were able to hit her between the eyes with an arrow.'

'You mean they killed it?' Said Billy who was jabbed in his ribs by Larry.

'But they were on friendly terms with the Witch and never attempted to hunt her herd.

'One day they was on the Saddle of Bwlch Mawr sitting on a large stone, called the Witch's Chair, from its shape. They had found it wise to sit here and think kindly of the Witch before proceeding, for they knew she was descended from Titania. One day Thunder Grass was lighting a fire with his flint when suddenly the Witch appeared at their side.

'Where did you come from?' They asked.

'I was on the top of Carn Fadryr when you struck the first spark on your flint.' She replied.

'Where you running?' They asked.

'No, only a bittie', she said.

'That's it for today lads, I've told you more than enough already, and you'd better get back before you get into trouble!'
'Awwww Dan! It was just getting good!'
'Dan we have things we must tell you. Strange things.'
'Oh yes?' So the boys related the events and strange happenings of the previous week.
'Hmmmmm! Strange indeed!'
'What do you think Dan?'
'Well I think somebody could be trying to sabotage Barron's plans for Flaxden Brig.'
'A Government operation?!'
'No, they can't organise a piss up in a brewery! There is a force here a real power at work.'
Larry dug in the ribs. 'Oh yes Dan and we have come across this.' And they showed him the disc star that they had seen on Walter's rump.
Dan's eyes opened up like saucers.
'Where? Where did you get this?'
'It appeared on Walter's rump. Crazy but true!'
'Can you make one and bring it to me?'
'We can try!'
'We should be so lucky!' Said Larry.
'This star we see at night sometimes, high in the sky.'
'Seems to follow us around!'
'And we hear this tune, 'Blue Danube Waltz!' do you know what this means?'
'Go boys and do that for me!'
'We'll I'll be glad of my bed tonight, surely we'll get some peace!?' As the boys left Charlie spoke in a quiet voice.
'You know I think Dan is pointing to something. I'm not sure but something.'
'Do you think Mad Mac is related to the Witch?' Said Billy.
The four friends headed off to Brecon and were silent as the lights were turned out and door closed. Even the light in the corridor was switched off. Still nobody fell asleep waiting for the inevitable. 15,30,45,60 minutes passed nothing. Why no pound? Maybe there was no pound? Strange. You could feel the relief in Conway as bodies began to go limp relaxing into peaceful slumber when a sound of blackeys clattering on the corridor

heading their way. They had heard this before but never in Brecon at this time. The door burst open, they had felt no need to put the wedge there, and the light was switched on blinding all who were now fully awake. There stood in the doorway were four Uppers, Blare, Braun, Ztirgeon and Horbyn, older a lot older than the Novus in Conway.
'Right you Brecon Hoosies! This is a scuddy mag raid! We have good intelligence that you have pornographic material in this dorm! Where is it? You have 45 seconds to declare!1,2,3………………..'
They all sat upright in their beds, nervously looking around at each other, not knowing what was going on. Silence.
'……………….26,27,28,29,30! Times up! Good we hate it when someone owns up! Right fellas search the place leave no corner out!'
And with that they were tipped out of their beds, sheets and blankets torn away, the lockers and cupboards emptied, with disregard. Could it be Walter's photo they were after? Troup, Pearson and Kerr couldn't have anything to do with this they had a truce; the picture was safely in his sporran, tensed as they opened the communal wardrobe flinging our kilts and kilt jackets to the floor.
'Nothing here!'
'Wait a minute look at these toy soldiers! Now who do these belong to? And this Piggy Bank! Wow this seems pretty full!' Said one, as he shook the Pig. There was silence.
'And what have we here.....a present nicely wrapped up! Bet this is an Action Man!'
'Whose is this?' There was no answer. 'See this Blare? Nobody owns any of these! I will have it then!' Said Ztirgeon.
'Closest you'll get to having your own army Ztirgy!' Replied Braun.
'Don't call me that in front of the Hoosies!'
'I'll have these!' Announced another of the Upper boys, taking the soldiers. Finishing their destruction the four boys coolly turned the lights off, taking their bounty with them and closed the door. Their footsteps faded into the night. Five minutes later they could hear the muffled sounds of laughter coming from the other dorms.
'Put the wedge in the door! Let's just get back to sleep we can tidy up in the morning!'
'Those were mine.' Billy said in a quiet voice, hoping that no one would hear but in the sudden silence there was a whisper.

'It wasn't an Action man, it was Yogi Bear........'

Remaking their beds they soon fell into a deep sleep.

At 6am Monday morning and in silence one boy gently woke each boy up.

'Wake up let's get ahead today!'

So they tidied up and once done they changed into running shorts and with still 30 minutes before Jimmy Crow would appear rested on the beds. The bugle went and quickly they were all up, made their beds and were out at front of the house before Jimmy Crow had finished the bugle call. Stopped in mid call at the surprise he smiled and raced to the other dorms. On his return after upending all the beds he returned to the front of the house.

'Right off you go!'

The other boys hadn't arrived so they took their chances and set off. Finishing the run before the Lowers had even started. With broad grins they knew they were ahead today but would it last? They showered in luxurious hot water, changed, did their housework and headed for breakfast all ahead of the Lowers, nobody was late that morning.

The final two periods that day were within the Jaw shack and the period could not have ended quickly enough. As they were leaving Billy was grinning broadly.

'What are you smiling about?!'

'Wait and see!'

They headed off to the Top o'th' Banks and Billy pulled out a small metal sheet roughly 4' by 4'.

'See I'm not just a pretty face!'

'What do you propose to do with that?'

'We can make this thing from Walter's bum for Dan!'

'Hey great idea!'

'I've got a nickname for Walter-Bum face!' An icy stare pierced into Billy.

'Maybe not!'

'Draw two circles with a compass and cut it out.'

'How do you cut it out?' Billy produced a pair of cutters from his pocket.

'Put it away!! Do you not think Jaw will not miss those?'

'Doubt it; he'll not even know they are gone! The cutters I got from Joe when he was boring me to death about football! And I'll put them back when we're done!'

So they cut the circle, but soon discovered that they would need to put a smaller disc on the top. Charlie figured out that there must be another

smaller disc on the top so to align the letters up. In art class a star was painted on the Upper disc just like the star that they had now all seen those times, well something like it. The letters of the alphabet were then scratched onto each disc and a screw was put through the centre of the discs to hold them together.
'Doesn't look too bad, does it? We can call it prototype one.'
'I think Dan knows what this is, don't you?'
'He certainly seemed very interested. Let's take it to him on Sunday.'
On Sunday they headed for Dan's shack, again they couldn't find it, certain they had been to in this place before. 'Quick down!' The boys dropped to the floor. A clashing of metal could be heard further ahead. 'Let's have a look!' Creeping slowly towards the sounds they could see a group gathered in a clearing in the forest. They were dressed in white, wore masks and had swords with them. 'Let's get out of here!' So the boys headed away in the opposite direction.
'We're lost again!'
'I think one of those boys was Horbyn.'
Eventually Dan's shack appeared out of nowhere, as if by magic. A blue plume of smoke came out of the chimney; his bike could be seen leaning on a tree by one of the large boulders... Wolfie came to the door to greet them. Larry dropped a piece of the chicken he had saved from dinner which Wolfie pounced on. Dan was inside warming his hands. 'Hi boys!'
'Hi Dan! We have made the disc!'
Larry handed it to Dan. 'You know what this is?'
'No.' The boys all replied.
'It is a secret cipher, coding machine used by the Confederate Spies in the US Civil War. Simple, but effective. Fooled Uncle Abe's lot, for quite a while!' Dan was excited.
'Wow! Is it still used?'
'Doubt it, but it could be useful! Thing I'm puzzled about is the star. I would've expected CSA-ss in the centre. How did you come across it again?'
The boys retraced their story, Walter's sore bum, and the appearance of the disc which only they appeared to be able to see. The strange happenings at the Brig, the Blue attack, the fire at the boatsheds, the chase by the UPPER boys in Myrtle Wood and the mystery blocked out window. Getting

trapped in the tower, hearing but not seeing the two men in the snooker room. The star appearing, Blue Danube Waltz.
'And now come to think of it every time this happens the bullies play their games.
'Interesting!' Dan said quietly.
'Where did you see the star the other night?'
'It was from the dorm window above…..' Walter angled himself such that he faced a North position. 'That way!'
Dan pondered for a time. 'Hmmm that is in the direction of the island in the middle of the lake, with the little castle on it. The Isle of the Gulls. Have you seen it?'
The boys shook their heads. 'Well there must be something there for you, information perhaps?'
'What is this island, can we get there? Where is it?'
'Yes you can but it is tricky, you need a boat.'
'We can't do that we got caught the other day and nearly got thrashed! And we still haven't those lines!'
'Well there is a causeway but it is risky.'
'What is the significance of the island Dan?'
'I don't know but you need to go there to find out. But I will tell you what I know.' Dan then related his story to the boys.
'The Carters who had been outlawed by the King had taken refuge on an island in the lake which in their day had been a good size and was suitable to withdraw to after their numerous raids. The island however was now much smaller and a local Landowner had built a folly on it. A little castle where it was it was purported that he put his wife there as punishment after he had found out she was unfaithful. Each day one of his workers would row out with a basket of food, mainly fruit, for her, but the woman soon seduced the man into falling in love with her allowing her to escape. The Carters managed to get to their island by a causeway, barely visible below the surface, zig zagging across from the shore, which only they knew and proved treacherous to those who tried it.
'So there you have it boys get to the island of the Gulls and ye shall find! Look for the causeway could be useful. Now away with you all and haste ye back! I believe you are getting corn beef hash tonight!'
The boys left the den; Wolfie was curled up at the door, his belly full with the feast that Larry had given him. They could see Dan putting wood on

his fire and humming to himself, as he placed his kettle on the glowing embers.

'What should we do? What is this all about?'

'Shhhhh! Hear that?

'Stop!'

'What?

'I can hear a train!'

'You're mad!'

The boys listened and sure enough they could hear the chuff, chuff, chuff, of a train. 'We'll have to find where that is! Where there is a train there will be a station nearby!'

'We could escape!'

'Where to? We're in the middle of nowhere!'

'Wales!' Said Billy in an excited tone!

'Remember when we were in the tower? Nothing but trees and hills!'

'Yes and also when we chased after McIver.' They all nodded, escape was fruitless they had nowhere to go plus they were beginning to enjoy themselves!

'Come on let's get back to supper I'm starved, I could eat a horse!'

On approaching the dining room Horbyn appeared in front of them, in his whites, foil and mask under one arm, blocking their path.

'Come here Flannigan I've got some debts to pay!'

'I owe you nothing I have nothing of yours!'

'You have, we want it and we'll take it and you'll be sorry you crossed us!'

Suddenly out of nowhere Beefy Bill appeared. Horbyn scarpered quick style.

'Flannigan, MacCloon, Digweed and Odhiambo! Session tomorrow at 5am! What did that scumbag want? Causing you trouble?' As he glanced in the direction of the retreating Horbyn.

'It's ok!' They lied.

'Don't forget 5 am!' Not really convinced, Fecitt headed for his meal.

After supper the four friends headed for the Top o'th' Banks. It was now getting quite chilly and the light was fading, the Autumn nights were now in full glow.

'What should we do?'

'Get our scarves and duffle coats on?'

'No stupid! Cobber can you never take anything seriously!? About going to that island.'
'Well I think we should. Now we know.'
'Yes it could have some meaning. Something important!'
'It does smell a bit fishy!'
'Thought that was Cobber's pants!'
'Shut it!' Larry playfully thumped Billy's shoulder.
'Well if we can get a boat or something we could get to the island see what's what and then go to the other side of the lake a visit the girls school!'
'Never give up do you Billy!'
'Never!'
'And you think they won't mind us turning up for afternoon tea?'
'Well Larry man……..'
'Come on guys let's go back to the house, prep is soon and I think we are being watched!'
Sure enough the unmistakable figure was at the window of his study. Jet at his feet looking adoringly up at his master.
'Hmmmmmm……..! I wonder?' The Head looked in deep thought as he headed back to warm his hands at the fire. 'Is there a link?'
Back in Brecon the boys collected their books and folders, an essay in Latin was to be done for the next day but their minds were far from thoughts of Julius Caesar and his Legions. That night there was a calm that the boys had not felt in the dorm. The four discussed their meeting with Dan and decided they had no option. Why were they really here? 'Ok let's build a raft! Easy to do! Let's get those drums and logs we found the other day.'
'Yes I agree, anyway what else can we do?'
'We'll need other things.'
'What other things?'
'A map of the area, a compass, a torch and a monocle, which we already have. Where did you get that Billy?' Billy grinned that broad smile beaming across his face.
'Least said! But I'll get the torch from the same place!' Shaking his head continued. 'Just be careful we don't want to draw attention to ourselves. Cobber if you can could you get a map or at worst make one?'
'Will do! Think I'll make one.'

'I'll get a compass and Charlie can you refine the discs?' All agreed with their purpose they soon fell asleep.

Walter was woken up by a prodding on his shoulder. It was McIver 'Come on its 5 to 5 am. We have practice.' Quickly the other boys were woken and they headed for the gym. All 3 1st xv boys were there, Puss, Cats and Beefy.

'We will now play basketball for 15 minutes then a game of touch for the remaining minutes lads, we'll join in, good work out at this time of the morning, will make you feel good!'

Afterwards Beefy cornered Walter. 'Is there an agenda here?'

'Yes there is! But it is for all of us. It's hard for us all, the beatings and bullying are constant, sometimes it is difficult but we take it. Some of the boys aren't as strong as others, but the others shoulder them and we stick together. We just want to all get along with everybody.'

'And you think that by playing this match you will? You've chance!'

'No such thing as that. We have to try. It has all calmed down, to a degree since the challenge was made, but an uneasy truce, but there are others.'

'Yes I saw the other night. You know there are only 13 of you and 26 of them? Law of averages says you will get a good tonking. The rules have been set, 13 against 13 and they have 13 substitutes, 25 minutes each way, no penalties. Big Jim set the rules.'

'No we didn't know that. When's the match?'

'A week on Sunday, pitch 2 straight after dinner!'

'I'll tell the others about the rule change later.'

Head down turned away, what had they let themselves in for? Indeed what was leading his friends and fellow Novus into? It was all his idea, complete novices against experienced Lowers and for what? To satisfy his own intentions? No definitely not! To help others? Yes but there was no alternative here. Beefy watched as the young boy headed towards his house, a sense of pity coming over him but as walked further away his head seemed to rise, body erect, powerful and determined and the pity turned into admiration.

'Guys I got some good news but I'll tell you later!'

On return the boys ran their morning run all together, 'Here let's do a bit more!' So they all ran down to the lake side. 'Come on let's all run in!' So they all did, right up to their necks! There was a camaraderie building and everyone knew it. Back at the house they raced into the showers and were out before the rest of the house returned from their run. Puzzled looks appeared across everyone, smiles from Monkey and Mony, snarls from Kerr and co.

'You wait till Sunday!' Said Troup.

At the Top o'th' Banks Walter related to his friends what Beefy had told him. Aghast at the conditions of the match convinced them it would be ok.

'Besides I have a surprise for you all!'

'What surprise?'

'Just wait! You'll love it!'

'Let's get that task done; we need to get that raft made. We can't take a boat from the lake side after last time. We can make one from all that stuff we found in the den.'

'Remember we need to do this quickly!'

'Tomorrow we'll start building after seeing Dan. Have you picked up anything for him? I got a few pasties! And a tub of that corn beef hash.'

'I got some baked beans and mash!'

'I got bread and butter and a carton of yoghurt!'

'Hold on to it!' The next day Larry came to Walter,

'Can't get a map anywhere.'

'Tell you what Cobber Let's make our own!'

'How?'

'From memory! Remember the tower? Well we could see the lake from there and I've figured out from the compass I've made that looking from the Top o'th' Banks as we look at the lake it is towards the north, south is behind us.'

'West is to the left and east to the right!'

'Yes

'Right!

'You made a compass? Wow! How?'

'Easy! Well, I got a large needle from our sewing kits and rubbed it along the magnet in the back of my radio, so I converted it to a magnet!'

'Yes I remember in Science the other day with Boot Jarvis and all those filings and magnets! Good thinking!'

'So from the tower we could see the lake and that we are surrounded by hills and forests, So there is our map! And Cobber you can now mark on it north, south, east and west!'

'Did you know the sun rises in the east and sets in the west?'

'Who told you that Charlie? Don't tell me!'
'ENCYCLOPEDIA BRITTANICA!!!!' The boys let out a loud chorus!
'Ever since the Ancient Egyptians!'
That afternoon the boys rolled down the three drums to the lakeside along with the wood and logs they had acquired from the forest. 'Right all we need is some rope!'
'Got it!' A glint appeared from Billy, 'Here!' And he suddenly produced rope, at least 150 feet from nowhere. 'I'm not even going to ask!'
With six drums they positioned two at the sides and one at the front and one at the rear, they soon had made their raft, fastening the wooden planks as a foundation to make a triangle and positioning the logs on top as a floor. Two sponsons were fastened to the sides to stabilise, 'Just like Donald Campbell's Bluebird!'
'Wish she had the speed!' A mast was erected in the centre.
'Why there?'
'Well we need a centre of gravity so we don't capsize!'
'Why don't we find that causeway instead? We could make the Isle of the Gulls our Haven!''
'Too dangerous! Anyway this looks good. What shall we call her?'
'How about..............., the Bounty?'
'You are planning a mutiny Cobber?'
'How about Escape from Botany Bay! Just trying to make you feel at home!'
'Nah we are not going to mutiny! What about Bluebird?'
'No way, she crashed!'
'Ok............. The Lady Rose?!'
'After Nurse Rose? Yes what a beauty. Sleek and curvy!'
'Here Billy, give us your can of Banta!'
'Why? I got a bottle of TC today. Cola!'
'How do you always manage to get served at the Tucky?' Said Larry.
'Yeah! How do you do it we've not got served there yet! Hand it over!'
'Why?'
'So we can christen the Lady Rose!'
Billy handed over the bottle, first taking a swig in turn.
'I'll do the honours! I name this vessel The Lady Rose!'
Larry then smashed the bottle against the single steel drum. SMASH and CRASH!

'Shit! I've cut myself!'
'Serves you right! What a waste all of that cola gone! And I'm not going to get my deposit back!'
'You'd better get that seen to its bleeding.
'It'll heal itself!' He wrapped a large leaf around his finger. 'Quick Let's hide her!' So the boys covered the raft in ferns, branch and rocks. 'There we can't even see!'
On their way back they passed Grappy cycling towards his house. A smile came over his face after a courteous greeting. 'I wonder what they are up to now. Those big grins show it all!' The second master thought to himself.
At supper the boys talked about the upcoming match with the Lowers. Walter was asked what his surprise was, for a moment he had forgotten but now realised an opportunity had arisen looking at his hand. He would go to the San after supper. Once eaten, the four boys gathered at the Top o'th' Banks. 'North is that way! We'll do it this Sunday after letter writing. Agreed!'
'Any other ideas?'
'Ideas?'
'Right we go!'
Kerr, Troup and Pearson came out of the front door, followed by Blare, Braun and Ztirgeon and on seeing the group.
'They are up to something, find out.' Blare ordered the three Lowers. And as they made a bee line for them they were stopped in their tracks as Beefy Bill and Puss Whiteford appeared up the banks. They had been preparing for Saturdays match, an exercise called 'Doing the Banks'.
'Don't forget match is this Sunday now! See you at 5am in the gym tomorrow! Final practice!'
'Shit! We'll have to go after games tomorrow!'
'No problem! I'm off to the San to get this cut seen to!'
'WHOOOOOO!' The others said in unison. 'See you in prep!'
At the San Walter knocked on the door. 'Come in! Come in! Oh you again, what can I do you for now!' The gentle smile was warming as Nurse Rose swung around on her chair, immediately leaving the pile of paperwork she was catching up on and directing her attention to her new patient.
'I cut my hand today Miss.'
'Now how did you do that? Don't tell me slipped and fell on some glass, whilst falling out of.....!'

'Well……..yes actually Miss, I was carrying a bottle of TC from the Tucky and slipped, the bottle smashed and I cut my hand, but I wasn't up a tree!'
'Here let me look my o my that will need a stitch or two!'
'A stitch…...'
'Yes its ok, just a little prick and you'll be fine!' Trembling Walter held out his hand, which she cleaned up, stitched, one only was required and as a tear rolled down his cheek Nurse Rose said, 'Now bend over you need this!' Pulling down the top off his pants and underwear she pressed the needle into his bum. 'Owwww. that hurts!'
'I hear your Dad is a Vet Master Flannigan? Well that is how those little puppy dogs and kittens feel!'
Pulling up his pants, she turned away and picked up her pen to continue her reports. 'Miss!'
'Yes? What is it?'
'I......errrmmmmr….. ?'
'Yes!!!!'
'Will you be our Nurse for the match on Sunday please? Like a Physio?'
'The match?' She pondered. 'Ah yes the match! The first formers against the second formers. I've heard about it.' Pretending to think about it she suddenly swung back around. 'Yes of course I'll be pleased to! I'll also organise the Ambulance Service to be there! Those second formers are massive, massive!' She giggled as she continued her work.
'Thank you Miss! Bye Miss!'
'Good bye Flannigan! And one thing more, just be careful out there! It's one big jungle!'
Closing the door Walter skipped out of the San and headed to the prep room. 'Yes!' He shouted to himself loudly as he punched the air! On arrival at the classroom everybody was taking their places quietly. An Upper boy was sat at the front, to supervise prep. There was no noise. After prep they headed back to the house and got themselves ready for bed. 'It's tomorrow then?'
'Sure is, get some sleep fellas.' Walter looked out the window from his bed, a clear night and then he could see the star again shining brightly over the same spot as before. North in direction or there about, how difficult could a castle in the middle of the lake be that hard to find? Would the

Lady Rose stand up to the test? Lifebelts! They had no lifebelts! 'Hey Guys we have no lifebelts!' Larry whispered across the dorm.
'Don't worry already thought of that!' Billy replied, you could see the beaming white teeth as he smiled.
'I won't ask!' And with that they fell asleep.
Again they attended the 5am gym session with the three older boys. 'Only a few days now boys!' Commented Puss, as he dropped a football on to the gym floor.
'Football? I thought we would be playing rugby.'
'This is to help with team work, a bit of five a side; we'll finish off with some touch.'
'You are starting to look better!' Said Cats. 'These boys will do it! They have a hunger and thirst! That's enough! Basketball next time.' 26 against 13 a mammoth task but the challenge had been laid down no turn back they had to go through with it. They headed back to the house and completed their morning run, did their house work. Walter had the toilets, Larry the boot room, not touching George, who now appeared to be in a state of dormancy, but could be woken at any time, now that would tempt fate! Charlie the common room and Billy the showers.
At dinner time that day, BONG! BONG! The Head strode in to make an announcement. 'This Sunday the Arch Deacon is coming to Flaxden Brig, to consecrate the ground as the Chapel has now be completed, for a guest appearance. In the afternoon we have a match of interest to be played on pitch 2. This is a challenge match within Brecon House as the Novus; the new boys have challenged the second formers, the Lowers to a game of rugby. Jim Powers our head coach will referee and although it is not compulsory to watch, it would be good to see support for this unusual first event as there is no home match this weekend, the 1st xv are away at Dunsforde and I am sure you will wish them every success!
On a sour note, there is no headway in the recent events and my intention to close Flaxden Brig is still there. Good day gentlemen!'
At the Top o'th' Banks they could hear murmurings, as the senior school poured out of the main door. 'Well I'm not watching those little shits, they are only Hoosies!'
'Here have a banana!'
'Go play a banjo boy!'

Taunts directed at Billy were now coming fast through. You could see he was hurt.
'Just ignore Billy; you'll have the last laugh!'
'It's ok Cobber, I'll hack it!'
'I think it will be great, something to do anyway! To see the Novus get battered will be a laugh!'
They stood in silence. There was a lot to do in the next few days, starting with the day's classes and a final two periods in Jaw shack.
'Did you see those Uppers in Jaw shack?'
'Fifth formers?'
'Yes I think so, possibly Uppers, well I asked what they were making and they told me they had a challenge in the summer. They are going to canoe down the lake and then do 6 more.'
'And they have to make their canoes first?'
'Yes, great isn't it! Do as the Caveman did!'
'By the way did you hear that no duffle coats in the workshops anymore?'
'Or wellingtons!'
'Guilty!' Cried Billy that broad grin again.
'Your fault! You!'
'Billy where have you learnt all these 'skills' from?'
'My Dad of course and his friends, but mostly Dad, he learnt them from Great Granddad and he from Great Great Grandad Odhiambo!'
'Woweeeeee!'
'Yes, Great Great Grandad was always in trouble with the British Authorities, getting locked up, escaping, locked up, escaping learnt a lot in the nick! Just been handed down! Comes in useful! Didn't really like you are doing this whether you like it or not attitude!'
'Certainly does! Yes it is better to be asked than told.'
'I think us wearing wellys on a sunny day might've given it away!'
'Well how did you think I got those nails out?'
'And no wellys!'
'That's how I got the metal sheet out!'
'Billy! You'll get us in trouble!'
'We're always in trouble!' Said Charlie.
'We needed them for the Lady Rose!'
'Just be careful!'
'Where there is a will there's a way!'

'Now what about the life vests?'
'Well, I was walking past the swimming pool, hey fellas a swimming pool with no water! Well the door was open and I saw this pile of rubber rings and floats so snatched a few. I also found this big inner tube. Took me ages to blow up!'
'Where are they all?'
'About 100yds away from the Lady Rose covered in ferns. I also took some vacant washing line, didn't have any clothes on it. Should be able to fasten things down. But we still have no sail!'
'Got that! Found this tarpaulin covering a boat by the lakeside!' Piped in Larry.
'Which boat Larry?'
'It had a B on it I think!'
'That's Mental Pete's!'
'Well we can put it back after!'
'We're all set then!'
'Let's stop calling the Head Mental Pete, he's a fair man!'
'Well he's not beaten us yet! Okay what shall we call him?'
'How about just Pete?'
The tension could be felt and the adrenalin built steadily throughout the day as the boys launched the Lady Rose into the lake. 'Right let's go!'
All four sat on the raft. 'She's floating! She's floating! A miracle!' Billy and at the sides with the paddles, Larry and Charlie at the rudder. Using the compass and the map they took a North direction across the water which was calm. 'Nothing. I can't see anything!
'Keep looking!'
'Look! There it is in the middle over there! Dan was right! Head that way!'
Paddling the raft towards the little island the boys became excited. 'Wow look at that!' They shouted, whooping as they did so. Suddenly there was a grinding sound. 'We're running aground!'
'No it's the causeway Dan was talking about! No it's the rocks remember he said the island was here. 'At the sound the gulls in the castle flew out angry at being disturbed, suddenly splat, straight on s head, 'Shit!'
'Yes it is! The bird crapped on your head!'
'I've heard it's supposed to be lucky that!' Charlie said.
'Not for, he got shit on!' Then as if in turn. SPLAT on Billy, SPLAT on Larry and SPLAT on Charlie! 'Don't think we're welcome here!'

'Come on guys let's see what's here.' Climbing into the structure they rooted around. There was nothing inside except rocks and a nest with eggs in it. This was what the gulls were mad about, only protecting, splat! Another bomb hit Billy. Suddenly Larry said, Must like you Billy! Wait there it is the letters *nafppn*, remember that that is what we must need. Now let's get out of here!'

'Quick down!' Two fast moving boats sped across the lake towards the Flaxden Brig.

'Down they'll see us! Is that the Lake Patrol?'

After the boats had gone they clambered aboard and pushed away.

'Do you think they saw us?'

'Nah Cobber! If they had they would've stopped!'

The water was now getting choppy and it had become cloudy. 'Hey let's check out the girls school it's only that way.'

'Ok, but Let's get going. It must be North East way.' And they headed off when suddenly they could see a pair of orange lights and bellows of smoke. 'The Beastie!'

'Let's get out of here!' Turning about they headed for the shore paddling like their lives depended on it.

'Keep going, keep going!' Tired and wet, they saw they weren't being followed. Slowing down, they paddled into a small lagoon. 'This is a great place to hide the raft and all our stuff. Were bound to use her again.' Dragging the raft ashore they covered her up with foliage confident she couldn't be found. On arrival at the road. 'Left or right? Must be left.' got out his compass.

'Listen..... I can hear that train again, sounds like its coming north east of us.' As Larry checked his directions. Yes they all could hear. 'Scotland!'

'Another time let's get back we got what we needed. Will see Dan tomorrow. How about a final practice tomorrow. Not seen the Lowers training have you? Come on let's move it. Quick in the bushes its Grappy on his bike don't want him to see us.' They then raced back just in time to the dining room. Famished they devoured their meal disgusting but tasty. They didn't care. After that they went to prep, showered and went to bed. It was strange the beatings were really tailing off. Had the second former bullies given up or had they just given them respite? A big weekend was coming up as they drifted in and out of sleep. Dozing , it was always going to be difficult to sleep, anything could come through the door, Walter

could see the half asleep figure of Billy walking across the dorm in his pyjamas, opening the door, 'he must be going to the toilet' he thought. Just before 5am the dorm awoke and dragged themselves up and out the door. 'Last session today fellas! We'll have them on Sunday! Listen they are all snoring their heads off!' A brief laugh came as the boys headed across to the gym. It was unusually mild as they jogged towards the Lower bridge, a metal bridge built by the boys in Jaw shack a few years ago, up the hill and into the gym where their coaches were already stretching themselves. 'Same again! Touch rugby but change over after one touch now. We'll join in 8 aside! Remember speed of ball from player to ball will beat them every time!'
'Think it's time for breakfast!' Larry nudged Charlie.
'Where's Billy Cobber?' The session was good as they went through their paces for 30 minutes. It could be easily seen that Beefy, Puss and Cats were going through their paces at a coast; they had a big game tomorrow.
'Right that's it see you Sunday, will all be there rooting for you!'
Thanking them for their help they headed back to the house for the morning run. 'Where's Billy?' Off they went around the school and back for the shower. Still no Billy. Back in the dorm went over to Billy's bed, the sheets and blanket had been pulled back, a dent in his pillow where his head had been laid. Larry came over and put his hands on the sheets. They were cold, looking at each other, their eyes widened. 'I saw him going out about an hour after lights out, thought he was going for a pee. Then I fell asleep.'
'He's not been here since then.'
'He's been kidnapped! Kerr, Troup and Pearson. Monkey and Mony wouldn't do that! Would they? For a laugh, to disrupt us?'
'I wouldn't put it past them but I don't think they would do anything that stupid!'
'Then it must be Blare and his cronies!'
'What about that storm we had last night? Do you think he was out in that?'
'How could he survive that. Thunder, lightning and rain, with only his pyjamas on?' They all looked blankly at each other, knowing the answer.
'Better report it. Let's go to MZEEE. He's on duty today.'
So the boys knocked on the door of MZEEE. He came into Brecon House and Conway, looked at the bed asked the rest of the house questions and

went quickly, stern faced without a word down to the main building. Seconds later Moaning Minnie started to wail, screeching. Boys were running from every direction, the V1 and V2 arrived, then the Quad, the Ambo and then the Hill Service. An anxious Head spoke to all the crews pointing in the direction of the Grap track, the Flaxden Brook and Krebs Quickie, the perimeters of Myrtle Wood. Brecon House stood in silence. Jimmy Crow came over and told them there was a serious issue, but they all knew a boy was missing. 'Go have your breakfast and continue with your day.' Jimmy Crow told them, but the three friends couldn't do that, one of their own was gone; a part of them was missing.

'They know something you know. Bugger breakfast I'm going to look!'

'Me too!'

'And me!' Said Larry. 'Can't have you going on your own!'

So after feigning going to the dining room, the rest of the house wouldn't miss them, just meant more food for them, the boys headed up to the direction of the Services. The Quad had gone up the tracks with the V1 to produce a cordon, within that, the Hill Service had made a long line and doing a sweep, were moving slowly inch by inch into Myrtle Wood with the Ambo parked nearby, its crew talking to a bleary eyed Nurse Rose. The boys watched with intensity following every movement. 'Let's go up the Brook, where we were chased the other day. I have a feeling. We won't be seen that way.'

'You think they had something to do with this?'

'Yes! They've been after something or someone from us for a bit now!'

'Let's go!'

Stealthily the boys shadowed the Brook, ducking down when they saw or heard someone or something. The crackling of radios, with the Hill Service, sweeping their way through the Wood. 'That's a negative.' Could be heard. Moving at a fast pace they managed to overtake the search parties, unseen. 'We are up near where we were the other day; we must be near the Flaxden Pool. Look there is that overhang we hid in the other day. Doesn't look safe does it? Keep moving!' As they passed by the shelter they could see part of the banking had slipped into the Brook.

They were now venturing into new territory, they had not ventured this far. They were pleased that they weren't being chased but were getting concerned for Billy. After climbing up a steep waterfall and overhang they

could hear voices. Sure enough in the distance they could see a small group of boys around a tree. 'I knew it! I knew I could smell something fishy!'
'I've told you change your underpants, Charlie!'
'Shut it Cobber! This is serious something's going on it's the ones who chased us!' Said Walter.
'I can count five! Four and somebody leaning against the tree! Wait its Billy! He's gone over! The traitor!'
'Right Odhiambo where is it?' Said one of the group.
'What?'
'That piece of paper with the information on. We want the information!'
'Even if I had what you are talking about I wouldn't give it you.'
'RIGHT HORBYN GET THE BEES!'
Hiding behind a fallen tree root upended from the storm, the boys hid in a stunned silence. 'He wouldn't, Billy just wouldn't. I' m not having that let's get closer!'
Getting closer they saw Billy had been tied to the tree. 'Look they've tied him!' Retreating behind another root. 'What are we going to do? We can't leave him. Tell you what Charlie you are fast, distract them, and go round their left and head straight up. The search parties are somewhere over there, they might chase you!'
'Ok what will you do?'
'We'll go around and start talking they may decide to move. Shout at them!'
Off Charlie went, quietly at first then dashing through the wood he turned and shouted. 'THERE THEY ARE! I'VE FOUND THEM!' By this time Walter and Larry had moved above the position and they shouted, 'LOOK THERE THEY ARE!' The kidnappers, for that is what they were, panicked and headed off back down the Brook, except one. A siren and the grinding of gears could be heard in the distance, it was the Quad moving through the undergrowth as though it was some monster and soon the other figure started back. 'I hope Charlie will be ok.'
'He'll be fine, quick let's get to Billy!' They ran towards Billy who was tied tightly to the tree, a weary head looked up, bloodied, bruised and dishevelled. His pyjamas were torn and shredded a few cuts could be seen on his arms and legs.
'Cobber! Walter! Is that really you? Boy am I glad to see your ugly faces, they were going to brand me, threatened me with all sorts, get me out of

here!' By the side of the structure was a small fire with what looked like a poker stuck in it.

Quickly untying Billy from the tree. 'What happened!?'

'Will tell you later let's get out of here. Stop! I'll have that rope may come in useful, we can improve the Lady Rose!'

'Billy!!!!! Forget that! The Quad is coming. Move! Come on!'

'Wait what's that?' Two pieces of corrugated iron were positioned over the structure.

'It's where I've been all night! It was like a court, they said I was guilty! God knows what would've happened, if you hadn't turned up. We can use the corrugated iron and the rope so we can get across the lake!'

'The whole of the Flaxden Brig Services are looking for you and you're still joking, you never stop do you? Ok let's take the iron and wreck the place so they can't use it!'

The structure was a hollowed out building, a fox hole, empty beer cans and a pile of cigarette stubs were inside. 'Wreck the place! Come on make sure they can never use it again! Bet these are the beer and cigarettes the Blue Ratings bought.'

'And look at this!' Larry picked up a jam jar with a number of large angry bees inside it, buzzing away and trying to get out. 'What do you suppose they were going to do with that? I'm going to let them out!' Unscrewing the top, the bees flew away disappearing in the distance, all but one.

'Cobber! There's one on your neck!'

'OWWWWWW!!!' Shouted Larry.

'Come on let's get back to Brecon.'

Dragging the corrugated iron towards the Brook they could hear voices in the distance. 'Shhhh! Don't worry they'll think it's the search parties, come on slowly we'll hide these at that place we found the other day!'

Eventually they got near to the playing fields, 'Billy you go through the Nature Reserve and walk over to the pitches, and pretend you're in a daze or something! Delirious.' Billy did that as Walter and Larry headed back to Brecon. 'We're in trouble now, it's nearly lunchtime and we've all missed morning classes! What will we say?' There was no need, the rest of the house had been instructed to search down by the lakeside. The boys changed and went into the common room as one by one the V1, V2, Ambo and Mountain Service returned to their sheds, only the Quad remained in the Wood. Then Nurse Rose appeared from the South Door with a

dishevelled Billy and headed up Magillycuddy Hill towards the Sanatorium.
'Lucky sod!' Quipped Larry and when he didn't come back they assumed he was being kept in.
'That must've been a shock! Imagine if he hadn't been found and something terrible had happened, his family and friends. That sort of thing affects many.'
'Let's go see him tonight.' After supper they skipped the banks and headed to the San and knocked on the door.
'Oh, you again Flannigan, broken fingernail this time?'
'No Miss, can we see our friend Billy? We are worried.'
'He will be ok…………..' she was just about to say no, 'Ok you can, it will cheer him up, 10 minutes only mind, he's had a big shock!'
They were lead into Billy's little room.
'Big shock my arse! Hey not bad in here. Now where's all the grub you malingerer? Awww...he's had a big shock!! What did you say?'
'Well I scrambled through the reserve like you said and wandered straight into the path of Miss Daphne the Heads secretary................WHAT a pair of knockers! Well, she put her shawl around me and took me to Mental Pete's office and sat me down by the fire, would you believe it! I was sitting on the Headmasters Chair! They asked me where I'd been so I told them I had fallen asleep and woke up in the Nature Reserve! Simple!'
'They believed you?'
'Yes! Miss Daphne got me a mug of tea, must have had 8 sugars in it! And a jam scone! Pete looked relieved! Then after about half an hour Nurse Rose appeared and brought me here, the Ambo was still up the tracks. Well you can't have everything!'
'Poor you. What really happened Billy? We were worried sick! We didn't even notice you'd gone till we came back from morning run. A jam scone you say? Strawberry or Raspberry?'
'Blueberry, thanks a bunch Cobber, really missed me then!'
Billy then told them the story that he got up to go to the loo and as he got to the door a tape was put over his mouth and a sheet around him, he tried to struggle but it was no use, there were too many. Barefoot he was lead up to where they had found him. They had torches, one of which he had commandeered, how he tied it to his willy, there they gagged him tied him up and left him when it started to rain. 'That lightning and thunder was

quite something.' He exclaimed. And in the morning when they came back one of them read out an accusation and said, 'GUILTY!' Tied him up against the tree and were just about to do something when you guys appeared as if by magic! He even prayed to Rita. He was sure glad to see them! 'Billy if we hadn't seen you tied against that tree we wouldn't have believed you!'

'Who's this Rita? What did they say?'

' I pray to Rita for impossible cases and she answered me! No idea I was absolutely knackered! Good job they didn't use the bees, they would've found the torch! My Willy comes in useful!'

'Do you think it could've been McIver they were after and mistook him for you?'

'It's possible! But we don't look anything like each other.'

'Now we have two groups on our tail!'

'Remember Mony told us to keep away from Blare, Braun and Ztirgeon.'

180 degrees

The Full Circle

'Was it them?'

'Yes and that one ......Horbyn!'

'Think positively, we are all back together Billy is safe now!'

'One thing at a time!'

A knock came on the door and Nurse Rose came in. 'Right boys times up, but would you all like to watch Dr Who in my lounge? I can make some tea and there are some biscuits!'

'Yes please!' They all shouted and trooped in. Miss Rose brought in the refreshments and turned on the TV, it was the return of the Cyber men, and was tense! Frightening to say the least. 'Hey Billy, what you doing behind the settee?'

The program finished all too quickly as the boys left to go back to Brecon.

An Upper prefect pounced on Larry for having his hands in his pockets.

'100 pd, 2 shillings or 50 press ups! You choose!'

He chose the press ups to the disgust of the prefect.

'You too!' Not just content with Larry he gave Walter the same punishment.

'Why? I didn't have my hands in my pockets!'

'You just happened to be there and now you will do 100 press ups for insubordination!'

Back in Conway, the others were keen to know about Billy and were relieved he was ok and even more relieved that he would be available for the match on Sunday. There was confidence in them all growing by the day. 'Put the wedge under the door tonight. Let's take no chances.' It wasn't necessary. A sound sleep was had by all. The bugle sounded and a rush came, everybody was up, the run, the shower, all went without incident.

After breakfast the bus taking the 1st xv to Dunsforde departed and could see Beefy Bill with thumbs up followed by a clenched fist as the coach went down the front drive, a big green coach with panoramic windows, morning classes followed. English, Maths, Latin, break, and then double Scripture finished off the morning. No teams were at home that day so the boys headed for the Myrtle Wood to find Hairy Dan, but no use, so they headed up the Brook past the pools and retrieved the rope and corrugated iron deciding it would be good to use Billy's idea and strengthen the Lady Rose, but she was still near the lagoon so they had to find a safer place, nearby and they would bring her back later. On the way down they noticed smoke in the distance and headed towards it, it was Dan's shack. Charlie had gone back along the lake side road so it was just and Larry now. 'Hi Boys! How are things? I heard about the events today is Billy ok?'

'Yes he's fine we've brought you some grub!' With the word grub out ran Wolfie meowing with delight! 'Come in, come in! Let's have a cup o char!' They sat around the fire warming themselves; it was the first time Dan had invited them in, telling Dan what had happened. 'Hmmmmmm…..! Those boys ran past me and asked if I'd seen anyone but there were only 3.'

'Only 3, there were 4 up the Brook!'

Wolfie tucked into the meet Larry had given him, purring as he did so whilst Dan chomped on the cheese and onion pie they had brought. 'Oh Dan we got to the Island of the Gulls! And we found the letters *naſppn.* Took some doing and we saw the Beastie again!'

'Good lads, have you seen the star lately? Let me know when you do!'
'What's it all about Dan?'
'You'll know soon enough!'
'You coming to the match?'
'Maybe I'll cycle round with Wolfie!'
With that the boys headed back, changing their route as they did so in case they were being followed. 'Let's see if we can catch a fish for Dan!'
'What with?'
'Our hands stupid! Come one of the Myrtle Pools is nearby!'
Larry and Walter headed for the Pool. They would be safe there with easy passage back to the school. 'Look at that big thing Cobber!' In the pool was a big fish, quickly jumped into the water, the fish going through his hands like a goalkeeper having a ball go between his legs. Larry then jumped in and they had it cornered, a stare out commenced when the fish turned about and jumped over the rocks. Its intention seemed to be to land in the smaller pool below and away!! It fell short trapping itself in the rocks they had it! Larry picked up a rock and SMACK! The fish was dead.
'It's a Salmon!'
'Can't be look at those gnashers!' It was a Pike. Lugging the big fish up to the big pool the boys suddenly saw a reflection and on looking up on the other side of the Brook it was Horbyn.
'Come here!' He growled but without a word they took flight taking their catch with them. They had a head start and headed across the Myrtle Wood where they knew there was a path there. They could hear splashing behind them! He was in hot pursuit but they were in the lead and came to the expected path. 'Does that guy never give up? Who's he trying to impress? You two go that way; I'll go that way with the fish! At least one of us has a chance!'
'Ok Cobber!' So they split with no idea who he would follow. Exhausted, with his fish up his jersey Larry slowed down to a crawl, when suddenly he could hear running steps behind him, turning around; Horbyn was no more than 30 yards from him. Suddenly from in front of him he heard a familiar voice,
'Now MacCloon what are you doing here?' Larry had never been so happy to hear that voice!
'Nothing Sir, just out for a stroll!'
'Have you been fishing?'

'No sir!' But suddenly he realised that there was this big fish tail sticking out of his sweater! Flapping away. It was still alive!

'Hmmmmmmm! What have we here MacCloon? My o my this is a big one!' The Head pulled out the fish and tucked it under his arm. 'I'll take that, no poaching allowed up in the Flaxden Brook it's against the law!'

'Sorry sir!'

'Now off you go!'

'Thank you sir!'

'WAIT! MacCloon! What do you want as a punishment?'

'A punishment Sir?'

'Yes, for stealing this lovely fish! You can have the Headmasters Chair or....'

'Yes Sir?'

'Or you can write me a poem!'

'I'll take the poem Sir!'

'The title is Flaxden Brig as seen through the eyes of a Novus!'

'Yes Sir, thank you Sir!'

'AND! One more thing MacCloon, where are your lines? And where are Odhiambo's and Flannigan's?' The lines..........they had all forgotten to do their lines. 'My desk the day after tomorrow! Along with your poem!'

Larry headed back down the track nervously looking over his shoulder every now and again. The Head saw this and wondered. 'He's running from something! Has he gone beyond the West Bridge?' And with that he also headed back down the track, the fish tucked under his arm as yet ran ahead of him.

Back at Brecon, Larry was relieved to see Walter had safely arrived. 'Where's the fish Cobber?'

'Mental Pete got it! Horbyn came after me, nearly got me, I was lucky running in to Pete! Never saw him again, couldn't see where he went. They really want something from us!'

'I don't know, but things are getting complicated all by themselves. Hey has Charlie told you what he saw earlier?'

'Never mind that! Pete wants our lines and I have to write a poem for him!'

That night they made a start on their lines and helped Larry with his poem.

'Pete must like poetry!'

'There! What do you think?'

The boys read Larry's effort. 'An excellent collaborates!'

360 degrees Michaelmas

FLAXDEN BRIG AS SEEN BY A NOVUS

AH WHAT GLORY IN THAT BUILDING
SEE HOW TALL ITS SPIRALLING TOWERS
WITH *its* SECRET ROOMS
HOW FINE ITS LAWNS
WHAT INSPIRATION GROWS
WITHIN ITS WALLS
CAREFUL LAD YOU'RE GETTIN' MAUDLIN!
AH, OUR WEARY MINDS ARE A WONDERING
NOW WE ARE ONCE AGAIN A MERE CHILD
THE PLAYING FIELDS
THOSE JOYOUS PATHS
THE ROLLING HILLS
A DENSE WOOD
ARE THEY PERHAPS THE ROAD TO
UNDERSTANDING
Cobber MacCloon

'That is superb! Couldn't have done better myself!'
'Think he'll like it? Think you'll have to remove the Cobber bit!'
'By the way Billy, he wants those lines too! Anyway what were you going to tell me?'
He hadn't heard so told him about seeing Pete's dog Jet running off with a whole cooked chicken in its mouth. Stolen from Miss Daphne's kitchen. It was going to be part of the dinner for the Arch Deacon tomorrow! Well now he had the fish! No wonder he was happy and lenient, he now had a

fish supper for his guest whilst they were having cauliflower soup, beef stew and a pear.

'Get something for Dan.'

'What about the film? It's Magnum Force.'

The boys piled over the bridge to the gym and queued, the 1st xv were conspicuous by their absence and as Cozy Powell's Dance with the Devil blasted out they took their places at the front. 'Heard anything about the Firsts yet?' Shakes of the head all round as the music faded and the projector clicked into life as the music came through the speakers and a big gun appeared on the screen, with the voice of Dirty Harry giving a full description of the weapon and its capabilities. About half way through there was an intermission, unusual, not today; everyone turned around it was the return of the first team. They had won 14-15! A tremendous roar went up as the team took their places at the front. Puss Whiteford led the way, smoothing his flowing locks with his hand as he proudly lead his men in an impromptu victory parade.

'Brilliant!' Larry directed his congratulations towards the three coaches who were behind them. Puss, Cats and Beefy ignored them, they were heroes to all! 'Should we tell them about Billy?'

''Is there anything they can do?'

'No not now.'

'Then they don't need to know do they?' All agreed, all they could do was wait and see. The film continued with Dirty Harry winning but only just. Theme One then blasted out to indicate that the film was over and in boisterous mood everyone left the gym. It was cold outside, it didn't matter and they were all pleased that they had their thick duffle coats. It was a clear sky and suddenly looked up and above the school building he could see the star high in the sky. 'Cobber see that? But don't point, we're being watched! Blare and Braun are over there.'

'Yes I see it! It looks to be East, in between those two hills.'

'Mark it on your map. Come on we can go to Dan tomorrow!'

'Just saw him cycle up the track, do you think he was watching the film?'

'Look its Ztirgeon and Horbyn coming this way!'

'Quick there's Spy, get close to him so they can't touch us!'

So they shadowed Spy, Dr Wallace the botanical genius of the community and the head projectionist. It was down to him that they could see a film at all. The two gave them a wide berth,

There was a big match for the Novus the next day. 'Let's get some sleep! Lucky Billy in there!' As the passed the San, 'Wonder if Nurse Rose is reading him a bedtime story!'
'Better still a bed bath!'
Nobody could get to sleep that night, the excitement and a simmering of adrenalin, and just as they were getting to sleep the door flung open, it was the whole of the second form, the lot! Frozen in their beds taken totally by surprise when WHAM! Walter was hit by a hard pillow, filled with books, the rest belt in hitting the others at will, some had rocks in, others rugby boots, 'There that'll soften them up, think they're smart don't they!' It was Troup. As they piled out of the dorm, it was over before anyone one knew what was going on or had happened. 'See you this afternoon!' Leaving the dorm Larry said after a prolonged silence. 'I think they are worried! Their guerrilla tactics won't work on us!' Nobody uttered a word, they were shell shocked thinking the worst was over it had all come back suddenly with a vengeance 'I want my Mum!' Said Darnley who was nursing a swelling on his forehead the size of a boiled egg.
'Here have this!' Said Charlie as he broke off a large icicle from the window.
They all dressed, made their beds, instructed everyone to leave the dorm together, keep together all today, it was important that they do that. So they all went down for breakfast and sat together. The Lowers were staring at them trying to frighten them, don't look, carry on, start chatting to each other. BONG! Leave together. Go to letter writing together. Supervised by Mzeee.

Flaxden Brig

Dear Mum and Dad,

It has been another exciting week here and although I miss you all, I have 3 very good friends here, Larry, Billy and Charlie, we are constantly with each other, and have a great time exploring the woods, climbing trees and yesterday we caught a big fish which was confiscated by the headmaster! His dog had stolen a chicken that was supposed to be for the Arch Deacons dinner today as he will be here today to consecrate the Chapel which has now been completed. Did you know it had been converted by the boys/? We seem to construct everything here. We were going to try and cook it for ourselves somehow! It will soon be half term but my friends have nowhere to go, would it be ok for them to come and stay with us? Larry and Billy live overseas and Charlie's family are away somewhere.

I must go now we have a game of rugby this afternoon against the Lowers and tonight there is a Service by the Arch Deacon.

Walter

Posting his letter he headed for the dining room and took his seat. BONG! It is announced that the match will kick off at 2 pm. The food arrived, the usual Sunday roast, beef, roast potatoes, veg and gravy. All too quickly the meal was over. They headed for the Top o'th' Banks, a quick chat, the rest of the school headed for bed rest. 'Hey!' It was Beefy Bill calling them over. 'Get the Novus together and go to the gym you'll change there!' The boys headed back to Conway and got their kit together. They all headed to the gym.

225 degrees

'Where's Billy? He should be here by now, are they keeping him in?' The boys changed, there were a screech of brakes as the familiar sound of the Ambo came to a halt, and in came Cats, Beefy and Puss effortlessly carrying a huge hamper. They gathered round curiously, it's the 1st xv blue shirts! All neatly folded, cleaned from the day before, and every Novus was handed a shirt by the 3 mentors. 'You deserve this after your efforts! If we could we would award you full colours! You have all proved your conduct on and off the field! You can and you will do it! You have the bulk of Flaxden Brig against you, including most of the first team but you

have the spunk in you and we are behind you all the way!' The boys listened as Puss addressed them.
'GIVE THEM HELL NOVUS!!' That was all he needed to say.
'By the way where is Odhiambo?' Asked Beefy Bill.
'In the San.'
'Hmmmmmm! Only 12 now. Not good odds fellas.'
Pulling on the jerseys, even though far too big, baggy on some, the boys felt a sense of pride. Each ran their fingers over the embroidery on the breast. It felt so good. 'Come Let's go now.' As the team filed out each got a slap on the back from the coaches. But there was still no Billy. As they jogged towards pitch 2 they see boys milling about and descending on the banks and the other side of the pitch. It looks like the whole school was turning out! The Ambo arrived, with the crew standing by the side, stretchers, gas bottle, oxygen, nitrous oxide and a large bag with bandages, splints sticking out and a bucket of water with a large sponge bobbing up and down in it. Some of the crowd were jeering and hissing but there was the odd, 'COME ON LADS!' No sign of the Lowers, no sign of Billy. There was a hush around as Whiteford strode over to the Novus. '12 against 26? Not much of a contest.' They gathered around the towering Colossus, he was silent for a moment. 'You have all walked the walk and not talked the talk, do not over complicate things, be yourselves, now see to this day!' He about turned smoothing his hair with the palm of his hand and headed towards Cattell and Fecitt standing behind the posts. The Lowers led by Monroe appeared to roars and cheers, waving and smiling at their support, all 26 of them took to the field, eyeballing the Novus. It looked like lambs to the slaughter. Surely they couldn't all be playing at once. No they can't. Big Jim strutted on to the field and blew his whistle.
'CAPTAINS!' Mony ran to the centre, the Novus didn't have a captain.
'Who'll be the Captain? You Walter?'
'No! You go Charlie!'
'No we're all the Captain here!'
'You go McIver! Take the toss!'
'Just shake hands?'
'Yes and say heads before Mony does, get an edge!'
He accepted went to centre, held his hand out to Monroe, who was taken aback but tentatively accepted. It was not that long ago they had met in different circumstances. 'Heads!' Shouted McIver.

'Yes! Heads!' Toss won.
'You can choose.' McIver said to Monroe.
'Lowers will kick down.' There was a slight incline. Nurse Rose appeared. She was looking after them. Masters appeared, more boys, and then more, everyone seemed to be there. Atmosphere built then suddenly Billy arrived in the nick of time. Big Jim blew the whistle. GAME ON! Larry kicked off. Lowers catch, run straight through and score! 4-0 then 8 then 12. The weary Novus stood behind the goal line. 'Cripes! We've had it!'
'Don't give up! Come boys think of all those early mornings you'll get to be a laughing stock. I'm embarrassed why did we help this lot. Come on Let's do something!' Shouted Beefy Bill standing behind the goal, with Puss and Cats.
Walter takes the ball, kicks! It is taken by Pearson who kicks up in the air. 'That'll scare em!' shouted someone from the crowd.
The ball headed down to Stevenson, he catches sidesteps one, dummies another. 'RUN STEVIE RUN!' He darts through an opened up gap, passes to Charlie and is flattened. 'PLAY ON!!' Screamed Big Jim. The ball goes to Holt to Gibson he sidesteps, shrugs a tackle and kicks into the corner pick up by MacCloon, he scores in the corner.
'Wow Stevie! Great sidestep!'
'Sidestep, I was bricking myself! I just wobbled!'
Monkey kicks off, Billy catches and sprints off.
'Billy the corner!' THWAP! Ball goes high to the corner Billy catches. He scores! Silence, a few feeble cheers for the Novus. 'See we can score if we move fast!' Ball comes back Larry catches, gets tackled by 4 at once. CRUNCH! Ball goes loose, picked up by passes to Darnley, quick pass, Darnley throws anywhere in panic Monkey catches and intercepts. He scores! Heads down they trooped behind the line.
'You've done it once you can do it again. Big effort now, big effort.' Puss advises them in a quiet voice. Restart, Kerr takes, THWAP! Clobbered by McIver! Ball goes loose booted on by Laing picked up by MacCloon passes to Billy it's a try under the posts! Under the posts! kicks 16-10 the Lowers lead. Whistle goes for half time the tired boys clump together. Monroe makes 5 substitutions, oranges come on, and Beefy comes on. Talks to the Novus. 'Speed of player to the ball wins this, remember you can do it, you have the advantage. Keep the ball away from their big men, keep at it! Win the crowd they are turning.'

Kick off catches passes the ball to Billy on the and off he went down the line when a foot comes out from the side, it's one of the three Uppers, Ztirgeon, hissing at Billy as he went flying,
'Here boy have a banana!' Said Braun, throwing the fruit at Billy. The crowd laughs, Billy got up but he had lost the ball and picks up the banana, mimics the banana as a banjo, unpeels it and eats, sticking his thumb up at them, 'CHEERS FELLAS!' The crowd go into spontaneous raptures. Scrum down near the Lowers line the Novus are pushed off the ball too quickly, too light, too small but the ball spins loose as Laing gets a toe to the ball and hacks it on, Billy picks up and he scores! As he ran down the touchline to cheers he passed Braun and Blare, breaking into song,

♫

A BANANA A DAY

HELPS YOU WORK REST AND SCORE!!!

'A big THANK YOU from the Banana Gang!' Their faces were purple with rage at this. 16-14 kick missed! 4 more substitutes made. Bodies are tiring' a free for all follows, Kerr gets sent flying gets up and lamped Larry in front of Big Jim, who grabbed him by the ear 'OFF!' Growled in his ear. 'Not on MY pitch BOY!!' Kerr is off. 12 against 13 now, the odds are getting better. Troup has the ball' Charlie tackles him ball and man lifts him up and runs fireman's lift style 10 yards SPLAT! As Troup lands heavily, winded, gasping for air the ball went loose picked up by , long pass to Darnley, to Gibson, to Holt, Stevenson, Digweed, McNut, Odhiambo who grubbers, picked up by MacCloon, a sidestep ball to McIver, Bowles, Thom, Melton inside to Bartholomew he catches it. 'RUN RUN!' He runs but as he's running his shorts fall down, wriggling down his legs to his ankles and he falls over ball goes out. Pearson takes it charges head on at Melton, THWAP! What a tackle! Melton's shoulder smacked on to Pearson's thigh. Mad Mac takes the ball heads for the posts at speed, through 1 then 2 then 3 a clear run Monkey and Mony converge on him one round the waist one round the chest ball went back gathered by Laing passes between his legs Larry takes a drop kick, it goes over between the posts 3 points! A cacophony of cheers goes up! 16-17 the

Novus are ahead. they think. They run back, Pearson is limping badly, Troup flat out on the floor and Kerr sat by the side of the pitch head in his hands. Whistle goes. Cheers all around, they lead! Their three coaches punch and jump in the air! 'You see that Puss?!! All of them handled the ball within a minute! Wait! Just watch this!' A roar goes up around.
Troup knocks on for the Lowers on the 25 yard line, sensing a chance Larry picks the ball up, passes to Flannigan, showing lightning acceleration running on to the ball, flicks an off load onto Billy as he is tackled, Billy dummies but the ball goes go to ground, MacCloon kicks on soccer style for Mad ma c to swoop and pick up he scores! Under the posts, it took all of 16 seconds!
The Novus_are now defending too narrowly their inexperience is beginning to show, Monroe drops deeper spotting the Novus pushing up the centre channels. MacKay stays on the right touch line knowing the quick pass is coming. The ball is sent high over the oncoming defence, he catches he scores!
'This is end to end stuff Puss! What do you think?'
'Hmmmmmm! They have potential Cats!' Replied Whiteford as he smoothed down his hair.
Stevenson passes to McIver he draws both Paterson and Kerr. The ball is dropped. Quick ball from the scrum, Digweed feeds Larry using Billy as a dummy runner, 3 Lowers fall for it but Larry passes behind Billy to. Stevie is first to Walter's left but does not get the ball instead his presence attracts Troup, leaving a gap for Mad Mac to loop around. Mad Mac passes to Gibson who draws Churches the last the defender and puts the scissoring Stevie through!
Line out on the 25. Melton throws in to Doig at the front, down to Digweed off the top. Digweed feeds a quick pas to Flannigan who feeds MacCloon and loops round, Stevie runs inside decoying Monroe and MacKay between Flannigan and Digweed combination before spinning out a long pass to Odhiambo who passes to the hurtling Stevie, it's falling apart not it's not! What a helter skelter! Stevie stumbles but picks up the ball in one movement. Everyone on the pitch stops to admire as he swoops the ball off the turf. He make ground slipping an inside pass to Mad Mac charging down the left wing handing off the any Lowers in his path. The crowd falls silent as McNut is tackled by 4 of the Lowers in a crunching pincer movement. A ruck forms, Billy plays scrumhalf and hits

Bartholomew who lumbers but his carry allows Digweed back. The Novus sense the line Digweed to Flannigan to MacCloon, a long pass to Odhiambo; he has Gibson backing him... Again McNut is there, takes the ball before finding Billy again but he still had plenty to do...
RUN BILLY! RUN! And he simply bulldozes his way through crashing by Troup and the despairing Kerr touching the ball down. Score! It must be all over now!
'WOW! SCOOP LOOP AND SWOOP! WHAT A GAME! Did you see that BEEFY?'
'Sure did Cats! GET YOU A CRATE OF TC FOR THAT ONE NOVUS!'
'Sure did Cats! Look look!! Look at Pete he's dancing around the Yew Tree! Even Dochan Do!!! They are doing THE DOCHAN DO!' Sure enough an unbelievable sight could be seen at the bottom of the banks. It was electric! All but four were ecstatic. The boys collapsed to the floor as the final whistle went.
'One minute boys.' Said Big Jim. 'I'm afraid I got the scores mixed up in all this excitement, the Novus lost by one point. NOVUS 16 LOWERS 17.' The coaches came over; the Novus were surrounded by the crowd. 'Don't worry lads the score doesn't matter! Great stuff out there! Great match!' What a day! Over on the other side was Dan with his bike, a little black head appeared out of the basket, it was Wolfie! They had both come to watch. looked over and nodded in their direction. Bloodied and bruised they left the field. The four were no longer to be seen. All shook hands, Mony and Monkey come over, they are accepted now, with a slight no backing down, the Troup, Kerr and Pearson shook hands they have met their match, equality but explain it is the senior boys pulling their strings, they had been the bullies in Brecon before and still had a hold. The house needs to stick together they could break it this way; these 4 have been at it for a long time, what can be done?
'What are you four up to?'
'Nothing we just like playing in the Myrtle Wood.' No they didn't take the beer and cigarettes from the Blue Huts and they didn't know who the 4th person was, except he was new and called Horbyn, nor did they know who had set the fire at the boatsheds but they were convinced that they were trying to be framed for it. A new found alliance was forming when Big Jim came in with Beefy, Cats and Puss. 'Great stuff out there this afternoon

Men, I was pleased this happened, the trial is now over I can now start on a team for your first match! Good job!!' Congratulating the whole of Brecon.
'Match?'
'Yes, when you come back from your break you have a game against Mumblemond! The whole house is in the squad now.'
Mony tells the Novus Mumblemond are a tough team don't like Flaxden Brig and have not been beaten for years. They won't play at the Brig so we have to go there! But it's a day out and we all get to stop at the chipper on the way back! Last year they hammered us.
Supper was enjoyed that night, for the first time since arriving the boys mixed with the whole of the house, there were no bullies here, Walter next to Kerr, Larry next to Troup and Billy next to Pearson. There were no apologises for the past but a veiled admiration for what they had shown that day. 'That was some tackle by Digweed! And that tackle on Pearson! Wow!'
'And the speed of Odhiambo! Wow! He goes like BillyO!'
'Hey Billy! Your nickname!'
'What's that?'
'BillyO!' And it stuck!
'Where is it you guys go? Everybody wonders.' They all glanced at each other.
'Just up the Flaxden Brook, exploring! Its fun and we can climb trees!' Said Larry innocently.
'But why all the secrecy?'
'What about Blare and his cronies?'
'Keep away from them, ever since they were given authority they changed and we will now. They are menaces! But there will be a backlash! We'll all have to watch out. They even change our Lower Logs. Easy to do when it is mostly tick boxing.'
BONG! Just in the nick of time the gong went and the Head walked in. Commending the Novus and all of Brecon on their achievements that day, and could see the pace, passion and power from both sides, he reminded them of their special guest that day and that full uniform with, clean, polished shoes were to be worn and that there was to be an inspection. The Service proceeded with an atmosphere, a good end to a good day. The boys headed to the Top o'th' Banks, their private meeting place, but it wasn't really that private, and they could be clearly seen. 'Hey look there is the

star, the same place as last night.' They needed to go and tell Dan about this. 'Mark it down Cobber!' Larry pulled out a crumpled piece of paper from his sporran and sketched the direction of the star. Yes East, Billy gazed out towards the other side of the lake. 'Come on BillyO! We'll get over there sometime. The Lady Rose will get us there!'

'Yes we can use the stuff we got from that den to make her more seaworthy, besides I'd like to go back to the island someday.' The week ahead had now become very busy.

That night there were no beatings, no mischief, a shield seem to be protecting the Brecon. Even George looked fast asleep in his position at the top of the boot room rack. Nor was there a bugle in the morning yet everyone seemed to gather on time for the morning run, all ran, mixing shoulder to shoulder, together, some thought a sudden surprise would happen as they ran by Sperrin House but nothing did, nobody was shoved down the banks or deliberately tripped up, just a couple of snide remarks from the dorms above, sounded like Ztirgeon maybe all three? Another banana was thrown in Billy's direction, 'CHEERS! I'll have that at break time! Saves me 1d!' Housework, breakfast nobody late, Chapel then, Latin, Geography and Maths. At break Walter and Larry queued at the Tucky, nobody pushed in; each taking their turn at last Walter could buy something, a bottle of TC, a Marathon bar and a bag of Golden Wonder crisps, salt and vinegar. Not much change left out of 2 shillings still he still had £2 and 15 shillings in the house bank, plus the rest of the money his Dad had given him. Walter and Larry sat down on the steps by classroom 8 and were soon joined by Charlie and Billy. When suddenly a commotion blew up on the other side of the quadrangle.

'Dull it isn't!' Commented Larry, as they all looked in the direction of the noise. 'What's going over there?' They had not been that way before but in the midst of a group of boys they could see another boy being dragged along the ground. 'Hey look! What's going on? They are dragging Horbyn! Shall we ring the bell?'

'No don't let's watch a while! Can you see Blare, Braun and Ztirgeon?' The boy was then ceremoniously flung into some water in a big splash,

'YOU SODS!' Screamed Horbyn, his shouts could be heard all around the classroom block. 'Hey Monkey what's that all about?'

Monkey was passing by with Mony. 'It's his birthday! Anyone whose birthday it is gets bunged into Magillycuddy Pond on his birthday! Thought you knew that!'

'I hope he can swim! Let's check it out before we go to lunch!' With that they went into the class for double English! Walter glanced out the window and he could see the large wooden hut structure diagonally opposite, 'What's in there?' his curiosity was now insatiable, into overdrive! He'll find out later he thought to himself as he opened his poetry book. After class they crossed the quadrangle and up a little slope to find the scene at break. There was a little summer house at the top and below were two ponds full of water, this is where the ducking had taken place.

'I'm glad it's not my birthday when I'm here!'

'Me too!'

'Mine was 23rd of August.' Said Charlie!

'But you'd be ok anyway, you're not in Magillycuddy!'

'Will do him some good!' It was all in good taste and harmless.'

'We'll have to think of something for you Charlie!'

'Oi! What are you lot doing? That is out of bounds! It is my turf!'

'Your turf what do you mean?' It was Blare!

'Your turf what do you mean?' Repeated Larry.' This isn't Harlem! You are in Sperrin.'

'Quick Pete's over there! Quick scarper!'

The all ran to the dining room just in time for grace. There was an unusual harmony about the place and it was welcomed as the boys recovered from their recent exploits. It was to be short lived! 'What is that music?' Asked Darnley again at bed rest. 'BLUE DANUBE WALTZ!' Shouted the rest of the dorm.' 'Why is that on all the time?' The boys changed and headed down to the pitch and Charlie whispered to. 'That's strange. Every time you have pointed out the star, Blue Danube Waltz music pipes through at bed rest.'

'Really?'

'And another thing.'

'Yes?'

'The bullying escalates at the same time.'

'Hmmmmmm....I see!'

'Yes, check for yourself next time!' Commented Charlie.

With that they arrived on the pitch. No rugby today just a big work out Big Jim wanted them fit for their big match. It seemed to go on forever with the finale being the sprint the full length of the two pitches. This time there was no punishment for the last one to finish and a sense of relief, there was a metamorphism taking place, a strength developing and it was welcomed. They changed, had afternoon tea, broken only by a scream when one of the Upper boys poured hot tea down another boys back, Blare had done it to someone not playing ball, the bullying hadn't stopped there but it had in Brecon. Gordon Ghylly in his hobnailed boots chased the culprit out of the dining room and as the crowd dispersed; Horbyn appeared gazing in the direction of Walter and his friends.

'Got a problem Horbyn? You still Blare's flunky?' Said Billy laying down their challenge, as Horbyn looked to the ground and started to walk away.

'We'd better not go to the Brook now or he'll follow.'

'We have to see Dan, we saw the Star last night.'

'Ok we'll go after supper there will be time before prep.' And so they did but this time they were followed. 'They are behind us. Horbyn perhaps?' No he had found someone else to pick on. 'It must be those Uppers. Double back, can't risk Dan being found by them.' The next day they went over the Brook knowing they couldn't be followed and eventually found Dan. 'Good match boys well done. 'As they handed a tray of food for him and Wolfie who dashed by with a mouse in his mouth, the mouse already dead from one bite to the back of the neck, dropping it down at Dan's feet, proudly showing off his kill. Double meal for him tonight!

'So what have you all been up to?'

'Well we saw the star Saturday night and Sunday night, at an East bearing as we face the lake in between those two hills yonder.

'I see.'

'Yes and there is one more thing. Yes, every time we see the star, Blue Danube Waltz is piped through the speakers at bed rest.'

'Hmmmmm! Interesting! Well now you must head down the lake and face the valley between the two hills and look for the Flaxden light. At this point you will see its actions and then you will find another clue and keep a clear eye, in front, behind, to the left, to the right at all times.'

'Do we have to cross the lake, we have the Lady Rose now and she is solid, ship shape,'

'No need this time. You head down the lake road until you get level and see the light but you must do it by tomorrow night, be quick. Then come back to me.'

'Dan what is this all about?'

'I will tell you more next time.'

The boys headed back with no interruptions, straight to the prep room. Their books had been taken there by the rest of the form.

'I want to get to the tower top again so I can get this map into more detail, anyone game?'

'Yes I think we should Cobber, remember the last time those legs we saw? We should look and see who wears shoes and trousers like that, pretty distinctive you know. Cobber Let's get up on the roof in the morning, nobody is around that time and it will be clear. Charlie and Billy will you be look outs? We'll go on the roof and take Joe's ladders!' It was agreed. The boys got up early and crept around the back by the old milk parlour where they had fallen the week before. Charlie and Billy positioned themselves at strategic points as they hauled the ladders against the side of the building. Eventually they arrived at the wooden planks and opened the trap door in to the tower. It was a clear day and Larry pulled out his map and drew all the points as near and as far as he could see.

'Done. Let's go down and see what's there. We might be able to find that secret room.'

'No, there isn't time!'

'Where's your sense of adventure?'

'But what about Billy and Charlie, looking out for us?'

'They'll be ok won't take long!' So they crept down the narrow corridor and slowly opened the door. Nobody there, but the table was uncovered and the balls are scattered about and two cues were on the side.

'Hey let's have a go!'

'No, no time for that!'

'Aww come on! So they had a quick play. Then footsteps were heard along the corridor and the boys dived under the table. A man walked in and went over to the bookcase took a book and headed out. It was one of the same shoes as before, brogues and turn ups. The door closed no click or key turning. The two boys looked at each other. 'Let's get out of here while the going is good!' Scrambling they heard two sets of footsteps and they dashed for the other door. Where can this go? Just as they closed the door.

Two men now entered. In the darkness Walter put his ear to do door Larry looked through the keyhole. Straining they hear the men say they are getting closer to completion, soon they will know definitely. Larry could clearly see the two men but only their backs. The men left the room switching the lights off as they left. Pausing, the boys stood upright and Larry moved to the side when the floor gave way and half of him vanished below, Walter grabbed him. They heard below him the unmistakable voice of the Head,

'Hey boy!! Come down NOW!!!' And suddenly swish! It was Flash that they could hear but the legs and cane could not connect.

'Pull me up! Pull me up!' And Walter with all his strength hauled his friend back up and they scarpered through the door. The other door was unlocked and they headed through it. As they reached the end they heard another set of running footsteps. It was Pete heading for the snooker room. Quickly they ran down the stairs and hid in the telephone booth. They saw the head coming down but he went straight past. They followed behind, he couldn't see them and they climbed out of a dining room window. Billy and Charlie saw them and they headed back to the sanctuary of Brecon. Job done!

'Boy I love this place! It's...............so exciting!'

At breakfast the Head walked in. BONG! 'I am today putting all corridors in the main building out of bounds to all boys.' At the Top o'th' Banks the boys met and Larry told them his story and they all laughed. Tonight they needed to get to that point but how?

'Well we can borrow some bikes.'

'Against the rules, junior house not allowed bikes till the summer term, Billy!'

'Only said we would borrow. I always put things back!' Billy piped up

'I know.'

'No we are not stealing or making them! No If we are quick we can borrow the bikes, cycle there and back within an hour, we can skip supper, ask the others to bring us some grub back, the bikes, well there is one outside the dairy block, I think that is Boot Jarvis's, he'll have had a few whiskies by then so that will be ok, Grappy is Master in Charge so his bike is up at his classroom, Neville's bike will be at Daphne's house, he will be having his supper there, and doing a piano and flute duet with her.'

'But that is only three,'

‘Neville’s is a tandem; saw him on it leaving the match on Sunday. Probably heading for Daphne’s place.’ After a brief argument it was decided who was riding what, Larry and Billy each had a bike and Walter and Charlie the tandem, who consequently argued who would be front and back.

‘At the sound of the BONG! We go. One at a time or in the case of you two, two!’

‘Ha ha, very funny! Use some excuse in minute intervals, pour tea down your shorts-you’ll be ok because it’s never very hot, feel sick, and need the loo. Sit at different tables, now we’re all buddies should be easy! Piece of cake!’

The time came Walter left first said he felt sick, Charlie said he would go with him just in case. Two minutes later Larry went accidentally knocked his cold mug of tea over himself and finally Billy leaving claiming that he was still feeling unwell after his sleepwalking and wanted to see the Nurse. All bikes were commandeered and they hightailed it down the back drive as fast they could pedal Larry and Billy ahead, Charlie and Walter bringing up the rear. Soon they had reached the point where the valley between the two hills was and they waited, and waited. Then a light appeared, a small sun like figure, a small ball of fire coming towards them.

‘See that?’ Yes they could and straight towards them, across the lake skimming along, just like Walter remembered doing with his brothers at the seaside with slate like stones. It was an amazing sight, it then hovered in front of them for a second and hurtled up and back in between the valley.

‘What do you make of that?’

‘I can’t see anything, what have we come here for, a goat chase?’

‘It’s a Goose chase Billy!’

‘Quick we’d better go!’ As the boys turned they look around. Next to the road was a stone litter bin with the letters *qcnnin* on it.

‘That must be it, write it down on the back of the map Larry and let’s get back!’

‘Hey look over there what are all those lights? To the left of us on the other side. Must be that girl’s place Billy keeps going on about!’ Billy punched Walter on the shoulder. ‘Better get back.’ The single cyclists arrived back quickly and the tandem two arrived in the nick of time, they could hear Neville and Daphne singing a duet whilst Neville played on his flute and she played the piano, ‘How appropriate! Do you have to fart so much?’ Said Charlie, as he put the tandem back in its place.

After prep they fell on to their beds, talking about their last trip.

‘What do you think? I mean what is all this about? The link between our new friends and Blare and his cronies. The men in the snooker room.’

‘Have any of you seen whose trousers or shoes they belong to?’

‘Hey!’ Larry said.

‘There I was in that little room with my body half in half out, Walter hanging on to me trying to pull me up, my legs dangling there and Pete shouting, ‘Come down boy!’ Whilst he was swishing Flash at me! Narrow escape that! I love this place!’

‘You’ve already told us!’

‘Me too!’

‘And me!’

‘Hmmmmm…. it has potential! Here is a letter for you from home. Mummy kins I think!’ Teased Billy who had not heard from home as he was so far away. opened the letter.

‘Great news fellas you can all come home with me at half term, it’s in two weeks isn’t it?’

‘Think so. That’s great news!’

The next day they went to see Dan. Wolfie greeted them at the door waiting for his treat. Charlie giving him some assorted meat pieces, he gently accepted them. ‘Dan what’s all this about we saw the light and got some more letters *qcnnin*. Heard the Blue Danube Waltz. Can you tell us what this all means?’

‘Well, the disc you have discovered is a cipher from the Confederate Army, a simple and effective way of people communicating in secret. I think there is a message waiting for you all. There are four of you and you will all need a key phrase. Use your names but change your middle names.’

‘There are four of us let’s use Ste, Dave, Nig and Bas!’

The boys proceeded to squabble who was going to have which name.

‘I’ll decide!’ Said Dan. ‘Walter you will have Barry, Billy you have Nigel, Charlie David and Larry you will have Stephen.’

‘Awww! I wanted Barry!’ Moaned Billy. ‘What’s that sound? It’s the Quad! This area is out of bounds just now. Quick let’s go.’

‘No time. You boys at the back I’ll go to the door.’ The Quad rumbled towards Dan’s shack, Dan went to the door Wolfie following by his side, voices were heard. One of them was the unmistakable voice of Aeronaut Fabius the boy in charge of the Emergency Services. Had he seen any boys in the area, any at all? No. Was he sure that no boys been here? No. Well they were under instructions to demolish any dens and places where or which could be used in an illegal way. They thought this den was ok. 'Thank you.' They heard Dan say. The Quad left, it had being doing a purge on all the illegal smoke holes and dens in the area. Who was driving the Quad.? No Masters it was the boy in charge of the emergency Service, Freddie Gibson a fair man who Dan seemed to know.

'But listen boys it is time to go. Come tomorrow and I will endeavour to show you how to use the cipher.' The boys left stroking a grateful Wolfie as they left.

'I'm completely lost here!' Said Larry.

'Puzzled isn't the word. We'll figure it out any or borrow anything; anyway we have the break to look forward to. It'll be fun and if we haven't got over to your imaginary girls Billy I'll introduce you to my sister and her friends! We'll have a great 5 days!' There were only 10 days to wait. They all had permission and were just happy to be together.

'I hope that star doesn't appear had enough of that!' But that was tempting fate. It appeared this time at the back of the right above the forest in an area that they hadn't seen before. 'Larry set your map out, south south west what could be there?'

'We need to be kitted out for all this!'

'What do you suggest Charlie?'

'Well we all have our rugby kits. Two sets actually and our tracksuits are all black, with our boots with have the ideal clothing for moving about quickly and effectively. Double up when it's cold, don't forget we have our duffle coats, balaclavas, scarf and gloves.'

'Yes it is getting a bit parky here. Just shows what we can do keeping it simple! Plus we'll look sleek and cool!'

'Poseur!'

'Let's get ready!'

'We'll have to ask Dan but there is no time there is a track there Let's follow it keeping SSW.'

'Worth a try.' so they headed up there right up the tracks they came to the large lake which they had seen when looking for McIver.

'I hope we don't see the Egg Man!'

'Just follow the path.' Soon the forest dwindled and the path continued up and away. 'This is going on too far the star is here above us.'
'Are you sure that is a star?'
'Course it is!' Looking around they could see hardly anything.
'Look there is a chimney stack on the other side of those trees, let's look!' Wading through the undergrowth they came to a small ruin. It was an old crofter's cottage, a man who looked after the sheep on the estate years ago. Looking around Charlie immediately picked out the letters above the doorway *ntadoavu*. They duly noted it and headed back. At least they didn't have to make anything. But they were late for supper and received the compulsory early morning circuit.
By now it had all become routine. The bullying in the house had stopped apart from the odd niggle, and the Uppers they were so far managing to avoid. They had gone quite quiet, maybe planning something, the morning run seemed to be looked forward to by nearly all, the house work done diligently, the boys had figured out to pay attention in class and do their homework, chapel, games, classes, prep and mealtimes all perfect harmony. Bliss. Boys attended societies learning new skills and disciplines whilst the junior boys had to wait for senior for all that. Big Jim was now relishing the preparation for the Brecon team for their 1st match and another tough workout was coming to an end when frustration boiled up between Troup and Pearson. A punch landed Troup on the side of the head BANG! He retaliated with a head butt in the back of Pearson, winding him up. All this done in front of Big Jim. 'RIGHT! You two I've had enough of this, to the gym! ALL of you! All of Brecon!' This was a big surprise but in silence they did as they were told, was he going to punish them all? They piled into the gym switching the lights on.
'Make a circle all of you.' Big Jim then went into the store room bringing out two sets of boxing gloves, throwing them into the inner circle, which was actually the basketball centre circle he yelled, 'PICK THEM UP AND PUT THEM ON!' The two stunned boys did so, without question. 'Now start boxing, you wanted to fight, so fight. I gave you a choice to play rugby or fight. There will be no rounds, come out of the circle and you will be beaten, fight until somebody loses, now fight!' The two boys came at each other hammer and tongue. Why? They had been such good friends, bullies in arms but that had all been sorted out, but why this sudden anger, had they been got at? Differing opinions? Nobody was cheering, just

amazement, silence as the two slugged it out, at first mimicking the boxers they had seen on TV, guards up, arses wiggling as though it was the customary think to do. The floor was now covered in sweat and splatters of blood, eyes were closing up and the two were now leaning against each other, breathing heavily, exhausted, arms down, rabbit punching against each other's side occasionally the side of the head, finding an extra bit of energy from somewhere, then as if a switch had clicked they came apart swayed in front of each other raised one glove each and aiming a punch at each other hit nothing but air and collapsed on top of each other. Troup then Pearson. In silence Big Jim walked over. 'It's OK! They are still breathing, right now listen you lot, there are no winners here, I am preparing you for a match and you will prepare properly, none of this wanting to fight each other, all the time Let this be a lesson to you all. Now go back and shower, get ready for classes.' The two contestants got to their feet nodded at each other and all headed out.

'Boy it's a tough place here but I'm actually beginning to like it, appreciate things more, take nothing for granted, feeling stronger!'. The comment came from an unexpected source, McIver!

'And I'm losing weight!' Added Blob Paterson.

'Good for you!'

'Hey look over there!' Walter looked over and sure enough there it was the star right above the Fairy Hill looming over the back of the Myrtle Wood.

'We better go and see Dan tomorrow. I'm thinking somehow he is involved in all this. Not telling us everything.' Blue Danube Waltz was again heard at bed rest. It was too much to be a coincidence now. 'I'm getting weary of this. Do you think Dan is some sort of spy? said Larry. 'I think we may be doing work for him!'

'That bearing is due West? Well let's see what Dan says.'

The next day they set off to see Dan and soon they realised they were being followed. Four boys, they up the pace and soon were away traversing the banks of the Brook whilst the other boys were directly above them. It was as though there were two floors, the friends were ducking in undergrowth and did this up past the Myrtle Pools and then above a small water fall they crossed, they still hadn't been seen. Why don't they come this way, one had, and Larry said, the one called Horbyn, but they had given him the slip thanks to Pete, why did they follow what did they want?

In the Clearing they hear the clash of swords,
'Hey it's the fencers let's go and see, maybe they'll let us have a go!' In the clearing they could see a group of Upper boys and two fencers all clad in white duelling. The scene was very atmospheric out in the open, shrouded by the canopy of tall Spruce trees and the two swordsmen were really fighting it out.
'ELA!!!' Shouted one of the duellists. The two stopped, brought their swords up and took off their masks, bring their swords to their salute, bowed and then another two came onto the field.
'Pretty honourable don't you think? Noble, Noble sport, all dressed in white. one is accepting defeat graciously! Think they will let us have a go?' They approach the fencers; their confidence has grown by the day. 'Could we have a go?'
'Have a go? Well you are too young to handle weapons; you have to be in the Uppers to do this art.' This was dè Menthon the fencing Captain.
'Art? I thought that was drawing pictures. It's not fair we're not allowed to do anything!' Protested Walter.
'No, to learn this craft you become an artiste`. But here have a feel of this Sabre, this is what we were using just then, they are now fighting with an epee! Here put the mask on and see how it feels.' Walter put the mask on and took a firm hold of the Sabre. Suddenly he heard
'ON GUARD!!!!' A sharp pain in his back and he turned around. It was Neville Chives, whose tandem they had commandeered the day before, dressed in full gear, all white. 'You seem keen to learn boy what's your name?'
'It's ....er Flannigan.'
'Hmmmm! Yes! I've heard of you! Brecon House So you fancy your chances do you Wally?'
'ELA!!!' Cried out the other fighter. 'Hold on! Flannigan! You take on the winner!' The winner didn't take his mask off. 'Frostwick you are in Flannigan's corner! Give him a briefing at to what to do. Let's see what he's made off.'
'But Sir we are not allowed.'
'Not allowed? I make the rules; here this is my play pen! Now, to your corner, SHARP!' Running through Walter's mind was Shaun Flynn in the Son of Captain Blood, a film he had seen. Six deep breaths Flannigan, he told himself beginning to hyperventilate,

'Go get him!' Shouted his friends.

'Here use my jacket.' Said one of the Uppers. 'You'll need this he's the Champion!' The two duellists met at the centre. Drew their swords. Chives came to the middle.

'You are duelling here as a point of honour and I am here to make sure you settle it that way. There will be no backstabbing. If quarter is asked....'

'NONE will be asked!!' Said Walter's opponent.

'Heck what is he talking about?' As it flashed through Walter's mind

'I only wanted a go.' He trembled.

'We're with you Walter, go get him!!!!' Quickly the duel began and Walter mimicked his foe. The Sabre was heavy as he managed to hold on to it at every strike, it was hot under the mask and he sweated profusely. The foe started to show off and toyed with Walter, the Upper boys started to jeer and cheer. Suddenly Walter lifted his weapon and swept it blindly across his path. His foe had not expected this and was caught unawares, off guard, catching the hilt of his sword s knocked the sword out of his foes hands. There was a silence. 'Finish him off! He's yours!' Walter raised his sword and presses the tip against the foes jacket. 'Go on say it!' He looked and could see Larry mouthing something. 'ELA!!!' He raised his sword and took his mask off and bowed to the fallen. He just lay there. The Uppers started to clap. 'Why are they clapping? They support him!'

'It's because they recognise that you have won fairly. And been lenient in victory! That will teach him to play! He is the Champion, well now he is no longer; you are the official Champion Flannigan. Bit off of a fluke but never mind you won!' Said dè Menthon. 'I will speak to the Head about this and see if you can all have a lesson, now off you go we need to get some practice!' Added Chives. As Walter turned his back the loser got up and lunged at Walter. HORBYN!!!' Shouted Mr Chives. 'Is it not enough that you are beaten that you turn into a backstabber?! Take your mask off and take your defeat! Remember where you are!' No wonder he was reluctant to take off his mask, slowly he takes it off and drops his head starting at the floor in shame. The boys made their way to Dan's place with the latest goodies.

'How did you learn that?'

'I didn't, I got it from watching Shaun Flynn in Son of Captain Blood. I must be a natural! It's in the wrist!'

'Was that not Errol Flynn?'

'No he did Captain Blood. And the Master of Ballantrae. Hey I might take this up. You heard him say he would talk to Pete. What do you think he meant by he is going to speak to the Head?'
'Dunno, but now we're going to have more trouble with Horbyn!'
'Nahhhhhh! He'll be putty in our hands now! That other boy was dé Menthon the fencing Captain, I think he is the real Champion, he'll love to get one up on him! But Blare and his cronies might step up the heat now!'
'Just think what the rest of the Uppers will say and think and you the new champion!'
'No show boating Cobber! Let's get a couple of fish for Dan and Wolfie.'
So they stopped by the pool and managed to catch a couple by hand, they found this easy knowing where to find them under the large rocks or tree branches expanding out into the Brook... Getting to the den they were grateful to see the boys, Wolfie purred around their ankles, calling them into the den, Dan in front of the fire.
'Saw the star last night and followed up the track and after passing a small lake and we came to a ruined croft in the clearing where we saw this letters over the door *ntadcavu*.'
'Good lads, you're learning fast, being resourceful. You found 20 Bell St?'
'Dan is there a meaning to all this? We have uncovered 3 sets of words now for you and are none the wiser. We are beginning to love this place but don't know why we are here.'
'You are here because you are here and you are learning to build with what you have, from first principles.'
'Again Blue Danube Waltz was piped through into Conway and again last night we saw the star, West this time right above the Hairy Hill at the back.'
'Then you must go there to BolyBrack and there will be another set of letters for you.'
'All this is strange Dan. We are always being followed by these Upper boys, Blare, Braun and Ztirgeon. There was another one called Horbyn but I think we have worn him out now.'
'Yes these are the ones you need to fear.'
'The boatsheds were burnt down the Blue attacked, Billy was kidnapped, the cipher, the star, the letters. What's it all about!' Repeated Larry.
'Well boys get to the top of the hill and you will be that bit nearer! Every step you take is a step towards the end point. Come to me when you have

the letters.' They finished their tea and headed away. Wolfie now curled up by the fire, yawned as he preened himself.
'How are we going to do this, you know it is out of bounds it is says so?'
'When has that stopped us, so far?'
'We can't cycle and we can't use the Lady Rose. We'd better check her soon and do some repairs, too much went into that. There is only one problem it will take five hours to do. So we go during the night. Nobody missed Billy till after morning run. Still got that torch Billy?'
'Sure do!'
'Well we have all our kit? We double up on our clothes and socks to keep warm, duffle coat scarves and gloves and rugby boots. Get some extra food from supper tonight, a couple, no, 4 bottles of water use, TC bottles and Bob's your uncle.'
'I've got four empties, was just about to take them to the Tucky for the deposit!'
'No, mine's called Arnold!' Joked Charlie.
'Who is Arnold?'
'My Uncle!'
'About an hour after lights out one by one we leave the dorm but fill your bed up with all your clothes from the lockers.'
'Why?'
'So that it looks like someone is in the bed in case they check. We don't want everyone up looking for us.'
'Right.'
'Then we meet up at the Summer House at the back of Magillycuddy Pond, moving in a group may cause attention but I doubt if anyone is around. If we all get there it's on, if not we are screwed, remember we're all in this together, leave no one behind.'
'Right. And then?'
'We strike while the iron is hot.'
'Like now you mean?'
'No it's just simmering just now,'
'What iron?'
'There isn't any iron!!!!'
'You mean like Bobs not your uncle?' Laughing away, then Blare and Braun appeared, Uppers, eyeballing them 'What are they doing now?' The friends moved on and prepared themselves. Food and drink was put into

two satchels and after lights out one by one they headed for the Summer House, Larry arrived first, then Billy. Then Charlie and finally Walter.' Sorry fellas I went by the San, could see Nurse Rose's figure silhouetted behind her curtains.'
'Did you get a good look?'
'No had to hide behind the Ambo saw Grappy cycling. But she looked great!'
'Grappy is nearby?'
'No he is headed home, we're ok. Come on let's go, sooner there sooner back to bed!'
The boys headed for the McInnis, straight up bisecting the M1 track and eventually coming to the lake.
'This is where we were the other day or was it night I've lost track now. Christ look! The hill's still the same size, we're no nearer. We've only be out 30 minutes keep going.' Soon they had reached the foot of the Fairy Hill, Billy leading with his torch scrambling through peat bogs and masses of clumps of heather. 'We're getting there, let's stop.' So they did taking on some food and water for 5 minutes. 'I can see the summit it's there!', when suddenly a red deer shot across their paths. 'Wow!' Then a grouse flew off. 'Wish I had a gun!'
'If I had a gun I'd shoot you!'
'Shut up guys let's keep moving.'
'No one can hear us! Shit this isn't the summit! It's there miles away! We can't go back come on.'
'Your compass is rubbish you Wally!'
'Don't call me that. Think you can do better yourself, Cobber?'
'Guys! Guys! Stop arguing, let's keep together.' Pleaded Charlie. And all of a sudden there they were on top of the hill. 'Billy search for the letters with the torch we'll rest and take some food.'
'Save some for me. Don't smash the bottles I want the deposits!'
'Don't stray too far it must be here somewhere.' They sat down drinking and eating in quiet whilst the beam of Billy's torch could be seen sweeping the area. 'Can't find anything!'
'Here give it to me!' Demanded Larry, tempers were now beginning to be stretched, they were tiring, he could find nothing, then Walter, then Charlie, no letters. They sat in silence. 'What is this all for?'
'I just don't know, here we are on top of this ....hill.'

'Yep we are sure here. And we don't even know why! We need explanations!' Suddenly the sun came up lighting up to give their stage a panoramic view.
'Wow can you see that?!'
'Yes it's made the trip all worthwhile!' Said an exhausted Charlie sarcastically.
'Yes more hills, forests and lakes. Where do you think Scotland is?' Walter went over to the trig point, a concrete marker to determine the summit and leaned on it, arms folded resting his weary head when,
'Look, by your knee.'
'What?'
'By your knee, look!' There they were, the letters *zwrſſ*! Jubilation, cheers went all round, punching the air, they were on the top of a hill nobody could hear them they could express their Euphoria as loud as they wanted.
'Any water left?'
'Just a bottle.'
'Take a sip and save the rest for on the way down, keep ourselves hydrated, we'd better go now, got about an hour and half left before we are missed, it's downhill all the way, just think of those greasy bacon, sausage and eggs waiting for us at breakfast!'
'It's cornflakes and scrambled eggs today! I looked at the menu yesterday!'
'We have a menu?'
'Yes there is a menu on the notice board every week!'
'Yuck! I'll have just have a piece of toast, tea and cereal! You know I'm beginning to feel better about myself all round.'
'Did you see what's for lunch?'
Quickly the boys made their way down passing down past 20 Bell Street, the small lake, the McInnis and to the back of the summer house.
'Quick inside, look, two men! Think they are looking for us?'
'Dunno. Listen we've got games kit on us. Let's strip down to that, hide our coats, track suits and satchels and get on to the road and pretend we are doing the circuit!'
'Great idea They'll just think it is a punishment.' The boys finished the water stripped down to their shorts and t shirts, 'Brrrrrr its bracing!' Hiding their clothes they headed to the road and started running. They'd done it again! Suddenly there was a well-known figure in front of them it was the Head with Jet by his side.

'HALT!' He put up his hand, 'Now what are you boys doing here at this time of the morning?'
'Doing a circuit Sir!'
'Clockwise? You know you can only do it anticlockwise!'
'Sorry sir won't do it again sir! We have a big match soon sir!'
'Yes I know I'm depending on you! Off you go, keep up the good work! Oh yes and where are those lines I gave you three and that poem MacCloon!? On my desk by tomorrow!'
'Look now we have to do the full circuit!'
'It'll do us no harm come on.' They completed the run, had a shower and headed for breakfast. Not a word was spoken as they chomped down their food. Outside they headed for the Top o'th' Banks.
'I need a rest! No one look at the sky tonight!'
'Yes siree!'
'Copy that!'
'Copy what?'
'That!'
'We now have four letters let's get Dan to show us how to use that cipher, he knows something.'
'Yes, even I think he is behind something, but let's get some rest, thank heavens there are no games today. What's on the agenda?'
'Grappy is taking us somewhere to put up tents. Well show us, should be fun I've not done that before. Is it the whole house?'
'No just the Novus, I think. Out for the night!'
'We can finish our lines then too!'
Classes followed smoothly another shilling was spent at the tuck shop, a little treat shared with others, a dinner of chicken curry was served up with a desert of apple crumble with custard, or was it rhubarb? The plates were cleaned, anything was edible. People would class this as survival but it was only the sensible way to live.
That afternoon they were shown how to erect a tent. Some found it difficult, some easy. These were Force Ten tents and looked pretty good with a fly sheet and groundsheet. That night they were to go up the Brook. They were given rations tea, dried milk, cheese and biscuits, cereal and some dried meat and veg, a Mars Bar and a tiny primus stove. They had rucksacks and sleeping backs told them to pack up and spend the night at a suitable place up the Brook The four boys headed for the Flaxden Pool

area. They would have a couple of hours light left and maybe they could go and see Dan they were sure he would be nearby. They had been given a torch so had two now.

'Bring your radio Walter we can have some music!'

'Yes we might get a connection.' Fully loaded they all headed off shadowed by Grappy they noticed, which was good. Maybe they would be left alone. Blare's lot wouldn't approach with him there, too lazy anyway. They needed the break. Lord knows. Finding a spot they pitched up. They made a bed of ferns and branches underneath the ground sheet to make things warmer. Charlie volunteered to be cook and made mince and veg for them all and a mug of tea each. Walter fixed up his radio at the tip of the tent pole using two guy lines as a support for the radio.

'Hey I got something here, sounds like……….the news, no Radio Caroline nope gone here again its Luxembourg!! Music came through the air which was filled through the air along with the wafting smell off Charlie's cooking. Billy went down the Brook for some water. 'Don't worry it will be clean and safe to drink. You can piss way up stream and it will be ok when it reaches here. But pee is a well-known drink.' Charlie stood up and walked up the side of the brook and disappeared, coming back about fifteen minutes later. 'Where have you been Charlie?'

'What are you Buster my Mother? Can a man not get a load off his mind in peace?!!'

'Ah right! I see! Doing the Continental?!!'

'You wait Buster I'll make millions!''

They sat around listening to the radio, the flowing of the water in the peaceful surroundings and did their lines, it seemed a world away.

'Tell you what we'll all have a pee and taste each other's!' When suddenly a familiar figure came into view it was Grappy. The boys stood up and they offered him a drink of tea which he accepted. 'Hmmmmm very nice! It certainly has plenty of nose!' They all sat down and he chatted to them for a while, asking how they were getting on and about life here in general. He seemed pleased at their efforts understanding it was their first time. Meanwhile Billy was sat there with a gigantic smile across his face. 'Well boys be back in time for breakfast and leave the place clear and clean. I'll be back to check.'

'What's the grin for Billy?'

'Well the water you used for our tea was actually my pee!' As it went dark the boys piled into their tent listening to the sounds from the radio, it all made for a calm atmosphere. The tired bodies soon were asleep. 'Everybody wake up! There's something going on outside listen.' There was a pounding of something, flashes, bangs and booms. 'Shhhhhh......! Don't put the torches on.' By now all had awoken, lying done listening, what could it be when WHAM! Something came down on the tent. 'Quick outside!' putting the torches on there was nothing to be seen, no pounding no noise no wind nothing on the tent. Straightening up the tent they stayed in their bags but kept them unzipped for easy exit. Unable to sleep anymore they waited till light and packed up, cleaned the area and headed back down the Brook. It was a warm morning, unusually warm,

'Let's have a dip in the pool maybe catch some fish.' Stripping down then all jumped in.

'Sure beats a shower this!' One fish was caught and they decided that they would give it and what was left of their rations to Dan. 'Let's pass by Dan! We could tell him what happened at the hill and drop this little lot off.' Decided they soon arrived at Dan's he was up and Wolfie came running as he heard the boy's voices.

'My my, you boys are changing in to young men already.'

'Here Dan we brought this for you.'

'Wolfie can have the fish I'll have the rest.'

'We got more letters *ntadoavu* right at the summit that one, spent the night climbing the hill just got back for breakfast. Saw those two men at the classroom quadrangle but their backs were to us. Blast we still haven't picked up our clothes. Can do that later, we can use these rucksacks. We need how to read the cipher Dan and half term is approaching, we daren't look up to the sky in case we see the star! We need a rest.'

'If you see the star you must follow it and find what is there. Yes I will show you tomorrow, can you come tomorrow?' They nodded eagerly, could they be about to find out what is going on? They then told him about the tent collapsing.

'It sounded like pounding? Horses hooves? Flashing lights? Ah that will be a skirmish during the 45 rebellion. Dragoons were chasing fugitives from the Highland Army around here and were last seen heading in that direction. Never seen again. Will you not have some breakfast me and

Wolfie?' There was no time they had to get back or they would be in trouble. Sorry would fall on deaf ears at The Brig.
'Tell you what we'll come this afternoon, we've no rugby today only playing football this afternoon. Used to like it but not anymore, much prefer rugby now.'
The boys headed off, stopping off at the HS store to drop the tents. Then picked up their clothes from the previous night, showered and went for breakfast. At the Top o'th' Banks they decided that they would go to see Dan but first they would go and see the Lady Rose, so after games they jogged at a double quick to the lagoon. 'Let's take her closer to The Brig, maybe not somebody is bound to find her but they could just as well find her here. Keep moving her from place to place starting now! Keep it KISS!'
'GIVE YOU A KISS? I am not kissing you Cobber! You sure are UGLY!'
'Keep it stupidly simple!' They dragged her into the lake and across to the place where they had launched her. It was here that they had left the rope and corrugated iron nearby. Billy and Larry dragged them over and they continued to make her safer.
'She's becoming quite a vessel. A carbon copy of our Nurse! Covering the raft up with ferns and undergrowth until they were satisfied she could not be seen the boys sat on the rocks at the water's edge, Billy pulling out his monocle.
'What you looking at Billy as if we didn't know!' Billy grinning, replied,
'Looking for the Beastie she is usually over that way at this time! Let's head back and remember don't look up!' As they headed for the road,
'Stop look over there! It's that big Stag we saw, look, there, in the road bellowing, calling, isn't he Handsome, Majestic, Proud?' Suddenly out of nowhere BANG! The boys dropped down was that a car backfiring or a gun. Then again BANG! BANG! The silence was shattered and the noise turned into howls of pain. A Land Rover appeared from nowhere, gears grinding being forced in position with one man on the back firing indiscriminately in the direction of the Stag. 'Billy run back and set off Moaning Minnie it might scare them away, they are not allowed to shoot in the Myrtle Wood. I saw it on the notice board.' The Landover stopped at the side of the road a searchlight on the roof swept through the darkening trees, in the dense Wood.

'There!' BANG! 'There!' BANG! Shouted the man on the back. Howls of pain could be heard echoing within the Wood. Then a wailing sound came from the direction of the main building it was Moaning Minnie. Quickly the men boarded the Land Rover and headed off away from them towards the lagoon. Billy joined them. 'They've gone but can you hear the Stag crying he's been hurt, he's in pain, suffering, Let's go and find him.' The boys came out of their hiding place and headed into Myrtle Wood, blood could be seen a plenty against the ferns against the trees on the heather already coagulating. 'He's hurt bad but where is he?' The wailing started to die down intermittingly, fainter, fainter and fainter till nothing, nothing, silence. 'LOOK! Straight ahead there he is!' Falling, getting up then falling again the beast staggered through Myrtle Wood. Then finally lying on his side head, trying to move, legs paddling about, the helpless, terrified animal saw the boys approaching. 'Slowly slowly fellas, he's scared!' They surrounded the prostrate animal, fear could be seen in his eyes blood pouring, pumping out from the gunshot wounds, one could be seen on the neck another around his spine, his rear leg shot cleanly off. 'He's dying. We need to finish him off for his own sake!'

'NO! We'll stay with him till the end. Look at those gentle eyes he trusts us he knows we're not to blame. It did not take long for the end; he had lost too much blood from his wounds. Larry had put his arms around his neck; the others stroked the handsome head. Moaning Minnie had stopped wailing in the background, blue flashing lights could be seen close by. Then suddenly a last breath could be heard coming out of the Stag, a slow drawn out exhalation. The boys looked at each other, there was no dry eye amongst them, and he was dead. The boys were finding this difficult, the beautiful creature had been alive only minutes ago calling for his mate and now he was gone, and for what?

'What shall we do, they'll come back looking for him.' They'd heard about these trophy hunters. 'Bury him.'

'No we can't do that, we need a big hole and we've no spade. Dan's not far from here I'm sure he'll help, let's drag him from here to Dan he'll know what to do. Quick before they come back.'

'They're not going to, the V2 is at the lake side and I saw the Quad going up the Service road.'

'Charlie you hold the antlers up keep his head off the floor we must show dignity here. Billy and I will pull him by the back legs, Larry try and cover our tracks. We're going to miss supper but so what. He deserved a better end than this.' Eventually they arrived at Dan's. 'What have you here boys? You did that?'

'No we didn't there were hunters down by the road we had been at the lake side when, bang, Billy set off the alarm they drove off and we tracked him where he died, we stayed with him Dan.'

'You're good boys, those two bastards!' It was the first time they had heard him swear but Dan too was visibly shaken. 'They're not even supposed to be shooting here because of the Brig.' Taking his hat off Dan scratched his forehead. 'Ok listen this will be the best thing.'

'Dig a hole?'

'No I'll cut him up.'

'Cut him up? That makes us no better than the next.'

'Now listen boys. You were with him at the end, I will cut off his head and we will keep that, he is a proud animal and we must preserve that. As memory. The rest of the body I will cut what meat I can and the rest I will burn and bury. Those hunters will want this head as a trophy and they are not going to get it, or profit from selling the meat. We will preserve it; I used to do taxidermy so I will need some things that you can get for me. I know Doc Wallace will have something in his lab. The meat we can eat but we have to act fast. I do not want those men around here. Let someone know at the gunshots were fired. They must've heard it. Remember you are the last things that he saw and you were kind to him now go, we can talk about the cipher later.' Reluctantly the boys went away, they knew Dan was disturbed and even Wolfie knew there was something wrong. After about 200 yards they could see a vehicle coming up the tracks and it sounded as though the Quad was still patrolling, upping the pace the boys crossed the bridge and paused at the Curling Hut. Sitting down on the steps, they agreed that they should follow what Dan intended. As they walked over they could see the V1 followed by the Quad heading back to their sheds. The Quad was filthy; it was the only vehicle that could drive through the wood.

At the supper table they could not eat their food, one of their favourites, sausage egg and chips. The scene of the dying Stag had made a lasting impression on them. They went to the Top o'th' Banks, not much was said. Billy commented on how did Dan know there were two men, had he seen what had had happened? Nobody spoke at prep; the rest of the night was in complete silence. It was difficult to sleep at all that night and after the morning run the boys decided to go to Dan at break time, stopping at the Tucky for some snacks they headed for Myrtle Wood. They were totally unprepared for what they would now see. Dan's shack was completely trashed, wrecked, ruined, Dan was sat head in his hands, beaten and bruised, as though he had been tortured. Wolfie was lying in front of him wrapped in a dirty cloth. 'DAN! DAN! What happened here?'

'Shortly after you had gone the two men appeared with two dogs, one chased Wolfie and bit him, I found him later over there hiding, I think he will die or lose his tail. Wolfie raised his head and looked at the boys, slowly putting it down, and a long drawn out meow followed. They demanded the Stag; it was where you had left it. They put him in the back of the Land Rover, wrecked my place and drove off.'

'This is our entire fault!'

'Nay lad you only did what was right for the beast.'

'But if we hadn't dragged him here they would not have found you, who are they, poachers?'

'Yes I think so.' Dan's attention had returned to Wolfie, tears flooded down his soiled cheeks.

'Let me look Dan.' And pulling back the cloth Walter could see a chunk of Wolfie's tail was missing.

'The sods.' Billy clenched his fists. 'Right! Dan let me take Wolfie to Nurse Rose, she likes us, and she will help.'

'But, but, but!'

'No buts, Cobber, Charlie, you get this place sorted out for Dan I want it looking like a nightclub when I get back! Billy you go and pilfer whatever you can.' Patting Dan on the shoulder he gently picked up Wolfie who struggled at first but then stopped when Dan gave him a reassuring stroke.

'We'll miss classes but we'll work it out.' Walter headed off straight for the San. At the surgery, luckily there was no one around. He knocked on the door.

'Flannigan! What are you doing here?' Walter took Wolfie over to the bench and unwrapped the cloth. 'Flannigan I'm a Nurse not a Vet!'

'Please Miss Rose, please!'

She looked at the boy and said ok but she wanted the full story,

'He's a feral cat isn't he?'

'Yes, he's called Wolfie.' She tended his wounds and decided she would keep him with her. 'No you can't do that.'
'It'll be ok, I'll look after him and when he is better I will let you take him back. So that is what all the commotion was about the other night?'
'Yes.' And told her as much as he was able to. Well I'll have to tell the Mr Barron.'
'But Miss, please, no.'
'It's ok I'll tell him about the poachers, or hunters they are not allowed to shoot there in Myrtle Wood and certainly not at the roadside. He will want to phone the Police, he will have to.' Walter understood. 'Now off with you young man, you can come and see him tonight.' He raced back to Dan's; the place had been cleaned and tidied up. Billy had got some food from Joe, enough for Dan for a couple of days.
'Wolfie is going to be ok Dan. Nurse is going to take care of him and he'll be back before you know it.' The boys sat around the fire. 'I think you need to relocate Dan, how about 20 Bell Street? Too far. How about the cave we found. Possibly.'
'No Walter, it was starting to collapse when we passed the other day, remember?'
'No wait there is another shack, the place where we got the barrels and rope.'
'You mean the Norwegian Commando's hut.'
'Yes, it's all over grown close to the Brook no one has been there for years. Yes we can use some of this place and make something good for you. Listen we have to go we will be back tomorrow and make a start and don't you worry about Wolfie.'
The boys left. 'We owe that man.'
'Yes we do'. At lunch the Head gave a statement for boys to keep out of the Myrtle Wood for the immediate future. There had been gunshots heard and an investigation was now under way, the emergency vehicles would be in the area periodically to enforce this.
'Digweed, Flannigan, Odhiambo and MacCloon are to report to my study after supper tonight.' This came as no surprise they would have been missed from double Maths and even their fellow Novus would be unable to account for them.
It was rugby that afternoon they had this match coming that they must win, this time there was no fitness session just rugby, moves passing,

scrimmaging team talk but the boys minds were far away. Big Jim pointed out it would be a full day out they were all going out all thirty nine but only 15 would take part in the game. The Head had ordered Jimmy Phillip's Panorama bus for the trip which was usually reserved for the firsts. They would arrive early have lunch with the opposition win the game and as a reward they would stop at the chipper for a fish supper before heading back to Flaxden Brig in glory. All seemed to be in agreement. The boys headed off for their shower and afternoon tea. Double Latin followed before supper, when they stocked up for Dan. The usual chat Top o'th' Banks then before prep a visit to the San to see Wolfie he was doing good. He meowed when he saw them. His tail was still sore but you could see he was comfortable. They tried to work at prep then headed to see if Dan was ok, give him the food and report that Wolfie was doing well and soon would be back with him.

'We've caused you a lot of problems Dan, we are so sorry.'

'Nay lad.' He would reply 'Your all good boys.' In the knowledge Dan was comfortable and safe for now the boys left.

'Let's get him away from here. We can do it Saturday then we are away next week, let's hope Wolfie is fine by then.'

That night after supper the gong went. BONG! 'Stay in your seats!' There was a silence as the Head walked into the centre of the dining room, head high, upright and direct. 'It has come to my attention that someone or somebody has caused an act of vandalism to someone's property. The Lowers and Novus can leave as this cannot affect them in any way.' The Lowers and Novus left the dining room but the four boys went to the Top o'th' Banks. 'Let's listen; we can duck down behind the windows.' So they did and listened to what the Head said. It was muffled but they clearly could hear.

'A boy has come to me and shown me damage to his bicycle. This is not only an expensive Raleigh model, but a present given to him by his family. The damage in question is that in two places the frame has been sawed into by ¾ of the circumference of the frame at each point. If the boy had ridden his bike at a certain speed, the frame would have collapsed and the rider thrown. At 30 mph or more this could have been fatal. Anybody could have been the rider; you could have been the rider, Mr Powers, Nurse Rose, you, even me. 'A laugh was heard. 'Take that boy to my study Gordon he will face the Headmasters Chair! Anyone else likes to laugh about it then there's the corridor to my study!' A silence enveloped the dining hall. 'Now I want the perpetrators caught, this is not a case of sneaking but a very serious matter. Health is at risk here! Mr Davie has also informed me a hacksaw is missing from his workshop.' He started to turn and said, 'I would like to remind you that the Myrtle Wood is still out of bounds to all. You may keep to the tracks.' With that he was gone.

As they walked back over the metal bridge they turned around, they could hear a vehicle approaching. It was the Quad. The Head was true to his word. Dan would be fine the poachers wouldn't be back tonight. The night was clear and without warning their attention was drawn to the Star. It was due West this time. 'Hey look over there! It's that flaming Star!'

'I see it. I was trying not to look! Listen say nothing to Dan about this he's been through enough. Let's get back I just want to sleep.'

Once in their beds music piped into the dorm it was Blue Danube Waltz.

'Well that's it then. No choice now.'

'We'll discuss it in the morning!'

There was an ominous trend developing.

After the routine was now an auto pilot event the boys headed towards the Top o'th' Banks. 'We've got a few minutes!'

'Right what shall we do? I think this time we'll leave Dan out of it for now and go and look for ourselves.'

'Yes I think so too.'

Nodding in agreement they left for their morning classes.

They decided to go that afternoon. After games they headed due west but were followed by Ztirgeon and Horbyn. 'Split up like we did before and head for the overhang. With Charlie taking the rear they set off and soon there were gaps between each appearing when suddenly Charlie was confronted by Ztirgeon and Horbyn?

'Empty your pockets Digweed!' Said Horbyn.

'NO!' Said Charlie defiantly.

'You'll do it now!' Ranted Ztirgeon, stamping his feet as he pushed him to the ground with a thud as Charlie's head hit the floor.

'Ok ok! Here have it all!' And two 3d and a sixpence were handed over.

'Don't make a fool out of me Digweed!' Ztirgeon continued to rant as he pulled Charlie up from the floor and rifled through his pockets, punching him in the ribs as he did so.

'Got it Horbyn! Here is the information! This is what they want.' He said as he threw Charlie into the dense undergrowth.
'Blare is going to be pleased with us!' Said Horbyn.
'US??You mean pleased with me, Blare will definitely let me into the BB GANG now........... if he doesn't I'll, I'll break away and start my own!' As the two Uppers left Charlie remained prostrate on the floor, winded. Quickly he gathered himself and jogged after his friends.
'Wotcher Charlie, gosh you look rough, what happened.' The boys listened.
'They ambushed me, took my money and my bits of paper. I think they took one of the codes. Sorry.'
'It's ok, don't worry, we don't know what they mean anyway.'
'Another thing, I think there is friction, trouble at Mill!
'What do you mean/'
'Well Ztirgeon is going to start his own gang if Blare won't let him fully join the BB GANG!'
'Looks like they have problems anyway let's get going!' Charlie rummaged through his pockets.
'It's ok I have the table code here I think he got one of my inventions!' Inadvertently they realised that they had started to play off Ztirgeon against Blare!
'What shall we do?' They could take the Lady Rose but somebody might see them so they will jog.
'We can use it as a training exercise in case any one sees us.'
'Good thinking batman!' At a quick pace they headed due West on the lake side road, still wearing their games kit they ran at three quarter pace from one telegraph pole to the next then walking at a brisk pace then running. We'll begin to enjoy this soon!'
'I thought we already were! Come on.'
'Do you think we are heading for the castle again?'
'No, it is definitely due West which means it is somewhere near the road.'
'Do we really have to go now?'
'Yes we do, we have to see what is there.' Soon the boys reached a little grave yard and had a look around the walls. 'It can't be here, there are too many inscriptions. Wait look on the other side of the road up that track, a cottage and some out buildings.' On the other side of the road about 200

yards a cluster of buildings could be seen. 'Hey look it's that Land Rover we saw the other day. The poacher's vehicle.'
'You sure?'
'Yes let's get them.'
'Hang on Billy. Stay back. Let's creep up. We don't want them to see us.'
So the boys headed up the track keeping close to the wall to avoid being detected.
'Hear that?'
'A train again?'
'No stupid it's the Land Rover starting up! Quick over the wall!' They ran up to the gate and hauled themselves over the wall. 'Shit I think they saw me! Bitch! Life's a bitch Charlie but we'll deal with it!' Cowering behind the wall they heard the vehicle coming to a halt. The dogs in the van are barking.
'Let them out!' The men let the dogs out and the boys heard them sniffing.
'We've had it now.' Whispered Charlie. Larry Let's out a 'BAAAAAAAAAAA!'
'MAAAAAAAAAAA!'
'Come on lads there's nothing there, back in!' The Land Rover rumbled down the track. Breathing a sigh of relief the boys laughed with relief.
'Hey you think they are heading for Dan?'
'I need a Strepsil!'
'Me too! A blackcurrant one would be good!'
'Nope too risky for them plus I saw the Quad at the Flaxden Bridge. Who do you think they are?'
'They were the ones shooting the Stag I'm sure plus I think I have seen the Land Rover before that. Come let's have a look around. This must where the Star was taking us.' Up the track they scouted around the buildings. Nothing about. Inside an out building they saw a freezer. Looking at each other they slowly open it. Cuts of meat sealed in see through plastic. It was the meat from the Stag, the hunters processing plant.
'No head, where's the head?' Looking into the cottage they see a roaring fire. A whisky bottle and two glasses on the table, a twelve bore shot gun at the side, looked as though it had just been cleaned, another smaller pistol close by and above the fire they saw it. That handsome head. 'Let's trash the place!'
'Billy we don't do that, we set the example.'

'They did it to Dan let's do it to them!'
'No!'
'Bet they are something to do with all what has been going on at the.'
'We don't know that for sure, see the 2 radios? This could be something bigger. Do that and we are no better than them. Let's think hard and long about this. But let's get back; we must see how Dan is.'
On their way back they jogged along the lake side road dodging out of view at the vehicles passing along. At one stage the Land Rover passed heading back to the cottage. 'They must've been back to Dan.' Upping the pace the boys race up the track to the Brook. The Quad was there parked by the bridge, suddenly the blue light came on. The boys stopped and hid.
'It's only a deterrent. Maybe the Land Rover saw the Quad and left.'
'Let's move.' They got to Dan's place; he's there to their relief. He's feeling better that's great. 'But Dan you have to move, they know this place and so do the two men. They left you and Wolfie for dead!'
'But they have known for a long time, even your Head gave me a pair of rugby boots when one of you boys poured water into my boots while I was asleep ruining them, it's these poachers who have suddenly appeared. They are the problem.' And the boys explained that they have been to the cottage, directed by the Star. 'Hmmmmm! That's strange. No letters? No message?'
'No we looked but we did find they had taken the Stag, mounted it on a plaque and cut the meat probably with the intention of selling it as Venison. Listen Dan even to us it can be seen that they took a big chance in what they did to you. I think they wanted you out of the way, there was anger here. You must move. How about that Norwegian Commando hut we saw? It's not too far away from here and we'll help you move.'
'Yes boys that would be good but you must find those next letters, you still have the disc?'
'Yes.'
'Well due West of here is the hill Chickory Hill.! 'Is there a story to that one?' Dan thought for a moment and said yes there was. 'Any of you like cricket?'
'I'm well, was, I think, a football man, we all like rugby now! Cobber you like Cricket?'
'Yes mate!'
'Yes I saw that the other day with..... Wolfie. Wolfie!!How is he?'

'It's ok Dan he is with the Nurse, she's looking after him. What's the story?'
'I like Cricket too, play on the beach back home.' Said Billy. 'Play it all the time at home with Dad's employees.'
'Well there was a Cricketer who played for England, real posh man, went to one of those Toff places, well he used to come up here and walk, climb about the hills and gills when he wasn't playing cricket, staying at the bed & breakfast near where you were today.'
'He still goes there?'
'No he died a while ago and his ashes are scattered on the top. He used to play cricket with all the children in the village in the garden of the B & B. The Australians didn't like him, two in particular because he invented bodyline.'
'Bodyline?'
'I have heard of him back home, they still talk about it!' Said Larry.
'Yes the bowler bowled directly at the batters. Needless to say England won but he got flayed by the press in Aussie Land. So the Star was leading you there to the top of Chickory Hill I think?'
'Another hill, we've already been to the top of one.'
'These will be easier there is a track up the back of Myrtle Wood that will take you to it; an afternoon no more. When can you do that?!'
'It will have to be Sunday, we go on a break on Thursday until Tuesday but we are going to make sure you and Wolfie are ok.'
'Thanks boys but I have been living here for a while now and had many escapes, but nothing like this.'
'Well even so we are going to help you, aren't we fellas?'
'Damn right!' All say at once.
'You are good boys.' He appeared to be relaxed.
'And we will go and see Wolfie for you. We will get some food for you after supper Dan, it's what is it tonight Billy, have you seen the menu?'
'Pasties, beans and chips, oh yes and cauliflower soup. We'll bring bread too. What do you do for food when we are not here Dan?'
'Well once every two weeks I cycle into the village and cash my Giro cheque and get some supplies. I have plenty of water from the Brook. Yes plenty of that! But when I run out of food and sometimes we do. Wolfie, cats are good for themselves, mice and birds, natural survivors. He even bring something back for me! Hunting wild animals is not my first thought

when looking for food, instead I use snares and traps. This stops me from using up my energy. Most animals can be snared with a wire noose in the right position, such as near a den or above a game trail, but do not set it close to a den as like we are and should be, animals are wary when they first emerge from hiding. Remember funnel the animal towards your trail, camouflage the snare, and mask your scent and then bait. Set many traps and the better the chance of success. The Brook is my first port of call for food. Look at that pike you got the other day, fluke but you still caught it! Now off with you all it must be nearly your supper time.'

Sure enough it was as Billy said, cauliflower soup, pasties, chips and beans with a welcome yoghurt to eat. They managed to get a few pasties and many chips and beans, bread for Dan. Charlie donated his yoghurt. The boys headed for the Top o'th' Banks and had their daily discussion. Getting closer to the tree, they knew they were being watched; they would move Dan to the new place on Saturday and go up the new hill on Sunday after dinner. They didn't have much time now they were leaving for half term on Thursday morning and there was a lot to do.

'What did Dan mean by many escapes?'

'What about the poachers?'

'It's ok we can deal with that later.'

'Don't forget we have tests on Monday, all eight subjects.'

'What!!!!???? Even Wood Work?!'

'Nah not that but definitely Latin, English, Maths, General Science, History and Geography. Think you've done enough?'

'Best do some revising!' As they left their position the three Uppers approached them slamming their shoulders into them. Billy turned aggressively. 'Leave it Billy.' The Uppers looked out from the banks then looked into the trees near their spot.

'Hey look they are searching the trees! What a set of idiots! Quick there's Pete let's go!' Back to the house they collected their books and headed for prep. It was quiet everyone was studying for their tests. Once over, 'Let's go see Wolfie.' At the San they were greeted by a tearful Nurse Rose. 'What's the matter Miss Rose?'

'Wolfie has gone, he was doing well and had just had his food, sat on my knee, I stroked him and he purred away then suddenly sat up and bolted out the window, bandages trailing behind him.'

The boys looked at each other in disbelief. 'I had become to like the little fellow!'
'Don't worry Miss he will go back to where we found him he must feel better. We'll go and see.'
'Listen from now on let's not move as a group, I will go first then just as I am out of sight the next and so on.' Soon they were at Dan's, to find Wolfie curled up by the fire.
'He's back boys! He's come home!' Said Dan as he gratefully took the sack of food.
'So we see. Miss Rose will miss him, but she will be happy knowing where he is.'
'Here Dan, I brought you some headache tablets.' Said Billy, as the others rolled their eyes.
'Billy you'll have to stop this pilfering, Nurse Rose will know they are missing!'
'And she will certainly miss these! These are contraceptive pills!' Said Dan.
'Contraceptive pills? What are they for?'
'Well lads it's all about the birds and the bees! I can be of no help with you here. You must take them back! She may need these. Right boys you get back now.'
'No story Dan?'
'I've told you enough for now!'
'Ok fellas same as before Billy you go first and somehow return those pills.' The boys headed back all but Walter arrived just as Big Jim was just appearing. 'Where have you been Flannigan?' He growled.
'Up the tracks sir. Definitely not in Myrtle Wood.'
'You know that is out of bounds, anyone with you?'
'No sir, only me.'
'Right after lights out report to the Georgetown!' Back in the dorm Walter told everyone he was going to get beaten, what's better knowing in advance or getting a summary beating? At least the latter is quick. Yes. He must be on the warpath.
'I thought all those beatings had finished, tailed off.' But he knew he deserved it, the wood was an immediate danger and the Head is charged with everyone's safety. Ah well.

'Hey, put a cushion down your pants, maybe not, he'll see your bum looks bigger!'
'What about your notebook, Latin, no, too stiff he'll see that one! Tell you what soak it in water and that will shape to your backside.'
'Hmmmmm! Yes that could work, I'll try that. 'Walter went to his cubicle and picked up his note book soaked it and put it down his pants. Perfect fit! He could say he dropped it in a puddle.
Sure enough the door flung open and Big Jim was there silhouetted against the light from the corridor, a fearsome sight George in his hands. was sure he could see snarling teeth and a staring eye coming from the Puma shoe, dying to carry out the sentence.
'Flannigan! Common room now!' Walter headed out after Big Jim, 'Good luck! Take one for me!' Nobody was laughing.
'You have deliberately violated a direct order from Mr Barron Flannigan; count yourself lucky it is me who caught you and not anyone else. The Headmaster has the weight of Flaxden Brig on his shoulders, its future depends on his actions. You have also avoided the Headmaster's Chair. Bend over!' Walter bent over when THUD! 'What the!!!!!?????' Another THUD! 'Flannigan take whatever you have down there, out NOW!!!!!' Walter did as he was told and dropped the soggy, now mashed notebook on the floor. 'Turn around, bend over and pull your pants completely down, I will not allow any boy to make a fool of me indefinitely!' WHACK! WHACK! WHACK! The first two were fine he, could take those but the third sent a pain throughout his body he had not felt before, excruciating, nauseating, blood curdling he went dizzy and awaited the next one, it did not come. 'Stand up boy, pull up your pants and get back to your dorm. I will give you full, however' marks for ingenuity. You'll learn from this!'
Walter did as he was told and got into his bed sore and in pain he bit his pillow. 'You ok?' Whispered a concerned Charlie. 'We have to be careful now.' The silence was so strong you could cut it.
At bugle call Walter struggled doing the morning run, almost at a crawl, nobody said anything except gave only sympathetic stares. But he knew he was at fault. Hearing of what had happened Kerr offered to do his housework but Walter politely declined, he'd be ok. A gingerly walk down to breakfast feeling like he had been riding a horse for hours, he sat down in agony and gobbled his food down, cereal, toast and a cup of tea. 'How many did you get? 3?'

'Two with the book then 3.The first two weren't bad but the third was terrible.'
'Maybe you should go to the San?'
'And say what? I'll be ok.' But unable to sit much longer he excused himself and headed out the main door. The others followed suit. At the Top o'th' Banks he reassured them, he was ok and they planned the next days ahead, this time next week they would be away and they wanted to tie things up, leaving no stone unturned. 'You know there is so much going on here we could write a book!' All Saturday classes were assigned to revision which the boys were glad off. After bed rest and piped music the boys headed for the Brook. 'Wait I can see one of the Firey's, it's Beefy Bill driving, it is over there and I can hear the Quad too, on this side of the Brook so Let's go up the Grap track we are still allowed that way.' Heading up in that direction the friends walked for half a mile and cut across through a new stretch of wood that the forestry commission were planting, young trees, spruce, it would soon be Yuletide commented Larry.

♫

DECK THE HALLS WITH BOUGHS OF HOLLY!
LA LA LA LA LA LA LA LA LA LA!

Billy sang breaking into tune. Soon the boys came to where the Uppers den had been destroyed. Thick tire tracks were around the spot and unless you knew it had been there it would have been difficult to see. The Quad and Emergency Service had been up here. Carrying out the instructions of the Head to the letter. 'Hey look no tire tracks further Southwest.' It was clear to see that even the Quad could go no further or maybe they saw no danger further up. 'There's a whole new frontier up there for us!' Looking away they saw just forest, thick bush. 'Hey fellas I need to rest a while.' Said Walter. Sitting down they talked and decided that when they come back after their break they will build a series of dens/out posts that they could use to hide if needed and if anyone would get cut off or isolated, to give them breathing space, a sanctuary. It was decided 5 in all, shelter is one of the top priorities in any environment, and it would help them conserve energy, precious energy. Don't waste time constructing a shelter if nature has already provided one. 'We must take advantage of caves, overhangs, hollows and trees. We need to make some shelters ourselves. Larry mark on the map where you think we should have them, I think we need to put one about 500 yards further up.' A life raft, safe wreckage, abandoned structures. Scavenge any man made materials we can Billy you are good at that, you have licence to pilfer, they will help in construction. Choose the right location so everyone look out for ideal places. Protection from detection and the elements must be our key in building these shelters. They must be stable and built to last away from natural hazards like wind, rain, flooding, rock falls, and insect swarms. I saw an ant hill back there massive it was! Study the terrain before choosing the shelter. We can do a lean to, an A frame like the tent, a tree pit and an earth pit and a sheet shelter. Anyway let's get going we have to get Dan moved. In fact if Dan sees a problem he could get to one of those easily. But this is for when we get back.'

At the Brook they discovered the water was in full flow, a new thing for them... This was going to be dangerous. Looking about they saw they were not near a junction where the flow would be split in two and they could cross above. Good there were no bends where the water may be deeper.

'Hey look it is wider there that may be good.'

'How do you make that out?'

'Well the water is spread over a wider area and will be the same volume, but look out for the dark parts that will mean it is deeper.' Said Charlie.

'Good thinking Brains!'

'Have a look around for some sticks, good sturdy ones and long, one each.' The boys found one. Billy seemed to have the strongest as Walter's and Larry's snapped. 'Ok Billy you won, you're first, face upstream, hold the pole vertically in front of you so you create a strong triangle. Move one foot at a time to the pole and resist the temptation to place it closer to the other. Then move the pole back to the apex of the triangle, make sure that you have a strong secure footing and pole placement before moving on. Take your time and once over throw the pole over to us.'

'Why me?'

'Because you got the longest stick.'

'Yes my mum always said I was a big boy!'

'Come on Billy get on with it!'

'Alright alright!' Billy went over and threw back the stick straight into the Brook and watched as it floated away!

'You twit Billy. My stick is too small. We'll try crossing together in a group. We'll do an arrowhead I'll go at the front and Larry and Charlie behind grabbing the straps facing the river flow.' Walter could feel the cold water on him giving him some comfort from his pain but Larry stumbles.
'Quick grab him and make a circle.' They do this and steady themselves getting across safely. 'You prick Billy!'
'Sorry!!'
'Come on let's get to Dan's! We've still plenty of time.' Walter by now was beginning to feel uncomfortable, he had to unloosen his belt and now it was becoming noticeable.
'Hey you got a bonar!!!'
'Shut it Cobber, I am not feeling that good right now.' The other three looked at each other confiding in themselves,
'You know Walter hasn't been too good after that beating last night.'
'COME ON!' Walter urged the others; he just wanted to get back.
'But you are……….'
'Forget it this is the only chance we have to get all this done for Dan.' Soon they were at Dan's place. Dan was already packing up with Wolfie at his side, non plussed at the activity at his home.
'Hi boys thanks for coming.'
For the next few hours the boys and Dan shuttled all Dan's worldly goods to the Commando hut. Dan was pleased as it was clear that there had been nobody there for years. The boys covered their tracks.
'You lot are becoming experts in this. I will call this place Myrtle Cottage!'
'Oh Dan, here's some nosh from dinner.' A fire was lit, providing the two with light, comfort and protection. 'Do you not think you'll be seen here?'
'No I'll be ok.' There are many ways to start a fire and with some dry tinder the boys observed Dan taking a piece of foil and attach the ends to a small battery he pulled from his pocket. A light ignited. 'Wow Dan! How's that?'
'Just making an electrical circuit,' And with this the kindle glowed at first then burst into life. The boys slowly put the dry pieces of wood they had collected onto the growing fire which soon filled the room with warmth and light, Wolfie moved to the hearth smiling at the flames. 'He's home now!' The broad smile on Dan's toothless face was worth all the effort.
'You boys are good at what you do,'

'How so for boys so young? We need a fire outside too, tell you what you go and choose the location as an exercise.' Choosing the location was easy for them, in relative proximity to the shelter and wind proximity being the most important considerations. They then built a base of green wet branches, in case the ground was wet, maybe they could dig a pit in case a wind arrives suddenly. The ingredients are easy, oxygen, fuel and heat. They gathered a good supply for Dan to use. Collecting wood off the ground, dead branches that would ensure the best chances of being dry, dead branches and twigs that they could break easily. We will need tinder to get the spark going. Fluffy fibrous materials like the dry moss and grasses. Once they got the flame going there would be enough to keep it going. The fire could be kept smouldering with soil or ash. As they were doing this Dan had boiled some water in his pan. A metal tray was over the fire and he was heating up the pasties form the night before. The boys sat down around the fire and told him what they would be doing after half term and that tomorrow afternoon they were going to climb Chickory Hill for the next letters. And they would come and see Dan a couple of times before they left for their break. They left to go for their supper but as they approached the main building doubled up and keeled forward smacking his head on the tarmac. 'Walter! Walter! Are you ok?' Reeling in agony the three other boys picked him up and said, 'We are taking you to the San, Nurse Rose will be there now surgery doesn't finish till 6 30 pm. Can you make it? Want us to call the Ambo.'
'No don't do that Moaning Minnie will bring everyone out, Firey, Quad n all! Just help me I'll make it.'
'What's wrong Walter?' They all made their way slowly up Magillycuddy Hill when a strange sight came in to the distance, it was the V2 and music was coming from it! 'Do you hear that?'
'What the music.'
'Music?'

270 degrees

'Yes it's Blue Danube Waltz.'
'Please NOOOOOO!' And as the V2 passed by a familiar figure was sat in the back playing a piano, it was Jaw. It was surreal! The boys stopped for a

moment mouths wide opened, jaws dropped. The remnants of the queue at the Tucky had also turned. Even, but only for a second. 'Guys go to supper you'll be late I'll make it.'
'No you won't, not without us.' So the boys carried on, each step for Walter became more and more difficult. Eventually at the San Miss Rose came to the door, not seeing at first she asked about Wolfie. 'He's ok Miss, he found his way home, he's ok, but Walter isn't.'
'Now what are you boys up to now?' Suddenly the redness changed on Nurse Roses face as she saw the difficulty Walter was in.
'Quick bring him in here, help him on to the examination bed. Lie him down, now what is it?' She looked down at the expanding crotch.
'Oh My God! What have you been doing?' Quickly she unzipped Walter's pants and pulled them down, exposing an enormous swelling. The three other boys eyes became as big as the Owl's. 'Just relax Master Flannigan, deep breaths.' Walter's testicles seemed to have expanded so much that they looked likely to explode any minute. 'How has this happened!!!??' Nurse Rose looked at the other three boys from one to the other, who in turn quickly acknowledged with a tired shake of the head.
'I jumped from the top of the wall near the Summer House and landed on my backside, it was sore, it still is.'
'Right........ You boys go to your supper.'
'But we want to stay with.................... .'
'You can't now here's a note to say why you are so late. Flannigan is staying here tonight for observation. You can see him tomorrow.' The boys filed silently out of the San and headed out down for their supper. The V2 could be seen in the distance with a couple of Uppers unloading the piano into the Chapel.
'Right! I will have to call the Doctor; you have a dangerous swelling to the testicles, very dangerous. I will need the Dr. Now tell me how you did this.'
'It is how I said Miss Rose, I jumped off the wall but I forget to put my underpants on this morning.'
'Last time Flannigan! And no joking!' the Nurse was getting impatient.
'I promise you I will deal with it my own way. I can see those marks on your backside!' Looking at her he could see she was being straight.
'What are you afraid of? Is it the bullies? Kerr, Troup and Pearson. We have all noticed.'

'No it wasn't, we are getting along now. They are fine with us.'
'Well what about the Uppers? I've seen a group follow you.'
'No.' So Walter told her about the beating the night before and how he came about to get it.
'Please don't say anything!' He told her he was in the wrong and deserved the beating and the extra beating for the notebook.
'Right I am going to put an end to all of this barbarity.'
'I need to be out of the San tonight Miss, I'll miss the film and I have things tomorrow to do before……..'
'Like what?'
'Well revision for Mondays tests!'
'Don't worry you will be ok, it is only a problem with your testicles not your hands, you can still write, I'll call Dr Shields now.'
Larry, Billy and Charlie ate their supper in quiet.
'I have a nickname for Walter now!' Announced Larry trying to break the silence.
'Not now Cobber, later.' Said Charlie.
'Yes, we don't have the balls for it just now.' Added Billy. The rest of the discussion around the dining room was about Jaw playing his piano on the V2. It was a magical moment but the boys couldn't help but think about their friend. After supper they headed to the Top o'th' Banks, only three tonight. 'Where's the other?' Shouted some of the Uppers. 'Not in love with him anymore!!' They ignored this and pondered what they should do tomorrow. No they would carry on and maybe would be ok with them. They would have to pass by Dan's to get directions for the route.
'How's the map doing Cobber?'
'Looking good, getting pretty detailed now! Think I'll become a cartographer! What's the film tonight, thought it may have been cancelled.'
'No it hasn't and it is Butch Cassidy and the Sundance Kid.'
'Great, sad Walter can't see it, but he's in good hands.'
'Yes I'd like to be in those hands too!' As the boys headed back to Brecon they could see Head observing them with a look of puzzlement on his face peering around looking for the absentee.
Lying down, Walter was looking up at the ceiling when a big burly man, with a gigantic beard came into the surgery with Nurse Rose.
'Now young man what have you been up to?'
'He fell off a wall Doctor.'

After a brief examination he concluded, 'Yes you are right Nurse Rose he has hydrocele.'
'I have what?'
'It is a build up of fluid around the testicles and what we will do now is drain out the fluid to make you comfortable. Nurse here will assist.'
'Will those orange Strepsils not work?'
'Nay lads, this is the only way!' The area was swabbed down with pre op solution by Nurse Rose, something that many boys had probably dreamed about and a small needle of anaesthetic. When suddenly the Doctor produced a large hypodermic needle stuck on to the end of what looked like a rubber tube. 'I believe your father is a Veterinary Surgeon? Well this is the same principle he will use for the cows!' Rigid with fear Walter closed his eyes as the Doc carefully inserted the needle into his scrotum when suddenly there was an immense release and could hear something like water from a tap spurting into a bowl held by Nurse Rose. Cleaning him up Nurse Rose asked the Doctor should he be kept under observation. Yes he should for at least two nights maybe more.
'Nooooo! I want to go out now! I want to be with my friends!'
'You can't!' Said Dr Shields and he resigned himself, then suddenly realised he may not get away for his break and have to stay in the San, all the time.
'Don't worry I will arrange for your night dress and books so you can study for your tests on Monday.' Puzzled. Did the beautiful Nurse Rose call him by his first name? Wow! 'Is there anything else I can do for you?' At this s eyes popped open.
'Well Nurse I've been having these strange dreams.....'
'That's ENOUGH young man! Besides I am not an Oneirologist.' With that she left him alone. 'Peace at last!' He thought to himself. 'What did she think I was talking about?'
That night Larry, Billy and Charlie attended the film at the gym, The Graduate, the Firsts and other away sides returned all suffering losses but the spirit that seemed to be enveloping Flaxden was evident to see. The next day the three boys visited Walter in his room at the San.
'You lucky sod, she did that to you?' As he related his story of the treatment he had received.

'Well I didn't have the chance to complain. I told her what had happened, told her I fell off a wall and that because I had forgotten to put my under crackers on they hit the floor before the rest of me!'

'Really???'

'Nahh she got it out of me, I had to tell her, but she promised to deal with it in her own way.'

'No choice. Wait! That means you sneaked on Big Jim. We're all doomed!'

'No I trust her, besides she has that Mum tone, she got it out of me,'

'What you mean you caved in to her,'

'Don't worry she won't do anything even told the Doctor that I had fallen off a wall,'

'Pretty tricky that falling off a wall and landing on your balls! What are the chances of that?'

'Heck man it was 12 feet up!'

'And which wall was that?'

'So come on where are the biscuits you've been hiding?!'

'Hey guess who came to the window last night?'

'Don't tell me, the Maidens from the across the lake, to have a view of you in all your glory! Singing blissful tunes to you!'

'Give it a rest Billy!'

'No, Wolfie!'

'Wolfie?'

'Yes Wolfie, came to the window meowed a couple of times then went! So what's the plan? When are we going up Chickory Hill?'

'You aren't coming, we are going.'

'But you need me,'

'It's ok, we'll be ok, we are going to Dan's after Sunday dinner and he will give us directions. When are you getting out?'

'Maybe never Doc says its terminal!'

'Heck, it's only your balls, anyone would think you've bust them!' 'I nearly did! Maybe tomorrow but better be by Wednesday!'

'Ok we'll keep you posted we need to get to letter writing. Hey did you notice Jaw was playing Blue Danube Waltz on the piano yesterday?'

'You mean when he was on the back of the V2?'

'Yes, do you think? Take a look at his shoes and trousers.'

'Nah I doubt it, but I've heard he used to be a Paratrooper.' At this Nurse Rose popped her head around the door,
'Time boys, he needs to rest he's had quite an experience!'
'Yes Nurse he sure has!'
'Hey! We've decided on your nickname!'
'WE'VE decided Cobber?'
'Yes WE have!' Said Larry.
'Come on spit it out!'
'BUSTER!!!!'
'Come on boys out!' Nurse Rose insisted smiling at them all.
After they left Walter pulled out his writing case and took out his writing paper.

Brecon House

Dear Mum and Dad,
I wonder why I am writing this letter as by Thursday I will be at home for half term with my friends and I wonder if I will get there before this parchment. Thank you for letting my friends come, everyone will like them. Over the last few weeks we have become good friends, inseparable, a group who can trust and rely on each other. We are in the sane classes and are in the rugby team, but not only that the whole of Brecon House is getting along. In our free time we play in the woods and down by the
lake side, we have a bantastic time, it is quite safe. Tomorrow we have our half term tests in all our subjects except woodwork, which I am really happy about as I am rubbish at it! The bird den I was building is so small now from all the planning it will have to be a small bird to get inside. Yesterday we saw an amusing sight it was Mr Davie on the back of the fire engine playing a tune, I had not heard before, somebody said it was called Blue Danube Waltz. I am hopeful I will do well in all the

others. I can't wait till Thursday when I can see you all, it seems so long now, well I must go and do some revision.
See you at the station on Thursday. I wonder who will arrive first, us or this letter!

W

With that he excitedly sealed the addressed envelope and asked the Nurse to post it for him. Looking at all his books spread across his bed he decided on Latin suddenly realising he couldn't use his note book from what he had done the night before. 'SHIT!' He said out loud and the door suddenly opened. 'Are you okay? Again!
'Yes I'm sorry, I'm ok. Could you post this for me?'
'Yes of course. Hey Wolfie came to my door, purred around my ankles so I gave him some food and off he went! I was so pleased to see him!' With that she closed the door and he opened his Geography book.
Larry, Charlie and Billy headed to Dan's taking the precautionary route that they had done the day before. They had seen the Quad and V1 heading in the direction of the Myrtle Wood. It was good to see that they were still policing the area. That should keep those hunters away. It wasn't long when they arrived at Dan's and they were given directions to the summit of Chickory Hill. They were to head further up into the forest until they came to a track. Follow the track due West as the Star had been the other night walk for an hour and they would see the first summit below whence they were to climb on to the top of Chickory Hill and look for the letters. At the top whilst walking along they would suddenly see the Isle of the Gulls, stop and look around and they would find what they were looking for the letters *qwniwd.* Leaving Dan they headed up when Larry suggested they build a small den on the way.
'Hey fellas!' Said Charlie. 'Have you heard of the Auxuliers? Well they were the resistance that we were going to have if Jerry had invaded during the war.'
'What's this?'
'Well they built these underground hideouts that were difficult to find.'
'So?'

'Tell us more!'

'Well they built a network of these tunnels, under directions from Churchill and mainly little underground dens where they would have other little dens and they would come out and cause havoc with the invaders! They had a life expectancy of about two weeks because the Germans had sniffer dogs who would soon find the secret hideouts. So we'll do the same! It'll be fun!!! We've got time let's get it out of the way now and surprise.' Working at speed they built a lean to, enough to fit 3 to 4 people in it. Satisfied it was camouflaged sufficiently they got on to the track and headed towards the summit of Chickory Hill.

'It's amazing that someone would have his ashes scattered. Well this is a place where he was happy, could relax, and find enjoyment getting away from the maddening crowd. Hey I see it, the island, stop and look around.' Astonishingly quickly they found what they were looking for; letters *zsruzrvp* had been etched on to a large rock. 'Write it down on your map Larry, by the way did you mark the den down on the map?'

'Are you my Mother now Charlie?' Yes he had. The view was staggering. 'Look what Buster is missing! The boys sat down on the rocks admiring their surroundings. There's was nothing better than getting on top of a peak.

'Hey Let's have a game of Cricket! In memory of the Bodyline Guy!' So they had an impromptu game. 'SIX!!!!' Shouted Larry.

'Six? It's gone down.....look down there isn't that?'

'Yes it is. Come on Let's go back that way.'

'BILLYO… NO!!!'

'Awwww come on you haven't let me go over to the girls, so......' After a lot of humming and ha-ing they all reluctantly agreed to Billy's demand. They still had a couple of hours to get back. The decent was easy, the boys were becoming fitter and fitter and they took the route in their stride coming at the back of the poachers/hunters cottage. There was no Land Rover. Shall they look inside Yes why not? The fridge was empty but it was clear they were still around. Guns were stacked in a case and on the wall were the head of the Monarch they had all seen die the other day.

'Let's take it!'

'We can, how's it stealing?'

'How can we steal something that's already been stolen? And we are in the enemy lair!'

'They shot and killed it, how can we forget that look on its face we saw?'
'Ok let's get it to Dan's or hide it somewhere. Quick we must go now!'
Grabbing the head from the wall they stood in stunned silence as they looked into its eyes. 'Is that.....?'
'Yes I think it is, let's get away from here.' They headed off down to the lake road. On leaving they suddenly see what looks to be a set of rags, dirty white cloth by the side of the road. On approaching they saw it was a white cat. 'They've run this over,'
'Now you don't know for sure, Billy'
'They are the only people here. Wait! It's alive!' Cautiously approaching a battered head looks up, one eye green one eye blue, a silent meow is let out.
'We're taking it with us; we'll go to Nurse Rose.'
'What do you think we are an animal sanctuary?' A scowl from Billy at both Larry and Charlie gave the answer. Slowly and gently they wrapped the poor cat into Charlie's sweater, he was blooded and battered.
'I hate those men!'
'BillyO calm down. Let's get this head away and the cat to Miss Rose.'
'I am going to make them pay for this!' Shadowing the lakeside road they checked on the Lady Rose, she was good when suddenly they heard a large growling noise so they hid by the road. Yellow and white lights in a cloud of smoke soon appeared. 'It's the Beastie! Shhhhh!' Billy jumped behind the large bush with the injured cat. Quiet, hearts were beating like the clappers. Yes it was the Beastie heading towards the Brig with Greasy Joe driving!
'Shit it's not a monster it's a big van with a monster painted on the side. We'll ask Joe about it tomorrow. Quick let's get this cat to Nurse Rose he's in a bad way. We can hide the Monarchs head near the pool and get it to Dan. Come on Billy you can come out now the Beastie's gone!'
'Wow! Did you see that?!' This they did without interruption and the cat was taken to the San.
'Hey boys this is a clinic for humans not a veterinary surgery! But looking at you lot I sometimes wonder!' Greeted Nurse Rose.
'He's in a bad way; I'll clean him up, get some fluids into him and some food and keep him warm. I'll do my best and if he is worse I will take him to the Vet, but we'll see. Look at those beautiful eyes looking at me!' Nurse Rose said with a gasp. 'I will call him Pocholo!'

‘Can we see Walter?’

‘Yes but not for long he and you 3 should be revising for your tests tomorrow, are you not?’

‘I’m ready!’ said Charlie!

‘We are all ready!’ added Billy.

‘Yes go on but 10 minutes only. The boys went into to Walter who was not studying but staring out the window, long to be outside.

‘Hey Guys how’s it going?’

‘Great Buster!’

‘Cobber!!!’

They related what had happened, they got the letters, they now had five sections and needed to work out how to use the disc so they could find out what this was all about, maybe Dan would help, and he knows something. They had built their first den South of Dan’s place; both Wolfie and Dan were good. They had taken the Monarchs head and found a white cat that had been injured on the poachers land. The cat was here now and Nurse was looking after him and he had been named Pocholo. They were excited about break on Thursday and could not wait!

They had Chapel that night the visiting preacher was from another informing us boys how last week he had been at St Georges girls and how it was a pleasant experience from tonight after seeing all those pretty faces.

‘Oh no you’ve set Billy off again. Ok Billy we will take the Lady Rose across on Tuesday after dinner. We have an afternoon off as all the Masters would be marking exams.’ Next day, Monday they had their tests. ‘God that was hard, especially Latin.’ Walter was happy with his efforts and pleased he is back with his friends. They went to the Top o’th’ Banks. Horbyn saw them and began to walk towards them. They headed away keeping well away from him. What does he want? Billy looked up at the blocked window. ‘Hey fellas we haven’t found out what’s there yet.’

‘Billy we will give you a choice, the room or the girls.’

‘No contest, the girls!’

After prep which was very relaxed they went over the Brook and saw Dan, He showed them how to use the cipher disc and a back up on a piece of paper that they can all eat and is not to be given to anyone else. Eat if you have to.

‘This is simple to use boys, it looks difficult but it is not so simple to decipher as it may seem so, I want you to copy this table down. To cipher take the plain letter X at the Right side of the table-in bock capitals and move across till you see your key phrase letter at the bottom Y and then take the letter at the intersection which is the cipher letter v.

'To decipher find the letter Y from the key phrase at the bottom of the table, then track up the column till you come to the cipher letter v, look to the right column and take the letter X. Simple!'

'Simple to you Dan. How do you know all this anyway?' Ignoring them Dan said,

'You should find this useful in many ways not only in deciphering the messages you are finding. It will also be useful for you to communicate with each other. Use different key phrases for each other but let each other know who you are, what your key phrase is. Change them from time to time and guard with secrecy so that no one but you, not even me knows what is said. It will be a water tight way, you may need this sooner than you think! It is very hard to decipher with the key phrase'

'What about the disc Dan?'

'Apply the same thing to the disc and see if you can work it out. No tell you what this is how it works. Take your key phrase say you Charlie-Charlie Digweed, ok, using the inner disc take the C to letter A on the outer disc then the first letter of your message read on the outer disc and see what letter it aligns with that letter is your first cipher letter. Easy and so on. Try it out and see what you come up with. You go tomorrow?'

'Yes.'

'Well, try and make a disc for each of you.'

'Why?'

'So you all have one!' Wolfie was looking at each boy for his stroke and once he had received, he curled up by the fire. 'You go on Thursday? Will I see you before?'

'Yes we will bring all we can for you before we go. Will you be ok Dan?'

'Yes I like it here it's peaceful, I cannot see anyone coming here.' The boys headed back stopping at the San to maybe see Pocholo. Hopefully he was doing well.

'But he hasn't ventured out yet. I don't really want him to, he might not come back.' The battered old warrior was getting his coat back and he was cleaning himself, it was clear that he was well on the road to recovery.

On their way back Nurse Rose called them over.

'Hey boys somebody wants to see you!'

'Who? Why? What have we done?' It was Pocholo! She took them into her lounge. He's there in a makeshift bed sitting up, looking at the boys from one to the other. His striking, separate, green and blue eyes happy, comfortable. He is looking better. 'Will he be ok?'

'Yes he will.'

'I want to keep him but he likes you lot.'

'That would be good he will be safe from those two Morons.' The boys were happy go back to Brecon. Dan and Wolfie are good and so is Pocholo. She asks if he is ok. Yes he is. They head back to Brecon. The excitement was rising as Thursday approached. At lights out Big Jim came in.

'I want you all on pitch 2 at 5 30am! We have a big match when you come back and not much time left.' There were groans throughout. Night was peaceful, no Star, no beatings, no Blue Danube Waltz. They seem to be tailing off.

They get up and are at pitch 2 at 5 30 am. An intense workout followed. What a sadist! Then the last fifteen minutes was pure rugby. 'I will announce the team when you come back from your break, keep yourselves fit during half term, do some running, go to your local club!' As the boys left the pitch somebody said blow that for a game of soldiers! We're on holiday!'

Classes were fun in the morning, some Masters were still marking the test papers, reading morning, and some fool around. After lunch bed rest, no Blue Danube Waltz. Phew! Afternoon off, Uppers were doing Services, final drills the ambulance hurtled off down the back drive, V1 and V2 were outside the main building and are about to put a ladder near to the blocked window,

'Not there boys, not allowed!' shouted Jaw. The Quad and HS Land Rover headed over to the Myrtle Wood. Brecon could roam about but were still not allowed to return to the house until 5 pm. Enough time to take the Lady Rose over to the other side of the lake. She's still there in the lagoon. A natural harbour. She's looking good! Walter informed the boys he was going over to the cottage whilst the others do some repairs on their raft.

'Ok be quick Buster!' Said Billy anxious to get to his promised land. Walter worked his way through the wood and comes to a hillock above the cottage, 100 yards from it, a good view. The Land Rover was parked outside and he watched. 'There must be a link' he thinks, when the door

opens and two men come out. No guns well dressed, not in fatigues. They got in and drive off. Once down the lane he approached the building and peeped in. The guns were in the locked cabinet, the whisky had gone and there was a chess board on the table, where it could be seen there was a game in progress, a small silver flask lay on its side by, a Pawn, Rook, Bishop and Knight spatially surrounded the Queen, a rucksack looped over the chair. He made his way back to the lagoon and saw Billy sitting down.
'Hi Man!' Billy said to Walter.
'What are you doing?'
'Eating some crisps, drinking some cola, catching the rays.'
'What are the others doing?'
'Well they are fixing the raft.'
'Why aren't you helping them? You're not at home now! I thought your Dad has a boat?'
'Well I only sail in them.'
'Billy get moving or we are not going!' The boys took her out. They are now becoming seamen.

♪

CAPTAIN BIRDSEYE!
CAPTAIN BIRDSEYE!!

Sang Larry. 'We'll have to get you a cap Cobber!' They got across; the lake was like a plate of glass.
'I reckon the girls place is about 1 mile that way.'
'Nautical or Land?'
'Land!' They started walking; they still had plenty of time.
'Shit it's the Land Rover, it's the two men. It stopped very close to the boys who were now hiding.
'Hey look isn't that Horbyn with them? And they are not the two who were in the forest either?'
'Not sure I can only see his back. We're too far away!'
'Yes I saw them leaving the cottage, not the same ones and they left their guns. Hmmmm.....I'm not sure. Look they have a map on the bonnet and they are pointing towards Myrtle Wood no Chickory Hill, no Isle of the Gulls, no Bell street, and no BolyBrack now they are looking towards

where we saw the Flaxden Brig light. Hmmm! We'll never get to see the girls.'
'Billy, were having a party on Saturday with my Sisters friends. I've got just the one for you.'
'What's her name?'
'Boo Boo Barclay!'
'Boo Boo! I like that name. Hey look they're leaving! Cripes its 4pm we need to head back!'
'Can we not go further?'
'No better get back.' They returned to the raft. A reluctant Billy was last on board, a longing look in the direction of the girls that were supposedly there. Half way across the water began to get choppy, very choppy but they arrived at the lagoon and they secured and camouflaged their boat to make sure no one could find her. Supper prep and the remainder of the day were without event. 'I am beginning to feel melancholy.' Larry said. 'We are having a great time! Beatings and all!'
The next day was results day. All results were posted at the South Door and a group of Uppers laughed as they looked at the results as they made way for their supper the Novus who crowded around, each other looking at their marks some good, some ok and some..
'Hey I came bottom in Latin!' Said Walter. '2 Percent! How can that be possible? Something's wrong there.' He had thought he would be top. In brackets was, (Flannigan come and see me- *Julian Ward*).
'Walter went to see him, and he was given extra work to do during the break.
That night after supper they took extra supplies for Hairy Dan and Wolfie and bid them farewell and say they would be back in 6 days. They popped in to the San and saw a good recovering Pocholo sitting up in his bed purring away, his front two paws kneading his blanket. Nurse Rose informed them he is hers now and he will stay there. After lights out they were so excited to be going away and chitter chatter all night when the door was flung open, it was MZEE, all hold their breath but he just tells them no talking. They drifted off in to sleep. At 1 am Moaning Minnie sounded, all out, they saw the flashing lights of the emergency vehicles as the Quad roared past them as they headed over to Myrtle Wood. It was too good to be true, what was going on?

'It's ok just an exercise!' Said Jimmy Crow who seemed to have changed overnight. He looked tired, drawn out. Maybe he was in a good mood at the forthcoming break? Back to bed. No morning run, just make sure that the house is tidy before they left. Were his final instructions. Breakfast chatter, crescendo. They go to the Top o'th' Banks and chat about the break. Horbyn watches. 'Look there he is again! He's the Spy!!' They got their bags and all piled onto the coach. It headed down the front drive and left for Flaxden Brig Station twelve miles away. To their horror they saw a flume of smoke rising in the Myrtle Wood. 'Is that coming from where Dan is?'

'No too near, sure of it but we can't do anything now.' They felt helpless as the coach took them away. On the way they passed near the lagoon where the Lady Rose was hidden, no chance of anyone finding her and then close by they saw the lane and cottage in the distance, no Land Rover.

'Hear that? It's a helicopter heading in the direction of The Brig. Must be for that Prince who got beaten after lights out. Ever seen him none had.

'Bit strange a Prince of the Realm and we haven't seen him. Helicopter is black? Wouldn't you expect a forces one or a blue one or something? I saw a camouflaged one on pitch 4 last week that's near to the Blue Huts.'

'Why are the Blue Huts there, there's no sea? Ah well let's get the train. Look there's Dochan Do! He's come to see us off!' The train arrived to rampant cheers from the party of boys like welcoming a conquering hero home. They piled on but got no seat, the older boys used their privileges and nothing could be done. They accepted and the guard allowed them to sit with the mail sacks at the back. Occasionally they got up and looked out of the windows. Nothing but hills, forests and lakes, a long viaduct sweeping majestically around the hill that lead into a station, Bridge of Orchy. A number of Uppers and Lowers got out vacating some seats.

'Right lads there are four seats back there you go sit there.' Said the guard

'Have you ever heard of this place?' Asked Billy.

'Yes it's the end of the earth.' At the next station a group of boy from Punglestock got onto the train and headed straight for the four friends.

'Right! OUT! SHIFT! You little shits! We want those seats!' Shouted one of the new passengers.

'NO YOU DON'T!!' The voice came from Harry Stoker a Cuillin Upper.

'But Harry! They are Novus!'

'Yes but they are Flaxden Brig Novus NOT Punglestock Jeremy! YOU sit on the floor!' The other boy was Harry Stokers brother, an Upper from Punglestock.

'WOW! Would you believe that!!?' Exclaimed Larry.

'The Brig IS the Brig! WE ARE THE BRIG!' Charlie said proudly.

They arrived at Queen Street and asked their way to City Central.

'Up the street, turn left, then right, and another left and straight down and it is on your right.' Eventually they get there and look for the train to Preston. They are early and get a seat. Many of the other boys live in Scotland.

The next stage of the journey began at City Central; Billy came back with a large haggis supper, a very big haggis and a large portion of chips. 'I hope you put plenty of salt and vinegar on those!' Said Larry. 'Can't taste the chips if you don't.'

'Sure did Cobber!' Charlie bought a paper the Scotsman. On the front page...

WHEREABOUTS OF PROTOTYPE JET A MYSTERY
ADMITS AIR FORCE

They all shared the food and paper. Walter bought a few cans of coke and Larry got a Commando comic to go with his extensive collection. 'Hey should we buy one of those?' He said pointing to the top shelf in Muncaster's News...

'Don't waste your money Cobber! Plus he won't let us buy one and if my Mum sees it she will kill all of us! We'll be mucking the horses out our entire break!'

'Well how about a beer, Buster?'

'A beer yeah a beer, we can change out of these kilts into our jeans and have a beer. Let's try that one we've still got a couple of hours before we need to get to the platform, right. Ok then.' So they headed to the pub outside the station the Trafalgar. They walked in with their bags and saw the pub full of suited business men either after work or a late lunch, with their mistresses and secretaries. Some are having chicken in the basket others, they were eating sandwiches.

'Bit posh this place.'

'Well we are posh in our kilt jackets and kilts, so Let's go to the bar!' They headed over to the bar and queued patiently. A tall man wearing waist coat asked them. 'Now what can I do for you boys?' Larry in his strongest Australian accent replied.
'We'd like 4 beers, 2 bags of peanuts and 2 bags of salt and vinegar crisps please!'
'Och, you do, do ya! Well boys can ya nae read?' He said as he pointed to a sign behind the bar.

NO ALCHOL
TO BE SERVED TO UNDER 25'S!
DRESS CODE IS SMART!

'So aff with yae all! Awae!!'
'But we are well dressed!' Protested Charlie.
'Aye lads you are a' wearing dresses! NA OOT YE GAE!!'
The four left to laughs from the rest of the customers mingling around the bar. As they were leaving a drunken man shouted. 'Try the Dockers Fist and they will welcome you boys wi open arms, it's just aroond the corner!' So the boys headed off lugging their bags over their shoulders and sure enough they soon saw the Dockers Fist.
'Funny name for a pub, the docks must be miles away!' So the boys headed in and walked into a near empty pub. A jukebox was mounted on the wall, Ride a White Swan was belting out of the tiny speakers and a dart board at one end with peppered dots around the board where the players had completely missed the board. Behind the bar was a large buxom lady cleaning some glasses.
'Hello boys have you come to change out of your uniforms? The lav is over there!'
'Can we buy a drink?'
'Are you all Novus?'
'Yes we are!'
'First time home? Well boys you should stay like you are for your Mothers, it is what they would want. I would! I think you look lovely. So much so I could eat all of you! Now how long is it before your train?' Walter looked at his watch.
'About 90 minutes.'

'Then you have time. What can I get you?' Larry spouted up. '4 beers, 2 bags of peanuts and 2 bags of cheese and onion crisps please! Golden Wonder! Please!'

'Nae lads it's more than my licence is worth! One of my customers is the Chief Constable and another the Procurator fiscal.'

'The Procurator what, who is that?'

'He is the Lawman around these parts! Tell you what you all can have half a Shandy each and some pork scratching on me! Do you want a cheese and onion sandwich each? Hmmmmm! What's that smell? Haggis neeps and tatties!'

'Yes! Lovely isn't it!' said Billy bringing out a squashed parcel of the haggis supper he had bought. '

Go sit down over there and I'll get you a plates and forks!' The boys did as they were told. The lady called Betty came over and set out the table for them and the boys quietly relaxed.

'Can we have a game of darts? We were kicked out of the last pub.'

'Were you now? Well if you are eating you are ok and I will get a jug of orange juice for you. Yes you can play darts.' They had a game and soon it was thirty minutes before their train. The boys left and gave Betty a shilling each. 'Awa with you boys it's ok, will ye come back?'

'Too right we will! Thank you Betty!'

Quickly they headed for platform 1 at Central Station. 'Come on Ladies, you'll all miss the train this is the last one!' Said a guard on th platform about to lift his flag to signal the train to leave. As the train pulled white smoke filled the sation to the rafters and Billy shouted out, 'Och Aye the noo!'

And the exhausted friends found a seat each and watched the world go by as they drifted in and out of sleep. At Preston they were met by Walter's Mum, and one of his brothers. 'Here he is!! Look at him! My Walter! Come here, to your Mum!' And she gave him a big hug and kiss. 'MUMMMM! Not in front of my friends!' Said Walter blushing and to his embarrassment.

'I have something to tell you Son, your Dad has had an accident.' It went quiet. 'Come let's get to the car.' He had been at Grimshaw's farm and as he was driving away a cow fell on top of his car smashing the window screen and knocking him out. He had a cut face and needed stitches. There was a headline in the paper.

COW SENDS HOSS FLANNIGAN THE LOCAL VET TO HOSPITAL!

It was headlines. 'He is ok, signed himself out and working, he is looking forward to seeing you tonight at supper. We also have a new vet with us; he is called Archie, a young man just out of University, City actually. I think they will be late tonight, they were both called out by the Police, Hoffman's Circus lorry had over turned up Brooks bottom road and they were just leaving as I left.' They headed off in the white Wolsey, but it was now getting dark and they could see nothing. They soon arrived at Crane Hall. This was a complete new environment to the other boys and not a single word was uttered. Walter's other siblings were there. His older sister Morag, shy, with suddenly being surrounded by all these new faces that she had heard so much about. The three younger ones greeted them and went off to play. Mr Flannigan came in after surgery and they all had a good chat, he took an interest in all of them, no favourites there. 'Go and help your sister and brother feed the animals.' They all trooped out, 20 cats, 9 dogs, 41, hens 34 horses, 26 ducks and geese, 7 horses were stabled in the back 2 of them massive! 'Those are shire horses! The big Grey is's the one kicking his door! He only likes him!' Morag told them fluttering her eyes in the direction of Larry. Charlie dug Larry in the ribs playfully.
'How do you ride one of those things?'
'Just like you would one of your camels Billy!'
Mr Flannigan and Archie arrived and related their experience with the elephants.
'Mrs Flannigan, you have one brave Husband here!'
'Really Archie?'
'Aye! Yes, we arrived at the scene, Police escort the whole thing, traffic tailed back for miles. When we got there the wagon was completely overturned and the elephants were upside down!'
'Upside down?'
'Yes they were still chained up, so Mr Flannigan was asked what he could do. The inside was like an oven and they were getting concerned for the elephant's health and what they might do if they panicked. So he instructed the Fire Brigade to cut holes and went inside.'

'Went inside? Wasn't that dangerous?'
'This man has no fear Mrs F! It was amazing the elephants were so calm! He gave them a sedative to relax them and the Circus handler unchained them slowly and led them out! What a noise they made with their trumpeting! But he soon hand them under control! '
'What then?'
'Well they were lead away to a farmer's field for the time being until another truck could be found. All the way up to Duxbury's field. Three elephants in a line. It was amazing! There were many people and in awe of the situation! And it didn't end there! As we were leaving 3 Ostriches escaped and ran off down the road! We had our own Circus Show!'
They rested and went to bed early when suddenly they were awoken by Mrs Flannigan,
'Boys we need your help a snake has escaped from the front surgery!'
'A snake?'
'Yes a snake!!!'
'I thought we were on holiday!'
'No time for holidays here young Billy!' In a trance they all got up and start searching looking in cubby holes drawers, under beds everywhere. There had been floods in the area and 2 snakes had been brought in by the Police. No one knew what they were and they were waiting for the Zoo to pick them up.
'It could be poisonous? Heck! Be careful!' After a while they were told by Mr Flannigan that it was ok it may have scooted out the house long ago. Then suddenly there was a scream. It was Mrs Flannigan standing in front of Phillip and he is holding up a shed snake skin. 'Is this it?' He had found it in Iain's cot where he had been sleeping the previous day.
They had another search but decided that it had now gone and was no risk. Mrs Flannigan now calmed down enough to compose herself back to her bustling way. 'Well boys Let's have an early breakfast now we are all up.' So they sat down to small mountains of food, eggs, bacon, sausage, black pudding, fried potato, beans, fried bread, toast and mugs of piping hot tea.
'Awesome!' Said Billy
'Hey you boys looked starved! What's the food like up there?'
'It's ok some good some bad.' They tell about how Boot Jarvis's dogs turned up their noses at some beef stew but the funny thing was they liked it! Roars of laughter followed around.

'Ach, you are all a blether.'

'Haggis is good!'

'That's not what you told me in your letters. !' That morning Morag went off to school, definite eye contact with her and Larry. She skipped off excitedly couldn't wait to tell her friends. 'Don't forget the party, tell them about it!' She had been planning this for months.

'I already have! Don't worry we'll feed the animals.' The boys were relaxed; there were no grumblings at the work they were doing, new experiences, especially mucking out! The party was going to be on Saturday night. Walter overheard his parents talking in the middle of the yard, 'I think we made the right choice,'

'Yes, and he has changed so much in such a short time, hasn't he got a wonderful set of friends? You were right Hoss!'

'He has, I think he'll do us proud. I think I'll take them up to Grimshaw's later and experience the farm!'

'Oh Hoss! They are on holiday!'

'Still it will be an experience!'

That afternoon Walter took them to the local baths. 'Hey I can see the bottom!'

'Yes it makes a change not to be swimming in that tea! We won't get lost from here.' On their way back they stop by the Famous Green and Blue stores on the Rock. 'Let's have a look see. Maybe we can buy something useful. They see pen knifes clothes, rucksack and 'Hey look a compass! We could have our own. Let's pool our resources and see.'

'I want the penknife.'

'We can't, not allowed. Anyway he won't sell to us.'

'Ok.' They go back and just as they are arriving Mr Flannigan is there, waiting,

'Come on boys we are off to Grimshaw's, I need to do a calving!'

'What's that?'

'Well a cow is struggling to give birth. Come on in you get! We're on the minutes!' They get to the farm after opening the 12 gates to the farm. They go to the farm door, 'Watch the dog he bites!' Surely enough the dog bites each boy in turn as he goes in. There is a roaring fire over a large range. In the corner there is movement and out of the shadows a figure stirs. Almost an identical image to Dan! A bigger man, his checked shirt was tatty and

his threadbare pants were held up by improvised braces made by bailing twine. 'Grimshaw we've come to look at your cow, now where is she?'
'Up thar, yonder!' He said going over to his cooker on the large open range. A frying pan is there warming covered by a plate. He shovelled the contents on to a plate and picked up a greasy fork. Nothing on the plate was recognisable as food.
'Are you having your dinner?'
'Dinner lad? Nay this is mi breakfast!'
'Ok Grimshaw, are you coming, I'm a busy man.'
' O Aye! Trouble at Mill Flannigan?!'
'Grimshaw!'
'Course I'm coming Flannigan, have to get value for my cash, don't want you stacking up your bill like you usually do!' With that he shovelled the burnt offerings down along with a mouthful of tea.
They got up to the field through three muddy fields and found the cow in the corner. They had dragged a bale of hay and straw up along with a couple of pales of cold water. At the cow Mr Flannigan examined and diagnosed a breech birth but he managed to get the calf delivered safely and in good health. Satisfied all was ok they headed back down but then suddenly Mr Flannigan discovered his watch was missing! All looked around even Grimshaw.
'Only one place it can be.'
'Where?'
'In the cow!' They went back up to the cow and calf who were looking good, mum was cleaning her new arrival and it was suckling well. Mr Flannigan had a feel. 'Blast! It's right at the horns Grimshaw. You have a go, I'm knackered!'
'OH AYE!!'Grimshaw tried but no luck.
'Any of you boys care to try?' Silence and shocked faces were seen. 'Come on, you try! You've done it before.' So Walter had a try but no luck.
'Come Charlie you have a go now!' Charlie had a go, carefully putting first his hand then his full arm inside the cow. 'Digging for England Charlie? I feel a nickname coming on!'
'It's warm in here Mr Flannigan! I can't feel anything my arm is too short!'

'Ok I'll spare you all! No alternative I will have to open her up! But let's wait a minute!' Then suddenly BLEEP! BLEEP BLEEP! BLEEP! 'There it is it's four 'o' clock!' He opened her up and retrieved the watch. 'I'll check on her tomorrow Grimshaw, but she'll be fine.' They headed back; the boys were relieved that they do not have to return to the farmhouse.
'Brrrrrr! It's getting cold now bit Brass Monkey here!' Walter felt a twinge in a certain place. 'Shhhhhh! They don't know what happened remember we sneak on nobody.'
'Dad where did you get that watch? It's smart!'
'From a rep son! Anything else Grimshaw?'
'Aye yes, Daisy's tits are summat chronic!' The boys looked at Grimshaw in astonishment.
'Well I'll give you something for that, its mastitis.'
'Ok, but don't be quick at sending yur bill! And I want something off for leaving your watch inside Blossum!'
On the way back to Crane Hall, Mr Flannigan announced they had to stop at Mrs Oddie's house to see her little dog Ploppy.
'Wait here boys! I'll just be a minute.' He was soon coming out 'Mrs Oddie wants you all to come in for a cup of tea.' The boys piled in to what was a house that was like a palace. She brought them into her living room and presented a large teapot with cream cakes and scones.
'Here boys tell me all about Flaxden Brig! We've heard so much about it!'
'Well Mrs Oddie we are by a very big lake which they call Flaxden Lake, there are large forests and we are surrounded by hills!'
'Well that was the best fruit cake I've ever tasted, thank you Mrs Oddie!' The little Poodle was now asleep on her lap.
'What is the parrots name Mrs Oddie?'
'He is called OBJ! That stands for Oh Be Joyful!'
'Does he talk?'
'Yes he does.' So Larry says
'Hello Oh Be Joyful! How are you today?'
'FUCK OFF!' Was the parrot's, OBJ'S reply!
'Oh I am sorry; I don't know where he gets that from!'
'Why don't you show the boys OBJ's friends Mrs Oddie?'
'Oh Mr Flannigan should I? I mean they are guests.'
'Go on just for the experience. Please Mrs Oddie!' So she brought in another cage with two other birds and almost immediately they started

trading insults with each other. 'They do this all day. I got the other two thinking that it would stop OBJ, but he just taught them to swear. It's incredible!' They thanked Mrs Oddie and all were now ready to pile back into Mr Flannigan's car.

'Mind the syringes!' They got up to head back for Crane Hall. 'I don't think I could eat anymore!'

'Hey Charlie I've got a nickname for you!'

'Now what is that Cobber?'

'Well after all the digging with that cow.............I know we will call you DIGGER!'

So now they all had their nicknames! Digger, BillyO, Cobber and Buster! They were to stick!

As the boys were getting ready to leave there was what they thought a knocking at the back door.

'One minute please!' And Mrs Oddie got up and went to the front door.

'It is the back door Miss!'

'Course it is! Silly me!' She went to the back door and opened it, looked out. 'Nobody there!' With a 'Whose there?' A gasp from them all as a little bulldog dashed into the room, straight through Mrs Oddie's legs and swept past them all and mounted Mrs Oddie's little Poodle and started banging away. The Bulldog was grunting away and the little dog of Mrs Oddie was yelping with cries of delight!

'Mr Flannigan! Mr Flannigan! Do something quickly he's going to come!!!' The boys tried to pull them apart with the little bulldog Jimmy snarling, snapping at them trying to ruin his enjoyment, nothing is going to stop him!

'Get some hot water Mrs O!' She got some hot water. 'Now throw it between them!' She did as instructed and the two separated at the agonising yelps of the two canine lovers. Mrs O's dog slinked into the corner and Jimmy is shooed out the front door back to his home.

'What a naughty dog he is! He only lives next door!'

'How did the little bugger get in?' They all go into the garden and see. back gate is Shut,

'Look! He's dug under the fence!'

'Oh Mr Flannigan! I don't want puppies looking like him!' As this is all going on the birds could be heard continually insulting each other.

'It's ok Mrs O, I'll give her a jab and she won't have any pups! Maybe a spaying, or a castration for next door!' What an event!

On the drive back Mr Flannigan related the story of an interview Archie had had with another practice nearby Pitts Paté Inc. One of these corporate organisations. Well he had been sitting waiting in this rather posh living room when Mr Pitts himself came in and sat down, accompanied by a rather mangy mutt. The interview started and the dog started sniffing around the room then sat in between the two and start cleaning himself, cool as a cucumber and then got up and started to sniff around, then suddenly cocked his leg up and proceeded to pee a on the most expensive wallpaper you'd ever seen! Well Mr Pitts continued to drone on and on and as the mutt peed and peed and peed! Not having got a word in Archie interrupted and said, 'Excuse me Mr Pitts your dog is peeing all over your wall!' Mr Pitts stopped and looked around, looked at Archie and said 'My Dog?? I thought he was yours!'

'Did he get the job?'

'Yes he did a sought after young man is Archie but he didn't take it! He felt something just didn't ring true.' Laughter filled the car as they arrived back at the surgery they were met by Miss Sherlock, well dressed elegantly lady calmly smoking a cigarette with a cigarette holder. 'Mr Flannigan you cannot go into the surgery yet. There are two irate men there threatening to kill you because you put down their greyhound last week. One has a gun!' It was amazing to see someone so calm and so serene at this.

'Ok you boys off you go into the house, dinner will be waiting for you, and I'll go and deal with this.' The four hurried into the main house, looking over his shoulder watching his Dad and Miss Sherlock walking calmly into the surgery. It was surgery time any way and the queue was beginning to develop. Then they could hear a screech of breaks and two capped uniformed Bobbies came into view. More relieved Walter headed to the house. But his Dad had gone into the surgery first, what if they were too late? They wait around the kitchen table in silence and could hear the clock ticking. About an hour later Mr Flannigan came across the back yard and was seen to be smiling. The boys took a deep breath of relief.

'Coffee please! All milk today, don't let Phillip do it, and the last time he watch the pan boil dry!'

'Hoss leave him alone! He's only six!' And he sat down with the boys and related the happenings of last week. He had been at the dog track and the race had begun but only three dogs had come out of the traps, well, one dog had overtaken the hare and turned back on to it, head on! BAM! The hare hit the dog and hurt it badly. Blood everywhere, bowels hanging out, no choice but to destroy the poor animal. 'Could you not save it Mr Flannigan?'

'No, impossible, it was a kindness. The two men were very angry than upset at losing the dog, and that was because it was a Champion dog and had won many races. They would lose a lot of money. Plus they had not insured it. So they had lost out. They blamed me for not being able to save it. Miss Sherlock managed to calm them down and the Police helped too. No worries it is all sorted out now!' The next day they met Archie Brinks again, an assistant Vet working for Walters's Dad. They piled into the back of his Morris Countryman. 'Watch out for that hypodermic!'

'You like those Buster don't you!'

'Ha ha! That's hilarious Digger! Did you write that?'

'Nope! Got that one off BillyO!' They got to a pig farm and watched Archie deliver a new born pig that was stuck in its mother's womb, when the farmer came to him. 'Hey Vitinary, you have to go and see a sick dog!' They all go right over, down a long dirt track to a caravan, Archie knocked on the door and a bunch of Hell's Angels answered the door. They all look at him, kind of funny, but he was tired and too worn out to care. 'Stay in the car boys I won't be long!' He examined the dog and saw right away it was distemper, so he took the dog out the back and shot it. BANG! The bikers paid him his fee, but they were still staring at Archie wide eyed, like he is some sort of loony.

'I think they are going to attack him.' It's not until he was back in the car and looked in the rear view mirror that he saw his face and hair are all blotched and matted with pig placenta. He looked like the psycho Vet from hell!

'Hey you could've told me! Want to hear another pig story?' Yes they do. 'I was once taking some foot and mouth disease blood samples from some infected pigs for this big meeting in DC' Archie told them. 'The pigs were being held in separate rooms'

'Sounds like the bed studies at Flaxden Brig!' Whispered Larry.

'Well I had to change and shower, change into a new set of clothes with each pig, so to save time; I just decided to do it naked. There I was going from room to room, crawling on my hands and knees with the squealing pigs, buck naked on the cold cement floor. Great fun!'

Then just at the end of the road the car stalled and wouldn't start again 'Quick boys out and push the bikers are coming after us!' Sure enough the bikers were following them. They piled out and pushed, the car started and they got back in, the back doors of the Countryman slamming shut just missing Charlie's foot.

Archie took them back to Crane Hall as he had a surgery to do. It was raining solid when suddenly the wiper flew off! Screeching to a halt Archie dashed out of the car in the pouring rain grabbed the wiper.

'Here put your foot on the accelerator so she doesn't stall and pass me that match box.' He takes a match and fixes the wiper on. 'There that'll do the job!'

Back at supper. Archie joined all the family and guests and the boys tell the table about their adventures with the cats and the Stag up at Flaxden Brig. 'Hmmmmmm!' Both Archie and Mr Flannigan listened with keen interest. 'Right boys now to earn your keep. Go had help your sister feed the animals.' They did this eagerly; Larry was first like a greyhound out of the blocks. The horses, the goats, the geese, the hens, the cats and dogs, 'It's a zoo here never mind out there!' Then looking up into the clear sky they saw the star.

'Hey look fellas up there. I can't believe this!'

'What can't you believe?' Said Morag. Larry elbowed Billy.

'Oh nothing.' That night they ask what is in that direction.

'Well that is the hill where they burned the witches, it is called Knowl Hill.'

'So we have to climb another hill on our holiday?'

'I think we should.'

'Ok we can do it tomorrow. All for one and one for all!! That's The Three Musketeers! There are four of us. I'll be Portos!' They asked permission to go. It was granted.

'Can we come?' Asked the siblings.

'No!' The boys headed off. There was nothing there. They searched for an hour. Nothing.

'Well it's picturesque; hey look what's that in the distance?'

'It's Bordello Bank, the telescope. Come let's go Mum will be worrying about us.'

'When's the party?'
'Tomorrow.' On their way down they got lost. 'We'll have to get our own compass!' They ended up in a valley. 'Do you know this place?'
'I think so it's known as the Forgotten Valley. Sometimes I bring Rebel up here, it also called Steeply Vale.' They came across about five Wigwams.
'Just like that film we saw in Soldier Blue. Don't tell your Mum, remember it was X rated! What happens in the Brig stays in the Brig. Do you think there are any Squaws around?'
'This must be where Davie FiveTrees is from!' Outside they saw people dressed as Hippies playing musical instruments and there was a stage set up at the far end with a set of drums. It was the swinging sixties after all. 'I remember now there was a pop concert in the summer. We are not supposed to be here, Mum forbade me. Made me promise.' Billy was looking in one of the wigwams when suddenly he was pulled in. YELP!!
'Hey Buster!' Shouted Charlie, 'Look!' At the top of each entrance to the wigwams was a letter. 'That was five letters *cetpc* Cobber. Digger can you write them all down?' Yes he could.
'Where's BillyO?' Suddenly he surfaced from the Wigwam with the letter c on it and was being chased by a woman,
'COME BACK! COME BACK!' She shouted. Billy's clothes were in disarray! The boys took flight!
'LET'S GO!' Soon they approached Crane Hall there was no one in pursuit. 'What happened Billy?'
'Well Buster, she pulled me in and started kissing me, then took my jersey off and unbuttoned my shirt and was just taking my belt off when I ran! I was in a panic! Hey what's that smell? I think its drugs. I've smelt it before somewhere.'
'Quick get changed, I'll bung them in the washer, and Mum will kill us if she knows what we have been up to.' Billy stripped and showered.
'Billy where's your pants?' Billy looked down, looked up.
'She took them!'
'Hey what about this party tonight? Remember Boo Boo is mine!'
'Oh yes he who runs from woman1 A freaky woman!'
After dinner they went into the town centre and into Norman Helms record shop to look at the latest records, singles and albums. Walter bought a T REX single and a David Essex album for the party.
'The girls are coming; they love this one, worth every penny.'

'Buster which one will Morag like?'
'Who's coming?'
'All my sisters' friends and some of my friends from my last year. There will be somebody for everybody!! Think you can cope Billy!!!' Suddenly they heard it, Danube Blue Waltz filtered through the record store.
'Where's that coming from? Seems to be following us around!' Six cubicles lined the back of the shop. None were occupied Charlie looked into each of them. Only one has a record playing, there is nobody in the cubicle. It is blue Danube Waltz. He took it to the counter.
'Excuse me Sir do you know who left this over there?'
'No idea Sonny, didn't see, don't remember.' Not even bothering to look up.
'Come on guys Let's go and get some burgers, there is a Wimpy Bar round the corner.'
'Wait on! The library is over there; let's see if we can find out what Chiral means. It's worth a shot. I think it's something to do with the cipher.' They headed to the library. Silence signs were everywhere. People were reading books, local and national papers. 'Excuse me Miss could you help us please?'
'What!?' A dizzy scatty woman peered over the rim of her inch thick glasses. Then a kindly old lady said.
'Well that looks like a science word to me and there is your man. He is Dr Gilmore a Chemistry teacher from the local college, he's even written his own books! Charlie, Larry and Billy while Walter did his Latin rework approached the man sitting reading a book who was only too pleased to help.
'Yes of course but you boys are very young but keen to learn, I can see. Here is my book.' He pulled out from a library shelf with pride, A Modern Approach to A level Chemistry, with an immense pride as it was his work, Neil Gilmore written on the front. He flicked through the pages and came to Chirality. He explained to the boys and the meaning of the word... Then asked if they would like to know about mechanisms. The boys knew this was too much for them and bid the Dr a good day.
'Remember there is no substitute for hard work! Enjoy your break!'
'You know what this means.' Said Charlie.
'What? That we are a non-super imposable mirror image that reflects plane polarised light!'

'Yeah right!' They explain to Walter what they had read, but that is four elements there is another one. They show him Dr Gilmores drawing.
'Well it's clear who the C is that's me.' Said Walter.
'No Buster! It must be me said Larry',
'Well I think....I think....It's a load of rubbish!' Billy added.
'Well I think it is none of us but I am sure we are the other four and if you thought about anything other than girls Billy, you would be able to have better conversations...........' Said Charlie ignoring Billy's comments.
'ENOUGH YOU TWO!' Intervened Larry.
'Then who is Chiral Five? Or what is Chiral Five?'
'Come on we can think about that later it's party time soon!' Billy saw a group of girls in their uniforms across the road white blouses, brown blazers with matching pleated skirt white socks up to the knees and black shoes all wearing a hat. With a white ribbon circling the rim.
'Wow boys look at the t'arse on that!'
'Shhhh! Don't point Billy.'
'Come on Buster! They are HOT!'
'Keep down don't go frantic! What's Digger up to?' Sat down at the table Charlie was reading a big book. 'What's that Digger/'
'I'm looking up something in Encyclopaedia Britannica! Be with you in a moment! Got an idea for Mr Flannigan.' As they were walking through the town centre again they passed the Army and Navy store. 'Hey let's look in here again. We'll get the compass and a monocle.'
'We need the knife but he won't sell to us.'
'Ok we'll ask Archie.' They do, and he buys them each one.
'Archie we can't afford.'
'It's ok a gift you helped me the other night getting away from those Hell's Angels! But keep them safe and only use when needed.' They got the blades engraved with the money they were going to use. Their first initial is put on to each blade and the inscription '*Aide toi et dieu l'aidera*.' Help Yourself and God will help you, on it. Walter's blade has the letters *wlcb,* Larry has *lcbw*, and Charlie has *clwb* and Billy *wblc*. They also bought a whistle each from the flea market at the Drill Hall, all trench whistles from the First World War and decided on an emergency blast Walter is one repeated every 5 seconds, Larry is two repeated every ten seconds, Charlie is three repeated

every fifteen seconds and Billy four blasts repeated every twenty seconds but use the whistle only if needed.
'These are very loud!'
'We need to get each other a disc made like Dan said. I know Tim Dampier is coming tomorrow morning we'll ask him to help he's the Blacksmith, coming to shoe the Shires.'
'Will we have to help?'
'No, but Dad will want us to help with operations, in the surgery. We have to earn our keep here.' The next day they talked to Tim Dampier and he agreed to their strange request as long as they hold the Shires for him. With trepidation they agreed and then the operation began. Mr Flannigan sedated the horse with a chloroform mask and it span wildly around the yard,
'Keep it near the straw pile for a soft landing!' The horse landed on its side and shook and vibrated. 'You sit on the neck, you others hold the legs!' Mr Flannigan gelded the horse,
'Wow look at that! He's cutting his balls off! Can you feel that Buster!' Walter felt a twinge! Mr Flannigan glanced at his son non plussed. The back gate opened, Archie walked in winked at the boys as he headed into the surgery. Operation over Mr Flannigan asked Larry and Billy to stay with the horse until he came around.
'I'll stay too!' Said Morag looking at Larry adoringly. Billy looked to the sky. 'When is my time coming Lord?'
'Soon, you will see Boo Boo!' Morag giggled away. They went into the operating room and a road accident had just come in. The dog was still conscious; the two vets sedated the dog and stopped the bleeding, did an x ray and decided they could save the dog. The boys stood by while the vets did their work and when it came to plastering the legs up they were asked to assist. The dog was heavily sedated and both Hoss Flannigan and Archie were happy that the operation was a success. Archie went to complete afternoon surgery while Mr Flannigan continued on his visits. 'Want to come boys? Ah I remember there is a big party tonight!' That afternoon they went and watched the local rugby club Export RUFC play. They were asked to play as the Vikings 4th team were short. They had no kit but some is found and they drew straws on who would play. Billy got the shortest and played on the wing,
'Wow look at him go! What's his name?' An onlooker at the side asked.
'It's Billy, we call him BillyO!'

'Well he goes like BillyO!!!'

After returning to Crane Hall the boys were sitting around with the Flannigan family having supper when the phone rang, Billy, Charlie and Larry jumped out of their skin. 'Answer that please Walter.' Said Mrs Flannigan as she bustled around the kitchen. Walter stopped eating and picked up the phone, 'Hello!' And he listened for a few minutes, 'Yes Ok I will tell him. Dad the Police are on the phone and want to bring in a dog for examination.'

'Well that's ok, just tell Jackie to let them know I'll be here for about an hour.'

'Erm Dad..... the Police say they want you to look at a dog whose owner has had sex with it!'

'Not in front of the little ones!' Said Mrs Flannigan.

'Mum what is sex?' Asked Phillip and a quick glance from his Mum showed not to ask that question again.

'Tell Jackie to inform the Police that she will phone them back. Could be a hoax, the Police should understand!' On the other line Jackie did as asked. Soon enough the request was confirmed and the Police asked to bring the dog into the surgery.

After tea Mr Flannigan went over to the surgery where 2 detectives were waiting with the dog.

'Now what have we here Jack?'

'Well Hoss a terrified owner came into the Station with this dog and was concerned he had made it pregnant! Is that possible?!'

'Come on Jack! Thought you knew better than that!' He replied.

'But it is still an offence so can you do a test to see if he is telling the truth?'

'Where is he now?'

'In a cell, thought we would let him stew for a bit!'

'Yes I can take a swab and examine it under my microscope in my lab.'

'Great Hoss. We'll leave you to it!'

'No Jack wait it won't take long, you can come with me. Jackie would you be so kind as to make these two Gents a coffee with milk please? Many thanks!'

Mr Flannigan took a swab and took it to his vet lab. After peering down the microscope it was confirmed. 'Yes, yes, yes many of the little blighters there Jack. What will you charge him with?'

'Some sort of public order offence, maybe a mild caution but we'll wind him up a bit!' With that the men finished their drinks and left.

That night the party started, about seventy turned up. 'Which is Boo Boo? Which is Boo Boo?!!'

'Calm down Billy, you're going frantic again! Where is Larry?'

'He is helping your sister with the food.' Mountains of food were on a long table in the pink room, a room usually only reserved for adult guests but this was a special event. There would be about fifty/fifty girls to boys, Morag had thought about this for weeks, planning to the finest detail. They all arrived in stages; the girls gazed at the boys from a faraway place as though they have come from Mars. The boys look them up, sizing up the competition for the night. Mrs Flannigan puts on the first record on to a cigar shaped like box, turntable in the middle. It was an album, Glen Miller. 'Now come on! All dance! Enjoy yourselves!' As In the Mood struck up! Boo Boo arrived,

'There Billy! There is your girl! A small girl with glasses and with pig tails walks nervously into the room on her own, they all look at Billy for a reaction but he just stares at her. His mouth drops and slowly the biggest grin and smile comes over him as eye contact is made. But this wasn't a smile of attrition it was a warming smile directed at Boo Boo for her only, as he headed towards her, nothing was going to break his stride...

'Hi! How are you doing? My names Billy what's yours?'

'It's Boo Boo.' She said in a quiet timid voice, her cheeks blushing a shade of crimson.

'Would you like to have some food and a drink, the orangeade is good? Or maybe a dance?'

'Whoa! Billy slow down!' Thought Walter. 'Don't rush it!'.

'Yes that would be nice.' They go over to the table covered in mountains of food and, sandwiches, sausage rolls, pork pieces and much much more. Next to the table are the drinks. Orangeade, Dandelion and Burdock, Sarsaparilla, Ginger beer, orange, lemon, lime cordials-the lot!!!

'Wow what a spread!' Complimented Charlie. 'Your Mum has done herself proud!!!'

'Digger what were you looking up in the library?'

'Looking up? Oh yes, those tablet's Billy whipped from the San, remember? The contraceptives. Well I looked it up and it is stop having babies and regulate periods.'

'Meaning if we take one we can control our classes?'
'Not exactly Buster, I'll explain later!'
The atmosphere changed as the Glenn Miller LP ended and the latest top twenty were put onto the turntable. Smaller singles stacked on top of each other, ready to drop down on the turntable once the previous song had finished. Charlie paired off with Sheila; Walter warned him that is where Steve, Dave, Nig and Baz came from! He'd be careful!
'You'd better they are all here!!!'
'Do you think Cobber will get jealous? He likes his Shelia's!' Walter mingled with the crowd, knowing most faces and looked around for Prudence Blaney. No sign, he saw his Mum at the door just checking. Have to warn them she will be patrolling the corridors tonight! He continued to mingle on his own and chatted with some previous friends.
'Here Riggers let me introduce you to my friends. This is Billy you see with Boo Boo, he will find anything you want or need, and watch his big antennae! He can pick up the slightest dialect! See he knows we are talking about him now! Charlie who is over there with Sheila is our intel/information man, knows everything, great conversationalist and Larry is our strategist, cartographer, who is with Rachel we refer all our planning to Charlie and Larry.'
'And what are you Walter?'
'Me? Well I'm...........' Suddenly he was cut short by another of his former school friends.
'You know, you are lucky going up there many are jealous, they say if they won the pools they would like to have a term there, without their parents!'
'You know Chaddy it's not easy, it's hard, we are laughed at most of the time but we just get on with it. We've learned to adjust and adapt to the environment. Your library at the Derby Low is better than ours; many are without their parents even here. Look at some of the pupils at the Derby. When they go home their parents are none existent, not there, never there.'
'You go to the library; you mean you use a library?'
'Yes, it is a useful and quiet place, Diggers is a whizz with the Encyclopaedia Britannica, if you want to know something he'll find it! The gymnasium you have is much better. It is very Spartan you know, tough, morning runs cold showers like that, caning, but that has tailed off. The Masters we hardly see, the boys run the show, they drive the fire engine and the ambulance in fact all Service vehicles!'

'Really WOW! I can't believe that on! Have you had a drive?'
'No Paul we are too young! And they constantly remind us. No vehicles are allowed on the site except the emergency vehicles and visitors to Flaxden Brig. The Masters ride a bike, walk or run as we do.'
'Never!! A boy driving a fire engine?' Paul repeated. 'Wow!'
'And no girls!'
'Well there are plenty here! Let's get the party going!' Paul pointed out as he headed towards a leggy blonde. Prudence didn't turn up; there was no sign of her. Suddenly there was a loud slapping noise.
'What was that for?'
'I've told you before Chadwick; keep your filthy hands off!!'
'Ah well the party went well and his friends were enjoying themselves, that was the main thing. 'Hey look Billy is snogging Boo Boo!!' At ten pm the parents started to arrive to take the guests' home it had been a great night. But no Prudence. They all tidied up for Mrs Flannigan before going to bed. 'Well Billy?'
'Yes Man great!'
'What about the girls across Flaxden Lake?'
'Nope I have a girlfriend now Boo Boo! I'm going to write to her! In fact I think I'll even marry her!' Walter smiled and was pleased. Boo Boo was a good girl.
The next morning they were again woken up. A dog was missing from the surgery. An Alsatian, 'Every one up and look for it.'
'We should be good at this; I don't think we'll be able to lie in again!'
'Hmmmmm! I think it would head to the river. Right Larry and Morag that way, no hanky panky. Billy and Charlie that way and I'll go that way and look in the woods.' They spotted the dog on the road works where the new motorway was being built,
'Quick chase it!' They chased it into an old air raid shelter at the edge of the works. 'Billy go to the top, there is a gap I think it was for a gun or something we'll go through the front.' Soon they have the frightened dog and took him back to Crane hall. They have a Sunday dinner Roast Beef, Yorkshire pudding, roast potatoes and veg. Mr Flannigan is not there he has been called out to an emergency by the RSPCA. A Swan had got into some difficulties at the Mill Lodge.
Suddenly there is a buzzer, Morag answered the phone, 'Yes Dad, yes Dad! , Dad says you are to go into the surgery he needs you to help him.'

'Anyone want to come?'
'No only you.'
'Oh ok!' Walter headed for the surgery and as he opened the door.
'In here!' The booming voice of his Dad could be heard as he peered into the waiting room and on seeing into the main consulting room he saw his father stood there rigid. 'Look!' He pointed down to his crotch. And as did his eyes opened wide, there stuck to his pants was an enormous cluster of fishing hooks of every design available. 'I can't get these off and I'm not going to the ruddy hospital! I'll be waiting for hours!'
'What happened?'
'Well I was at Tranny Lodge and a Swan had got tangled in a fisherman's line and they were doing something illegal.'
'But there must be over a hundred there!'
'Yes! Now cut these off! I took them to dispose of and as I was getting in the car it caught and one got stuck then another then another. Grab a pair of scissors from my case and cut them away.' Walter did this. 'Now just go and get me another pair of pants! That was a narrow escape. Wonder what your Mum will say when she sees these!' Walter got the fresh trousers. 'Now why were you in the hospital at Flaxden Brig and tell me the truth young man!' He tells his Dad of the beating and the events that lead up it. 'Hmmm! Well you were in the wrong and deserved punishment, but I think that he went a bit too far.'
'I'm ok Dad.'
'Look at it this way you just nearly lost your balls and I nearly lost mine!!! Like Son like Father!!!!'They both laughed. 'Enjoying it up there?'
'Yes it's great!'
'I thought you would! It was just a question of finding the right place for you. Come on let's join the rest for dinner.' As they arrived there was only Phillip, Fairlie and Chirsty. Mrs Flannigan served Mr Flannigan with his roast. 'Sorry I wasn't there to cut it for you dear. Slight emergency. Where are the others?' At that moment a road traffic accident came in. A Retriever had been hit by one of Hoss Flannigan's friends from the Hack Horse Inn... The owner, a young girl, followed. Bone was sticking out of the badly smashed leg, the dog howling in pain but with his friend helping it was stitched up and plastered in no time.
'Thanks Hoss, how much is that. I'll foot the bill.'

'That will be £53 shillings and sixpence Omar, but we'll keep her in overnight. She'll recover well. Won't charge for that but the next round is on you.'
'Walter, why don't you take Rebel out for a ride? Since you left he has been terrible, banging his head and kicking his door, breaking his shoes, Dampier's been back many times. Omar and I will go and have a.............. coffee! Right Omar?'
'Ok I'll do that, I think Morag will come? I'll ask the others.' But alll were otherwise engaged. He saddled up Rebel alone and off they went! Rebel seemed pleased but soon found himself on the floor! Again, again, again and finally again, five times. Walter decided to take him back. He felt all jumbled up. Puts him in the stable and gave him some water and fed him. Back in the house Hoss Flannigan was sat the kitchen table peering over his glasses. 'Back so soon? Here have a taste of this.'
'What is it?'
'Well Archie has just breezed in with this chicken that he cooked. Have a taste. Tell me what you think.' And he picked up a fork and pulled a piece of breast away from the steaming chicken.
'Hmmmmmm that tastes good! Nice and tender!'
'Pulled Chicken. You have something there, it might catch on. Well he brought it in wrapped in tin foil and presented it on the table but he had to dash off to a calving at Wilkinson's, so he said try some but left it for me. Guess how he cooked it?'
'How?'
'Well Grimshaw gave him the chicken, he bought the tin foil from the corner shop and put it on his car engine and by the time he got back here, BINGO! It was cooked!'
'Wow! Really!?
'Yes really, now what happened with Rebel?'
'He chucked me off!'
'Come on let's go see and have a word with him. Look he's laughing at you!!!' And sure he was whinnying and smiling at Walter and kicking his door. 'He's done that because you have ignored him! Try again.' Reluctantly he did as his Father said and got up back onto Rebel and set off, no problem. As he rode he could see Morag and Larry walking nearby hand in hand towards Oak Wood. He took Rebel up to the Steeply Vale escarpment, that's strange all the Wigwams are gone! He decided to take

Rebel down into the vale where he could stretch his legs. A trot developed into a canter and then a full gallop. The remnants of camp fires were clearly seen around, slowing down as they reached the head of a small wood Rebel came to a dead halt and Walter was thrown clear over, arms and legs flailing as he hurtled through the air to his uncontrolled landing. BANG!!!! His head landed with a heavy thud, CRACK! As he came to a halt rolling down an embankment, winded. He heard Rebel whinnying and the pounding of hooves. Unable to move he saw a blurred vision of Rebel coming towards him, anxiously urgently wanting to see if his friend was ok. Then he saw flames licking around him, a steering wheel, greenery, red........

'ARE YE ALRIGHT LAD?' He heard a voice but lapsed into oblivion. He saw a woman, sultry, with long wavy hair cascading over her shoulders and, a brilliant white sheet wrapped around her body, she seemed to be saying something, then, NUDGE NUDGE NUDGE, he opened his eyes and saw the mouth of Rebel, nudging him and making brief brrrrring noises. Slowly he turned on to his back and realised he was ok nothing broken, drawing air into his lungs, he was battered and bruised but what was new in that ? He felt a massive thirst and got to his feet gingerly. Rebel nudged him again. 'It's ok fella, I'm ok, and It'll be alright.' He realised that Rebel had stayed with him and felt grateful. Yes now he remembered a gunshot. 'Not your fault Rebel.' He led Rebel to the nearby stream and they both drank together. He could hear the voluminous quantity being drawn into Rebels body as he took his libation. Finished, he turned his head and was astounded to see Rebel had also turned his head to look at him, simultaneously. Getting up, he lead Rebel back to the track but there was no need Rebel would follow him without being held so putting the reigns over Rebels head they walked side by side. At the track they see two horses approaching a boy and a girl. He recognised the girl as Prudence Blaney. His head feels on fire as he takes hold of Rebels reigns. The two approached and at the last minute Prudence recognised the ruffled figure.

'Oh .... I didn't expect to see you here!'

'Yes you are a surprise to me too.' He said looking her in the eye. Sheepishly she continued.

'This is John, John Conroy. He has, since......... been my boyfriend since...........'

'Since September?'

'How did you know?'

'Just an educated guess. I thought, hoped you would be at the party last night.'

'We went to the theatre with Mummy and Daddy isn't that right Prudence?'

'Yes it is John, I.......'

'I must go now, Rebel stumbled and I fell off.'

'He's getting a bit old he's gone grey!' Laughed Conroy. On hearing that Rebel heavily nudged the others horses causing a mini stampede.

'He's grey because he is a Grey! Pure Grey Eagle stock.' With that mounted and turned,

'WALTER.........' He did not reply and headed home.

When he got back he questioned Morag,

'Why didn't you tell me?' She didn't know. 'Never mind, it's ok.' Larry chipped in. 'You should've seen what happened whilst you were out. Your Dad asked us to help with a foaling. You should've seen Billy!!! He fainted!'

'As soon as he saw the hooves and head coming out he was gone! SPLAT!' The next day was the final day of the break.

'Hey lads look what I've got, 4 tickets for Export City v Fortvik Town! It's the start of City's Cup defence and no Larry, Morag you can't go!' That day the boys prepare themselves for leaving, help Mrs Flannigan around the house, feeding the animals, bedding them down and helping Mr Flannigan with his rounds and in the surgery. 'You know we've had a fantastic time, thank you.' Agreed all the boys. That night Mrs F prepared their supper. It was s favourite. Chicken breast cooked in a sauce made up of tomatoes, mushrooms, Babysham and double cream, boiled minted potatoes and assorted veg. Beautiful! Afterwards they were all taken to the match by Archie. It was cold and rainy and the match ended in a 1-1 draw. John Connelly scored the goal for Export City. 'At least they won't go down this year!'

'Not much further they can!' Commented a group of elderly spectators as they made their way to the orange and cream Double Decker outside. Leaving the ground suddenly they realise that their break is coming to an end, could you possibly believe that they could pack so much into such a

short time? A melancholy feeling spread amongst them. Breaking the silence Larry said. 'Billy what was the TV program you were watching?'
'It was this guy called Jake Starwood doing impersonations, it was good! I fancy myself as an impersonator!'
'We've been saying that ever since we met you!'
'Ha ha!!!!'
'I watched the news; did you know Apollo 8 is going to circle the Moon?' Said Charlie.
'Hey Billy you could teach us all our own character any ideas?'
'Ideas? I'm full of them; hey look what I acquired at the rugby club!' It was a book of rugby songs!
'We can learn these but cut out the rude words of course! I like this one in particular! It's called Sweet Chariots.'
'Billy you know you shouldn't do that!'
'Come on Buster it was on the floor by the pitch! FINDERS KEEPERS LOSERS WEEPERS! CAN'T HAVE IT BACK!'
'Sing it for us Billy, go on!' Cried Larry and Charlie.
'Ok here goes! Buster you conduct!'
'Left hand Buster!'
'Left hand Diggers? Where did you get that from? Don't tell me!'
'ENCYCLOPEDEA BRITTANICA!!' They all shouted in unity.

♫

SWING LOW SWEET CHARIOTS
COMING FOR TO CARRY ME HOME
SWING LOW SWEET CHARIOT
COMING FOR TO CARRY ME HOME

WE LOOKED OVER FLAXDEN
WHAT DO WE SEE
COMING FOR TO CARRY US HOME
A BAND OF ANGELS COMING AFTER US
COMING FOR TO CARRY US HOME

WELL WE'RE SOMETIMES UP
AND WE'RE SOMETIMES DOWN
COMING FOR TO CARRY US HOME
BUT WE KNOW OUR SOULS ARE HEAVENLY BOUND
COMING FOR TO CARRY US HOME

SWING LOW SWEET CHARIOTS
COMING FOR TO CARRY US HOME
SWING LOW SWEET CHARIOT
COMING FOR TO CARRY US HOME

WELL IF YOU GET THERE BEFORE WE DO
COMING FOR TO CARRY US HOME
TELLALL OUR FRIENDS WE'RE COMING HOME TOO
COMING FOR TO CARRY US HOME

SWING LOW SWEET CHARIOTS
COMINGFOR TO CARRY US HOME
SWING LOW SWEET CHARIOT
COMING FOR TO CARRY US HOME

WELL NOW THEY'RE COMING FOR TO CARRY US HOME.
HOMEEEEEEE!

'Put a sock in it Billy! Hear that? You can hear Lucky howling!!!'

Valette

The next morning arrived and the boys were taken to the station by Mrs Flannigan, all splendour in their uniforms, kilts and kilt jackets. With a tear in her eye Walter's Mum spoke breaking the silence. 'It is a pity you won't be here next week; Her Majesty the Queen is coming to the Town to see of Operation Spring Clean.' It remained quiet to the station and as they all said their goodbyes and getting his big hug from his Mum.
'MUMMMMM!!!' His protests fell on deaf ears. They looked out the window as the Clansman pulled out of the station heading north, Mrs Flannigan waving with Morag, getting smaller and smaller then suddenly gone. The boys find their seats for the 6 hour journey, straight through this

time. In silence and looking out the window at the passing Lancashire they soon come to Lancaster, Oxenhope before stopping at Carlisle. 'Strange this feeling, it's as though we've have never been away.' Said Charlie with a sombre note, they had had such a great time. No stop at City as the train is changed from electric to diesel for the final leg of their journey, Stirling, Perth and finally Cronkley. They had a seat all the way. Billy has been writing a letter to Boo Boo! Jimmy Phillip's coach arrives and takes them back to the, this is a new route for them they see Queen's view more lakes, hills and forests when, 'Hey look isn't that.....?'

'Yes it's the Fairy Hill. Hey Larry, can you recollect all this for the map.'

'Uhhh! What Buster? Sorry thinking about Morag. Ok will do Captain!' As he saluted. Walter thought about Prudence and envisaged her with John Conroy, the boy who has it all, but there was still that longing look in her eye as he rode off that evening. 'Ah well can't do anything now.' Not that he really wanted to. After about an hour the coach pulled into Flaxden Village. 'Hey fellas look at this!' They saw two hotels, a cluster of shops and a bank in a square around a small monument. 'We will have to come here one day. I didn't think we were that close to civilisation!'

'Like when? We have lots to do.'

'Yes I have that test with Pansy Ward.'

'Will you be ok?'

'Yes I'll pass I'm bound to. Something strange happened I do not know why I only got two percent.'

'Coz you're a Dumbo !' They all laughed. The coach was now full of boys of all ages and a mad dash to get off as they pulled up in front of the main building. The four waited until everybody is off and watched their bags thrown to the side. 'Hey hope all that grub we got from your Mum is ok!'

'Yes we must get it to Dan somehow. Let's go to the Top o'th' Banks and breath it all in.' They did this and stood in silence looking out towards the lake and hills, not a word was said. So calm. 'No Head in his study maybe not back yet? Come on.' They entered Brecon and at the boot room saw George on the top rack. 'Hey he looks to be sleeping! And long may it so be!'

'Shhhh! We don't want to wake him up now!' They got a courteous greeting from Mony and Monkey and a brief nod from Troup, Pearson and Kerr as they headed towards Conway. In Conway they see the other boys plus a couple of new faces.

'Odhiambo, Digweed and MacCloon you are no longer here in Conway. MacCloon you are in Mersey, Digweed in Shannon and Odhiambo you are in Thames.' The four looked at each other and without saying a word made their way to their new quarters. They had been separated! 'Why have we been separated?'
'Usual thing this happened last year too!' Said Mad Mac.
'I know we can communicate with Morse code.' Said Charlie and he began to explain how, International Morse code worked.

1 The length of a dot is one unit
2 a dash is three units
3 the space between parts of the same letter is one unit
4 the space between letters is three units
4 the space between words is seven units

.A. _B _ . . . C _. _ .D _ . .E .F . . _ .G_ _ .H . . . .I . .J . _ _ _K _ . _L . _ .
M _ _N _ .O _ _ P . _ _ .Q _ _ ._R . _ .S . . .T _U . . _V . . . _W . _ _
X _ . . _Y _ . _ _Z _ _ . .
1 . _ _ _ _2 . . _ _ _3 . . . 4 . . . . _5 . . . . .6 _ . . . . 7 _ _ . . .8 _ _ _ . .
9 _ _ _ _ .0 _ _ _ _ _

'Heck Digger do you not think we have enough to do!'
'Here. I've written it all down for you all!' It's an option agreed the friends. 'We can tap on the pipes or the walls we'll have to work on it. Let's concentrate on the numbers first, no, let's have just one message for all,-.......----.'
'And what does that mean?'
'It says LET'S GO! Tap it or flash it.'
'Or. -- . --. --, that means WE GO!'
'Hmmmm!' muttered Billy.
'Flash it with your torch, idiot!'
'Don't call me that! I know what to do. Teach me shut your cakehole!'
'Charlie! Billy! Stop it! We're all in this together right? Good tool, great tool, we'll use it! Just get some practice in. Remember practice makes perfect!' Intervened Larry, defusing the situation.
'Yes just memorise those two.'
'What with the cipher, and now this. I really am getting confused.'

'Well it's an option. Tell you what we'll just concentrate on the numbers!'
'What do you think? Well even if we don't get it right we can still use it. It will confuse the others if someone really is on to us. We've all got torches now so we can use those too.'
'Say if we are stuck in the woods at night or something?'
'Yes like that. Look what we've got our knifes, whistle, communication, compass, we're ready for war! I want those poachers!' Exclaimed Billy.
'Hey enough of that war is senseless.'
'Yes I know, just joking. So you can take on the Beastie now then Bill.'
'Ha ha!'
'Well you were scared about the Vulcan the other day when we were on top of Chicory Hill. Have you noticed we spend most of our time outdoors?'
'Yes its great isn't it! Keep's us busy! By the way how's Latin going?
'I am through, still, strange that yes it was 2 % when everybody got over 50! I reckon somebody spoiled it. Mony told me that his LOG had been tampered with before. So that's it ok, we'll memorise the numbers. Let's have our own number so we know who is flashing. Hey that's against the law! You'll be put in jail for that ha ha! Larry? I will have 8, lucky Chinese number. Billy? I'll have number 1! Charlie? I'll take 3. Well I'll take number 6! Come on now let's get to Science class Spy is taking it today we might learn something!' The boys and the rest of the Novus piled into Spy's Biology lab.
'Well boys today's lecture is about Sphagnum moss, Larry whispered to Walter. 'Sounds like a Rock Group,'
'Quiet Digweed! That's a strange name for someone.'
'It was my Great Great Grandfather; he was the gardener for the Duke of Marlborough sir.' Replied Charlie even though it was Larry who had been talking.
'Was he now? Well if you don't pay attention to me I'll have you digging the weeds in my garden!' Dr Wallace continued...........
'Sphagnum moss is a bog builder extraordinaire! '
'You mean he builds the toilets!' Called out Walter.
'You are quiet a stand up Flannigan! Think you're smart?' He continued.
'The Moor is a special type of peat bog – a blanket mire The country's blanket mires are very precious as they represent between 10 and 15% of the earth's total blanket mire area. The moors vast expanse of wet blanket

peat is of such ecological importance that it is designated as a site of scientific interest and a special area of conservation. Part of the moor is a national nature reserve. It is so special that it has also been listed ramasar site- this means it is a wetland of worldwide importance.
'The Sphagnum moss is the living surface of the moor blanket bog is a dense carpet of different kinds of sphagnum moss. Who's that snoring?' A quick look round and he sees that all seem to be upright and paying attention. 'The moss plants produce new buds and leaves at the surface while the older, buried parts of the moss die and eventually form a new peat. Sphagnum moss soaks up moisture and can hold up to eight times its own weight in water. People have made the most of this absorbency. For example Inuit's have used Sphagnum moss to make disposable nappies and it was also used to dress wounds in the first world war.
The moor acts like a giant sponge, the moor's healthy carpet of sphagnum moss soaks up rain and slowly releases it into the streams and rivers that drain the moor. In this way, the moor helps to reduce the risk of flooding or drought in the surrounding area.
Growing peat lands like the moor are also described as carbon sinks because they absorb a lot of carbon dioxide gas and store it as peat, playing a vital part in helping to keep the composition of the earth's atmosphere content. Any questions?'
'Yes sir what is the film on Saturday!'
BRRRRRRRRRIIIIIIIING!! The Bell for the end of class brought the boys to life. Thank heavens for that! 'I want an essay on my desk tomorrow by 5 pm, that is your Science prep! You Odhiambo will do 161 lines, 'I will not ask stupid questions in class!'
'But Sir!!'
'When is Mr Fowler coming back?'
'When he is better!'
'Where is he? At home? '
'No he'll be recuperating on the front lawn!'
'Word is he had some sort of poisoning, whisked away to hospital.'
That night a rumbling was heard throughout the house and voices are prevalent, the doors flung open, it was MZEE 'Right NOVUS! All report to the common room now!' Bleary eyed and putting on their dressing gowns the boys headed for Georgetown. At the common room the Head walked in. It is 1am what can all this be about?

'Right boys you are to pack all this gear, and report to the South Door in 15 minutes sharp, you are going for a little break!' And with that he was off! They all did as instructed and made their way to the South Door jealous that the others were all still fast asleep. After 15 minutes of waiting Joe pulled up in the little green minibus and told them to get in!
'Where are you taking us Joe?'
'To the station!'
'We've already come from there.'
'Well you are catching the Royal Mail Train to Mallaig where you will link up with Captain Hum; you are being taken on a cruise!'
'A cruise?'
'Yes all Novus have to do this, its part of your curriculum!' They got to the Flaxden station and the train soon arrived, it was pitch black and eventually the train rolled in to view out of the darkness and the boys piled in. There were plenty of seats this time. At 7 am the train arrived at Mallaig. The thirteen boys headed down to the harbour where a large yacht is waiting. On seeing the boys walking down the hill a figure appeared and strode towards them. 'THE GOOD SHIP VENUS FELLAS!' As Billy once more burst into song.

♫

TWAS ON THE GOOD SHIP VENUS
MY GOD YOU SHOULD HAVE SEEN US
THE FIGURE HEAD WAS A WHORE IN BED
AND THE MAST WAS A RAMPANT PENIS
FRIGGING ON THE RIGGING
WANKING ON THE PLANKING
THERE WAS FUCK ALL ELSE TO DO

'Have you learnt all the words Billy?'
'Sure have, may come in useful! Keep the book under my pillow!'
'Not going to give it back to the Rugby Club Billy?'
'Like when you are serenading Boo Boo!'

'Nahh they know all the words, think of me as spreading the Gospel! And not a word to her Cobber! Or I'll............'
'You'll what?'
'I'll.....'
'You'll......'
'I'll.....'
'Oh yeah!'
'Yeah!'
'Yeah!'
'Christ you two give it a rest! Try a cut out the swearing Billy!' Ordered Charlie, as the boys headed down the slip way to the boat. 'Billy she won't like the swearing!'
'I'm not comfortable with all these rude words. It's painful to the ear.'
'Nothing to do with me I didn't write them! Just having a bit of fun!'
'Do you know what they mean?'
'Right boys climb on board! WELCOME TO THE FLAXDEN BELLE!' Shouted Captain Hum.
'You mean we are going for a cruise in that?'
'A cruise? Who said anything about a cruise?' The boys climbed aboard and were taken to their bunks, well some were beds others hammocks.
'Cast away!!' They heard from the Captain and then, 'All hands on deck!'
'Come on Let's get up top and see what is going on and where we are going. Captain where is the crew?'
'Crew...What crew?'
'Yes Captain, the crew.....'
'You lot are the crew lad!!!' Quickly they were taught the skills of seamanship, and after that first day they were all glad to sleep, some with bloodied fingers and others feeling seasick and funny legs. The next few days were spent at sea in horrendous conditions, with waves crashing over the Flaxden Belle.
'Good job we're not in the Lady Rose!' The boat leaned to 45 degrees to starboard, and then 45 degrees to port, the boys are fastened to the sides as the Captain wrestled with the Belle's wheel and vomiting could be heard coupled with the sickly smell. Eventually the calmness came and the boat moored in the bay near a small town. There were many trawlers there and the boys explored, the hulls were empty the smell a terrible stench. 'This is a creepy place Let's get out back.' On the way back they found a record

store in the small village. There are now cassette tapes being sold. Two boys come out laughing but are followed by the shop keeper. 'Hey you little American shit! I'll call the Police! One of you has taken a cassette!' and Charlie walked back to the man and asked how much it was, 'Four shillings and six pence.' Walter fumbled in his pocket and pulled out the ten shilling note.

'Here take this.'

'I'll get your change.'

'No, it's ok keep it, we are sorry that happened, just a mistake, easy done.'

'Ok boys thank you! Hope you don't sink!'

'It's Mad Mac who took it. We'll sort it out later.' In the rowing boat Larry drew up his oar. 'Right who took it?'

'It was Mac!' He handed the cassettes over to Larry.

'Middle of the Road? Poor taste Mac, you keep it!'

'But I took this too; it's One In Every Crowd by Eric Clapton.'

'That's more like it! I'll have this one, it's been paid for now!'

'Well his till be ok now!' The next morning they were woken up with a bell, DING! DING! DING! DING!

'Up boys and to the decking.' All the boys were lined up. 'Now face starboard and look at the beautiful view.'

'But Captain Hum there is nothing but the sea!'

'Exactly! Now strip!'!

'Strip?'

'Yes strip!'

'Why?'

'Because you'll get your clothes wet!' They all stripped down to butt naked. 'Now jump!!!!' They all jumped into the freezing water!

'Christ! My balls are where my throat used to be!'

'My knackers have shrunk!'

'I used to be 8 inches!'

'Yeah! In your dreams Billy!'

'Hey look Stevie is struggling, he can't swim!!!!' They all swam around the stranded boy and helped him back up the ladder.

'Why didn't you say you couldn't swim Stevie? We're all here to help.' The boys then see the Star. 'Heck how do we do this one? Is there no escape?'

'Well its shining over that island with the big house, well take that little rowing boat at night. The Captain will be flat out, drunk with his rum!' That night they get over to the island and creep up the little beach 'OI! What are you lads doing?'

'Heck, look at that Giant! RUN!!!' About, 100 yards away a giant of a man was striding towards them at speed, behind him followed a smaller man.

'Quick over there in the rhododendrons, dive in!!!' He didn't notice and ran past. A few minutes later, 'Wow did you see the size of him! The smaller one looked fearsome too. Looked like those two men chasing McIver remember? Must be his house come on, how do we get ourselves into these situations?'

'You know something; they look like the men who were chasing McIver that night.'

'Just said that but yes Digger I think you are right!'

'Yeah, did you see the size of his head?! I've seen them before.'

'We don't create problems, they come to us. Think he has seen the boat? Let's have a look round.' They found the letters carved on to a tree *uJzpa* and carefully made their way back to the rowing boat and back aboard the Flaxden Belle unseen. The fumes of rum could be smelt coming out of the Captain's cabin.

'Now we know why he is called Captain Hum!' Quipped Larry. In the morning after their dip they asked the Captain. 'Who lives over there?'

'No one lad, used to be a big house by a very tall man and his butler and he died many moons ago.' The Clipper turned to port and headed out to sea.

'Hey, look at that hill range, fancy a hike across there?'

'Not today Cobber!' After the five days were over the Flaxden Belle berthed back at Mallaig dock and the 'cruise' is over. The boys bid farewell to the Captain as he shuttered up and headed for the local shop to replenish his now depleted rum supply. The boys headed for the station but the train was not to leave for two hours.

'Let's have a look around.' They saw the shops and went into a cafe and see a pool table.

'Hey look someone has left these florins on the table, must have forgotten them. Let's have a game!' So they do, then two big men came in and said, 'Where is our money? I put it there TerreRouge!' It was the same men from the other night.

'Quick the train is leaving!' And the boys sprinted to the station chased by two burly men, only just making it. The train set off and as they peered out the window they could see the men shaking their fists, 'Don't worry lads I left a few shillings on the table as we were leaving.'
'Heck Charlie that was big of you! Are you sure that's all they wanted?'
'Yes, it was wasn't it? Well somebody has got to look after you lot!', and a few hours later arrive they arrived at Flaxden Station. The doors were locked.
'Hey we can't get out!' The guard came out,
'Sorry boys you have to go the other side. The platform is too easy for you. And by the way the way we have had a call from The Brig that you are to walk the two miles to the bridge where you will be picked up by Mr Delgrano!'
'Nothing is easy for us here is it? Always difficult.'
'Life isn't like that. Well it's not impossible! So easy is a walk in the park!' So they did this and as they were walking along the road although dark they could hardly see in front of them only the outline of the boy in front. Suddenly there was a noise in the sky above and they all look up it is a big bird. 'What is that?' A large like object is screaming across the sky.
'It's the Vulcan Buster; we saw it when we were on the top of Chickory Hill!' That night they met after supper at the Top o'th' Banks. 'We've been separated, why?'
'It's something to do with rotation and mixing everyone. Shouldn't be too bad for us except Cobber, Clyde has Kerr, Troup and Pearson there.
'I'll be ok. We're kindred spirits after all now!'
'Hey listen.......' But before they could continue a wind suddenly blew up, as a helicopter descended on to the front lawn. A boy got out and was accompanied by two men carrying his bags. They headed to the main building and the Head suddenly appears from the office. 'Isn't that the Prince?'
'Yes think so. Just look how the other half live!' But it was time for them to get back, no prep but they all headed to the library.
'Wonder why Nurse Rose needed those contraceptive pills?' After there was no one around, so they could chat freely. 'Listen we are not going to be able to communicate as well as before now they've split us up, so we'll use our discs, agreed, yes.'
'We could also use the Morse?'

'Right we need to get to Dan. Did you see the sign on the South Door?'

'Yes Myrtle Wood is still out of bounds.'

'When has that stopped us? We can go up the Grap track right to the top where that bridge is and cut down the Brook and cut across to Dan's, dropping down across the Brook, near the den we built. We can do that tomorrow after games. We have to see if Dan is ok.' They got to bed, it was quiet but they are not woken by the bugle, but by the new Housemaster Târpnam tipping all the beds, morning run, but no pushing down the banks, the cold showers as cold as ever but it was becoming a pleasure now. 'Why is he Housemaster now Mony?'

'Well, we've heard that Jimmy Crow is on leave, poorly, some sort of food poisoning, taken away during the night, nobody saw, so Târpnam is interim, nobody likes him, only arrived this year and a tyrant! Was a tutor in Sperrin! Blare, Braun and Ztirgeon's House.'

'No Horbyn?'

'No he is Cuillin but hang s out around Sperrin.'

'Must be the reason we are all separated?'

'No that usually happens. Dochan Do's idea to integrate us more.' After Chapel they headed for classes, Latin was first and was given his retest whilst the others did Roman History, DAMNATION! Walters favourite! Double Maths, break no Tucky queues English then French it had all become comfortably routine. Dinner approached and they were happy that they could all sit together. Bed rest then games. Showered and preparing themselves to go to Dan's they suddenly heard a piercing scream. It was McIver, yelling at the top of his voice! He was the last to go in the shower room, 'The door is locked! I can't get out and somebody has put a bomb in the shower room!' All laugh, 'A bomb? Shhhhhh listen! One moment. I can hear a fizzing sound. Go to the corner McIver, by the windows we will break the door down!' It took four to break the door down, Troup included.

'Cripes we've damaged the door and frame now! We'll get a thrashing!'

'No we can't, Pete has banned it!' The door flung open for them to see a rocket in a milk bottle aimed at McIver who was now screaming and climbing buff naked out the window when the rocket took off ZAP! Straight through the open window and singeing his backside as he just escaped. The boys ran to the window to see him streaking and screaming around the building, Quick! Get his duffle coat!' He came round; they covered him in time as Big Jim appeared out of his cottage.

'What's going on here now?'
'Oh nothing Sir!' Replied Mony. 'Just all excited at being back at The Brig now!'
'Good! Good! Good!' The four headed off up the Grap track and eventually come to the den, it was intact, 'Good den well done, fellas!' They crossed the Brook and moved with animal like precision and stopped to get water from the Brook. Dehydrated Walter took a long slurp direct from the flowing water. Billy started telling a joke. 'There was an African, Australian, Irishman and an Englishman...............'
'Ahhh! That feels sooooo good!' Said Walter as he closed his eyes, swishing water around his face, sucked a mouthful into himself and pictured Rebel by his side, drinking with him after his fall, opened his eyes expecting to be back at Steeply Vale and see his horse gazing into his eyes. That's odd Billy had stopped talking, there was now only silence but in the water he saw the reflection of a dark figure in front of him, legs shoulder width apart, he closed his eyes quickly and looked again, no it was not a dream, he was still there, he was now aware of the deafening silence around him now, he wanted to call out to his friends but was paralyzed by fear, he steadied himself and as he put out his hand to get himself up, it landed on a large black boot. With knee jerk reaction his head looked up to see him surrounded by six men, his friends were to the side, also rooted to the spot. The men were dressed all in black and their faces completely blacked out with what looked like shoe polish heads covered in balaclavas. He was pulled firmly to his feet. All they could hear was the birds and the running water of the Brook, gurgling away. The silence was broken with a Cockney accent. 'Now what do we have here?!!' Riveted to the spot the boys could not speak, mouthing a response but no sound. 'Well!??' A more clipped and authoritative tone from another of the group.
'We are only just exploring Sir!' Blurted out Charlie, the others eyes had now become like saucers.
'Hey I like it when boys talk like that!' Said another in an Irish accent. 'You know proper like.'
'You mean with respect Paddy.'
'We come up here a lot Sir and play in the Myrtle Wood. We are from the Brig.'
'Yes we know where you are from.'
'Who are you?'

'Who are we? Well now that would be telling! What shall we do with these four, men?'
'Let's take them with us!'
'We are heading for one of the old commando huts; we have a friend living there.'
'Commando hut, where?' The men looked from one to another. 'Yes it is over that way.'
'Right and who lives there?'
'An old man, and his cat??' The boys then related their tale of adventure from before the break.
'Hmmmmm! The old man? An old man you say?' You know what this means men?' The boys stood scared stiff again rooted to the spot. 'What have we got ourselves into?' Larry whispered to Walter but the look was explanatory on each other's face. 'What time is it?'
'4 30 pm Sir!'
'Hmmmmmm.....Soup time I think! Come on boys join us and less of the Sir! We are all equal here!' With that the group sat down and the men started a fire, so quickly it was unbelievable. One took out a knife, another a thick wad of cotton wool,
'These tampons are certainly handy!!!' Another grabbed the bits of wood a spark and they soon had the fire going. Small pans came out and a watery but nourishing soup was made. Oat biscuits and wedges of cheese appeared and the boys sort of relaxed. Who were these men? 'Listen boys we know about the old man and his cat, its ok, he will be ok but we are interested in the poachers over the hill, but what do you know?' The boys related their story with the Stag and the destruction of Dan's shack.
'Yes they are going to pay!' Said Billy in an angry tone, 'And for what they did to Wolfie!'
'Listen Lads leave them to us!'
'But!' Protested the boys.
'No buts!' All the men listen intently, nodding at each other but not replying to the boys. 'Well boys' thanks for that maybe we'll meet again?'
'It's a large wood sir!' With that the men packed and picked up their guns and they were gone as soon as they had appeared. The boys made their way to Dan's cottage and there at the door was Wolfie! The meow was incredible! He was so pleased to see them. With this noise Dan came to the door a broad smile revealing the toothless grin that they had missed,

leaning against the doorframe in his customary pose... 'Here Dan my Mum got you all this.
'Wow! A hamper!' It had lots of goodies for them. They were thrilled Wolfie was fully recovered and Dan had been good with no problems. They told him about the final message and that it had read you are the Chiral Knights. They had found out what that word meant but believed there was a fifth element and explained what Doctor Gilmour had said.
'Hmmmmm! Beginning to make sense! How did you get the phrase?'
'Charlie worked it out. To make sense? Would you mind telling us about it?! We have no idea' They all say without telling Dan about the men they had seen in the wood. The fire had been the Forestry Commission flattening his old place the day before they left and a fire had caught hold. They told him about the men at the cottage and they had seen different pairs. One pair had Afrikaner accents the others clipped English accents. The plot was thickening. No the Star had not appeared nor had they heard Blue Danube Waltz. The last time that had been heard was when they were at Steeply Vale. The boys bid their goodbyes and headed back they passed the San where Nurse Rose was at the door majestic in her uniform and Pocholo sat by her ankles looking at his rescuers with admiration. 'Hope you are behaving yourselves!'
'Course we are!'
'Buster shall we ask Nurse Rose what a tampon is?'
'No!!! Let Charlie look it up!'
As they were approaching the Service area they heard the Quad starting up, the unmistakable sound of gears grinding, 'That's a double de clutch going there!' Said Larry. 'Hey look! The doors on the shed are still shut they.............' But before the sentence was finished the shed moved away from them straight into a reverse mode and on to the tennis courts. Two figures emerged from the wrecked shed. 'That's Braun and Blare!' The shed now was relocated on the tennis courts. The Quad could not be seen as it was still in the shed! 'Hey that's? Yes it is! Quick let's get out of here they will think it's us again!' They boys departed just in time as crews of the Fire Service and Joe Delgrano descended on the Service area. From the common room, minutes later they could see Aeronaut Fabius heading that way, stomping with clenched fists, he was fuming as apparently he and Freddie Gibson were the only ones permitted to drive it, not even the Emergency Service crew.

That night at supper Mental Pete asked for information on what had happened, reminding that the Brig was on borrowed time already. The man looked weary, no longer straight as a ramrod he was starting to stoop; it was one thing after another. 'Until the people are caught all of you will contribute to the demolition of the cow steading and byre at the front of the new Chapel entrance, so as to assist the Building Service.' The building of Flaxden Brig was continuing as normal.

'Do you think the Brig is being sabotaged for some reason?'

'Yes Diggers it is looking that way!'

That was to be a light punishment the boys realised as he had banned the beatings before half term. 'You know fellas I think there definitely is more to all this than meets the eye.'

'What do you mean?'

'Well how about sabotage?'

'Yes sabotage! The spokes of Flaxden Brigs machinery are being tampered with. Yes I think those bullies are something to do with all this and they are causing so much disruption look at poor Pete.'

'Yes they are certainly putting a spanner in his plans for the Brig.'

'Well they don't like us that's for sure!!'

On their way they saw Ztirgeon with a fellow Novus, Stevenson, against the wall but they were too far away to see what was going on. They ran quickly and stood in between them, WHACK! SMACK! As both Buster and Cobber take on Ztirgeon, taking the punches for Stevie. Suddenly They were grabbed by Mony and Monkey. 'Stop it! They are more trouble than they are worth!' Ztirgeon struggles free and spat into Cobber's face. 'Quick move on Grappy is coming!' Quickly they all dispersed, a beating from Grappy was nearly on the cards and as they were going into supper a frightened Stevie tells them what has happened. Ztirgeon had 'bought' his watch off him for £1, a silver hunter which had been a present from his grand dad. He had already sold it to another boy for £10, it was worth much much more than that but priceless to Stevie. 'Don't worry we'll get it back for you!'

'Oh WE will, will we, how do you propose that?'

'We lure Ztirgeon into the nature reserve tie him up, give him £1 and take the £5 off him. Two of us do the luring, then you take the £5 and get his watch back! Simple!' 'You know the plan could work. Let's do it! We can put all our skills into work here.'

The boys were all separated now but see they are still together, they are still in the same year, same teams same tables and they can communicate easily. They also understand that they can use this turn to their advantage as a form of intelligence as to what the others are up to gain more information.

That night Troup and Kerr tell them everything. Blare and Braun are running a racket, as Mony had said, as they probably know they pride themselves being known as the BB GANG, started when they were themselves in Brecon, Ztirgeon is just out for what he can get but they are all school authority so be careful, Horbyn they don't know, he just seems to be tagging along, harmless really, don't know why he is there. Blare and Braun have got the place tied up, even more this year since they gained authority, taking money with menaces. They have many on their side who don't want to be, just waiting to get out. The auctions are a way of paying them off, keep them out of Brecon. McNut gives them nearly all of the profits. They said they would stay away but haven't. They are for some reason targeting the Novus. The three are nothing to do with them now. Blare is furious. Ztirgeon seems to be doing all the grabbing now. They've been like this for a few years now but there is intensity now. Keep away from them. But it is not just them, there is a Mr Big.

'A Mr Big? You mean one of the Masters?'

'No another boy, nobody knows who he is and they take instructions from him.'

'A Flaxden Brig myth maybe?'

'No, if it wasn't for Mad Mac McNut and his pay offs from the auctions we could have a problem. And now they have increased the payments by 50% also threatening with a 20% surcharge if we are late with payments. Brecon will end up penniless!'

'Can you not go to Pete?'

'No they have sweet talked him too, have you not seen them doing his garden?'

'You mean getting others to do it.'

That night they came back from prep and saw Braun and Blare leaving Brecon, Ztirgeon could be seen keeping a lookout.

'Hey they aren't supposed to be there!' They soon find what they have been up to. They have put a turd pie bed into McIver's bed. Billy also found a hacksaw under his mattress. 'Quick let's switch mattresses with

Stokes. He's the link to all this. BillyO can you get that back to Jaw Shack, that must've been the saw that they used for the bike. They are setting us up!'
'What's an Upper boy doing living here anyway?'
'They'll be searching the dorm tonight I'll bet!'
'But will he be there now?'
'No, remember Târpnam he is with the new housemaster.'
'New housemaster?'
'Yes Jimmy Crow has left!'
'Great no bugle in the morning now! Maybe no morning run.'
'Quick Let's do it, tell Mony and Monkey though.' The boys switched the beds and rushed back to their dorms, All are wide awake as they hear Stokes going back to his bed study.
'SHIT! What is this? Who has done this?' They heard the door slammed as he went out of the house. Five minutes later a double set of footsteps were heard, then,
'RUDDY HELL!' It was the unmistakable voice of Târpnam. Then Stokes went around to all the dorms, 'GEORGETOWN NOW!!' Soon the whole house was crowded in to the common room. The angry Târpnam came in, 'Somebody has put human faeces into this man's bed! I want to know who is responsible! I am also going to search all the dorms in Brecon!' Though everyone knew nobody sneaked. He couldn't prove it. The next morning on their way to Chapel Walter said to Larry.
'Did you see those trousers that Târpy was wearing? Well I'm sure he is one of the men who were in the billiards room that night.'
'You think he may be involved in all this?'
'Well Cobber look at it this way he hates us and is very nasty. Some connection. Remember we weren't supposed to be there!'
'Who could the other one be? Do you think it is anything to do with the Prince and those two men who are always near him?'
'No those men are his body guards, those were the ones we saw when we were looking for the girls when Billy was hiding behind the rock from the Beastie. Pardon the language but Târpnam is such a bastard he must be behind all this. Well these bullies have to be dealt with first. It can't go on.'
That weekend the coach pulled up to the main entrance. They were off to Mumblemond to play their long awaited match, a grudge match, they were

excited, Flaxden Brig had never won but they are very optimistic this time, with their new recruits. But this time the whole house was going, a day out, and fifteen in the team and the rest as supporters. As they were waiting to go the familiar figure of Târpnam got onto the coach.
'Why, where is Big Jim?'
'Don't we see enough of him, constantly snooping around?' They didn't like Târpnam, in fact detested him, for many reasons.
'Unfortunately Big Jim has got flu and is confined to bed so Târpnam will be with us today.' Monkey confirmed. On the way the coach pulled into a coach stop at a little village called Amulree.
'You have 5 minutes! Nobody can go into the shop!'
'What is the point of us stopping then? There's NOTHING HERE! NO ACTION, SIR!!' Târpnam looked at Billy,
'I'll deal with you later boy! Don't speak to me like that.' The first snowflakes of the year hit the boys on the head.
'Hey we might get stuck in the snow.'
'Maybe they'll put us up at a nice hotel!'
'You think??? Come on Digger! This is Flaxden Brig remember.' In the middle of nowhere they get back on to the coach and sang a couple of rugby songs, Târpnam sat straight ahead at the front and said nothing. The mood is joyous and they are all happy together and within 60 minutes the coach pulled up at the sports fields of Punglestock. The Mumblemond team play here and are a feeder for Punglestock... 'Isn't this where the Firsts won the other week for the first time ever, gave them a bit of a battering from what I heard Cattell saying?'
'Yes when they came back late and missed the film and Big Jim was singing that song he likes? What is it, Trampled underfoot?'
'Who sings that?'
'Led Zeppelin.'
'Led Zeppelin? I thought that was an aircraft!!! The boys changed and Mony is the captain. All four friends had been selected to play. They took their positions and the match kicked off. caught the ball, passed to Mony, to Monkey, to Stevenson. 'Run Stevie run! You're in the corner!' When suddenly he is sandwiched by two players, lifted up and speared into the turf. 'Argggggghhhhh!! Shouted Stevie.
'Hey ref! You can't do that! It's dangerous, look he's hurt!'

'Any more of that and you are off this is my pitch! Now get him off! He's not fit to be on the pitch!' With that Charlie and Larry help Stevie to the side of the pitch.
'Here Stevie just rest and enjoy the match!' The game had only been going for 3 minutes.
'Right now kick off!'
'Kick off?' Said Mony, 'We need to reorganise!'
'BEEEP! Penalty against you!'
'But!'
'10 yards!'
'I must......!'
'Right you! OFF! Arguing with the ref!' So Mony left the field and went over to Stevie.
The team was in disarray. Monkey took over the captaincy.
'Right lads, it's 13 against 15 now!' THWA! The opposition score the penalty. 'We'll regroup. When we are attacking we have no forwards, when we defend we have a full scrum.' But the plan takes time to adjust and at half time the boys they are 35 to nil down. At half time they rest.
'It's 16 to 13, the ref is against us!'
'What should we do Monkey?'
'Stevie are you ok?'
'Getting there, sore but I'll be ok.'
'Think you can come on later?'
'Let me run it off.'
'Ok. Right we fight and don't give up!'
The game restarts and the plan is working in attack they get the ball to Mad Mac who scored! Taking out three in the process!
'Well done Mac, but watch the hand off!' Then BillyO scored under the posts!
'We got em here they're starting to panic!'
'Slowly they pulled back in the second half and manage to get to 35-29.
'Stevie you ok to come on?'
'Yes Monkey!'
'No he can't!' Said the ref.
'Yes he can he is ok now!'

'I sent him off!' At that point an elderly gentleman stood on the line intercedes, 'No Sir! You did not send him off, it was the other boy! Who you shouldn't have sent off anyway! Shameful!!'

At this the referee beckons on Stevie. Play begins. Troup takes the ball in the lineout a ruck is formed and moves towards the half way line. The ball passes to, Buchanan, to Flannigan, to Monkey to Pearson then Troup, 'Here Stevie take it and go!'

The ball was caught by Stevie who was in a bad way, struggling to run.

'Quick BillyO get to his side we'll guide him to the line!' said Kerr They crossed the line, put it down Stevie! Two hands!' Encouraged Kerr

Stevie pole axed himself and scored!!!! TRY!!! The conversion is added and the match ended at 35-35.

'You've blown 5 minutes early!'

'You arguing with me again, I can still send you off!!'

The game was enjoyed but the Mumblemond side do not shake hands, unable to accept the draw they tell the Flaxden Brig boys that they will get them. Luckily there was a member of the Punglestock 1st xv who was watching the match. 'You'll be ok lads they will not cause trouble! Your boys beat us fair and square! I'll watch.' In the shower room they burst into song

♫

WHEN WE RUN THE BANKS OF FLAXDEN....

picked up from hearing the Firsts singing in their changing room after their match, but only if they won. 'Well we didn't lose, so Let's sing. The final chorus of

♫

BALLS TO MUMBLEMOND!
BALLS TO MUMBLEMOND!

could've have been heard for miles about. They finished their showers and all headed for what they thought was going to be refreshments but are told to go straight for the coach. After waiting 10 minutes Târpnam came from

the pavilion stony faced, looking like thunder but as he is just about to board he was called back and he goes to the caller. An intense conversation is going on, with Târpnam just nodding his head, his face going purple as they speak, and the boys sit in silence. The complexion on Târpnam's face was by now fuming and about to explode. He tells Jimmy Phillips. 'Straight back no stopping.' As the coach pulls out of the park, the boys break into another song.
'Hey Let's do that medley we've been working on!'

♫

FOUR AND TWENTY VIRGINS CAME DOWN TO FLAXDEN BRIG!
AND WHEN THE GAME WAS OVER THERE WAS FOUR AND TWENTY LESS!
SINGING BALLS TO YOUR PARTNERS ARSE AGAINST THE WALL
IF YOU'VE NEVER BEEN SHAGGED ON A SATURDAY NIGHT
YOU'VE NEVER BEEN SHAGGED AT ALL!
AND WHEN THE BALL WAS OVER
THEY ALL HAD TO CONFESS
THEY ALL ENJOYED THE DANCING
BUT THE FUCKING WAS THE BEST
SINGING BALLS TO YOUR PARTNERS
ARSE AGAINST THE WALL
IF YOU NEVER GET FUCKED ON A SATURDAY NIGHT
YOU'LL NEVER GET FUCKED AT ALL
DINAH NOW!
A RICH GIRL RIDES A LIMOUSINE
A POOR GIRL RIDES A TRUCK

BUT THE ONLY RIDE THAT DINAH GETS
IS WHEN SHE HAS A FUCK!
DINAH DINAH SHOW US YOUR LEG
SHOW US YOUR LEG SHOW US YOUR LEG
A YARD ABOVE THE KNEE

Suddenly Târpnam stood up, face contorted with an expression that they had not seen before.

'PHILLIPS! STOP THE COACH! NOW!' Jimmy Phillips did as he was ordered. With a heavy jolt the coach came to a halt, only the sound of the engine could be heard now. 'SHUT YOUR MOUTHS! YOUR FILTHY MOUTHS! YOU HAVE ALL EMBARASSED ME! SINGING THAT VULGAR SONG IN THE CHANGING ROOMS, YOU WILL ALL NOT SAY A WORD UNTIL WE GET BACK TO THE BRIG. YOU'LL ALL PAY FOR THIS!' His screaming could be heard back at Flaxden.

The journey back seemed to take forever; seconds seemed like minutes, minutes felt like hours. Most slept exhausted from the game, the others gazed out of the window into what was now pitch black. As the coach pulled up at the South Door. 'STAY THERE! NONE OF YOU LEAVE!'

Târpnam went into the Head's office then a couple of minutes later went to Big Jim's cottage. Jimmy turned and said, What have you lot being doing?'

'Nothing, only singing rugby songs.' Soon Big Jim and Târpnam could be seen heading for the class room block. An Upper came down to the coach.

'You are to unload your bags and go straight to classroom 3.' They all did as they were told and all piled into the room.

'Right, Târpnam relate back what you have just told me!'

'Yes I will! I have never been so ashamed in my life! I was called back to speak with a master in the pavilion, only to be informed that the changing room you had been using had been vandalised. Coat pegs removed, shower fittings broken and missing, as were the light fittings... dirt and water all over the floor.'

'Right Mr Târpnam. Have you lot anything to say?' They boys look around at each other, incredulous shock, eyes wide open and alert. Mony looked over at and opened his hands, frowned and shrugged his shoulders. 'Right

OK! The punishment is that you are all gated and may not go out of the Brig perimeter which is within the circuit, except for the ACE and you will all do that tomorrow at 5 30 am in lieu of your morning run. As I am still recuperating Mr Târpnam will check you all out and in!'

'What? Me? Is that all the punishment they get?'

'Yes Mr Târpnam! It was on your watch this happened. Now you may all go! Except for, Monroe and Flannigan. I want a report on the match.' The boys left silently and then there was only the four left in the room.

'YES? You still here Târpnam? This is rugby talk, not your scene. The incident has been dealt with you may go now.' Târpnam left the room but he was obvious he was fuming further humiliated at being asked to go.

'Right you two what happened?'

'Well we drew 35-35 points each sir. We were 35 nil down at half time and pulled back to even the match, would've been more but Monkey left his kicking boots behind, BillyO scored four tries, 16 points!'

'No, I mean what happened in the pavilion? There is something hid from sight here! I can't just put my finger on it.'

'Well Sir, Flannigan and myself were the last to leave the changing room, Flannigan had collected the shirts and I swept up the changing room, it was as spotless as could be, there was no vandalism done by any of the boys from Brecon. Impossible!'

'Are you sure? Where were the others?'

'They had all gone onto the bus Sir; no one was left there in Pavilion except us two. They were all excited at stopping at the Chipper in Punglestock.'

'Hmmmmmm! Yes I see! Right you two that's all. Remember Nelson at Trafalgar?'

'No sir I wasn't there!'

'Flannigan! Well he put his telescope to his blind eye, this is what we are doing here, we know your quality you boys didn't do it, the Head agrees with me, but Punglestock have blamed us directly. Phoned and they will be writing an official letter, I believe what you say and we will write to them and disclose our findings.'

'But Mr Târpnam?'

'Ignore him! He will give you a tough time but you'll cope, use the ACE as a training exercise, I'm sure you are up to it. Now off you go!' The boys get up and are leaving when,
'Good result, good result! But remember one thing here at the Brig you can only sing that if you win!'
An Upper boy knocked on the door and came into to the room. 'Yes boy? Can't you see I'm busy?'
'Sorry Sir but I have a message from Mrs P!'
'Well? What is it?' The boy handed a piece of paper to Big Jim who opened the folded paper. Looked up at the boy and then glanced at Mony and Walter.
'Yes I know! Very good, very good, you are making progress! Now go before I find something you are guilty of! NOW SCRAM!' And with that he got up and left.
Followed by Big Jim humming and rubbing his hands together.

♪

BALLS TO MUMBLEMOND?

YES!

BALLS TO MUMBLEMOND!!!!!

He laughed as the two headed out of the room.
'You know Mony I think it all had something to do with an episode we had on the train.....'
'It's ok Buster tell me later we'd better get back!' Buster...Mony had called Walter by his nickname! Mony and headed back down to the South Door to pick their bags up, who would have thought that a Lower and Novus walking together... As they approached the bottom of Magillycuddy Hill they saw the figure of the Head coolly smoking his trademark cigar at the door to his office.
'Enjoyable match?'
'Yes sir! But we could only manage a draw!'
'Yes I know! Very good, very good you are making progress!' And with that he went into his study.
The messenger passed the two and they asked him what it had said.

'Nothing to do with you fellas, it just said. Have reached 97 Fahrenheit BIG BOY, I NEED YOU!!! NOW!!!'
'That's why he is called Big Jim!' The boys picked their bags up and headed around to Brecon and said to Mony. 'You see that? Pete? He just mouthed,

'MY BOYS!'

After supper they gathered at the Top o'th' Banks when they saw the Prince sitting at the second tier, breaking a twig branch and throwing it aimlessly, gazing into the distance.
'That was a close one with Pete! I thought we were for it!'
'Hey isn't that?'
'Yes it is it's the Prince.' He heard the friends talking and started to climb the banks and the boys froze, should they stay or go. They couldn't see why or what his intentions were. As he nearly got to the top he slipped and fell sideways into one of the Yew trees. The boys helped him out and onto his feet. Charlie noticed something out of the ordinary but kept it to himself. He put his index finger up to his lips, to indicate silence.
'Hi! I'm Christopher.' They introduced themselves, not sure how to address him and said they had seen him before but don't know much.
'Were you the boy beaten and the cane auctioned?' Yes he was. 'Why?'
'For talking after lights out.'
'But you are a Prince!'
'Doesn't seem to matter here at the Brig. We are all equal.' But nobody speaks to him because of who he is, which form was he in that? Just another Upper.
'Why are you here?'
'Don't know. Dad wanted me to be different from the status quo.'
'Can't fault him there. You arrived in the helicopter.'
'Yes!'
'Why do you follow us with those other Uppers?'
'I was only just tagging along, only done it a couple of times, wasn't comfortable.'
'Oh........Ok.' Their meeting ends courteously.
'A shame that he has no friends but as they walk up Magillycuddy Hill Charlie hits them with a bombshell.

'I think he is a plant.'
'What sort of plant Digger?'
'How about a tree.'
'BillyO I'm serious!'
'Hey look there is the mail van. A letter from Boo Boo??!!!'
'Guys, listen I saw something in the tree. I think we are being listened in on.'
'What do you mean?'
'Well, when he slipped I noticed something in the tree Buster!'
'We'll have to check it out. Say tomorrow morning during morning run?'
'Good idea.' Another peaceful night and the next morning they were up and out Charlie dashed ahead and ran straight into the tree surrounded by the other 3. In the shower room they ask what he has found. 'It's a microphone.'
'Any camera, no, need to check the other trees though!'
'How long do you think it's been there?'
'Must've been put in when we were away, not before. Nothing when the Blue Ratings attacked.'
'Hmmmmm! They've been listening to everything we say. Right, no discussing anything but normal life or home life at the Top o'th' Banks, we can use this against whoever is listening to us, but why are they doing this? Why the interest in us?'
'Those hunters, the men in the billiard room, the men up the Flaxden Brook, we must be on our guard from now on, Cobber! It's closing in.'
That afternoon they headed over to Dan's with some supplies. Grateful to see them, as always, they tell him what they are going to do about Horbyn. He laughed and thought it was a scream. The next day they put their plan into operation. Charlie took the lead but the others stayed behind, Horbyn took the bait, he followed, Charlie started running, Horbyn gave chase, Charlie slowed down then speeded up detouring into the nature reserve. The others fan out behind. Charlie led them into the centre and suddenly the 3 jumped him. Wrapping cello tape around him but not letting him see them. They all had their tracksuits and duffle coats on with balaclava masking their faces. Tied around a tree with vines they had collected early They gagged him and blindfold him. They find the pocket watch on his hand and took it. They give him his £1 back and take £5 from him as he had already been paid by another boy for the watch. He struggled like mad

threatening, expletives through the gag. Then suddenly, 'My fellow American! How do like this taste of your own medicine!' Blasted out, it was Billy impersonating Richard Nixon. 'Leave the Brecon Hoosies alone, you have been warned. Do not attempt to follow us with have set traps in the wood, go back the way you came.' Then turning his voice instantaneously into Prince Charles, then into Bridget Bardot, they left. A shaken Horbyn struggled then stopped tired out, too exhausted to fight back.

'You've not lasted long!'

'No staying power!' They loosened his vine but not the cello tape. Then shouted. RUN!' He can't follow and as looked behind he sees the defeated Horbyn sitting with his head in his hands.

'That's twice we've beaten him now!'

'Wish it had been Ztirgeon!' The boys raced back to Brecon, changed and cleaned up and gave the watch back to Gibson and suddenly heard a loud jeering noise. They raced to the common room window and could see about 30 boys following behind a hopping Horbyn as he headed for the main door of Sperrin House. Alerted by the noise outside the Head followed and soon they saw Horbyn arise with the Head and headed for his office still hopping. Thirty minutes later a furious Horbyn came out, staring in the direction of Brecon.

'Wow he is steaming!' Some of the Uppers hop kangaroo style past him and he took a swing but missed.

That night the Head came into the dining room, greeted the boys back from their break and asked everyone at The Brig to be on lookout for a masked gang who speak like Richard Nixon, the Queen and Prince Charles! The whole room erupted in laughter!

'I thought Pete was going to call for us there! Horbyn will be furious now.'

'Not to worry we can cope with it, just another thing to deal with, we are many steps ahead. Horbyn never learns the Fencing and now this!' They went to the Top o'th' Banks to talk but only discuss their prep and games.

'We have this match coming up.....' but just as they are heading to the house they see the Star.

'Where is that over?'

'We'll have to ask Dan. Take a bearing, Cobber mark it on the map.'

'Will do! I am going to redraw it and make it better.'

'How about putting a couple of rhinos or elephants on it?'

'Why?'
'Well then it will become a decoy.' Another decoy. Prep was good; there was no trouble these days every one getting along Troup Pearson and Kerr now seem good friends everybody pulling together. Then the door swung open, five boys seen before but not appearing to be the bullies dashed in.
'There he is!' Everybody froze. They pointed at Brookes, got him, they do and frog marched him out of the classroom and headed towards the summer house, suddenly the second formers start laughing and singing and burst into happy birthday! They dragged Brookes up to the Magillycuddy pond, one, two, three and splash!!!!!! A big soaking everybody cheering as they surrounded the pond pushing him back in as he tried to get out of the pond. 'Glad my birthday was on the 23rd of August.' Said Charlie.
'Lucky you!' Replied Billy. 'Sorry I forgot your present! I'll get you something!'
'You'd better!'
Walter turned around and saw the Head looking that way, admiring what is going on, not interfering, it is tradition. Nurse Rose walked past. 'Is this another part of the new order too Headmaster!'
'All good for Flaxden Brig Miss Rose! All good!' They got ready for bed and lay down listening to the piped music, Billy was reading his letter from Boo Boo for the 20th time, Larry was reading a Commando comic-'The Chef who went to war', Charlie a novel-the Day of the Triffids and Walter was staring at the ceiling when suddenly Blue Danube Waltz piped through walls. All stopped their relaxing and listened until the end. They must see Dan, find out where to go. The next day they arrived at Dan's but he was not there,
'Let's build another couple of dens further up the Brook, while we are waiting.' Which they do but leave behind the supplies for Dan.
'He has probably gone for his Giro which means he may not be back for a few days. Gets his £24, buys his whisky, beer and some food eventually getting back here. Wolfie goes with him but come on we'll catch up.' They build another two dens. They build an A frame with branches and strong branches, heavily camouflaged and a lean to and again heavily camouflage that. They come across their cave and go inside. Mark this one down as a den on Cobber's map and Let's drink some of BillyO's TC.' Orangeade this time. They discussed the map. It is becoming detailed and they must make sure it doesn't fall into the wrong hands. Larry agreed to make

copies. They headed back down the Brook and come to Dan's place; he was now home and thanks them for the food. 'The Star? That direction, it is Chickory Hill. There must be a message up there for you.' The boys now have to go there but can no longer go at night as they would be missed and someone would drop them in it. On their way back they are flanking to avoid detection when suddenly. 'Vot are you lot doing here?' They look around and see nothing then suddenly a head appeared out of what appeared to be a big bush. It was Aeronaut Fabius, head of the Emergency Service and he was sat in the Quad which was hidden underneath the dense foliage. 'We're lost!' Piped up Charlie. 'Uh huh!! Zat vay, Snell! Ze Myrtle Vood is still out of ze bounds! Herr Barron said Vyrtle Vood VERBOTEN!! SCHNELL!SCHNELL! The boys scurried away and headed back.

Suddenly they heard a noise behind them it was the sound of something they have heard before, PHUT! PHUT! PHUT! The boy swizzled around, it was Archie and that unmistakable sound of his Morris Countryman. 'Hey boys told you I'd pass by! Just up from Export thought I'd have a few days up here before going back down to the Zoo!'

'Hey Archie!' And the boys crowded around him, happy to see a friendly face. They tell Archie of their latest adventures, but will he take a look at Wolfie and Pocholo? Yes he would, good; his case was behind the driver's seat as usual. So they headed to Dan's where they had a cup of Dan's forest tea. The taste had now become acquired. Wolfie was checked over and Archie was pleased and confirmed he was in good health. He queried who the Doctor had been and they told him about Nurse Rose and that was where Pocholo was now and that she had got him better. 'Well would she like me to look?'

'Yes I'm sure she would!' So he left his car at the bridge,

'Remember there are no cars allowed into the grounds.'

'Why is that?'

'No idea, not even the Masters can. Bicycle only. The only vehicles are allowed are the Service vehicles.'

'So you do have a fire engine here, and the boys really drive them?'

As by magic the V2 passed, Beefy Bill was driving and he acknowledged the boys with a clenched fist as he passed by. They arrived at the San and knocked on the door, a couple of minutes later the door opened it was Nurse Rose dressed as they had never seen her before! Barefoot, and a

tight white t shirt hair down and no glasses. 'I knew it would be you four!' Then with jaw dropping silence Nurse Rose's and Archie's eyes locked on to each other's. It, what must have seemed like an eternity, Walter nudged Billy and raised his eyebrows.
'Nurse Rose, this is Archie who works with my Dad he has looked at Wolfie and said he would look at Pocholo for you, you know to make sure he is ok.' A blushing Miss Rose said, 'Yes, yes of course please come in!' They all trooped into the small lounge. 'Here Pocholo, we have some guests!' Archie gave him a check over and some precautionary jabs.
'Again he was in excellent health! You have worked wonders from what these boys have told me, the St Francesca of Animals!' Miss Rose blushed, 'Right boys I believe you have your dinner to go to now. 'Mr Binks, would you like to have something to eat here it isn't much but you are most welcome to join me.'
'Yes that's very kind of you Nurse Rose but less of the Mr Binks, call me Archie.'
'Now off you boys go! Now!' Her eyes firmly locked on to Archie's.
'No biscuits?' She said her face not moving.
'OFF!!!'
As the boys were almost out the door, they overheard Archie say to their Nurse, 'Lovely a face, perfect in attributes of grace she comes like the fullest Moon with a happy face.....' With Miss Rose replying,
'1001 Nights, Scheherazade..............don't call me Miss Rose or Nurse Rose I want you to call me....................'
'Could you feel it? I think we weren't wanted Buster!'
'Dead right Cobber! 1001 Nights? Come on let's see what is being served up to night!'
'Billy did you catch that? Put those ears to good use! What Nurse Roses first name was? BillyO, you must have?' None had and they headed for dinner.
At the Top o'th' Banks they sung their latest rendition very loud. 'Hey we are getting good at this; they'll be asking us to join the choir next!'
'Us in the choir? Nahhhhhh! It will cramp our style! We would ruin our street cred!' As they were turning Archie walked down and greeted them.
'Just got to go and see Mr Barron before I go, be right back.' He came out and said he must head back now. 'I am going abroad when I get back. It was only a short spell at Crane Hall but I'll come back and help out when

I'm back in the country during recess. Your Dad is thinking about sending some horses here, I was just putting the idea to Mr Barron.'

'What did he think?'

'Well he likes it and will put it to the Board. I must go.'

'Where are you staying tonight?'

'At The Flax Bar, Flaxden Hotel. I have a date boys! Miss Rose is coming with me to the Festival Theatre and we will have dinner afterwards.'

'And?'

'And then I will bring her back! Come and see me off!'

'Do you think Pete will buy the horse thing Buster?'

'Hope so Digger! It'll be great!'

'Can you see the fun we would have with horses up here?' So they walked to the back Service road and Archie got into his Morris as it started to drizzle he switched his wipers on and POW! The wiper flew off and hit Charlie in the side.

'Whoops Charlie sorry about that! Any one got a match!' Archie had his own box now for emergencies. Then PHUT PHUT PHUT PHUT! He stalled 'Hey lads give me the big push!' Into second gear, raised the clutch slightly and off she went.

'Hope that doesn't happen on his date, think Nurse Rose would like pushing his car Cobber?'

'She can push my car any day Digger! Right up to the bumper!' They watched till he has disappeared down the drive.

'Some Guy that Buster!'

'Yes I bet Dad is upset he is leaving.'

'Where?'

'Not sure, overseas somewhere, a big Government job!'

'Think they will get married?'

'Who?'

'Nurse Rose and Archie.'

'Dunno BillyO, maybe.'

'Cobber said he wanted to marry her!'

'I want to marry her! Mind you I think the whole of Faxden Brig does! Have you seen the queue for the San lately, any excuse to see her!'

'Cobber you are a young man many more fish in the sea! You'll get over it. Anyway we have more pressing business, and....................'

'Yes?'

'You are not in her league!!!! No chance!!'
How were they going to get up Chickory Hill? It is past 20 Bell street. They decide to go on Saturday. There were no matches and they would get back before supper and the film. Butch Cassidy and the Sundance Kid. Also there are Sailors from HMAV Caledonian coming they have been invited to help rebuild relations. That Saturday with layers of clothing to keep them warm they set off. Up the McInnis, past the small lake and, then 20 Bell Street but had to dive into the bushes as they hear voices. Peering through the dense forest they saw Blare, Braun and Ztirgeon heading up the track towards Picklewick. 'Don't tell me they have now taken up hiking!'
'What a pity they will ruin the countryside! Litter like them!''
'Looks like they are heading in the direction of Bell Street, that's our way but we must keep way back.' They followed and suddenly they were gone.
'Must be moving fast, as long as they don't see us, BillyO!' They crossed the Curie Brook and over the tree line, and onto 1968.
'That's great look it's easy walking now just straight across! Do you think they are after these messages too?'
At the summit they found what they were looking for but this time it was a group of letters *yghjkerxcsdqcplzggvvvvvv*.
'Cripes what does this mean, Digger?'
'Looks serious, Let's get back and try to get it translated. This looks a quicker route, straight down! It's not very dangerous.' Eventually they reached a path and came across a walker with all the tackle. A courteous greeting with a nod but no words. 'Must've got out of the wrong side of the bed today or problems at home.'
'Maybe just doesn't like chatting! Hey Buster! Look he's leaving a trail of paper, a treasure hunt! Wait a sec these aren't just pieces of paper they are £5 notes!!!Shout him!'
'HEY! MR! YOU'RE DROPPING YOUR MONEY!' No response, again, no reply, 'Blow the whistle! One long blast!' No response, again, he just carried on,
'Ach he's got more money than sense, leave him to it, leave the trail he might be using it for something, and it is not right to take money for yourselves that someone has just dropped! He might come back looking for it.'
'We could do a lot with this Cobber!'

'BillyO listen to Buster, he's right, it's not ours! We can't take money that is not ours. We must earn it.' At the end of the trail they came to a small lay-by in a clearing near the lake side. There was a note and a fiver with a stone on the top of it. Walter read it out loud.

"I am lost and am going to find my way back over the hill. I need my medication."

'There's something wrong here, he was confused, look at the way he ignored us, didn't want to engage and he's dropping all his money on the floor.'

'Lots of people are like that.'

'Quick Digger you run and set off Moaning Minnie. We'll head for the red phone box at the end of the back drive, phone the Brig and 999. Billy you speak put on one of those ridiculous accents you've been practising like the one you did the other day. They call the Police on 999 but they give the Brigs number as they can deal with it. As the boys are making the call to the Brig they hear Moaning Minnie wailing away and the movement of vehicles and people ahead. Billy made the call using a Scouse voice.

'Urmmmmmm! Ello Chuck! There's a man in problems at the top of 1968!'

'Billy do you think they will believe that! Try something else! Look at that response!' Which he did. They dash back to the roll call. In time they see the Hill Service vehicle followed by the quad, V2 and Ambo heading for the tracks that lead to 1968.

'Ok boys supper time.' The boys said nothing, skip the Top o'th' Banks and get ready for the film.

'What about these letters Digger?'

'We'll decipher tomorrow afternoon at one of the dens.'

'Agreed.' They headed to the film, it was delayed. The V1 and V3 attended along with the Fergie. As they are waiting they see a group of men walking casually up the Service road and are headed into the gym.

'Hey isn't that?'

'Yes it is!' It was the group of men they had shared soup with in Myrtle Wood.

'They must be from the Blue Huts, HMAV Caledonian. Dressed like they were they must be Commandos but these aren't the ones who attacked Flaxden Brig, these are a lot older.'

'But why are they here? The sea is miles away?'

'They have the lake. forests and hills to train. Plus they do their operations on any terrain. I suppose this is where they train.'
'You mean where WE train!'
'Well I can tell it's them by the way they walk!' Sure enough as the boys took their seats at the front they can hear familiar voices from the days before, they look at each other. The Brummie and Cockney voices being particularly loud. The clipped English accent could also be heard along with the Scots, Irish and Welsh but just as before they were all in relaxed mode. The film started and about half way through the song Raindrops are falling on my head the film stopped,
'Awwwww.......!' A large groan could be heard throughout; they were all enjoying their night and in came Pete, up onto the stage,
'Must be serious Cobber. Pete doesn't usually do this!' Walter whispered to Larry.
'Boys I have the honour to announce the success of our glorious Services in rescuing a climber from the top of Chickory Hill, we responded to a call from a Lady on holiday from Liverpool and were on the scene in minutes, I'm pleased to announce he is now at Bridge of Allan recuperating under medical care, after being taken there by Flaxden Brig's Ambulance Sevice. A juvenile onset diabetic, he had run out of his medication and had become confused.'
Suddenly a voice went up
'3 cheers for The Brig!!' It was one of the Blue men, the Welshman. The roof nearly lifted off. Laughter and cheers went up. Fences were being mended. Suddenly Billy stood up....
'And 3 cheers from the lady from Liverpool!!' A silence followed then laughter then 3 cheers! The film continued and at the end as they were leaving Walter was grabbed by the arm and a whisper in his ears was 'Are you the masked gang?' Walter turned around, it was a Scottish accent and he immediately recognised the eyes that were staring at him. The man winked, smiled and let him go.
Exhaustion took over again as the boys rested in their beds the piped music of Frank Sinatra's

♫

I'M DREAMING OF A WHITE CHRISTMAS.....

faded away and they drifted into a welcome sleep. That day Walter had received a letter from his Mum.

Crane Hall

My Darling Walter,

We had a letter from Mrs Odhiambo thanking for letting Billy stay with us at the coming break and she has invited you to go and stay with their family after Christmas if you would like to do that? She sounds a very nice lady. I think she has written to Larry's and Charlie's parents too. You all made quite a stir Export Just a quick letter with your comics, Scorcher and Score, 2 Commandos and a Beano, were all that was in the newsagents today. Yes everything here is fine. You don't miss anything when you are not here, in fact there is an empty space, Archie has gone now, and we think he has fallen for the Nurse up there! The animals are all well. Rebel continues to kick his stable door and as soon as Morag Let's him out of his stable to muck out he heads straight to the wall and whinny's and darts around the yard. He is looking for you it is clear. Your father has been on to the head at Flaxden Brig and they are looking at the possibility of some of the horses being stabled up there, including Rebel!!! He is so noisy! here! Everybody is talking about you all. And could you let Charlie know your Dad is putting his 2 inventions to the test! Your friends from Fairfield are also more active, what did you say to them?
Well it won't be long until you are back for Christmas!
With all my love

Mum

ps We have noticed your letters are getting shorter!

At letter writing Walter thought what to write, he could see Billy writing furiously, Larry also looking vacantly around what to say, Charlie already done and was sealing his envelope.

Flaxden Brig,

Dear Mum and Dad,

We are now back into our routine and the place is just as exciting as before, even more so. All my friends enjoyed their stay and adventure at Crane Hall, Larry has written to Morag and Billy I think is just about to finish his 8th letter to Boo Boo! Who would ever have thought? The copious supplies you gave us all were very welcome but somehow food doesn't seem so bad now. The longer I am here the stronger and more positive I feel I am getting. We have been on the Flaxden Belle and drew our rugby match, achievement after achievement and the good thing is we are all involved now, everyone in the house. I love this place but I do miss Crane Hall and all the animals, including my brothers and sisters. Yes we saw that Archie took Nurse Rose out on a date! It is a shame t6hat he has gone abroad. Rebel's behaviour is strange but he must be annoyed that I am suddenly there one moment and gone the next. He seems to be part of me and yes he was laughing at me but he did make me get up when I had fallen.
Bye for now!

ps Sorry I am in a rush!

W

He quickly sealed up the letter and gave it to the post boy. 'Heck Billy what's all this? Must be an inch thick letter there and two other letters?'
'Well this is to your family, this is to my family and this is to my Boo Boo!' The thickest one by far was to Boo Boo!
'Billy you are going soft on us!!' Charlie to and Larry had written letters.
'Tell you what!' said Billy, 'I'm going to ask my Mum and Dad if you can all come to my place next summer!' 'Hey that would be great BillyO!' decided on not breaking the news he had heard fr0om his Mum, so not to steal Billy's thunder.
'Come on let's get moving. After dinner we will go to the Myrtle Wood, see Dan build another den.' On their way Horbyn follows. 'Does he never give up, look at his knuckles they have gone white!'
'I think he's mad about something. I wonder what.' 'It must be from that beating you gave him Buster!' They head into the wood easily giving him the slip. 'Look on the good side, he's focusing on us now, hopefully he'll leave the others alone.' After seeing Dan and Wolfie they head up to the end den and sit by the Brook taking in water. 'Let's follow the Brook and find its source!' 'Yes ok, we don't have to be back for a few hours and we are into new frontiers. Got your map Cobber?'
'Yes! I'm marking everything down as we go.'
'Must be quite a masterpiece! Don't forget to rub out the Giraffes and Rhinos!'
'I put those in to make BillyO feel at home!' On their way up they follow the banking. There is no path or visible route to take. They come across a number of pools, 3, all further up from the Flaxden Pool. 'These are good, looks like man has not been here for years, be a great place to have fun!'
'We could swing across there; land in the pool, bet there is fish here too. Our own private natural assault course!'
'Shall we build another den up here?'
'Well we are quite far away from the others now. Could make it an outpost?'
'Could be useful one day.' So The boys built a tree pit.
'Hey why don't we build other dens?'
'Haven't we enough?'

'I mean decoy dens, like traps. I know a good one near that big ant hill, did you see that? Ants everywhere!'

'Yes that's where Digger had a crap and they all got onto his pants!'

'Agreed!' After an hour they decide they are getting too far away and head back.

'Let's try this track. I think it's the M1.'

'Isn't that a motorway they are thinking of building in England?' 'Yes, but I heard that this is also called that. I know it leads to the McInnis, we can then cut down to the back of Brecon.' As they were walking along the M1 they had a magnificent view. 'It really is a beautiful place!'

'Yes it is we are lucky.'

'Lucky?'

'Yes, I feel we are we have gone through a torrid time but we are here and having fun. The forest is ours!'

'Wait I can hear voices!' As they approach the McInnis they jumped into the fire break and could see the four bullies, Blare, Braun, Ztirgeon and Horbyn, turning down the track. Horbyn and Ztirgeon had large black sacks on their back. 'What are they doing here?'

'Let's see.' They walked further and come across a den very similar to the one destroyed near Dan's.

'They have moved their place. Let's have a look in.' They saw dog ends, empty milk cartons and beer bottles strewn about.'

'God what is that smell?'

'It smells like the pub we got that Shandy in the City. Yuck!' They could smell beer of sorts and the dog ends were rolled up and the whole place smelt of sweat. 'Argghhhh! It's disgusting, I am feeling dizzy.'

'I like the Dockers Fist! Betty makes a good butty!'

'Shall we wreck it?'

'Nah they are well away from us, they must be doing this to get away from being seen.'

'Shall we drop them in it?'

'No, they are leaving us alone at the moment. We'll ask the Prince he might know, do you think he is the 5th person?'

'What about that one in the library? I've seen him speaking to Blare.'

'Not sure Diggers. Got to be careful can't befriend him too much. He may be a plant. Look at this. It's a crucible.'

'What's that used for?'

'Grinding things up. Now why would they want that?'
'Yes you've already said that but which one?' At the end of the McInnis they come out of the wood and can see the buildings in the distance.
'Have you noticed there is a ditch running along all these roads?'
'Yes, just like the one we jumped in when following McIver, we could use them for getting about without being seen.'
'I think we should follow them sometime.'
'You stink Digger!'
'So do you!'
'Hey we all stink! What is that smell?' Suddenly Billy said.
'I know that odour it's cannabis!'
'Canna what BillyO?'
'It is a drug the mild form of marijuana, like at Steepley Vale... A drug that makes you go high!'
'Ever tried it?'
'No and I would never, my parents would kill me!'
'What does it do?'
'It makes people happy and content, so they can have a good time and supposed to have a medicinal effect.'
'You-We don't need that. Is it dangerous? Sure it was like the smell at Steeply Vale?''
'It can be apparently. Yes it is the same.''
'Can you imagine the whole of The Brig strung out on that? Maybe that's what they intend.'
'You think Pete knows?'
'He can't Buster or they would be expelled immediately remember what he said he would expel anyone who smokes inside a building and he then extended it.'
'What should we do?'
'Well we have to get rid of this smell, if Billy knows then others will know, and they may accuse us.' So they all decided to throw Larry into Magillycuddy pond and then they all jumped in. 'Wait Let's roll about in the mud a little. That should get the smell away. Then we can wash our clothes and hang them in the drying room.' This done they showered and cleaned up, they headed for dinner, roast beef not bad but not as good as Mrs Flannigan's. They had bed rest, Blue Danube Waltz came through the walls, but there had been no Star. That afternoon they checked on Dan and

built another den, using a sheet and again heavily camouflage the area. Larry marked down the site and they headed off to check on the Lady Rose.

'Hey we've got time let's check out the girls!'

'Nawwww!' Said Billy. 'I'm a one girl man now!'

'Come on we're going!' They headed across and got to their landing stage, they were about a quarter away across the lake when suddenly Billy shrieked.

'It's the Beastie, quick behind that rock!' Billy dived behind.

'Shit! We didn't tell him, let's play along.' They followed but were laughing

'Why are you laughing? What's wrong? Can you not see the Beastie?'

'No Billy it's you being so scared! If only Boo Boo could see you now!' Quickly they made their way to the building.

'Yes I think she's gone now!'

'Yes this is it, we are right opposite the boat sheds and pier, there's the new Lake Patrol Boat. Get down I can see Boot Jarvis!' A large building stood in front of the boys 'Quick duck there's a car coming!' A Rolls Royce approached and glided into the driveway of the large granite house. They didn't see who got out but heard girls voices and saw four figures, foreign not from these parts. 'There I told you so it's a girl's house!'

'But Boo Boo?'

'Well she's miles away! You won't tell her will you? You know all for one and all that!'

'Let's get close, come on quick style! Climb that tree Digger.' Charlie did can't see anything, so they skirt around, nothing.

'Come on Buster, stop drooling, we must get back, leave this for another time or I'll tell Boo Boo!' They headed back to the Lady Rose. She was adrift, 'Heck who can get her?'

'I can swim!' said Billy.

'Ok you are elected!' Billy got there and managed to get her back. The boys reached the other side safely.

'We haven't deciphered the code yet, and look there is the Star, South South West. There's no hill there it looks like 20 Bell St.'

'No that is West. We are slacking. What's this all for? We don't even know what any of these letters mean!'

'I don't know but something is going on and we are slap bang in the middle of it. Write it on your map Cobber!'

'I think Dan knows the key phrases and isn't telling us.'

'Maybe. But maybe not. 'After Chapel they assembled in the library. Charlie volunteered to decipher then explain the next day. 'No we decipher all together then see what each comes up with. No solo work here, only use the cipher for an emergency.' They sat down and each worked out what the cipher was encrypting. 'Use our key phrase, Walter the letters are *asudrrofomsecvanbjmyvjamul.*' They deciphered, it was getting easy for them now RENDEZVOUS AT THE WEST BRIDGE 9 DAYS The boys looked at each other. Puzzled, what does that mean? That night the Star appeared again. It was directly over the building. At the end of the library a boy was sitting on his own. He looked up and was staring at them. 'Shhhhh! He is trying to study!'

'The code must be on the top of the building.'

'How do we get there?'

'Well Let's go straight for the roof, borrow Joe's ladder. Saves the problem of creeping around inside. Getting locked in.' The boys did this and got onto the roof. As they were crawling in the rafters, they can smell that sweaty smell up ahead and bright lights.

'Hey they are growing that stuff right here. The den by the M1 must be their processing place. And look what's this?' A big transparent jerry can/bottle of fluid could be seen with froth covering the top layer and a clear golden fluid underneath.'

'It's a brewery! Quick someone's opening the trapdoor!' The boys moved into and darkened far corner of the rafters and peered into the loft, it was two of the Uppers, Ztirgeon and Braun, who they had seen up the tracks and one had cornered Charlie...

'Looking good! Blare will be pleased!' It was Ztirgeon's voice.

'Yes there is going to be a good yield on this one! They also will be pleased! A good Pound value here.'

'Great! Let's go and tell Blare. I'll give him that information I got off that Novus Digweed, I wonder what Pete would say if he knew we were doing this right under his and their noses, and using all this electricity!'

They laugh and closed the trap door.

Without ado the boys left getting off the roof just as Joe came around the corner.

'Hae ye seen ma ladders boys!'
'Yes Joe they are aroond the corner!' Said Larry, in his Australian drawl.
'Less o the lip lads! Funny, a dinnae remember them owa thaur! Ha ye seen the Beastie lately boys?' Yes they had early that day, exclaimed Billy.
'Well next time a hope she bites yer!'
On their way back to Brecon they discussed what to do.
'What a racket they are running! Money, beer and drugs. All of Sperrin must be under their control. The beer is ok but the drugs we must do something about.'
'How are they getting away with it? '
'They have positioned the farm above the changing rooms and toilet's. Easy masks the smell and noticed that they are always have a coffee jar with them.'
'What does that do Digger?'
'Throws off the scent.'
'They have thought of everything. We still have to get the code. When did we last see the Star, two days ago? Then we have one week to find out what the rendezvous at the West Bridge means. Right so let's do something about the drugs at least, ok, yes and they are the ones who robbed the Blue Ratings and set fire to the boatsheds.'
'Decoys for some reason, Buster?'
'Maybe!'
'I thought we could challenge them to a match?'
'Won't work. Pete nor Big Jim would not allow us to play against boys older and bigger than us.'
'So we go back and wreck it?'
'No we go back and sabotage it.'
'How?'
'Well you saw the pipe coming out of the bottle, we block that and we get a couple of milk bottles of piss and pour it all over the farm plants!'
'You know this might just work. Good plan Digger! Will be a bit ironic for them after what they did to McIver!'
'Yes Buster but we have to get them caught at the time.'
'That will get them kicked out! You want to be responsible for that?'
'Well look at it this way. They have caused a lot of shit here, and are a danger to this community, our community. They only have themselves to blame.'

'Do you think they have anything to do with the codes? Think they will understand the code they got?'

'No not intelligent enough, they are lackeys for someone.'

'But there are 4 of them, and 4 of us, chiral, mirror image, non super imposable on us like Dr Gilmour said, you know what I mean?'

'Digger you are getting technical, you mean they are our mirror image? We are the good and they are the bad? Nah! Can't be! Anyway we have an opportunity here to strike while the iron is hot; they said it was all nearly ready. Don't complicate. '

'Then let's go now!'

'No the iron isn't quite hot yet, it's just simmering.'

'What iron?'

'Yes what iron?'

'There isn't any iron!!!!! Right we go tonight. Billy gets a banana from supper.'

'Why?'

'You'll see and all piss in a milk bottle.'

'I'm not carrying that, your suggestion Buster you do it!'

'Ok I'll do that.' That night they climbed back onto the roof and headed into the rafters.

'They must all be in prep.'

'Of course they have 2 hours, we have 1 hour.'

'Stop talking come on!' Stealthily they crawled into the farm. pours all the piss over the plants, through his improvised watering can and the boys can see the spray in a Brownian Motion effect.

'Now that's a beautiful sight!' Said Larry.

'Anyone need a leak!'

'Shhhhh! They'll hear us.'

'Must be a strong crop you can't even smell the piss! Billy the banana! Unpeel it and push it down the pipe on the brew kit!'

'What good is that going to do?'

'Well with any luck it will explode! The pressure will build up so much and then BANG! Now come on let's get out of here. Shit they are below.' The boys headed towards the trap and got on the roof just as they were through they could hear the Uppers inspecting their laboratory.

'Great nearly done, another twenty four hours and we'll be there. Do you think they will be happy with it?' With that the Uppers left. The four

friends now had to get off the room and a drizzle was coming down steadily.
'Let's go to the tower and through the billiard room. We are going to slip here.' In the tower the boys looked around.
'It's like camera obscura guys! I saw it in Portmerion where that film the Prisoner was filmed and the big balloon chased after him, Rover. Well the camera had 360 degrees vision! Let's go through the billiard room.' They went down the narrow winding staircase but put his hand up indicting to stop. They could hear the knock of balls on the table and 2 different voices talking.
'Listen I can hear balls knocking, must be Buster's!'
'Shut it Cobber! Listen!'
'Well........ I think........ it's all....... going...... smoothly!'
'Yes, but what about............ those new............. boys? They.......... seem to.......... be........... everywhere........... we.... go; you............ think they.......... know........ something? Have they seen it? I think we should move in, say about four at a time? It would be most effective.'
'Well if they do it will soon be too late and remember they too are expendable!'
Ears pressed against the door Walter and Larry listened intently. The voices tailed off and they left the room. Cautiously the boys entered the room. The shutters were closed but there were still balls on the table.
'We should have a game soon, wouldn't that be great!'
'Yes how about 5 o'clock tomorrow? We can only get into trouble after all!' They left the room and Larry explained what they thought he had heard.
'It was patchy couldn't make out everything. Four at a time? What did that mean?'
'Could be the four druggies they are after and not us?' 'Maybe but we are sliding into something that is well, we don't know.'
'We haven't even got that code yet. It's in the building somewhere. Maybe the sealed up room?'
'We'll have to come back. How many days till the rendezvous? Six or seven.'
'We'll have to work it out, we need to be precise. Something's going down and we are in the middle of it.'
'Maybe we should just go to Pete or somehow contact our parents?'

'No if we do that that they'll shut up shop. Plus they won't believe us!'
'And we will spoil our own fun!'
'When do you suppose the beer will blow Digger?'
'Sometime in the next 24 hours I presume.'
'Right we'll do that and let's wait for the fun to begin!'
Sure enough at about twenty hours later Moaning Minnie sounded throughout the Brig and they could see the fire engines all of them clustered around the main building. Ladders up onto the roof, the ambulance standing by along with the HS.
'Where one goes they all seem to go. They take no chances!'
'It's ok no fire but they found the illegal brewery which had exploded.'
'What about the plants?'
'Yes, but what about the plants?'
'The drugs, that was the point of this to drop those fools in it.'
'They must've moved them. They would've moved them not long ago.'
'Must've been to their den at the M1. We can check later. The still isn't theirs and the fire Service would've found the farm when going through the loft they have been up there sometime since we were there.' Monkey and Mony came up to them.
'Were you anything to do with that? Well they will soon have another still set up if not tomorrow the day after. Pete will denounce it first of course!'
'It's not the still we were after it was the cannabis farm they have! These are the boys who are causing all the trouble, the Blue attack, the boatsheds, pouring piss into McIver's bed, the black balling, and the honey jar.'
'Well they must've moved it!'
'If we think of something we'll help you.' They all nodded in agreement. Everybody had now had enough. As they sat on their beds discussing the options Stevie comes into the dorm and collapses on his bed, burying his face into his pillow biting it. 'What's up Stevie?' Asked Larry. After a few moments he sat up, clearly distressed, his eyes filled up and red raw, his fingers bleeding and sore. 'Stevie?'
'What's happened Stevie? The BB GANG?'
'Ztirgeon gave me PD.' He said falteringly and in a hushed voice. 'He made me cut the grass and hedges in Pete's garden. Blames you Diggers for embarrassing himself with Blare.'
'But he can't give PD, not to Brecon anyway.'
'Yes he can he's a Brevet.'

'What did you do?'
'Nothing, just walked by him. I just happened to be there.'
'Look at those cuts and blisters did you not wear gloves? And what's that mark on your neck?' A red swelling with a small head in the middle was prominent.
'Yes but he took them from me. I got stung by a Bee.'
'Get yourself to the San Stevie.'
'Sorry Stevie, I didn't mean..................WAIT A MOMENT!' Said Charlie standing up.
'That piece of paper, it wasn't the code it was my squatting invention! I wondered where it had gone!'
'Don't forget my additions Diggers; I'm on this, want a share of your millions!'
'Your additions?'
'Yes Billy's additions. He drew Blare's head sticking out of the rubber ring plus a few other minor details.'
'Stevie I'm sorry!'
'It's ok, worth it to hear all that!'
'Stevie go and get cleaned up, use warm soapy water that should do it. If not go and see Nurse Rose.' With that Stevie left Conway.
'It's escalating, but why? Why don't we just go talk to them, address it, before we just get used to it. You know... negotiate.'
'Are you crazy Buster!!? That's just like the man who told his Wife he was just getting out of the car so he could take a closer picture of the Lions!'
'You have a point there Billy but do you have the answer?'
'Stay in the car? Problem solved!'
'Digger? Cobber?' After a short special of quiet thought.
'We become the Lions! We hunt them down!'
'RIGHT!' They knew they would have to do something and soon time was getting short.
Crowding around the notice board that evening they saw a note from the Head.

THERE WILL BE NO PLAY THIS YEAR......
ANY IDEAS? SEE ME!

Peter Osmund Dougal Barron ESQUIRE

Charlie sprouted up. 'Let's do our own play, the whole house, get all involved somehow!'

'Who do you think you are Digger? William Shakespeare?!!'

'Yes! Tell you what, we could be the Knights of the Round Table who rid the land of this pestilence saving the Kingdom of Flaxden, we be can be the good Knights they can be the bad ones and the end of the play we can drop them in it!'

'We have an opportunity here.'

'Will take a bit of doing.'

'Yes but we are good at that!'

'Well your idea Digger you arrange it, you are Le Directeur!' To their astonishment they got permission to do it but for one night only and straight away think of a title. 'How about the Chiral Knights'

'Nah, too complicated, say the Knights of the Flaxden Brig Square Table?

'Too obvious, remember we are trying to be serious here! A means to an end.'

'I think...........' Said Charlie quietly and coming from deep thought. 'That we should call it....'

'Yes....' asked the others expectantly.

'I think we should name our play...............THE BANANA TRAP!!' Silence fell in the room and after a few long seconds of silence, then laughter,

'Brilliant!' It was decided.

'We must be mad to do this, yet there is method in it.'

'It's decided then!'

'Right Let's plan this now, by stealth, under the radar, let them all think it is some sort of joke.'

'No fear of that!'

'Digger besides directing you go and ask Jaw if he will be the Serpent.'

'Me, why me! I have enough to do sitting in the Director's chair!'

'Because!!!'

'You do it Buster!'

'No! I approached Beefy Bill to train us so you can do this.'

'What about BillyO and Cobber? Ok, ok, I will do it after woodwork, let's just hope the Novus behaves itself!'

'Larry you do the casting make sure everyone in the house gets a part. Billy you are responsible for the props.'

'Props?'

'Scenery, wardrobe all that stuff.'

'What are you going to do Buster, besides tell us what to do?'

'I will write the play!!! I will work with Cobber, in fact we will all work together!' So they set about their tasks.

Charlie approached Jaw after woodwork.

'Huuuuuh?!! You want something Digweed?'

'Yes sir! We are having a play as there is no play this year, Mr Barron has agreed and we wondered if you would like to take a part?'

'Me? Huhhhhhh!'

'Yes sir!'

'Well I am no actor!'

'Well Sir, it really isn't acting as such but a big role.'

'Go on Digweed! Continue!'

'Well there is this Serpent who is fearsome and is causing a menace to society. No one sees the serpent but sees glowing eyes and hears his hissing voice.'

'Well that I can do!'

'Thank you sir.' As Charlie was leaving Jaw asked.

'How are you doing the scenery?'

'Billy Odhiambo is in charge of that sir.'

'Well send him to me and I will see what I can do.' Charlie headed off to Billy and told him that Jaw wanted to see him but didn't tell him why.

'Jaw wants to see you BillyO!'

'Why?'

'Didn't say! But you better go now! He looked mad!' Charlie informed Walter and Larry of his success.

'Well we have got Boot Jarvis to do the sound and the electrics. He will do the music and the glowing lights and he can also do some smoke.' Billy comes back.

'You sod Diggers! I was shitting myself!'

'What did he want?' Said Charlie laughing.

'As if you didn't know Diggers! He has given me loads of wood. All I need and more if we want it! I can make up four horses for the Knights, yes who are the Knights?'

'Us of course!'
'Who are the others? The bullies from the Upper you mean?'
'Yes! Well we've asked Troup, Kerr, Mackay and Pearson.'
'They agreed?'
'They sure did. Only happy to! Mony is going to be the King and Monkey the story teller. Everybody else has agreed to take a minor role. Who is Horbyn?'
'That will be McIver maybe?'
'Maybe, we'll think on that. The others have agreed all to take minor parts as peasants and the crowd, even Stevie?'
'Yes he was thrilled to be asked!'
'What about music to the Wigwam dance? Well Nut bush City Limits? I need input here.'
'How about T REX?'
'I've heard of a song called 'Hands Up', I'll look into it'
'Well we will need a couple to do it. Hey what about our own band? We will call it Sphagnum Moss!'
'Something outrageous, the more outrageous the better, we have the stage for a couple of hours to put our case. We have musicians in the house! Trombone, French horn, tuba trumpet, the lot! Anyone know where the early morning bugle is? That could be used to start and end the play!' Yes reveille in the beginning and last post at the end.'
'Would that be proper to do so, I mean the last post.'
'We could do the play in remembrance?'
'Good idea.'
'Eat your heart out Hollywood!'
'One thing is sure we must have everyone on stage at least a couple of times.'
'I've a lot of 2nd formers wanting to help with the scenery.'
'You think this will work?'
'Yes it's bound to!'
'Why you say that?'
'Because if it doesn't we've had it. Come on let's get moving.' The house set to it, scenery is built, lines were learnt, costumes were made, sound checks carried out and the gym prepared.
'Hey have you seen this notice?'

ALL OF FLAXDEN BRIG
TO ATTEND THE BANANA TRAP!
7 30 pm tonight

Peter Dougal Osmond Barron ESQUIRE

'We have em!!! They have to be there!'
'Where are you off to Buster?'
'Just going to ask dé Menthon if he'll help us with some sword techniques, you know primary techniques and positioning, practise makes perfect!'
The big night arrived and peering through the curtains they located the position of the three. 'They are over there to our left.'
'Yes, tell everybody where they are, they all know what to do, we've learnt our lines, set the scene, this is it fellas! The reckoning is a coming!'
'I'm not sure they are going to like this much!'
'Bit like getting Al Capone.'
'What's that Diggers? You been at the Encyclopaedia Britannica again?!!!'
'Yes I've got a great idea how to bring the Bees into it...........'

315 degrees

THE BANANA TRAP

The Story Teller came on to the stage:

"Once upon a time in days gone by, there were four Knights who had just returned from removing a very bad group of men from the forest, they had built a den where they could do very nasty things to others, cause havoc in the communities, but the Knights had now cleared them away in order that the area stays natural and untouched so the wildlife and ecosystem could remain safe and sound and the population live in utopian

Harmony. Each Knight brings back a trophy, Sir Fecitt brings back a packet of cigarettes, Sir Cattell brings back a crate of beer, Sir Whiteford brings back a packet of biscuits and a black ball but Sir Phillip brings back nothing!

Standing in front of the King, the King says, 'Why have you no trophy Sir Phillip?'

'I saw the group had many plants and I wanted to bring back the plant and bring it back to you.'

'Oh dear, well never mind we will have a big feast and party for all in our community to celebrate our success! We will invite the girls on the other side of the lake to come too! I now declare 7 days of partying! We will now begin with the Wigwam dance so Knights choose your Damsels!'

The wigwam dance begins to music of Nut Bush City limits. With the brilliantly tuned music of Sphagnum Moss, to the enjoyment of the audience.

'Introducing the band Sphagnum Moss.' Continued the storyteller. 'We have Bowles on the tuba, Darnley on the fiddle Mad Mac McNut on guitar......' The 4 Knights dance running through a small figure of eight pattern, then in a circle always completing the formation but heading off in a tangent across the stage in the direction of the trio. the wigwam dance followed by a turn to the right to circle back to the starting point, another wigwam dance, followed by a turn and circle to the left and so on in a regular alternation between right and left turns after wigwam dance runs, thus releasing testosterone into the air to attract the damsels. The direction and duration of wigwam dancing is closely correlated with the direction and distance of the resource being advertised by the Knights. The source for our gallant Knights is the banquet table and the nesting site of the damsels. They wigwam excitedly towards the damsels, grabbing their attention but only 3 get the girl as Sir Phillip is left out.

The celebrations continue into the night but Sir Phillip is sad and subdued,

'What's wrong Phillip? You have helped to defeat these men and remove the pestilence from this Land.'

'Well I didn't get my trophy for the King!' So they all go to the King.

'Well I have heard the group have relocated to the other forest on the other side of the river and have befriended the fearsome Serpent and are now under his protection. The Serpent is fierce with glowing eyes and eats Knights for his breakfast! He can rise up to ten feet high bigger than a man! They have made a deal and are making life hell for the locals holding kangaroo courts and dishing out summary punishments. They have also taken control of the cottage at 20 Bell Street where an old man called Dan lives with his cat Pocholo. They say he can get his cottage back if he gives them £100, but he will need to sell all he has and still he will not have enough. His watch has been taken by one of the gang and it is worth £101 and he was given nothing. He now has to live under a tree.'

'Well I will go and remove them totally from the land!'

'But Sir Phillip, the Serpent is fearsome and no Knight has returned!'

'I will take on this task and rid once and for all and rid the Land of this pestilence, and return with my trophy the plant I saw for my King.'

He leaves the stage doing the Wigwam dance in the line of the sun in a vertical direction, the band striking up simultaneously strikes up.

'What do you think Sir Fecitt? Shall we follow/'

'No let him go Sir Cattell!'

'Let's party party!' Says Sir Whiteford.

'Sir Phillip heads for the New Forest and the group. He endures hardship in his quest, climbing the hills, swimming the rivers and lakes and getting through dense dark wood on his faithful steed Rebel.'

'The group hear of the imminent arrival of the Knight and decide to sweeten him up get them on his side.

'Let's use some of the leaves to make him a pot of tea! We can use this crucible we took from that peasant to grind them up, and then we can boil it up. He will be in cloud cuckoo land and will do anything we want to! He will be ours to command We can tell him that the Serpent wants to be his friend and that he can go and visit him for afternoon tea. That will kill two birds with one stone! Then we will be the Masters of this whole forest. The Knight will be eaten and the Serpent will be so spaced out we can slay him too.'

'Bob's your uncle!'

Sir Phillip arrives and the gang befriend him and it is not long until he is persuaded to have a refreshing cup of tea after his long trail.

Sir Phillip soon becomes very happy and merry after drinking his tea, so they wine him and dine him with chocolate biscuits and cans of beer. They even offer him a cigarette but...Sir Phillip politely declines. 'Never touch them!' Then their Hench man arrives wearing the watch of Dan.

'Hey he's expendable let him take this Knight to the Serpent and we'll be rid of that oaf too! Three birds with one stone!'

Before he goes they show him the farm and Sir Phillip sees a whole crop of plants, we will give you one for your King! In fact we'll even give you one of our Christmas trees too! Spaced out, Sir Phillip challenges the henchman to a duel.

Dan suddenly appears and has managed to raise the money; he has sold everything and has determined to use his giro money to good use, foregoing his usual basket of whiskey and beer. At least now he won't be homeless. He sees Sir Phillip is heading with the henchman to the Serpents lair, but Pocholo races towards the Serpents hole and tells Sir Phillip Dan has raised his money so his home is saved.

'You won't need to fight the serpent!'

'I don't want to...... to fight the serpent I want to make him happy!'

The Henchman sees the error of his ways, he realises they are using him.

'I can't do this these men are bad apples. I will help you!' The henchman and Sir Phillip go into the lair.

A loud hissing noise is deafening,

'Ssssssssssssssss! NOT CANNED MEAT AGAIN!!!! MY STOMACH IS VERY SENSITIVE!! And there is a commotion. A few minutes later they come out with the head of the Serpent.

'Here Sir Phillip this is your trophy!'

'You take it, not my trophy, without your help I could not have achieved this, it is the plant I want that for my King.'

'But the plant is not good for you!'

Storyteller:

In the meantime in the Myrtle Wood, Sir Facet, Sir Catelli and Sir Whiteford have become bored with partying for so long and they wonder what their fellow Knight is up to. So they ask the King if they can go and see how Sir Phillip is doing.
'Yes I think that is a great idea, I will come too!' Said the King. And the entourage set off taking the same route. 'I can now make my Kingdom safe and comfortable!'
'Yes Sire you can also increase your lands!'
The Knights arrive just in time there is news just filtering through that the Serpent has been slain. The King rides in on his magnificent steed to great acclaim. But Pocholo tells the three Knights that that Sir Phillip and the henchman are descending on the cottage at 20 Bell street to arrest the group and destroy the farm. But they need help quickly as there are only two of them and 4 of the group.
'Well Let's even the sport up what!' Says Sir Cattell.
'I'm quite ready for a brawl! How about you Sir Whiteford!'
'Yes Whato, Sir Fecitt we can't have Sir Phillip having all the fun now!' And with the King being greeted by his subjects, to great raptures, the Knights head for the cottage in the forest. The constable accompanies them they surround the den. The Knights quickly surround the cottage and the gang surrender without a blink.
'Please let us go, we promise we will be good from now on.'
'What do you think Constable Stevenson?'
'No! Let's hold a court now!'
'Constable Stevenson you can be the Judge and we will be the Jury!' Say the Knights.
Storyteller:
A bench is brought out and the Knights sit down.

'You four are jointly charged with, disturbing the harmony of a peaceful kingdom, stealing beer and cigarettes, setting fire to property of the king, stealing biscuits from the local store, practising the gruesome act of blackballing and growing a substance that will cause serious harm to the people of this land. How do you plead?' In low tones, whimpering, a barely audible sound. 'Not guilty?' As if asking the Judge and Jury a question.

'I KNEW YOU'D SAY THAT! I will have to think about it! I HAVE! The sentence is GUILTY! GUILTY! GUILTY! GUILTY! GUILTY! On all indictments!'

'You show no remorse, in fact you don't give a SHIT! You have no sense of shame, no sense of damage and no sense of regret. You will be sentenced by the King! Take them away!'

Larry whispers to, 'Buster look, they are getting un easy in their seats! It's working!' Sure enough Blare, Braun and Ztirgeon could be seen squirming.

Storyteller:

They tie up the culprits and head down to the cottage, collect the plants and give back the cottage to Dan and Pocholo. They take the hoard down to the King and as Sir Phillip give his King the plant.

'What is this Sir Phillip?'

'It is the plant I promised you Sire.'

'Where is the head of the Serpent?'

'I gave that to Henchman Sire, he is now reformed, and he did the slaying, for I could not kill!'

'Admirable! Very admirable! Yuck what is that smell?'

'Sire?'

'It is a hazard to the Kingdom! Brook it! And what of these men you have here? How did they plead?'
'Guilty my lord!'
'Banish them from the Kingdom!'
'Aye my Lord!'
'We will now eat, drink and be merry to celebrate our success!'

Story teller:

'And as it should be!'

They all then perform the wigwam dance, the Knights in a circle and the rest of the cast in a figure of eight both going off in a tangent, slowly edging towards the position in the audience where the 3 bullies are sitting until all on stage are at the tangent in the exact direct they all point towards the locus when suddenly the band stops..............the curtain goes down. Larry peers between the curtains. 'Look, look, look at the face on Târpy!' All the boys look as the noise of the audience became deafening.
'MORE! MORE! MORE!' The noise is bringing the house down!
'What about Braun, Blare and Ztirgeon?'
'They seem to be enjoying it! Think we we've done enough?'
'We've got them now! Can't believe they don't have a clue what's going on!'
'Let's put the icing on the cake!'
'It's now or never Brecon! Strike up the band! They want more, let's give them MORE!' The Storyteller came back on to the stage as the band started up! Here we have Mad Mac McNut on drums, Thom on Saxophone, Darnley on keyboards, and Walker on base, Vocals is McIver and Mad Mac McNut.....take it away Brecon!'
The audience fell silent.

♪ ♪♩♩♩♩ ♫

THERE WAS A LOT OF MOVING ABOUT GOING ON THAT NIGHT

360 degrees Michaelmas

CRUISING TIME FOR THE YOUNG BRECONITES
DOWN BY THE SOUTH DOOR AT THE KITCHEN PANTRY DOOR
THE BB GANG WERE CREEPING ALONG
THE SATURDAY NIGHT FLAXDEN FILM HAD ALREADY STARTED
BUT THE HEART OF THE HOOSIES WAS ABOUT TO SPRING INTO ACTION
AND YOUNG STEVIE WATCHED IT ALL UNDER THE STARRY STARRY NIGHT
AND SAID
TONIGHT OF ALL NIGHTS WE'RE GOING TO PUT IT ALL RIGHT'
AT FIRST STEVIE DIDN'T LIKE BEING HERE AT THE BRIG
HE SAYS THE TRAPS WERE SET FOR HIM LONG BEFORE HE ARRIVED
HE SAYS 'MY HOPE BIT THE DUST BEHIND THE TUCK SHOP SLAMMED DOORS
AND THE DECEIT AND SLIME OOZED FROM FOUR SCAB CRUSTED UPPERS
THERE'S BEEN SCREAMING AND CRYING IN THE BRECON ROOMS.
IT'S A BANANA TRAP STEVIE BUT WE'VE ALL BEEN CAUGHT
BUT WE CAN ALL MAKE IT IF WE WANT TO OR IF WE WANT IT BAD ENOUGH
WE'RE YOUNG AND HAVE THINGS GOING AND THEY KEEP ACTING TOUGH

ANYWAY FOLKS IT'S SATURDAY NIGHT AND TIME TO SHOW WHAT'S GOING ON
PUT ON OUR BRIGHT SHINY SUITS STEVIE
AND HEAD FOR THE LEFT SIDE OF THE WOOD
IT'S ALREADY 9 'O' CLOCK AND WE'VE NEVER GOT BORED
WE DON'T KNOW WHAT IT IS BUT KNOW THERE'S A LOT LOT MORE
WE'LL SORT IT ALL OUT AND TEAR THAN THOSE WALLS
IT'S A BANANA TRAP AND YOU'VE ALL BEEN CAUGHT
IN FLAXDEN BRIG EVERYBODY TRIES TO TELL YOU WHAT TO DO
IN FLAXDEN BRIG EVERYBODY SAYS YOU HAVE TO FOLLOW RULES
YOU HAVE A MORNING RUN AT SIX
YOU'RE BREAKFAST AT EIGHT
AND YOU CAN'T AFFORD TO BE LATE
SO YOU SHOVEL DOWN YOUR PORRIDGE
AND JUST WHEN YOU FEEL ALIGHT
YOU HEAR
RUN DON'T WALK
TALK DON'T SHOUT

HEY STEVIEEEEEE!! TAKE A MORNING RUN WITH ME
NOW DIGGERS TRYING TO WATCH PETROCHELLI ON TV
AND LITTLE STEVIES JUST GOT BACK FROM CUTTING THE GRASS
BUT IT IS CRACKLE CRACKLE CRACKLE SO HE HAS TO PASS

HE PUTS ON HIS DUFFLE COAT AND WALKS ALONG THE FRONT DRIVE
IT'S FREEZING OUTSIDE BUT HE CAN FEEL THAT FLAXDEN JIVE
DEEP DOWN IN HIS POCKET HE FINDS A 3d
NOW IS THAT ENOUGH FOR TO SPEND AT THE TUCKEE EE EE
'I'M GOING TO GET THROUGH THE BRIG AND GET TO DO MY DEGREE,
AND EARN MY OWN MONEY NA NA NA NAAAAAA....'
HIS MINDS MADE UP HE WALKS TOWARDS THE FRONT DRIVE
HIS HAND IN HIS DUFFEL COAT POCKETS PROTECTED AGAINST THE FLAXDEN BITE
HE SOON FINDS STEVIE SITTING AT THE TOP O TH BANKS
WHEN HIS MOUTH IS FULL WITH CHOCALATE BISCUIT
IT'S HARD FOR HIM TO UNDERSTAND WHAT STEVIE SAYS
HE MUMBLES THEN HE SUDDENLY ROARS
"IT A BANANA TRAP!! AND THEY'VE ALL BEEN CAUGHT!"

"And so our story ends!" Or does it?!!"

THE END

There were gasps followed by a stunned deathly silence.
Then to cheers and roars of adulation, the audience rose to their feet like a wave rising to full height.......... except for the BB GANG. The house took their bow, but the four boys made a dash for it. The Head who appeared to be enjoying the show with intense interest in the impromptu play, Dochan Do nodding in contentment, the atmosphere was electric. The Blue Boys at the back followed the four boys to their farm at the M1 cross roads. In a

panic the 3 bullies busily tried to hide their crop, whilst Horbyn pretended to watch. 'Quick, we will be in trouble if we can't deliver!' Said Braun.
'Forget them just get rid of it, I don't want to be found out! I'm not taking responsibility for this!' Expressed Blare, desperately trying to cover his tracks.
'Well I'm going to hide some; I want the most I can get out of this! I'm owed!' Said Ztirgeon.
They began to start hiding their crop under the spruce trees nearby as the Blue boys arrived. 'See what they have WOW! This is some stash boys what was your next move?'
'Well we found this......' Blabbed Ztirgeon.
'It won't happen.'
'Please don't say it was us, we will let you have it all, and it wasn't just us! Please let's do a deal! We can come to an arrangement.' Said Blare.
'Really!' The Blue Boys then made the boys fill up three black bin liners and force them to carry back to the. 'Pretty good entertainment that play lads did you enjoy it?! You were perfectly framed there!'
Without a do the boys, who were shitting themselves are frog marched to the Heads office, carrying the plants with them.
'Please, please let's do a deal!!' Blubbered Braun.
'Yes you can sell it on the open market, forget about payment you can have it all.' Quivered Blare, Ztirgeon just said nothing.
'SHUT IT!!'
After the play the Head came around the back. The boys were in fantastic mood with testosterone flying about.
'That was BANTASTIC!!' Whooped Billy.
'Do you think it worked?'
'I'm more worried about using Cats, Beefy and Puss's names!'
'We went close to the knuckle there!'
'Yes I think we went close there about the chocolate biscuits too!'
Well we certainly took the biscuit!' Then suddenly you could hear a pin drop as Pete appeared with Mrs Pete, his lady friend, followed by Dochan Do all dressed to the nines as though were at the Opera, a deadly silence. They were for it now. 'I told you we shouldn't have imitated Masters voices!' Larry whispered.

'But Willie Kerr was brilliant at imitating Târpy!' Pete's appearance was as though an Angel of the Lord had suddenly appeared, silence descended around the room backstage.
'Well done! Well done! Brilliant! Superb! I had my doubts about this when you came to me and I now wish that we had 3 performances for all to see! WELL DONE! Who is the Maestro? The Impresario?'
'I'm SPARTICUS!' rippled around the room from every boy's mouth. Walter looked at the Head he could swear there was a tear. He mouthed something. Walter thought he could catch it. 'That's my boys!'
As he was leaving they overheard Pete talking to Mrs Pete, 'Is there no end to this group's talent? They put on a play on their own and well, did everything! Quite remarkable! This is a unique set of boys, there is genuine care here, that they are not only giving to each other but reach out to everyone, they don't just talk about it they do it. Their values have become deeper than talent; the relentless setting of daily standards has become an example to each and those around them. The biggest strength is the genuine care they give to one another. They don't just talk about treating each other well; they live it because they know that works. They inspire and encourage each other to broaden their horizons! What a breath of fresh air they are to Flaxden Brig, raw but brilliant!'
'It's all down to you dear!'
'And this isn't just about being nice to each other; it's taking care of everyone around them! The whole of Brecon took part!'
'You've encouraged them to stay busy.'
'Yes we have encouraged them to broaden each other's perspectives and they have grasped it! The trick is when genius is in your hands is to help it along but keep out of it!' But the next sentences were drowned out by the roar of the V1 returning to its station. It had something to do with the Brig and girls.

'Did you see Târpy's face? He didn't like us being so successful and in the good books of Pete, he just doesn't like the camaraderie that has spawned here. Better watch out though he'll pin anything on us.'
'I think there is something more here. Something we can't see.'
'Remember he said he would beat us for even farting if he caught us. Very threatening isn't he?'
'I'm sure he is another one of those men I recognise, his trousers. Well how did he manage to take Jimmy Crows place?'

'Well he must've have sweet talked the Head and the Board of Governors.'

'Tell you what let's see if we can sting him too.'

'How?'

'Well we could deliberately get into a situation where he can beat us. So who'll volunteer...? Suppose I do!' Said Walter.

'Well it's your ass Buster!'

'My ass? Ha ha! Yes I just got it! You should write all this down Cobber!'

'Remember the Head has banned it now so let's test him.'

'Ok, how?'

'Well I will go and admit to the turd pie bed, the one that the BB GANG did.'

'Don't forget he turns up the music on his record player when he beats someone.'

'You will admit it?'

'You would? But it wasn't you.'

'I know that, everybody knows who it was. Just too afraid to say. Today we go and catch a Pike up at the small pool near Dan's you know Cobber where Pete confiscated the one you got?'

'Yes.'

'Well we'll get one of those. Now we all know Pete takes Jet for a walk over the golf course in the afternoon?'

'Yes.'

'Right, we get the Pike gut it and then cook it on the engine of the Ambo, which is always parked outside the HS shed. The keys are always left in the ignition in case of an emergency. I also noticed that at a particular time of day the engines are left running for about 10 minutes.'

'Will that be enough to cook it?'

'Should be nicely done, remember Archie's chicken?'

'Why do we need to cook a Pike?'

'Well when you see the Head going for his constitutional put the fish on the ambo engine and start her up , he takes about 40 minutes. While this is going on I will go and confess to Târpnam about the turd pie. You get the cooked fish and take it to the common room. Invite the head for a bite and he will accept.'

'Then Billy you go and switch off the electric so the power to Târpnam's record player gets cut off. Don't forget!
'Pete won't be pleased we will all get punished.'
'Not if the plan comes together!'
'Why do think that?'
'Well if he doesn't we're screwed. Me most of all! If we do this without breaking ranks we have him.' They carried out the plan and the Head accepted the invitation as he was pleased with his boys from the night before.
'That music isn't it The Blue Danube Waltz boys?' When suddenly the lights went out, there is no sounds and just as he is taking his second mouth full he hears, WHACK! Then another, then another. He recognised the sound of a beating lord knows he has carried out enough of those in the past before arriving at Flaxden Brig and the sound filled him with remorse...
'Where is that noise coming from?'
'Sounds like Mr Târpnam's study Sir!'
'It sounds like someone is being beaten.'
'Yes Sir it does sound like that!!' Said the boys nodding vigorously in agreement.

In the office Walter has confessed to the turd pie incident and Târp has told him to bend over. And switched on a record turning up the volume to 12 on the cigar box shaped gramophone.
'Why sir?'
'Because I say so, I am going to punish you my way. Not Barron's!'
'No sir, why the music. Why The Blue Danube Waltz? We keep hearing that.'
'Mind your own business! So nobody can hear you!'
'You can't sir!'
'Who says I can't? I'm going to wipe that stupid grin off your face once and for all Flannigan and your friends will follow! Well would you prefer expulsion?' So Walter bent over, thinking, 'Has the plan worked, PLEASE! PLEASE WORK! Let the plan work.' A fishing rod was taken out of the cupboard and he could see wire coil from the top to the bottom around it, he couldn't use George, he was too crafty or sly for that, WHACK! The blood rushed up into Walter's head, this was no soft hit, the

man was deranged, a sadistic maniac, it had been a long time since the beatings stopped, but Târpnam had not. He stood up, the music stopped suddenly as the symphony was about to get into full swing.
'You can't do this sir!' Walter said eyes watering as he stood up straight, praying that his friends had done their bit.
'Who says I can't? You..............'
'I DO!' Saved! It was the booming voice of the Head; three other faces could be seen peering from behind. The Heads knuckles were clenched and the whites could be seen clearly.
'Mr Barron this boy has...................'
'I don't care what this boy has done Târpnam, I will not permit this senseless barbarity in this community! Go get your hat, coat and suitcase! No not you Flannigan, GET OUT!' Walter left and joined his friends.
'WOWEEEEE! I love it when a plan comes together!'
'What do you think will happen?'
'No idea, it is in the hands of our Lord now! I hope You don't have to explain the turd pie bed! Looks like he has got his cards from Pete!'
'Hadn't considered that!'
'Let's go finish the fish.' Suddenly the door flung open and the Head came out slamming it behind him. 'Now where were we? Ah yes the fish!' They went back to the common room where he confiscated the fish. 'Jet and I will have this for our supper. Yes lovely, just lovely!' And with that he leaves.
'Well it worked!'
The next morning the four went to the Top o'th' Banks, sang the Brig Hymn into the microphones but this was interrupted by a commotion round at the South Door. They walked around and saw Joe with the little grey Fergie linked to the trailer. Then the South door opened and the three boys, Braun, Blare and Ztirgeon could be seen dragging out their trunks and going back in for more bags. Blare dropped his bag and the contents spilled out. 'Look look! Blare's dropped his toy soldiers!!!! Can't see a Yogi Bear though!' They were jeered and laughed at by the boys who surrounded them in a circle, as they prepared to leave and put their trunks on to the back of the trailer, they looked around and stared at the Novus.
'Don't worry Billy we'll get you some more!' Said Larry.
'What's going on?'

'They were caught with drugs, quite a stash too, they have been expelled!' A boy from the Upper told them. Once everything was loaded on to the trailer the boys tried to get aboard but they were stopped and told to follow behind by Big Jim A solitary drummer came out of Cuillin down Magillycuddy Hill and walked behind Blare, Braun and Ztirgeon as the cavalcade progressed at a snail's pace. Joe set off to cheers as the tractor puffed smoke out of the exhaust then pulled its cargo away snaking its way round the corner to the back drive. Many boys followed, mainly from Sperrin, jeering. There was then the unmistakable sound of the Quad arriving and followed the group. The crowd broke into the Flaxden Drum.

'Why the Quad?'

'Ironic isn't it!'

'Where are they taking them?'

'To the phone box at the end of the drive. This is what happens with instant expulsion. Pete disregards the culprits immediately and will have nothing more to do with them.'

'Quite right, look what they've done, the Blue attack, the black balling, the boatshed fire and the drug stash; they deserved to be drummed out.'

'Don't forget the biscuits!'

'Yes but look what got them caught. It was the drugs.'

'But it hasn't been proved that they did the other events.'

'Yes and Horbyn is still here.'

'We'll just assume. Don't worry about him he's on his own now. It's just like how they got Al Capone, nailed him on tax!' The boys all headed to a point where they could see the red phone box and as Fergie and the Quad pulled to a halt, they saw a blue light come on. 'What's that?'

'It's the Police, I think!'

'Yes they are in real trouble now.'

'Bet they thought they could phone Mummy and Daddy to take them home.'

'Come on boys you'll be late for Chapel and we don't want that.' They were now rid of them. Gone within twenty four hours. Their troubles were over.

As they are heading for Chapel, Billy overheard Pete saying to Dochan Do.

'I'm glad that's sorted now, I could not have closed Flaxden Brig down, and it would have broken my heart.'

'And the transition of going coeducational is going to be difficult enough at this place...............' Suddenly the Housemasters door opened and Târpnam appeared, carrying a suitcase and a holdall over his shoulders, he snarled at the four friends. Soon news was out that Târpnam was no longer in his position in Brecon and he too was now gone. The Head had relieved him of all his duties immediately, as he headed down towards the back drive. 'Now that is what I call killing four birds with one stone.'

'It's great I love this zero tolerance and I love this place!'

After Chapel they headed for their French class, Joe could be seen sweeping the leaves, the tractor and Quad were parked down at emergency shed; it seemed like any other day now. The cavalcade was over now. 'We can now discuss our next move. We have 3 days but where is the West Bridge?' They had seven days to find the final Chiral word too. 'I think we are on the wrong track here, red herrings, ruses all over the place. It was a big puzzle. The star shone over the Carie area, Blue Danube Waltz piped through the walls. They still haven't got the code from the Star. Where could it be? 'Look there it is the weather vane.' It was right above their heads. 'You know what this means?' They looked at Charlie. 'The answers are right here. And who exactly has put that there?'

That afternoon they went to check on Dan, Wolfie and Pocholo. All were fine and Nurse Rose invited them to watch Dr Who and the Cyber men. They also came behind Spy's lab and saw Jock BugBee with his bee keeping suit on. Jock was the grounds man and had five hives. The boys curiously gathered around and when he was finished he came over and asked the boys to come and look.

'Somebody has been throwing stones at the hives, know anything?'

'No Sir!'

'If the bees get upset they get very angry and they will chase you a long way then sting you. I hear one of you boys got stung in the Myrtle Wood the other day.'

'That was me.' Confessed Larry. 'We found a jar with a few bees in it and they were very annoyed and let them go. One stung me.'

'A jar now? Let me tell you about my honey. I get combs and honey from my bees. And every year I sell it to the local shop in Flaxden Village and beyond. A lady once told me that for her urine sample at the hospital she puts it into the Pure Flaxden honey jar! This led to the Nurse asking about The Brig and then realised she goes camping up here by the lakeside! Not

bad my honey boys and I'm no judge of a honey jar of pee!' Laughing to himself he then gave them a quick description of bee keeping and let them try some of the honey. 'Is the wigwam dance done here?'
'Bet that Nurse is one of the women we saw earlier!'
'You mean the one's sunbathing starkers?'
'Yup!'
'Yes it is, and always in the dark, your play was done to perfection! Excellent! Come down some time boys and I'll show you, let you watch. But it will be different from your Wigwam Dance, great play boys! Magnificent! Well done! How did you find out about it? You sure you haven't been here before?'
'No Sir, it was Digger here, he is our intellectual genius, knows everything! Well everything in Encyclopaedia Britannica anyway!'
'Yes flicking through the pages, surprising what you can learn.' Said Charlie.
'Is that a hive on the Chapel lawn?' Asked Billy.
'No that is a Stephenson's screen. It is where temperatures and below rainfall are taken, recorded to the metrological hut at the back of the San.'
'So no honey there?'
'Nay! No honey lad.'
'Thank you sir.'
As they were walking away they saw Dr Wallace walking up the Grap track with his dog Sputnik.
'Where do you think they are going? He walks up the track the same time every night!'
'Well Billy he probably is only just taking his dog for a walk!'
'I think I'll follow him Buster!'
They headed over to Chickory Hill, to the lagoon and saw the Lady Rose she was good and so well camouflaged that they themselves had difficulty finding her. 'Hey fellas look! Somebody has been here.'
'She has been reinforced sturdier than before. Who could've done that? Do you think it is those men at the cottage? Let's go and see if they are still there.'
'Ok let's stay here longer; I want to see if Boo Boo has written back!'
'Give it a rest Mr Testosteroné! Come on.' They hid the raft and headed into the forest to the back of the cottage.

‘I still want to get them for what they did to Pocholo and Wolfie. Their time will come!’ At the cottage they got into earshot.
‘We’ll have to do something about those kids. They know-I’m sure of it. Send a message and find out what we have to do.’
‘Wait a minute. They are cosy with that Nurse, you know the sexy looking one, and maybe she will be persuaded to help us. How about we ask her out get her on our side use her, try a sting?’
‘I don’t know. We’re supposed to be undercover.’ The boys crept back into the wood taking a different route.
‘We need to do something Nurse Rose is in danger, she won’t believe a word we say, nobody would if told anybody listened to what we had to say they would have us committed.’
‘And you would be right. What are we getting in to, whatever it is we have to see it through? Too late now! Let’s think of everything we have done and seen, put 1 and 2 together.’
‘And I thought it was all over.’ In silence they got to the lake side road and followed the drainage ditch undetected. ‘Look over there! The tent!’
‘Cor blimey! See that!’ There were two naked women, in their thirties/forties naked by their tent!
‘Hey you can see the lot! Look they’ve seen us!’ They are waving at us! The boys waved back and dashed away.
They looked up at the skies and saw a flock of birds flying their formation, in an arrow with the point leader taking a rest moving out and another taking its place. ‘I want to be a pilot,’ said Larry and as his eyes follow the near perfect and precise formation his eyes flash over the top of the main building a place they had now been many times. His eyes are suddenly drawn back.
‘There!’
‘Where?’
‘What?’
‘Eh?’
‘It is the weather vane that’s where the code is, that’s where we need to look!’
‘Another? Going to be difficult this.’ That area will be watched but if they get up and find the code. Instead they used the monocle and picked out the letters *ppavoexhptdeuixgpeveavwwsnscgtyindernkkmkn.*

'This is getting too much for us, so many letters. What do you think Diggers?'
'No problem!' And they deciphered it as CHANGE KEY PHRASE YOU IDIOTS THEN WAIT FOR FINAL INSTRUCTION.
'Heck that is going to cause us a problem; it must be 1 in 14 million chance of finding that phrase!' Said Charlie.
'Prince is the key. Must be. You think he is connected with all this?'
'Nah can't be he's being friendly, feel sorry for the guy.'
'Don't feel sorry for anyone or you will start feeling sorry for yourself.'
'Have you heard what is on tomorrow? The Duke is coming. There is going to be a Service display. What day is it?'
'Tuesday.'
'Dr Who might be on let's go and see Nurse Rose, we need to look out for her.'
'Hi Boys, come on in, someone is waiting to see you. My very own man!' Going into her little lounge they saw Pocholo; he sat up and started purring.
'My, my, Mr P you have your own place now!'
'Yes he feels safe and at home. I wonder what he was doing there anyway.'
'Do you think he belonged to those men?'
'Yes, he likes his box but always when I wake up he is in my bed with me.' They boys think alike, then settled down to watch TV. Pocholo goes from boy to boy purring, tail up rubbing against their shins. 'Look at that!' They watched the episode, Billy hid behind the sofa, 'Have they gone?'
'Never seen a Cyber Man before?'
'No!!!!!! There's no Dalek's there either??'
'Wait a minute Davros is coming through the screen!'
'We'll tell Boo Boo!'
'Aw Guys please don't!' The boys tell the Nurse about their break, the trip on The Flaxden Belle and their adventures falling short of the cipher disc and their slowly building around equipment.
After they go and see Dan and Wolfie, tell him about the play and the expulsions, and the departure of Târpnam. 'Good, good, we are rid of him now. We saw the play!'
'Even Wolfie?!'
'Even Wolfie watched!' Without asking why or how or where from they continue.

'Where is the West Bridge?'
'The West Bridge?'
'Yes we deciphered Rendezvous at the West Bridge; it will be in 3 days from now.'
'Well you know you followed the Brook the other day/'
'Yes?'
'Well, continue up and you will come to it.'
'I've seen it said, that day we got Billy away, and it's just up from the furthest den. We've all walked over it!'
'Den 5. Cobber built that one, the tree pit. Nearly across from the anthill den!'
'That's some way to get to, very isolated.'
'But not if you have a transport or a truck, or Land Rover. The hunters! Must be, they have a Land Rover.'
'Why is it the West Bridge? It's West, directly.'
'Well not if you are coming from the south though.' Said Dan. The boys leave, each going back to their respective dorms in Barron. The house is alive with atmosphere, a real good feel factor.
'What did Dan mean we are rid of him now? Hey we are going to have a do tonight! You joining in?' Kerr asked. Kerr, of all people would they have believed this was even possible only a few weeks ago? 'We are having a party to celebrate getting rid of the pestilence! It is all down to you guys.'
'No it's down to us all, Kerr.'
'Call me Willie!' Walter was exhausted and lay down on his bed and closed his eyes and listened to the music coming through the walls, who plays that music who decides what is played. Hmmmmm! Export are playing today let's go and see if the results are coming through. He twiddles with the knobs on the radio and gets the sport Huddersfield City 5 Southport United 2.........eventually Rochdale 2 Export City........; suddenly he was interrupted as the channels change... blast! A music channel came on, ahhh.......... radio Luxembourg. He decided to listen to the channel while he tidied up his locker, the top 20 countdown began, at no 20 we have T REX 20th century boy, at no 19 it's Mungo Jerry in the Summer Time……….. he saw his compass and penknife at the back, he made sure his picture of Pans People was fixed firmly on the inside of the locker door and gazed at Dee Dee. Prudence flashed into his mind, was that a longing

look she gave him? Ah well. He looks at the picture of his favourite footballer John Connelly there was a silence and the Blue Danube Waltz comes out of the radio speaker. It was too late to see the others so he went back to Conway. MZEEE turns out the lights, ‘Good night boys!’ Walter looked out the window and there she is the Star, shining brightly back at him. He looked and rolled over. ‘Maybe if I look away it will not be there............no..... still there!’ He tossed and turned but she remained. He went to the WC and there was Billy, Charlie and Larry. They looked at each other. No acknowledgement was needed; they all saw the Star and heard the music. ‘We must go now we are running out of time. They dressed into their gear. The Star was shining over 20 Bell St. They headed up the McInnis at a double quick. ‘No it’s over the reservoir.’ They followed a Sherpa track around the side to another large pool; they had not been here before. ‘Hey look this is great; we could swim in here and look at the scenery! No one will bother us.’

‘You mean now. It’s freezing?’ The sky was clear and the hills provided a natural amphitheatre a serene back drop, silhouetted in the clear starry night sky.

‘Look around we are not leaving until we have those letters.’ They keep looking,

‘Here look at the tree, carved into the tree is the code, *wiysrjhjjexsfpsy*. I’ve got the disc with me let’s decipher now.’

‘Come on its 3 am it’ll be 4 before we get back. I want to go back and go to bed.’

‘No now!’

‘Good let’s stay here longer.’

‘Shine the torch over the disc.’ Charlie deciphered the code quickly. NURSE ROSE DANGER.

They looked at each other. ‘Nurse Rose danger, a threat, a plant? Never!’

‘Maybe. Listen we have to do something. Remember we go and look and find out for ourselves.’

‘We can’t just go and ask her.’

‘No we must be careful. Listen we have to do something let’s move! Maybe she is, maybe she is not. Let’s get back have some rest and deal with it later.’

As they are cutting down the track they come to a clearance and their jaws dropped.

'What the............?' Exclaimed Billy.
'Cobber!!!!!'
'Buster what shall we do? It looks like....' After a long stare and silence, 'It's a parachute? A cover of some sort?'
'No too big no strings, no harness. YUCK! It feels sticky.' Larry looked and touched it.
'Feels like a skin, feel it everybody.' They did and spread it out, forming a huge bat like shape, doubled over. They looked in silence.
'Where are we now Cobber?'
'Roughly 2 clicks above the West Bridge, thereabouts.'
'Clicks?' Questioned Billy.
'Kilometres. What will we do? I don't like this.'
'Nothing, just do not say anything, let's get back!'
'We must tell Pete! Over there! It looks lik....'
'Yessss! Yes it does.....'
'We could use this as a cover for something in the future?'
'No Billy! Come on! Let's get out of here, we are way off track.'
Ignoring Walter Billy folded the massive cover and flung it over his shoulder. They got back, a few hours' sleep were gained, bugle, morning run, breakfast, Top o'th' Banks, 'Let's sing the Brig Hymn today, you be the conductor today!'

♫

DING DONG MERILY ON HIGH
AT THE BRIG THE BELLS ARE RINGING
DING DONG! VERILY THE SKY
AT THE BRIG WITH ANGELAS SINGING
GLORIA HOSANNAS IN EXCEL SIS
GLORIS HODANNA IN EXCELSIS

'That's not the hymn! What about this one? Remember when Cats took our music class the other week? Those Beatles songs?'
'Yeah! Let's do that!'

♫

IT'S GETTING BETTER ALL THE TIME
WE USED TO GET MAD ATTHE BRIG
ONE MASTER WHO TAUGHT US WASN'T COOL
HOLDING US DOWN TURNING US ROUND
FILLING US UP WITH HIS RULES
WHOA! IT'S GETTING BETTER ALL THE TIME! YEAHHHH!

♫

GOOD DAY SUNSHINE.....
GOOD DAY SUNSHINE.

'Now if anybody is listening from the main building they'll come out now!'

♫

A RICH GIRL RIDES A LIMOUSINE
A POOR GIRL RIDES A TRUCK
THE ONLY RIDE THAT DINAH GETS IS WHE SHE GETS A FUCK

'Quick the Brig Hymn Buster!'

♫

FATHER HEAR THE PRAYER WE OFFER;
NOT FOR EASE THAT PRAYER SHALL BE,
BUT FOR STRENGTH THAT WE MAY EVER
LIFE OUR LIFES CORAGEOUSLY

♫

360 degrees Michaelmas

AND DID THOSE FEET IN ANCIENT TIME WALK UPON

ENGLANDS

SCOTLANDS

WALES

NORTHERN IRELANDS

AUSTRALIAS

AFRICAS

AND FLAXDEN BRIG'S

PASTURES GREEN

'Quick Pete's coming out of his office!'

'Ah ah ahhh! Not so fast! Wait minute Boys....... Come on boys, off you go, better get there before me! It's good to see you practice your singing! You need to be careful they'll be asking you to join the choir!'

They headed off to Chapel. 'Do you think the microphones are still there?'

'Maybe they have something to do with the Dukes visit?'

'Possible! But maybe somebody is listening to us!'

'Well they're not getting much sense out of us if they are!'

After Chapel they went to the San, there is a cluster of boys outside. 'What's up?'

'The Nurse isn't there, still all locked up. Very strange Nurse Rose is always so efficient and always on time.'

'Look through the window, no sign, Charlie called Pocholo.'

'POCHOLO!!!'

'No sign of him either, he always answers. This doesn't seem right. Let's go and see Dan.' Walter then tells the boys that he heard the hunters talking about Nurse Rose when they were fixing the Lady Rose.

'Why didn't you say?'

'It's not important now.'

'Not important? Are you kidding?'

'Well straight after dinner we go to Chickory Hill and down to the back of the cottage she must be there, stuff games, the most we can get now are lines and the ACE'.

Yes did you see what he did with does lines we all did? Straight on his fire!'

'The poetry did it Cobber!' They attend classes and as they approach the South door there is a notice that Nurse Rose had unexpectedly had to go away. The boys didn't believe it. They overheard the Head saying that he thought it was strange that she would do that, and to leave without seeing him but she must've had good reason to do that and he will await her return.

'Hear that? It's those Hunters, they do have her. Screw dinner!' And they headed over to the Hunters cottage scouting stealthily along the drainage ditch. They see the men through the windows; Nurse Rose is tied up and looked at the opposite window. 'Can you believe that!!? Look over there!' They could see Pocholo also looking in. 'He must've got here somehow. Do you think they've harmed her? Touched her?'

'Billy!'

'What are we going to do? She looks distressed.' They listen to what the men were saying and catch bits of words.

'I've always fancied a bit of Nurse, pity you didn't put your uniform on! Is it true what they say about Nurses?!! Well we are about to find out.' At that point Pocholo saw the boys and started meowing, very loudly.

'MEOWWWWWWW..........'

'It's that stupid cat! Thought I'd got it when I ran it over.'

'Touch him and you'll regret it!'

'And you'll do what little lady? We have a feisty one here Thorsveldt, just what I like! You see, you, little lady are in a position to do nothing, we are in a position to grant you everything that we desire!'

Pocholo cries got even louder. MEEEEEEOWWWW.......'Shoot the damn thing Thorsveldt!!'

'Shoot?'

'SHOOT IT! KILL IT! Just like we killed that Stag!'

'And that old git in the wood!'

'Shut it Thorsveldt!' TerreRouge glared at him.

'THAT was you?!!!You...you.....you......BASTARDS!!!'

'Come on little lady the codes or we shoot the cat!'

'What codes? What are you talking about?'

'We know you talk to those boys a lot and that they know that old git, we know they are always visiting you.'

'I, I....I'm their Nurse!'
TerreRouge grabbed hold of a twelve bore shot gun and went out the door. BANG! BANG! A loud MEOW was heard piercing the after silence. Pocholo must be wounded or dead. It was a long drawn out pain
reminding the boys the day the Monarch died. The sadness pierced their bodies with a shuddering wave.
Nurse Rose started crying. 'You.....YOU BASTARDS! What had he done to you?'
'Now be quiet little lady or we'll have some fun with you! Everyone is expendable, animal, mineral, vegetable even you. Even Thorsveldt! Now tell us what you know!! Now! Where is it? Now that's all we want to know. And all your problems will go away! He screamed at her slamming his gun on the table.
'I don't know what you mean!'
'Don't give me that! Tell me now or by God I swear I'll skin each of those boys alive one by each! I'll give them an Exodus to remember!'
The boys slunk back down, sweating profusely, trembling with fight in them. 'They were the ones who got to Dan. They think they killed him.'
'Now they have Nurse Rose. Christ this is our entire fault! We must act now. We cannot stand by! What are we going to do? Well get more than lines for this! Mum will kill me!'
'Digger the plan please! Now! And remember we're not on any bloody Crusade!'
'Let's just get her out.'
'He's going to pay for that! If he has killed Pocholo! I'll............'
'Billy calm down, wait..... everybody listen. Buster you go ahead to the top of the hill, that little round one, the rocky one over there. Cobber you take the left flank I'll take the right. On my whistle sound, followed by Cobber after me we all start throwing rocks at the cottage and draw them out.'
'A diversion?'
'Yes, once they are out Buster you blow your whistle from the rocky top ,then Cobber, then me, that will draw them away in different directions, separate them, BillyO you go in and get Nurse Rose out and take her with you to the lagoon. They won't find you there, but make it quick, no stopping or looking for Pocholo or us... We'll continue confusing them and draw them further into the forest but Buster you come around and blow your whistle around at the cottage. They will think we have doubled back. We will all meet at the lagoon. Let's go in 2 seconds........1... Now! Start with one long blast.'

PEEEEEEEEEEEEEEEEEP!

The men came out.
'What's that?' Then the rocks began hitting the building, smashing the windows and landing on the roof. One hit Thorsveldt on the head. The boys took up their positions. 'There they are running into the woods!'
'Stop scratching your head. Get them Thorsveldt!'
Billy got in behind them and into the cottage cut the ropes and freed Nurse Rose. On the table he saw they had left a gun and a pistol. On the cabinet was a radio with a voice coming from it. 'Johan Strauss, Johan Strauss this is Henrietta Treffz, the message is, your mission is to eliminate all of them, eliminate all, over............Johan Strauss Johan Strauss the message is.................' The next message came in coded letters. Another voice came from a smaller radio.
'Billy what is all this about? Codes? Henrietta Treffz? Johan Strauss? I think they have killed Pocholo!'
'One minute Nurse Rose.' Billy picked up the receiver, took a deep breath and in an almost perfect Afrikaner voice. 'Henrietta Treffz Henrietta Treffz...this is...........Johan Strauss......*bsejoonvcyuovdf*.....over and out! BEEEEEEP!'
'BILLY! WHAT IS GOING ON?'
'Not now later! Don't know about Pocholo. Come on let's go! Follow me, not much time, they will be back soon.' As they left they could see Walter coming towards them. 'Go now!' Said Walter and he started to blow his whistle. 'To the lagoon the others will be there I'll follow, behind.'
Larry and Charlie continued to blow their whistles and suddenly stopped. The men headed back. 'Blast she's escaped! It's those new kids. I knew they were trouble and those idiots didn't manage to do anything. Quick, into the Land Rover we'll head to the Flaxden Bridge and intercept them there! I want them, all of them; let's write them out of our page!'
The boys saw the Land Rover heading down the lake side road. That has cut off a route back to the lagoon. They have no option now. At the lagoon they find that Billy and Nurse are safely there, Walter arrived last. 'I thought I was going to die!' The boys were now breathing heavily. 'Let's take The Lady Rose.'
'The Lady Rose?'
'Yes The Lady Rose! We'll explain later!'

'You have a lot of explaining to do.' The boys uncovered their raft! Nurse Rose's eyes popped out!
' I…I'M NOT GOING ON THAT THING!! I can't swim.'
'Its ok, that 'thing' is The Lady Rose and Billy swims like a fish! You are quite safe.' And Billy lifted her with one movement on to the raft!
'We'll tell Boo Boo!'
'How can you joke now?' Exclaimed Nurse Rose. They all got on the raft and are just pushing away when they see a white figure moving through the undergrowth, there one minute, gone the next. Then suddenly a pair of green and blue eyes came into view.'
'It's Pocholo!'
'Hey she's only designed for four there are 5 of us!'
'Well we'll kick you off Cobber! Six now with Pocholo and what's this?'
'It's another cat! Wolfie?'
'No, looks like Pocholo has a girlfriend, let her on, don't turn her away, he's not going to leave without her....' As they pushed away Nurse said
'Oh Pocholo, Pocholo!!! I thought I'd lost you!' As she cradled him in her arms...
'Is he ok?'
'Yes he is ok!'
'We'll keep as close to the shore as possible, she'll be ok, the Blue have reinforced her for us.'
'The Blue? What is going on? You mean this is the Blue's?'
'No, we built her, they reinforced her!' They moved off and took her to the middle of the lake then back towards the shore and headed towards the boatsheds.
'Look out for the Beastie!'
'Billy there is no Beastie!'
'No Beastie!'
'Yes no BEASTIE! As there is no girl's school on the other side of the lake!'As if by a stroke of luck they heard Moaning Minnie going off and seconds later they could see the Hunter's Land Rover heading back towards the cottage.
'Think they saw us?'
'They had a radio there with a message, Henrietta Treffz is to eliminate all in the way. Sent them a message back too! No Beastie?'
'That's it!' Shouted Charlie. 'That's the key phrase!'

'Yes Billy NO BEASTIE!! Can you not give it a rest!!!??'
'How so? Just like that Diggers?'
'Yes its clear, The Blue Danube, Henrietta Treffz is the first wife of Johan Strauss!''
'The music? So what/'
'Strauss wrote it!'
'There's something else, there was a smaller radio and a voice said something about a dog going to the fair.' Interrupted Billy.
'You mean Dogger Bank and Fair Isle?'
'Yes that's it!'
'That Billy is the weather forecast! They are listening for that for some reason.'
'Thank heavens for you Digger! You know everything!!'
'Yes just love my Encyclopaedia Britannica! That's me! Ain't it great?'
'Check when we get back.'
'No, not now, they are not coming, the siren has deterred them. They'll miss us at roll call though.'
'No look, see the 2 helicopters, it's the Duke arriving. Remember it's the Service display, come on, we'll see it if we get back soon, it should be good!' They get to the boat sheds without being seen and hide the Lady Rose, in the foliage nearby. 'She sure is a good ship!' Nurse Rose has Pocholo in her arms and Billy has the new arrival in his.
'I think she's pregnant!'
'Me?' Gasped Nurse Rose.
'No! We saw you take the contraceptive pill, it's Pocholo's girlfriend!'
'RIGHT!' She said, eyes blazing boring into each of the boys in turn as the boys turn around. 'BEASTIE, GIRLS SCHOOL, KEY PHRASES, CODES, JOHAN STRAUSS, THE BLUE, tell me what this is all about! NOW!'
The Mum tone shocked the boys reminding them of home when they had been in trouble.
'We can't Miss Rose. Not yet! You wouldn't believe us anyway!'
'Try me!'
'You'll be ok here, we will follow, Billy you take the cats to the San!'
'Ok! How come there is no Beastie?'
'Ok ok ok we'll tell you later! '

'Boys I have to take this to Mr Barron, somebody is going to get killed! These are dangerous men. They kidnapped me! They have guns. I thought I was going to die back there! They wanted information about you boys, something you have and made me write a note.'

'We are sorry Miss Rose we don't know anything.'

'You are lying! You know how I know?'

'How so?'

'Because your mouths are moving! I know you boys!''

'Please don't say anything just give us some time!'

'Ok, but only till tomorrow.'

The boys headed for the Top o'th' Banks to watch the display and sat down together.

'I've worked it out; it is definitely 1 am tonight, the West Bridge Rendezvous. I think they are going to kidnap the Prince! Those other 2 are plants they are not the men who took Nurse Rose. The weather vane indicates the Prince.'

'Yes Digger, it's all falling into place now. You sure about the code?'

'Yes definite!'

'Right, so here is what we do. We can hide in the Yew trees from about lights out.'

'Don't forget their lights out is later than us.'

'Yes. The Prince's bed study is near to the Top o'th' Banks. So if there is an abduction to take place. It will be near then and there. Keep our eyes on the Prince all through the Service display and as much as we can till then. Let them take him and follow them to the rendezvous at the West Bridge, rescue him and head down the Brook, get to lakeside road. Remember that this is our Land, we know every rock, tree, clump of heather, pool, and we have the temper of the forest. Simple!'

They headed for the display, suddenly there was a loud explosion. 'What now?!'And they ran to the sound as flames could be seen shooting into the air; at The Top o'th' Banks they could hear Boot Jarvis with a megaphone his booming voice giving a running commentary. 'No need to worry folks! The rioters have just exploded a car and hurt some people! No worries, we have just the thing!' Then the Quad roared down the pitch side with water cannon aimed at the rioters who were washed aside with the powerful jet. The fire Service then came in with the V1 and V2 putting out the fire, then the ambulance comes in and piles all the injured onto stretchers closes the doors and races off in the direction of the San. A group of men stood on the bottom bank, observing and clapping their approval, one was clearly the Duke. 'Isn't that the Prince? Then he must be the Dad, which means he is married to the Queen?' Boot Jarvis then directed the crowd to the front lawn when Moaning Minnie went off again. Here there was smoke coming from the second floor and soon the V3 appeared and ladders were placed against the walls as they rescued the trapped people, and put out the fire. 'But look there is somebody still on the roof!' Enter the HS, their Land Rover raced into action and with the help of the V3 crew brought the trapped person to safety, which was put into the busy ambulance which then raced away with the injured. Turning around the wooden horse was on display and Big Jim Power put the gymnasts through their paces. Next to them were the Fencers duelling. The Duke seemed to be enjoying himself and the Head too was smiling his biggest grin ever, his stoop of the recent months had now gone. As the party made their way into the main building the Duke stopped and chatted to the boys and singled out the four friends, 'Now boys how are you enjoying life here at Flaxden?' The boys replied they were having a great time. 'Well remember you must also be thinkers as well as stinkers to ensure achievement!' He headed away and the Head nodded at the four, realising they have probably been up to no good. Somewhere.

At the end of the display they heard the Duke talking. 'Well done Dochan Do and you too Barron, very impressive, very impressive. You have built something very special here a unique idealism and you are to be commended, a Fire Service, an Ambulance Service, Hill Service, Emergency Service, and do need I go on? All active and for the Community not only here but miles around. Now Barron, what I want to know is do you think these boys are ready.......................? Hilary is just around the corner.........................' Billy's ears were straining as the conversation tailed off as the men, followed by the Duke's entourage strode away down the banks their voices drowned out by the rotor blades of the Duke's helicopter sat on pitch one. The Duke got in and took the pilot's, seat saluted to the waving boys and the bird slowly lifted off and headed away. The second helicopter did an impromptu display around the grounds to the cheering of the boys.

They visited Dan and the Nurse after the display. She was ok but she will still go to Mr Barron in 24 hours and tell him everything whether they like it or not and make sure the Police are involved. Pocholo was fine.

All day they were watching the Prince throughout the display, he sat on the banking as the helicopters took off, the Duke taking the controls of the lead chopper, hovering in front of the boys and taking a bow in acknowledgement of their standings, waved at the boys who were singing their latest hymn JERUSALEM into the Yew trees.

♫

AND DID THOSE FEET IN ANCIENT TIMES

WALK UPON ENGLANDS AUSTRALIAS AFRICAS PASTURES GREEN

NOT FORGETTING WALES SCOTLAND AND IRELAND

'Must be driving whoever is listening to us potty!'
'Glad to see you cut out the swearing Billy!'
'Well......I didn't know what they meant anyway!'
On the way to supper Billy told the boys about the big pistol on the table.
'That sounds like a flare gun Billy!'
'A flare gun?'
'Yes, it is a distress pistol used on ships and the like, seen a few before.'
'How do you know that?'
'Haven't you seen the film Titanic?' The Prince was still in view, a solitary figure, and no friends a lonely sad figure. Is he really a Prince? They have supper, prep and almost immediately after lights out they sneak out, it didn't matter tonight if they were caught the disruption would help their cause. Another chat about the end of term, looking to be home for Christmas and that they are all going to Billy's for the last week of the holidays. You can go to Billy's for New Year then straight back to. You must be home for Christmas everyone should be with their family at Christmas Mrs Flannigan had insisted. All 4 boys' parents would be in agreement. They would fly to Billy's for the last week of the holidays. The concert was going to be in a few days too and congregational practice had

been in full flow. Glad they didn't ask us! And all that practise we were doing at the Top o'th' Banks!

♫

AWAY IN A MANGER

NO CRIB FOR A BED

OUR LITTLE LORD JESUS LAY DOWN HIS SWEET HEAD

They checked on their ropes and vines on the Brook and checked all dens. They were untouched no one had found them. A couple of signal fires were also built ready for fast ignition if needed, they covered them with vegetation to keep them dry and hidden, damp and living wood was at the side with leaves to create smoke. 'I hope we don't need to do this!'
At lights out the four lay in their beds waiting for Charlie to signal. It suddenly came a tapping on the heating pipes.

-- . --. -- -. -- - . - ... - - . - - ... - . - - . --. - --

This was it WE GO! COAST CLEAR! NOW! They left quietly and headed for the Top o th Banks, arriving almost simultaneously. 'SPOOOOOOOKYY!'
'Quiet Billy! Keep a clear eye!'
'Just having some fun Buster!' It was now 12 midnight, the silence could have been cut with a knife. 'I wonder what people would think especially the forestry commission.'
'What if they knew what was really going on in Myrtle Wood. Is this just one giant set up? I've found out what SINE PRAESIDIO means.
'Yes it means PROTECT WITHOUT FEAR So let's see to it! Quiet'
Suddenly they heard muffled voices behind them. It was the unmistakeable accents of the hunters making no attempt to be silent.
COME ON THORSVELDT! GET WHAT YOU WANT!' They entered the building and emerged 15 minutes later with a small bag and a body, hood over his head and slung over the shoulders of Thorsveldt like a rag doll, kicking and mumbling... They went back the same way and their plan must have looked to be perfect to them. The boys come out of the trees and watch them head to the Land Rover parked on the lake side road. With

dimmed light the vehicle set off and heads up the Service road by the Flaxden Brook. 'Yes! They are heading for the West Bridge. Billy you follow! I think its Pete they've got not the Prince! The Prince is smaller. We'll head up the other track and try to get near before you arrive.'

The lifeless figure was bundled into the back of the truck and they headed up the tracks. They got there after the Land Rover arrives but Billy was already there as with clockwork timing.

'How long do you think the chopper will be Thorstveldt?' Said TerreRouge as he got out of the Land Rover.

'They said 2 am.'

'It'll be here. Just think £200,000 in our pockets, split two ways! Yes would've been better if we had the Nurse ....'

'Yes Thorsveldt £150,000 for me and £50,000 for you! Just think of all the Boerewors and Mullerpop you can get for that!'

'Seems a fair split.' Replied Thorsveldt, obedient as ever...

'Forget the Nurse, we got what we came for, just can't wait to get out this damn place, arse hole of the earth! It's freezing, rains all the time and midges! There will be plenty of women back home.'

'Just a pity those kids who were disrupting the place for us got caught, let alone that stupid idiot Târpnam. To think we were going to pay them!'

'Pay them? Did you think we were really going to do that? And as for that idiot Târpnam, must be a knob if he has a hat in his name, they were all mugs! The one person who was supposed to be in charge wasn't. Greedy like us but gullible. Give them a little and promise the rest later they'll do anything, like a flock of sheep. Sheep that's all they are, SHEEP!'

'Those others seemed to know everything we were doing. Did we really need to do this? We got what we came for.''

'Just insurance Thorsveldt, insurance. Forget it, you got what you wanted and it's gravy all the way now! Think of the 868.938.22 Rand you'll have in your pocket!'

The boys arrived at the West Bridge and saw Billy. 'How did you do that Billy? Get here so fast?'

'Jumped on the truck as they drove by the gym. I stayed in the back and jumped off about 100 yards back.'

'We are turning into some unit! The Prince is he dead?'

'That's a negative!'

'Come BillyO speak English! Stop reading those Commando mags!'
'He's ok! I could hear him breathing and he farted 7 times, I counted them all, what else could I do, I got bored!? Good job there is air conditioning he would've stank the place out! And I read the magazine, not just look at the pictures!'
'Air conditioning?'
'Yes no roof!'
'Where is he?'
'Still in the back of the Landi. I heard them talk about a chopper and fifteen minutes, also talking about £200,000. And Charlie I've got a belated present for you it's a thermos flask with your initial and date of birth written on it, C 238. Pretty cool eh?!!! Want to see it? Nice silver colour too!'
'Later Billy!' Interrupted Larry as Billy was just about to give Charlie his present.
'Chopper? You don't think they are going to escape on bikes?'
'No you twit, he means a helicopter.'
'It is a kidnap then! We have to stop this; it was all the cipher is about. Good job you picked up that key phrase Billy but we have no time to alert everyone now!'
'Too far away now! What will we do? Remember a whole in our butts will not be a good thing!'
'You have your whistles; right same as at the cottage but in reverse, you all know the plan. Take your positions! Billy starts with the Wolf whistle. Use our call signals if one is in trouble and we all descend on that noise. I will flash Let's go using Morse code, the one we practised.'
'Practised?'
'Yes Billy PRACTISED! Tell you what I'll flash the light and you blow your whistles and we GO!'
'Billy0 you take the Prince and straight to Shed 5. That's the one closest and one they won't find, not even the Blue boys found that one. Digger you go on the east bank and Cobber the west bank and I will go down the Brook. Once we are well away, take the Prince to Dan's he'll be secure there.' Off they go the Wolf whistle followed by .--.-...---- with Walter's torch.
'What's that? That whistle and that flashing light!''

'Stay! The chopper will be here soon.' Again a wolf whistle from another direction.
'No it's over there now, no there, no over there!' Then a long blast directly in front of them from.
'MY FELLOW AFRIKANERS!'
'BILLYO!'
'Let's get them they seem close!' They headed straight into the ant hill, close to shed 5.
'SHIT! FOK! I'm covered in ants!'
'Forget the ants and get these boys leave the one they call Flannigan to me!'
A deathly silence followed as the boys hid in their positions. The men started moving down the Brook. 'If you hear the chopper we go straight back to the truck, understood TerreRouge?'
'Don't tell me what to do Thorsveldt! I tell YOU what to do! Let's have some sport!'
'YEEEEHAAA!' As Larry swung across the Brook and landed on the same bank as Charlie in an attempt to lure them away from Billy. 'Look there they are! They are using torches!' And they head that way. The Hunter grabs the rope and s right across but lands in the pool losing his gun, 'Blast!' But he pulls out his bowie knife. Comes out of his den and headed down the Brook wading through the cold water, up to his waist 'There he is I want him!' The other hunter took aim and fired. The bullet ricocheted off a rock but missed. 'Those are real bullets Charlie! Aren't they?' Larry and Charlie started blowing the whistles. 'Forget them he's the prize! That's Flannigan! In the water! He's the leader!' And they chased after. But they were not used to this sort of chase.
'TerreRouge! Forgot to tell you, I went back he's gone. Everything! Gone!'
'What do you mean he's gone? How could he just go? EVERYTHING? ARGGGGGGHHHHHH!!!!!! FOK! I'm going to kill him, get them, and kill them all!'' And they continued their chase after. A light drizzle now begins, soon it became a torrent, followed by lightning flashes and thunder but the moonlit night still lights up the scenery, all black and white.
'There he is! BANG!' As he fired off another barrel. 'Heck those are real alright!' All boys think at once as they move down the brook.
'Cobber they are not coming for us they are heading straight for!'

'Yes I can see that Diggers. Let's collapsed that overhang it's about to go anyway, that'll stall them but keep blowing the whistles and flashing the torch.' Moving quickly they heave at the overhang, it did budge but the men were approaching fast. 'Here move back I've got these.' Larry produces two bags of flour as Charlie looked at him incredulously.
'Don't ask Diggers!' As the men approached they poured the flour on to the top of the men from the overhang.
'What the FOK?' As they got showered in flour. 'Keep moving I can see him splashing about!'
Safely in den 5 with the Prince, Billy listened to the distancing sounds of gunfire, whistles, he could also see the beams of flashlights and soon decided it was safe to head to Dan's. Charlie and Larry were now on the other banking and shadowing the chase in the Brook, there was nothing else they could do. 'We must be with Buster! They are targeting him!' They understood the whistles were not doing any good just now; the flour had only delayed them slightly. Suddenly there was a loud crashing sound behind them as the overhang slid into the brook instantly increases the flow of water down, knocking and one of his pursuers over, then damming the Brook parting the waters below. 'Too late! It may give Buster an edge!' Exclaimed Larry. But they got into the water and followed the chase and continued to blow their whistles. Eventually they came to the lake side road. 'Walter must be hiding.'
'Or hurt, drowned maybe.' They headed for the Flaxden Bridge, just as the stars vanished and the darkness swooped all around. Walter was sheltering moving through the pools and crouching in the dens they made inadvertently, the flash flood of water had dropped as the landslide dammed the Brook. The waters receded and suddenly it was easier to move. The heavens opened and a torrent of rain soon became a deluge. Suddenly frogs started jumping around making loud noises and then a slow rumble at first as the damned waters were breached and a rushing could be heard, and the two men were swept off their feet down the fast flowing Brook grabbing themselves on rocks but Walter struggled and was taken over a small water fall into one of the Lower Flaxden Pools below. How many lives has he got, Walter thought as he clambered to the banking. It then went dark and the rain came down again but stopped, the air seemed to stop, followed by midges all over him. It felt as though there were a million at the back of his head devouring him. He could feel and see the

blood on his cuts dripping into the waters. Rivers of blood, insects, floods, darkness, darkness, torrents of rain, he suddenly remember they were all the first born males, the Plagues of Egypt? He remembered his Scripture lessons. No this couldn't be happening, it is not happening. He could hear voices.

'Come on Thorsveldt he's here somewhere! The water is decreasing!' Suddenly the water started to flow and was rising faster as he came out near the bridge he must be nearly safe. He heard a helicopter above up from the forest with search lights on it, sweeping in all direction, looking, hunting... It was the pickup up, the hunters extraction. He heard the hunter's voices. 'FOK!' But it was an acoustic shadow and he was fooled into thinking they were far away. He came into the middle and they were right behind him. Walter stumbled and fell into the water trapping his leg, he couldn't budge it but he was above the water line. He turned to see a twelve bore pressed against his forehead. Breathing heavily exhausted, lungs bursting unable to go on now, his muscles completely drained of lactic acid he was going into anaerobic respiration, hyperventilating, but he was happy they have made amends. The Prince was safe.

Billy took the hooded figure to Dan's and woke Dan. 'Off........... with his hood!' Said Dan. Billy's jaw dropped...

'YOU!' A thud was heard on the floor. 'Dan, look after him the others are in danger! There seems to be something wrong with our plan.'

'THEN PUT IT RIGHT!' Replied Dan as Billy headed for the door, picking up what had been dropped on the floor.

Larry and Charlie clambered up the banking to the top of the hill and looked over the Flaxden Bridge at the lakeside to see Walter prostrate below. They heard a gurgling noise but it was not the familiar gurgling of the babbling Brook. It was Walter he was hurt, have they shot him? He looked bloodied and cleaved. He couldn't move. The pitch black sky, the ants everywhere, the now torrent of the Brook, he could see blood pouring down into the Brook, it was his blood, he was the first born male, Moses in his reed basket coming by now would confirm? How could he think of his Sunday school lessons now? He was beginning to hyperventilate, finding it difficult to move and breathe. There must be one more thing he could do, there is always one more thing you can do, there is always one more thing, when suddenly the two men approached him, wading knee length through the waters, their gun and knife poised.

'Don't move! We've got you! You FOKING little shit! You'll pay for the loss and grief you've given us!'

'Yes I was looking forward to some Borrowers!'

'What good will that do you? Killing me? You failed, I heard the helicopter. It's gone.' Walter was now on his knees waist high in the water, head bowed, and body like lead, helpless he was breathing heavily and looks around him, searching for his friends at the top of the ghylls. He couldn't see them.

Pressing the gun against Walter's head TerreRouge pulled the trigger. CLICK! Nothing. 'Well I was having so much fun I forgot if I had one or two shots left. Must've been only the one.' How can this be happening, NO this is not happening! You are not going to do this! He started praying, 'Hail Mary Mother of God.....' Closed his eyes tightly, at least it will be quick; he had heard that they don't feel it but how do they know? Unless anything has happened to anyone how do they know what it is like? Time is running out. He heard the click then POOMPHF!!!!

Suddenly the whole area became floodlit. A group of men surround the scene, heavily armed, all in black with blackened faces, assault rifles directed at the hunters.

'DROP IT!!!'

'DROP IT NOW!!'

'FOK! NOOOOOO! I want this one, means a lot to me! He's ruined everything!' Screeched TerreRouge.

TerreRouge pulled the trigger; slurry trickled out of the barrel over Walter's forehead, as the barrel pulled up catching the back of his head. SPLAT! Missing a heartbeat he felt a searing thud to his temple, his heart missed a beat as did his friends watching at the bridge.

'FOK! What's this?'

Quickly the two men were surrounded by the Blue, their weapons taken from them and thumped to the ground, handcuffed and forced up the banking to the road. Walter was helped to his feet. 'Alright boyo!?'

Unable to say a word was still ventilating heavily.

'Suck it in lad! Deep breaths! Deep breaths! You'll be ok!' His mouth was filled with blood and his head was sore as though there was a Frenchman running around in it.

At the road the men were shackled, punched in the back, forced them on to their knees as their wrists were tied. Billy appears! 'My fellow Afrikaners. Always check gun for Big Banana before firing!'
'We'll get you!' Growled TerreRouge.
'Yeah we'll get you!' Repeated Thorsveldt, mimicking TerreRouge
'Shut it Thorsveldt! This is your entire fault!'
'That will be only in your dreams!'
Heads Lowered the men were led away. 'MOVE IT you two! Mustn't disappoint your Masters shall we?! Get that ruck sack Ffolkes! It must be in there. Did you get it Te................? ?'
'We've been after these two...........mercenaries, bounty hunters, whatever they call themselves for a while now. Thanks to you four they are now out of the way. They are or were professional assassins, ex South African forces if anything this looks like a kidnapping.' One of the Blue interrupted.
'Hey but guess who they kidnapped?'
'The Prince?'
'No, the Prince left with his Dad the Duke; I couldn't believe it when the hood came off. He had been in the kitchen, jersey inside out and his initials on his back collar! We have found the biscuit thief too!'
'Meaning?'
'He had a packet of chocolate digestives on him! Hidden under his jersey!'
'So the BB Gang were wrongly convicted of that?'
'Seems so!'
'What a shame!'
'Did you know the Tucky is getting a freezer?'
'So what was all that for? Who was it Billy?'
'You're not going to believe this it was......................M....' Suddenly Billy was interrupted by one of the men.
'Well boys, that's enough fun for tonight! This.......well it never happened. The reality is far away. You say nothing to anybody ok? I suggest you four go back to your beds and get some sleep I believe you have a busy morrow ahead of you. Enjoy the day!' Yes it was the end of term now and they had much to look forward to. The Christmas Dinner, the Carol Service. They also had a lecture on the upcoming decimalisation.
'What shall we sing into the microphones?'

'How about Silent Night? I'll have my present now Billy, where is it?' Said Charlie.
'Nah! Away in a Manger! How about you Buster?' Billy said as he rummaged through his satchel. 'It's not here! Must've dropped it somewhere. I know I left it at Dan's. We'll get it tomorrow. But look what I have found!!' Inside the sack were about 6 packets of biscuits.
'Let's have a feast with those biscuits! Rich tea biscuits and a can of Banta!?'
'Pity Billy hadn't brought that flask for Charlie! Wonder what was in it.'
'Makes a change from,

♫

2 RICH TEAS

AND A CAN OF BANTA!!

'You know something? This is all connected somehow.'
'Let's swing by Pennine and have a look around, no one will see us they are all asleep!'
'I just want my bed! Have you noticed its getting colder? I'm freezing.' Replied Walter now beginning to recover. The four boys headed back, the place was unusually calm, surreal, balmy, no sound, no smell, a clear starry sky. Unusual for a December night. They didn't exchange words as they opened the door and each separated on entering Brecon House, George looked down on them from his pedestal.
'We really have been grooving the danger tonight!'
Billy headed to Thames, Charlie to Shannon, Larry to Mersey and Walter to Conway.
Not long ago they had been pale leggy young men of all shapes and sizes when they had arrived at Flaxden Brig; they had now turned into strong sturdy young men.
Walter got into his bed with all his clothes on, thinking to himself. 'Been there done it, got the experience, we put it around us, saved the day, certainty, what we are and have been doing, what could we do to improve, what we could all bring to get the job done, we looked at the bigger picture required, we did it!' He gazed up through the window and watched the first

snowflakes to come from the sky, one fell on his nose and he drifted into a deep sleep, the music was piped through the walls.

♫

O LITTLE TOWN OF FLAXDEN BRIG
HOW STILL WE SEE THEE LIE
ABOVE THY DEEP AND DREAMLESS SLEEP
THY STAR IN THE SKY GOES BY

The next morning he forced his eyes open. His lids were stuck to his eyeballs and with a bit off pain he did and bleary eyed he scanned around the dorm. Where is everybody? There was nobody here, all the beds were made. He listened for any voices, any movement, and any music, there was no sound. He dressed, and looked around the house, Conway, Shannon, Mersey, Thames; he found Billy, Charlie and Larry, stirring on their beds. They look in the changing room, common room-no one, in the boot room they saw George in his cabinet, he looked asleep, and he had been for some time now, hibernating, retired weeks ago. Walter checked his watch it had stopped at 4 45 am, tapping it, had his Sea star 7 finally packed up? Nobody uttered a word. He tried to wind it up but it was stuck at that time. He put on his duffle coat, they must be at breakfast. Why weren't they called or woken up, the bugle call, they never heard it, the steady increasing rumbling building up into an avalanche should have woken them? On their way to the dining room, they saw the Quad, V2 and Ambo parked outside their sheds. In the dining room there was no one, all the tables were set for mealtime. They must be in Chapel; they headed over to the Chapel slid open the doors slowly and peered in, no one. Now they picked up pace and heads to the front lawn, the pitches, Top o'th' Banks, the class rooms no one, the San, the place was deserted. They looked towards the front drive and see a white cat heading away, 'POCHOLO!' Walter shouted but the white cat slowly strolled way looking around once then turning away and out of sight. They ran towards him but when he gets to the spot he is gone, vanished. They ran over to the gym it was locked, up to the Brook there was no sign of Dan, Wolfie or the cottage, he called Wolfie, all that was heard was the gurgling of the Brook, and the calling of the birds. He went over to the San there was no one there, the classroom block, they peered into the class to room to find empty desks and clean blackboards. The shutters were down on the tuck shop, they all headed down Magillycuddy Hill to the front lawn where they saw nothing. He sat down on the bottom bank joined by Billy, Larry and Charlie, couldn't think, couldn't do anything and shaking their heads, they walked into the middle of pitch Suddenly a drum beat started but they could not see where, there, no there , over there maybe. They heard a slow humming followed by;

♪

WIN NA YA HO

WI NA DE YA

WI NA DE YA

HO HO HO HO

HEY YA HO

Then the whole of Flaxden Brig seemed to suddenly have turned out. 'On the line Flannigan! MacCloon! Digweed and Odhiambo! You shrinking violets!' The voice of Big Jim bellowed at them, pushing, exhorting these exhausted beings to one more supreme effort, they turned around and saw everyone moving onto the other try line. 'Line up Flaxden Brig. You know the score! Odhiambo, Flannigan, Digweed, MacCloon!' Said Big Jim in a calm and understanding voice as he rolled the ball towards the 25 yard line, it span around like a top and stopped dead. 'PLAY ON!' The others charged fiercely towards the ball, sounding out the battle cry.

BRIG! BRIG! BRIG! BRIG! BRIG...

FLAX!FLAX!............FLAXDEN

BRIG................................

FLAXDENNNNNNNNNNN!!BRIG!

rooted to the spot Billy suddenly ran and got to the ball way before the advancing mob, scooping up the ball and feeling how heavy it was, he quickly remembered it was supposed to be like this but his mind was moved as he saw the advancing mob bearing down on him, there was rage in their eyes, an anger they had not encountered, he picked up the ball in one movement and with the ball in two hands raced towards the advancing pack, breaking through the first line of attackers he put the ball under one arm, the attempted tackles came in thick and fast, handing off and barging with his shoulder through the melee he had no one to pass to, he was on his own, a heavy blow to his arm, chest, head, his nose crunched and blood flowed down into his mouth as he spat out broken teeth, then a thump on his thigh leg, he shuddered and could feel the blood arising in his nostrils, he was hit hard, the ball ran free in front of him, the noise was deafening, 'STOP HIM! NAIL HIM! BATTER HIM! TAKE THE BALL!' Everyone he passed has to drop out, that was the only rule here, soon there were only a few left as Walter managed to gather the ball and focused on the try line he could see he is only 30 yards away, one comes in then another leaving only 3 in front of him, it was his friends Billy, Larry and Charlie snarling stamping poised like the bulls in the ring, the matador stops and leans his body and summons the strength to accelerate as his opponents did the same, there was now a paradox, they were the immovable object and he the immovable force, someone has to win and someone has to lose, they headed for him, bloodied and slowing down he lumbered to the line, still a power, still a force, he couldn't feel his legs they were like jelly now, one came in as he managed to hand off Charlie but he had him by the arm, he could keep running he was still moving but there was still Billy and Larry who sandwiched him one Lower and one Upper, the crunch was heard all around the field strewn with bodies who were now all cheering him on, but why was he pushing his friends away? He now had the ball in two hands and as the bone crunching tackles came in he fell out stretched dives and the ball is grounded firmly down over the line under the posts. 'He's done it!' A gigantic roar went up like a Lion and instantaneously it goes quiet as they touched down, their heads slammed against each other, with a bone crushing clash the thigh of Charlie who has hold of his arm. Their heads split open and they clutched their heads with both hands in an attempt to stop the pulsating vibration, he rolled away from the crumpled heap of his friends who sat up and started clapping him, turning his head to one side he saw Big Jim with his whistle blowing in his mouth and arm in the air then Lowered pointing to the ball but he could not hear any sound, he looked behind and saw the whole of The Brig behind him jumping up mouths open and shouting, punching the air, he struggled to his feet head in his hands, raised himself to his full height they were all there, around him, Uppers, Lowers and Novus all in pure blue, the Masters, the kitchen staff, Joe, Nurse Rose, Rebel, Jimmy Phillip, he turned straight into the piercing blue eyes of Dochan Do who said, '**Auxilium te, et auxiliatus sum tibis Deus**!'Then suddenly the world started spinning round and round, it went darker and darker as the surroundings faded, he was aware of flames licking around him,

'Are ye alright lad?' He looked to his left and saw an motionless Henrietta blood at the corner of her mouth, the wavy hair stuck with her blood onto her forehead, her eyes staring in one direction, pupils fully dilated, closed his eyes, the two men in the cab laughing and then saw Hennrietta and himself having afternoon tea, she was smiling and laughing, he looked ahead and they were on top of the hill, he looked over the hill and they were in each other's arms asleep. He turned around and they were chatting at the bar, he was now in Gharry's bar with Geoff and Emma, then the exam room, the scratching of Timmy Tiens writing. The regimental posture of Professor Brown, the two security guards, Hairy Dan collecting cans.

Lions
Lions
Lions
Get back to room 37
What can I do you for
What are you looking at
Trump pulls out of Kyoto Treaty
Fish Chips and mushy peas
Yes can I help you
She got her pound of flesh
Something better for you Cliffie
It's another glorious day down by the Quay
Are ye alreet Laddie

360 degrees Michaelmas

CLIFFTON! WE'LL PUT IT RIGHT!

PARTIR

He woke up in his apartment, bolt upright, the pizza with the engagement ring on it, BLEEP, BLEEP, BLEEP, BLEEP, he heard the electric milk float, and he fell out of bed and saw he had no milk in the house. Turning on the TV he flicked through the channels.

MAY CALLS SNAP ELECTION! JUNE the 8th

NOT ANOTHER! That's four years running. A morning film started but almost as soon as it began the adverts came on. Insurance, funeral and life, PPI, My supermarket is cheaper than yours, The Bank that likes to say YES! But look at the small print! Cruises, weed remover. 'Hmmmmmm.....weed remover!' Cliffton said to himself. He flicked again through the channels, nearly all reality programmes, and people airing their dirty laundry. Same old, same old'. Stretching he thought to himself. 'Communication? Hah! What a joke! A load of bollocks! OWCH!!'

Cliffton shouted out loud, looking at his arms and legs he saw cuts and bruises. How did they get there? He pulled on his jeans and t shirt, feeling sore as he did so, gingerly touching his bruised ribs, face and thigh not remembering how he got them he quickly descended the stairs heading for the local grocery store. He picked up a carton of milk and went to the counter. The girl behind the counter was chatting to someone

As he headed into the local grocery store. He picked up a carton of milk and went to the counter. The girl behind the counter was now also chatting to someone on her phone as well as the one at the counter so Cliffton glanced at the Newspaper paper stand, shaking his head as he did so. It was the same old same same old...........

'Give us 20 fags Chelsea, pack of Always size 3, there's a love; oh and a bottle of that cheap Spanish stuff!' The cashier still ignoring Cliffton;

'And how's Jezza........?'........

PYONGYANG TEST FIRE SECOND
INTERCONTINENTAL BALLISTIC MISSILE

HONOLULU BANS TEXTS
WHILE CROSSING THE ROAD

IT WAS SEX SEX SEX
AFTER LEAVING ISLAND

ARSENAL CHIEF'S
SICK TV SHAME

BIG BEN TO BE SILENCED FOR 4 YEARS
Due to health and safety

EXPORT HOSPICE LOSES OVER £200,000
IN ONLINE FRAUD

COST OF LEAVING EUROPE TO TOP £50 BILLION

Cliffton shook his head, as he finished scanning the headlines, just all good copy for the press 'YES! WELL WHADYA WANT? AVEN'T GOT ALL

DAY!! YE KNAAA!' The cashier demanded as though he was the one inconveniencing her, as she looked at the till whilst continuing to talk into her phone, saw the picture of a milk bottle on the screen, touched it. '55 pence!' Cliffton put his hand into his pocket and pulled out some loose change and handed it to the cashier. 'What's this? You trying to con me? What is this anyway? Roman? American? Monopoly? You a forger? I'll get the Manager, no, I'm going to call the Police!' He looked down and saw he had given her a ten shilling note. He put his hand into his other pocket and brings out some loose changes and handed it to the girl. She snatched it out of his hand as she said, '...YOU TAKING THE PISS?!! What foreign stuff is this?' Cliffton looked at his hand, shocked at the language, he saw 2 half crowns, 1 florin, a shilling, sixpence, 4 pennies and a half penny, another shilling with an indention on it. He looked closely and saw all the latest had the date 1967. He eventually found a £1 coin, one of the new ones and gave it to her, and as she snatched it out of his hand. 'WANNA BAG?' He shook his head without a word and headed out of the door back to his car. The bruises? The money? He returned home, made himself a brew, English breakfast tea. Pulling out all the coins, he emptied his other pockets and saw a £1, £2 and 20 pence coin with a couple of coppers. He felt something in his back pocket it was the pouch dropped by Hairy Dan. He looked over towards his packed bags, flask on the table and then turned on the TV. A holiday programme, it was Huerden Smythe flaunting her body across some beautiful sands, a couple of girls were sunbathing topless under a coconut tree. He looked outside and got up and walked over to the phone, dialled 02089 56666789 as he pressed the keypad his fingers were tender. 'Hi good morning, I would like to know if it is possible to book a ticket so that I can travel tonight to......................., it is quite urgent please..'The call was drowned out by the sound of the bin lorry emptying the rubbish. 'Did you get that? Good when is the next available flight? This afternoon? Great well book me on that. Here' my card details 6785 9812 0987 6341...security code 999, £414.29? That's ok. 24 hour trip? 5 pm? Right many thanks bye!' As simple as that.

He saw the lights flashing on his answer machine. Five messages. 'Hi Cliffton hope everything went well in the exams, enjoy the holiday!' That was from his Aunty Marjorie.

'This is John from Coniston Picks. We are answering a call you made to us in relation to your asbestos insurance claim.'

'This is the Royal Bank of Conland, we would like you to come in and discuss your account so we can shaft you some more.' The banks not interested in the needs of the customer, only interested in their needs, can't, ever be trusted, he mused.

'Hi this is Parys in relation to your Life insurance.' Never heard of her don't have it from them.

'The next message was over 4 minutes long.' Announces the voice on the machine. He let it run. There was an agonised silence, a deep breathless sigh and hush, a breath being held. ', I just....I just wanted to say sorry for the other week, I have made a mistake and I want to try again with you. Please ring me. It's Porsche.' No Cliffton my man how are you? No how did the exams go?

He erased all the messages.

♪

I'M DOING FINE NOW WITHOUT.....

He hummed in low key to himself glancing at the engagement ring still in the pizza box, taking root with the spinach seeming to wind itself around and around, closing the lid down as he headed to the bathroom, he'd sell it. Cliffton changed his bags and packed them into his car. He got to the airport and parked up in the long stay section. Handed the keys to the office and headed towards terminal 5. He wandered around the terminal, a group of women were at the bar all in fancy dress, drinking cocktails, must be a hen night, in the next bar was a group of men on a stag night, already started their drinking, he bought a paper,

RUSSIAN FLEET REFUELLING IN SPAIN

MARRIED PREMIER LEAGUE FOOTBALLER IN SEX SCANDAL

DROP AGE OF CONSENT TO 15

BREXIT WILL GO AHEAD SAYS PM

360 degrees Michaelmas

NUCLEAR CRISIS ESCALATES

WESTMINISTER IN SHOCK AS PM GOES TO THE COUNTRY AGAIN

He bought a novel, Catch 22 he'll read it sometime and glanced at the Daily Shit and read.

MY CRAZY 8 HOUR DRUG BENDER by......

He shook his head and sat down, gazed out to the runway watching flights landing and taking off. 'I'VE GOT TO GET OUT OF HERE!' A group came and sat near him and were very loud. Money, money, money, disposable income this, disposable income that. 'Is there really a word such as that, disposable income? Who can really afford to waste like that?' He glanced around, there were many all dressed up, dressed up especially for the trip, a big day. He opened his book and read a couple of pages. He boarded the flight tapping the fuselage 2 times, as he headed to his seat directed to by the smiling stewardess. The plane is full but he falls asleep and after a while he reaches his destination. A tiny airport, the plane stopped on the tarmac and the passengers descended the steps and walked over to the terminal building, they can see the hold being emptied and the bags being thrown on to the trolleys, he collected his bags from the antiquated carousel the first one arrives quickly great he will be through in no time, but his second bag is last through, eventually he went through the customs and his bags were searched thoroughly, funny that that last bag seems to have been opened. Handing his passport over to the immigration officer, the man wearing a pair of Ray Ban Aviator calmly informed he had a page missing. 'A page missing!? What do you mean?'
'Yes sir you have a page missing!' Cliffton glanced around and in puzzlement he said that he did not and a tap on his shoulder from the passenger behind raised his passport to reveal a note sticking out of his book. 'Ahh!' Nodding he understood now. Quickly he picked a £5 note out of his wallet and puts it in between. The officer raised his eyes, shook his head and looked at Cliffton's wallet. Cliffton only had £20 notes so

reluctantly slid that in to the pages and removed the £5. An icy stare from the man and Cliffton put the £5 back and the passport was stamped.
He came out of the airport and the heat seemed better on him than coming out of the plane, there were trees and shade. A long line of ageing taxis were parked there touting for trade from the new arrivals. Cliffton approached one, 'Sir! Sir!' His bags tossed into the boot and he got into the back. 'Where to Sir!'
'Hotel Sahara please!' The taxi set off rattling away, at a ferocious speed. The driver chattered away, in broken dialect, giving Cliffton an impromptu sightseeing trip. Cliffton sat in silence soaking up his new environment and soon the car pulled up outside a ramshackle place with the sign Hotel Sahara, in red flashing lights but hanging precariously off... He paid the driver with a wad of local currency, not sure if it was right or wrong. A porter appeared and carried his bag in. A receptionist sat dozing behind the desk.
'I have a reservation under the name Breeze...Cliffton Breeze.'
'Ah yes Mr Breeze, we were expecting you Sir, please sign in! Your room is 37 on the second floor your bags will be taken there for you!' He signed in and asked if there was a bar, when suddenly THWAP!
'Yes there is, right through that door Mr Breeze.' She said, just as he turned t around, touching where he had felt the hit. There was no one there.
'Thank you.' He walked in and saw two men sat on chairs around the bar.
'Yes........Grass......Tero.......'
'You sure? Thunder.............right.....Red.........' Their conversation passed in one ear and out of the other, background noise, none of his business. Three others sat at the bar were in deep discussion each gave a courteous nod of acknowledgement. An enormous fan was rotating on the ceiling providing a pleasant breeze, welcoming after being in all that traffic. He went to the bar and a big barman, hands the size of shovels looked at him.
'A Beer please!' He picked up a bottle of the local brew and took of the lid slamming the beer on the bar, all in one fluid motion.
'That will be 20 Rand.' He handed over the money and sat down. The other three turned their heads as he emptied his pockets and put the 6 shillings, half a crown, 2 sixpences, 2 shillings, 2 pennies and a half penny and the pouch, down. The three men saw this, acknowledge Cliffton and nodded their heads once as if an understanding existed, finished their beers and one by one left the bar. At the table of the two men was an empty beer

bottle spinning on the bar, it stopped and pointed directly at him. Cliffton, none the wiser, drank his beer slowly; staring at the stationery bottle he relished every drop.

'***Tujunga nag young sari at nag Days ay makaktulong sa iyo***!' He looked up and standing in front of him was a barmaid. 'Another one Sir?'

'Sorry what did you say? I didn't quite catch that.' He said with a puzzled look.

'Would you like another drink Sir?

'Sorry, just before that, I thought you said something else.' The girl shook her head smiling as she did so.

'Yes...........Yes please! What's your name?'

'It's Constanze.'

'That's a pretty name.'

'Thank you Sir, what is your name?'

'It's Cliffton............Cliffton Bree..........

.__ __ ._ _ .UNFINISHED. .SEE HILARY in

360 degrees

0 degrees

CORONACH

Shores where we came and went,
Heartfelt the hopes now spent,
Chronicles severed, traditions laid waste
Punished saws scruple, member, pupil,
Painful the ending, dear friendships displaced.

Chapel of cheerfulness, washed in new tearfulness,
Worked on by boys-now in sharp city suits,
Self-respect-justly swollen, achievements,- both stolen,
Wrested in mid-life,
their memories and roots.

Teachers will suffer too, every old buffer who,
Stapled his craft to the vistas of youth,
Their prayers have been said, every tear has been shed,
You have failed them, yes failed, that is the truth.

snſdeonepLdrsatnocmoaa
trcistnrnytsBeſzerabor
beſohaomnrrhvayetrrjhF
bfroauwrnotrſbefjdadaſ
iaaurrahvmnrſiawrwriua
naanniſqnrdirdoeimmRti
tgrqſnedirdinstonnsues
arcsttaimKmiiniptnuciu
hmenkieſneoaſiGiryitmr
eieBodrmgreeaeibzryeea
orpiiwhſſEatcotccueePh
ancſiedaofnIrwsakcachh
viwdcecdabwdeeeeperinr
ehgoDbrnnsrrnepefaoeew
jIeiknnshiſIjanonjgmmc
dRmoinnnsrrnenqGunoayy
tmasundrycnyiiunhytbtn
cdriavardyiyutjgdnKfqj

360 degrees Michaelmas

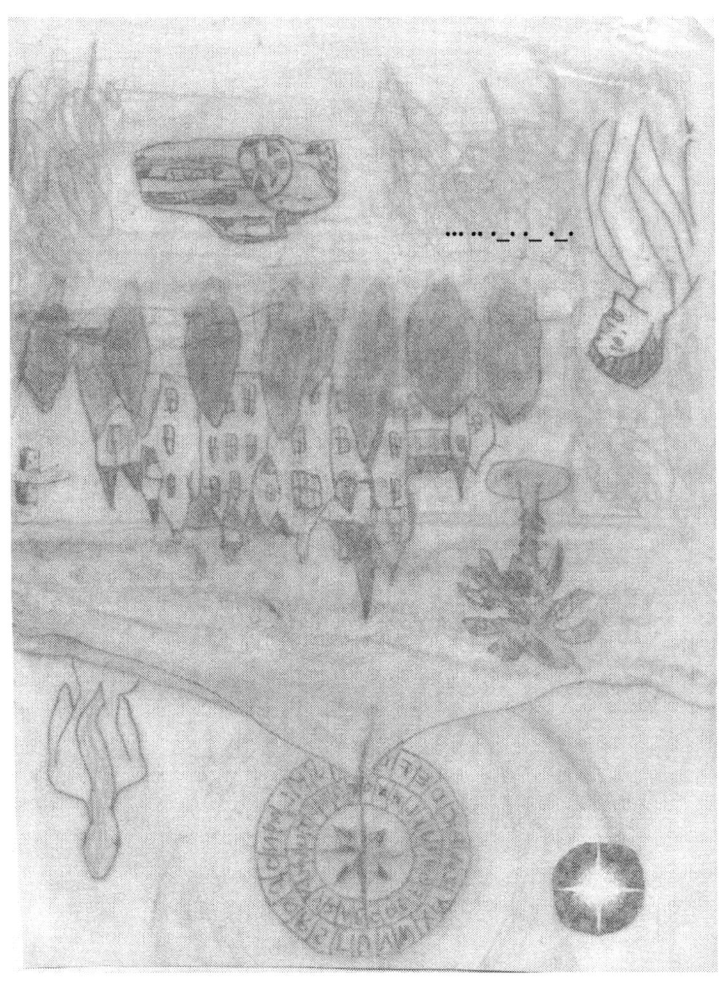

360 degrees Michaelmas

Now read 360 degrees!
Hilary!
then
Trinity!
followed by
Recess!

Oh yes! Not forgetting!
Festive Edition!

AND!!!
If you want them all in one!
Get 360 degrees The Quadology As Was

Roger